I0600187

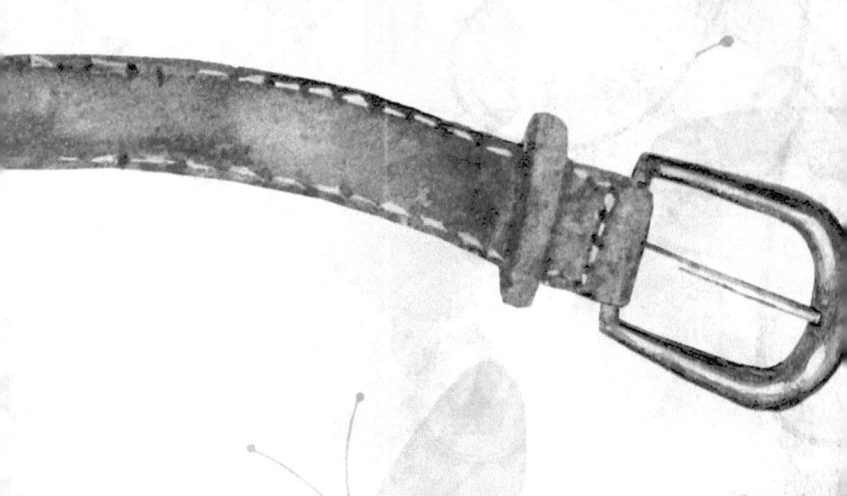

THE HEART LIES SERIES

LOVING QUEEN

SAFFRON BROOKS

Loving Queen Copyright © 2025 by Saffron Brooks

All rights reserved. No part of this publication may be reproduced, stored in or transmitted by any form or by any means, electronic, mechanical, photocopying, recording, scanning, or otherwise without the prior written permission of the publisher, except for brief quotations in critical reviews or articles.

This is a work of fiction. Names, characters, places, and incidents are either products of the author's imagination or used fictitiously. Any resemblance to actual persons, living or dead, events, or locales is entirely coincidental.

ISBN: 979-8-9986557-0-8

For permissions or subsidiary rights inquiries, please contact:
Saffron Brooks
www.saffronbrooks.com
Proofreading by Andrea Halland
Formatting by Halle with AJ Wolf Graphics

To my Queens— may you always know your worth, embrace your power, and accept nothing less than a King who honors and cherishes you. You deserve love, respect, and a throne beside someone who sees your greatness.

CONTENT WARNING

This story contains themes of domestic discipline, possessive protection, consensual degradation, and mentions of Alzheimers. It also includes depictions of stalking and kidnapping by a secondary character. If any of these elements are distressing or not your cup of tea, please feel free to skip this story. Otherwise, proceed with caution... and a hint of curiosity.

Inès Dubois has it all planned out, her studies, her career, and a life free from distractions. But one distraction has been impossible to ignore: Kingsley Ashford, her friend and unrequited crush. For years, Kingsley has kept her in the friend zone, leaving Inès frustrated. When the handsome Nathan Salvatore asks her out, Inès believes it is time to move on from Kingsley. But is she ready to let him go?

Kingsley Ashford's life has always been about control, duty, and hiding his true feelings for Inès. But when Inès agrees to go on a date with another man, it stirs up possessive feelings he has been trying to ignore. Scared he will lose her, Kingsley makes a confession to Inès: he wants her. They are thrust into uncharted territory, risking their friendship as they navigate their newly revealed feelings.

Their relationship is soon tested when secrets come to light, and Inès struggles with unwanted attention from Nathan. Can their love survive, or will they lose each other forever?

PLAYLIST

- *Everything Has Changed* – Taylor Swift & Ed Sheeran
- *More Than Friends* – Jason Mraz ft. Meghan Trainor
- *Say You Won't Let Go* – James Arthur
- *You Don't Own Me* – C. Grace & G-Eazy
- *Best Part* – Daniel Caesar ft. H.E.R.
- *Endless Love* – Lionel Richie & Diana Ross
- *Somebody's Watching Me* – Rockwell
- *Earned It* – The Weeknd
- *Hrs & Hrs* – Muni Long
- *Play With Me* – Rendezvous At Two
- *First F*ck** – 6LACK & Jhené Aiko
- *Santa Tell Me* – Ariana Grande
- *Tell Me It's You* – Aaron Pierre & Tiffany Boone
- *Traitor* – Olivia Rodrigo
- *S'il Suffisait D'aimer* – Céline Dion
- *Heartbreak Anniversary* – GIVĒON
- *Skin* – Rihanna
- *Elastic Heart* – Sia
- *I Love You* – Dadju ft. Tayc

DICK-A-PEDIA

AKA YOUR ROADMAP TO THE STEAM

For those of you who'd rather jump straight to the spice or skip it entirely. This is your handy little guide to the chapters where things get a *bit* heated. Whether you're here for the emotional angst, the slow burn payoff, or just came to see who ends up naked first, I got you.

Spicy scenes ahead in:
Chapter 14
Chapter 15
Chapter 18
Chapter 19
Chapter 20
Chapter 21
Chapter 23
Chapter 26
Chapter 35
and the Epilogue.

Read at your own pace. Skim, savor, or skip. No judgment.
Just bisous. 💋

PRONUNCIATIONS

Inès — *ee-NESS*

The "s" is pronounced, and the emphasis is on the second syllable.

Camille — *kah-MEE*

The "ll" is soft like a "y" and the "e" at the end is silent.

Daronne — *da-ROHN*

Used informally to mean "mom" in slang. The "e" is barely heard, and the "n" is nasal.

Hélène — *ay-LEHN*

The "h" is silent, and the final "ne" is soft and barely pronounced.

The hardest part about loving you secretly was pretending that I was okay with just being friends when all I wanted was to be more.

— *Unknown*

INÈS

FASHION FAILS AND FURRY FRIENDS

C*hips.*
Soda.
Salsa dip.
Paper towels.
Spicy pickles?

I adjust the strap of my tote bag as it slips off my shoulder, staring at the list Meghan sent me. Spicy pickles? She doesn't even like them. Maybe she's trying to throw me off, wouldn't be the first time.

The snack aisle at Walmart is crowded tonight. It's like every shopper here had the same brilliant idea I did, to stock up for tonight's game night.

Meghan is my best friend. We met during freshman year of high school. I was tucked away in the library, lost in a fantasy book during lunch break when she stumbled into the corner I was hiding in, making out with someone. They didn't even notice me until she literally stepped on me. She thought I was some kid hiding in the library. To be fair, I did look the part, small, skinny, and with a face that hadn't quite caught up with my age. I was twelve at the time, and she was fourteen.

Later, we ran into each other again in class. She just smiled and, without missing a beat, decided I was going to be her best friend. Ever since, she's been trying to pull me out of my shell, to make me more like her, outgoing and free. So far, she's succeeded…at least a little.

Meghan and I are now juniors at Ashford University, one of the most prestigious schools in the country. She's majoring in criminal justice, dreaming of becoming a lawyer, while I'm pursuing a double major in biology and psychology with a minor in math, aiming to become a neurologist.

As I turn the corner, I mentally brace myself for game night. Just as I reach for a bag of pretzels, my phone buzzes in my hand. I glance down to see Meghan's name flashing on the screen.

"Hey, Meg," I say, balancing my phone between my shoulder and cheek while grabbing another bag of chips.

"Inès! Please tell me you're still at the grocery store." Meghan's voice comes through, bright and cheerful.

"I am. I've just been debating on which snack I should get for myself."

"Oh good, can you grab the strawberry jam I like? We ran out," she says. "And don't forget to grab some dog food for Beau while you're at it," she adds, referring to my black terrier puppy.

"Strawberry jam, got it, and I already got his food."

"Thanks, babe. So, are you ready for tonight?" she asks, her voice bubbling with excitement. I can't stop the sigh that slips out.

This is the first time we're hosting a game night, something Meghan insisted on to impress her boyfriend of two years, Justin. I went along with it because, well, she's my best friend and I love her. But if I'm being honest, I'd much rather lock myself in my room and work on my assignments.

It's not that I have a problem with Justin, quite the opposite. I actually like him a lot. He's great for her, patient and funny, and they're perfect together. My problem is his best friend, Kingsley Ashford, the great-grandson of the founder of Ashford University.

I've had this ridiculous, unhealthy crush on him since I first met him at a party during my freshman year. The worst part? He's never shown an ounce of interest in me. Not in that way. In fact, he's been more of a big brother, always acting protective and watching over me, just like Justin. But while I'm fine with Justin treating me like a little sister, with Kingsley, it just feels… awkward.

Which is why I've made it my mission this year to spend as little time with him as possible, hoping these feelings will fizzle out on their own. Unfortunately, that's easier said than done. Not only are our best friends dating, but we also share custody of Beau, the most adorable little pup.

"Meg, I've been thinking. Maybe I should just stay in my room tonight, and you can say I'm out or something," I reply, tossing the chips into my tote bag.

"What? Why?" Meghan's tone turns serious.

"It just feels…awkward, you know? Like it's a double date or something." I sigh, moving to the next aisle. "Every time we hang out, I'm just the odd one out. It hurts, Meg. I don't know if I can handle another night of pretending I don't have feelings for him."

Maybe I just need to date someone else so I can move on from this crush.

"Inès, listen to me." Meghan's voice softens. "You never know what might happen. Maybe tonight will be different.

3

Besides, you're my best friend, and I need you there. Who else will help me cheat at Pictionary?"

I laugh, shaking my head. "Because nothing says friendship like criminal-level cheating at charades."

"Exactly. See, you have to be here, plus, you live here, too."

"Fine. But if he so much as looks at me like I'm his kid sister, I'm leaving."

"Deal," Meghan says. "And maybe accidentally spill a drink on him. That'll get his attention."

"Very funny," I reply, grinning.

Turning the corner, still chuckling at Meghan's joke, I collide with someone, causing both our tote bags to fall to the ground. Groceries scatter everywhere, cans rolling under shelves, and a carton of eggs splattering across the floor.

"Oh my God, I'm so sorry!" I exclaim, dropping to my knees to gather the fallen items.

"Shit… No, it's my fault. I wasn't paying attention," a man replies, crouching down to help me. He looks to be in his early thirties, with dark hair and a chiseled jawline. He has an air of confidence about him, despite the current chaos.

As I reach for a cracked egg, he glances at the mess and mutters, "Well, there goes my cake."

I pause, glancing at the assortment of cake-making essentials spread across the floor: flour, sugar, eggs, even frosting. "Was it going to be chocolate or vanilla?" I ask, biting back a smile.

"Chocolate," he says, smirking. "Although now it's more of a scrambled egg cake with a hint of aisle dust."

I snort, half embarrassed, half amused. "That's… definitely a bold flavor profile."

"I was going for 'unique.'" He hands me a box of cereal

with a wink. "I'm Nathan, by the way. Usually, I'm better at keeping my groceries in the bag."

"Inès," I reply, feeling my nerves spike. "Nice to meet you, even if I just destroyed your dessert plans."

"Well, Inès, it was a pleasure to talk to you," Nathan says. "Even under such… interesting circumstances."

I grin. "I promise I don't go around wrecking people's meals regularly."

"Good to know. My poor cake can rest easy." He glances at the mess and then at his watch. "I should probably go get someone who works here to help clean this up."

"Oh yes, uh, thank you, and again, I'm so sorry. I can definitely help pay in case they charge you for the damages," I say, wanting the ground to swallow me whole. Of course, it's just my luck that I bump into a very good-looking man and embarrass myself in the process.

"Don't worry about it," he says, hesitating as he looks from me to the checkout station, then back to me. Now, he looks awkward, almost boyish, it's cute. "I, uh… shit, this is weird. Believe me, I don't usually do this, but would you… I've got to run, but maybe I can get your number? I'd love to ask you out sometime."

That came out of nowhere. My first instinct is to laugh awkwardly and say no, because I don't date, and I don't date because I am hung up on someone, but didn't I just say I needed to date someone else to forget about Kingsley? And Nathan is hot. Sure, he seems a lot older than me, but what's the worst that could happen?

"Sure," I say, and he hands me his phone. I quickly type in my number. "Here you go."

With a smile, Nathan takes his phone back. "Great. I'll text you soon. And don't worry about the cake, I think you owe me one now."

I raise an eyebrow, smirking. "That's fair. Chocolate?"

"Definitely," he says, flashing me one last grin before heading off. I watch as he walks away. My heart is still racing, and I take a deep breath, trying to calm myself.

"You okay?" Meghan's voice comes through the phone, making me jump a little. I forgot she was still connected.

"Yeah, just bumped into someone," I say, shaking my head. "Literally."

"Yeah, I kinda heard everything, and it seems you gave him your number. Attagirl. Is he at least cute?" Meghan asks.

"I don't know, I guess," I reply, feeling my cheeks burn.

"Hell yes! Maybe this Nathan will make you forget all about King's stupid ass," she says, and a small feeling of guilt tries to take over, but I push it far, far away. I owe Kingsley nothing; he is not my boyfriend.

"Maybe."

"Now, hurry up and get back here. We've got a game night to prepare for."

"Alright, alright," I say, smiling despite myself. "I'll be there soon."

Meghan's and my apartment is in a charming four-story building just five minutes from campus. It's a new building, and I'm still amazed we got it for such a great price. Freshman year, we were required to live on campus, and I hated our coed dorm, need I say more?

As soon as freshman year ended, Meghan and I started hunting for an apartment. But this is Boston, and everything is expensive. Most of the apartments near school were out of reach since I work as a tutor and Meghan waitresses at a diner, neither job pays well enough to cover steep rents. And with our families not exactly rolling in money to help us out all the time, we had no choice but to sign up for another dorm. It was either that or live in a less desirable neighborhood. I needed something close to campus since I don't have a car, and while Meghan does, our schedules are different.

Then we saw a flyer for a new building in the area. When we saw the rent, we thought it was a joke or something was wrong with it, that's how cheap it was. But when we checked it out, it was too cute and clean to pass up.

It's a spacious two-bedroom, two-bathroom apartment with an in-unit laundry, a modern kitchen, and a patio. We were the first to move in, but over the past year, others have moved in as well.

Our apartment is a cozy haven, centered around a stylish sectional in a neutral shade. Colorful throw pillows and a soft, textured blanket on the arm of the sectional. A multi-functional coffee table, complete with storage, sits atop a plush area rug in a geometric pattern. The walls are adorned with a carefully curated gallery of framed prints, personal photos of Meghan and me from high school and some from college, and inspirational quotes, all softly illuminated by string lights.

As soon as I open the door, my black terrier mix, Beau, comes bounding toward me, his tail wagging furiously. I can't resist crouching down to greet him with my free hand, letting him shower me with kisses. "Hello, Beau! Hi, yes, I missed you, too." I laugh, giving him some love as I head to the kitchen to unload the groceries.

I found Euler Beau, yes, I named him after my favorite mathematician, Leonhard Euler, on my way home eight months ago. He'd been abandoned, so tiny and helpless, just a newborn lying in the snow. His pitiful whimpers broke my heart. I scooped him up, tucking him inside my coat, and immediately called Kingsley since Meghan was at work. I needed a quick ride to the vet. Kingsley arrived in no time, and together we rushed Beau to the clinic.

The plan was to make sure he was okay and then head home, but I couldn't leave him. Every time I thought about how cold, hungry, and scared he must have been, I couldn't hold back my tears. So, we stayed. When the vet told us he was fine, just in need of warmth and food, I felt a wave of relief. Then the vet asked if we wanted to take him home. I didn't hesitate. The paperwork was signed, and I was surprised when Kingsley signed it, too. That was the night we officially became dog parents.

"Meg?" I call out as I finish unloading the groceries and start getting Beau's meal ready.

"In my room!" she shouts back.

I crouch down again, petting Beau as he digs into his food. "I'll take you out when you're done, okay?" I say, deciding that finishing part of my assignment before game night can wait. Experience has taught me it's never worth risking a bathroom accident with a still-learning puppy.

I head to Meghan's room, making a beeline for her bed before flopping onto it. She's rummaging through her closet, pulling out clothes with a mix of frustration and determination.

Meghan is… how do I put this? Messy. There are clothes scattered all over the floor like a fashion hurricane just swept through. Honestly, she has more clothes than closet space. Some of her stuff even ends up in my closet because she's completely out of room. I glance at the clock and realize we have just enough time to get ready.

"Oh, finally! Here, put this on," she says, tossing something at me. It lands right on my face. Pulling it off, I realize it's a pair of short black overalls. I frown at her.

"Meg? I'm already dressed," I tell her, and we both look at the sweats and T-shirt I have on.

"No, you're not. Put that on, Inès, you have a bang-up body that most people pay for with that small waist and big ass, you just have to stop hiding it under those baggy clothes," she says, taking my hand and pulling me up. "And if you put this on there's, no way King won't notice you. You are unforgettable, Inès, you just need a little help getting out of your shell."

I snort. "Unforgettable in the way a particularly embarrassing moment is," I say, nibbling on a piece of dried fruit I find on her dresser.

"Stop that," Meghan admonishes. "And give me that, you know you can't eat sweets like that," she says, taking the fruit from my hand and popping it into her mouth.

I roll my eyes. It's true, I shouldn't indulge like this, especially with my type 1 diabetes, but sometimes I can't resist.

"Fine." I sigh dramatically, stepping into the black one-piece and adjusting it as best as I can.

Meghan gasps like she's just seen a celebrity. "Holy…"

"No, nope!" I cut her off, glaring at my reflection. "This is more appropriate for a strip club, Meg! My ass is hanging out!" I throw my arms in the air as I stare into the mirror. Sure, my backside looks amazing, but it's practically one wrong move away from a wardrobe malfunction. And don't get me started on my boobs, they feel like they're being vacuum-sealed.

"Ugh, you are no fun," she groans, pouting like she's the one who has to wear it. "Fine, but I'm not letting you wear anything baggy tonight." She's already on her way to my

9

room before I can protest. I follow her, because I have no choice.

After a few minutes of digging through my closet like she's on some kind of fashion treasure hunt, we finally agree on a simple yet elegant navy-blue dress. It hugs my curves in a way that says "classy" without screaming "desperate for attention."

"You look amazing," Meghan declares with a grin. "Kingsley won't know what hit him."

"Right," I reply, oozing sarcasm. "I'm sure he'll be just thrilled to see me in something that doesn't make me look like a cocktail waitress." I grab Beau's no-choke collar from the table. "I'm taking Beau out for a walk. Be right back."

Beau perks up, tail wagging like he's ready for an adventure.

INÈS

LOVE, LEASHES, AND CHOCOLATE

Back at the apartment after taking Beau out, my phone buzzes with a message from an unknown number. Curious, I unlock it and can't help but smile when I see the picture, a perfectly frosted chocolate cake, glossy and rich, with just the right amount of sprinkle flair.

> **UNKNOWN**
>
> A piece is yours if you want it. Tomorrow, during a date. — Nathan

I stare at the message, biting my lip to hold back a grin. He actually made the cake. And now he's using it to ask me out, smooth. I mean, who could resist?

"What's that look for?" Meghan asks, her eyes twinkling with mischief. Before I can turn off my phone, she snatches it out of my hand and reads the message aloud.

"Give me my phone, nosy!" I protest, reaching for it, but she darts to the other side of the sectional like a squirrel avoiding a dog. "What are you, five?"

Beau, my faithful little sidekick, lazily lifts his head and glares at us, as if to say, *Really? Can't you two keep it down?* But just as quickly, he flops back down, returning to his nap on the couch, blissfully ignoring our antics.

"Aww, he asked you out on a date! How cute!" Meghan says, her voice full of excitement. "I'm still salty that you didn't take a picture of him."

"Right, because that makes perfect sense. *Hey, I know we just bumped into each other, but can I take your picture? My best friend is going to want to see you,*" I retort.

"Exactly!" she replies, laughing.

I chuckle at her antics. "Give me my phone back, crazy."

As I reach for my phone, the doorbell rings. I know Meghan gave Justin the keys to the apartment building and our place. I don't mind at all, I love Justin. I've known him for two years and trust him completely. The same goes for Kingsley. Even so, I appreciate that Justin still rings the bell when we're home, it's a small thing, but it speaks volumes about his respect for our space.

Meghan hands me my phone and heads to the door. She opens it, and her delighted squeal fills the room as Justin sweeps her off her feet and plants a kiss on her lips. He carries her into the apartment, holding a bouquet of her favorite flowers. They're so cute together and truly perfect for each other.

Justin is the epitome of tall, dark, and handsome. He has striking light-brown skin that complements his tall, athletic build. His presence is both commanding and warm, with a charisma that makes him instantly likable. His features are sharply defined, and his smile has a way of lighting up the room. Both he and Kingsley are Québécois and have been friends since they were kids.

Justin's family owns one of the largest media conglomerates in the province. Their empire includes newspapers, television networks, and radio stations dedicated to promoting the French language and preserving Quebec's cultural identity.

"Get a room, you weirdos," Kingsley quips as he walks in, holding a huge bag of something in his hands.

I have to stop myself and force down the lump in my throat as I stand here awkwardly, wishing I could just be normal. I don't know why I act like a mute around him. I mean, it's been two years, and we've hung out plenty, so why am I still tongue-tied? Every time I look at him, it's like I've been hit by a freight train of awe.

Kingsley Ashford is a living, breathing masterpiece. He's not just tall, he's six-foot-five, a towering force next to my five-foot-four frame. His piercing blue eyes? They're like galaxies, pulling you in with a magnetic intensity that leaves you dizzy, lost in their depths. Broad shoulders, a chiseled jawline, he doesn't just look good; he's flat-out irresistible. And then there's his smile. Oh, that smile! It's lethal, made even more dangerous by those dimples that deepen with every grin. God, the dimples… I'm a sucker for them. Every single time, they undo me.

I'm completely starstruck every time I see him, like I'm the only one in a room full of art. How am I supposed to act normal when he's standing right there?

"Hi, butterfly," he says in that deep voice that without fail makes my knees weak.

Butterfly! He started calling me that almost the moment we met. I don't know why; I've never been brave enough to ask. But I am not mad about it because it, is all I feel when I'm around him.

"Hi," I manage.

Beau hears Kingsley's voice and jumps up in excitement

and bolts toward him. Just as he's about to leap into Kingsley's arms for a hug, Kingsley holds up a hand and gives a simple command. "Sit."

To my surprise, Beau obediently sits right at Kingsley's feet, his tail still wagging like a propeller, clearly thrilled to see him. It's unusual for Beau to listen to me like that, but for Kingsley, he's like a well-trained puppy.

"Good boy!" Kingsley praises, scooping Beau up immediately, showering him with kisses. I can't help but sit on the sofa, watching with a swoon as they love on each other. Kingsley and Beau are like two peas in a pod. I guess I'm not the only one who missed him while he was away on his work trip in Paris.

Kingsley's family didn't just found the prestigious university Meghan and I attend, they also own several successful businesses, including EcoTech Innovations, the company Kingsley works for. He started working there when he was just fifteen, which still blows my mind. He was supposed to officially take over as COO after graduating last semester, though for some reason, that title hasn't landed yet. Still, he's constantly traveling for work, and in the past five months, I've seen him less than ten times, not that I'm counting or anything.

Kingsley is impressive, to say the least. It's one of the many things I really admire about him. At only twenty-two, he carries so much responsibility on his shoulders, yet he handles it with such ease. And from what I can tell, it's not because he's obligated to work for the family business, he genuinely loves what he does.

"How do you make him listen to you so easily?" I ask, shaking my head in mock disbelief.

"I have my ways," he replies with an exaggerated air of confidence that's honestly so sexy. "I'm very talented at making people do what I want." He locks eyes with me brief, but intense, and a wave of heat rises up my neck, settling in my cheeks. His words hang in the air, carrying the weight of both a promise and a threat.

I clear my suddenly dry throat. "Right."

Kingsley sits down on the sofa next to me with Beau in his lap. "Who's a good boy? Yes, you are!" he coos, scratching Beau's belly as the pup's tail wags furiously. "That's why I got you something," he says, handing me a big bag. "Actually, I got you both something."

"Me? Kingsley, you didn't have to do that," I say, feeling my heart warm.

"I wanted to. Go ahead, open it," he replies, still scratching Beau's belly, which only makes Beau wriggle happily against him.

I open the bag, and just from a peek inside, I spot some luxurious dog accessories. One by one, I pull them out, first, a gorgeous plaited leather collar with Beau's name engraved on it, then two hand-painted, round ceramic dog bowls, and finally, some gourmet dog treats that look fancier than anything I'd ever buy. "Oh my God, Kingsley," I say, my voice filled with awe.

"Do you like them?" he asks, watching as Beau snuggles closer to him.

"I *love* them! Look at these bowls, they're so cute. Beau, say thank you!" I nudge Beau, who barks happily before nestling his face into Kingsley's lap.

"The last one's for you," Kingsley says, a knowing smile tugging at his lips.

Curious, I reach into the bag and pull out a small box. My breath catches. *No, he didn't.* I look at the box and back at him, and he's still giving me that beautiful smile that always makes me want to melt, but honestly, I'm already a puddle.

The box I'm holding says *A la Mère de Famille*, the oldest chocolate shop in Paris. I remember casually mentioning it in passing, that it was one of the things I missed from home. And he just… remembered.

"You remembered," I whisper, my heart swelling with affection.

"Of course I did," Kingsley says softly, his eyes twinkling. "I knew you'd appreciate a taste of home."

Beau barks again as if to say, *Yeah, thanks for the fancy new stuff, too!* Kingsley chuckles, giving Beau another belly rub.

"I… don't know what to say. Thank you! This means a lot," I exclaim as I open the box and see that Kingsley has chosen most of my favorites. "I've been craving these so much."

"You're welcome," he replies, looking back at me. "Just make sure you don't have too many, and always check your blood sugar first."

And *there* it is, the perfect example of how he does something incredibly sweet and thoughtful like a boyfriend would, but then immediately follows it up with big brother energy. I know he is just being overprotective, and sometimes it makes me feel special, but most of the time it makes me feel like a child.

Before I can answer him, Justin sits next to me. "What's up, Inès?" he says, giving me a warm, tight hug.

"Hey, J. Are you guys done making out, or should we give you two some more privacy?" I tease with a grin.

"Are you guys done pretending there's nothing here?" Justin says, waving his fingers between me and Kingsley. I know he's joking, but my heart rate spikes and my eyes dart to Kingsley, who is glaring at his best friend. My heart sinks at the look on his face, it's as if the mere idea of us being anything more is horrifying to him. *Don't cry. Don't cry. Do not cry.*

Sometimes, I let myself believe that Kingsley actually has feelings for me. The way his body language shifts when we're close, the lingering looks that last a second too long, and the fact that Meghan swears up and down that he's into me. It's enough to make me think maybe, just maybe, there's something there.

But then, without fail, someone will say something, and he'll do that thing where he stiffens up, his smile fading, like the idea of us makes him uncomfortable. That's when reality slaps me back down to Earth. It's like he pulls me in with one hand, but the moment I get too close, he pushes me away with the other.

And I'm left standing there, trying to decode a guy who seems fluent in mixed signals.

"Actually, Inès met someone," Meghan says. My eyes snap to her, stunned. What on Earth is she trying to do?

"Is that so?" Kingsley's tone has shifted, and I desperately want to gauge his reaction, but I force myself to keep my gaze fixed on Meghan. I shoot her a glare, annoyed that she's trying to make Kingsley jealous. As if he'd care if I met someone.

"Yup," Meghan continues, avoiding my eyes. "It was such a meet-cute. They bumped into each other at the store, and he asked for her number. Isn't that adorable?"

"Wait, you gave this stranger your number?" There's a note of judgment in Kingsley's voice that instantly puts me on edge.

I look up at him, my scowl deepening. "And what if I did? He asked, and he was cute, so I gave it to him," I reply, switching to French as my frustration flares.

"Butterfly, you don't just give your phone number to

strangers. I don't care how cute they are. What if he's a creep? Tu connais mieux,"[1] Kingsley responds, his tone firm, following me into French.

I roll my eyes. *Yes, let's all make sure no stranger harms his precious little sister, nope, not crushing at all!*

"Well, it's a good thing I didn't ask for your opinion. It's my life and my decision. It has nothing to do with you. I can give my number to whoever I want!" My voice rises, anger bubbling over. Okay, maybe that was a bit juvenile. I rarely talk to Kingsley like this, but this is just getting ridiculous. I have never met a person who sends out mixed signals like Kingsley Ashford.

He arches an eyebrow, and I catch Justin muttering, "Oh, shit," under his breath.

Meghan, sensing the tension, jumps in. "Uh, can we switch back to English? I'm sure all this yelling can be... yelled in English." She's the only one in our group who doesn't speak French, and though we usually try not to leave her out, I'm too pissed to care right now.

Unable to keep holding Kingsley's intense gaze, I huff in annoyance and move to sit next to Meghan.

"Alright, Pictionary time!" Meghan announces, yanking out the game board like it's a lifeline. "Inès and I are on a team, and you boys are on the other."

Justin grins. "Prepare to lose."

"In your dreams," Meghan fires back, clearly trying to diffuse the situation.

As the game goes on, I can feel Kingsley's eyes on me. It takes everything I have not to break and apologize for snapping at him. But no, I won't do it. Why should I? If anything, *he* should be the one apologizing for thinking he

---

1. You know Better.

has any right to dictate who I give my number to, or when, or why.

I steal a glance in his direction. His jaw is tight, but he stays silent, focusing on the game.

Good. Let him stew on it.

But still, that lingering tension between us makes it hard to concentrate. Beau comes to me and sits by my feet, offering me comfort, and I can't help but pet him.

KINGSLEY

KING OF REGRET

The words echo in my mind like a relentless drumbeat: *I am such an idiot.* After Pictionary, Inès practically ran to her room, mumbling something about an assignment, but I know she just doesn't want to see me. So, I respected her boundaries, no matter how much I want to go in there and make her talk to me.

I've always prided myself on my control, on my ability to keep my emotions in check. But when Meghan casually mentioned that Inès gave her number to some guy at a grocery store, that control shattered like glass. I know Meghan was mostly trying to provoke me, to see if she could get a reaction from me. I doubt her boyfriend has told her anything, but something tells me she doesn't need much to put the pieces together.

I've been in love with Inès since the day I first saw her, before she even knew I existed. I mean, who wouldn't be? Inès Dubois is the most beautiful woman I've ever laid eyes on. I've traveled the world, seen women who could easily be on the covers of magazines, but none of them hold a candle to her.

Inès embodies elegance and natural beauty. Her skin is a rich, warm brown, glowing with an inner radiance that catches the light perfectly, giving her a perpetual sun-kissed look. Her large, expressive eyes are a deep, velvety brown, framed by long, thick lashes that flutter with every blink, drawing me into their endless depths. Those eyes can speak volumes without her ever uttering a word, revealing emotions that captivate me completely.

Her petite frame is delicate yet strong. She might be small in height, but she is all woman with curves that are nothing short of mesmerizing. Her high, pronounced cheekbones give her face a sculpted, almost regal appearance, while the gentle slope of her nose leads down to full, luscious lips that, when they part in a smile, can light up an entire room. Her dark, curly hair frames her face perfectly, adding to her natural allure.

But Inès isn't just beautiful, she's brilliant, a genius, actually, though she'd never admit it. She'd just shrug it off and say she has an advantage most people don't, that she can recall almost everything she sees. But her genius goes far beyond a sharp memory. She graduated high school at just sixteen. Technically, she could have graduated at fourteen, but according to Meghan, when the principal suggested she start college at fifteen, her mother panicked, insisting Inès was still a child who wasn't ready for college. So, they waited until she turned seventeen to let her start. Talk about impressive. I've studied this woman for the past two years now, and yet every time I look at her, I learn something new.

She is not only brains and beauty, she's also kindhearted. She's the type of girl who sees a whimpering abandoned puppy in the snow and not only decides to take the puppy to the vet, but also stays to make sure he's okay and ends up adopting him. She's the kind of girl who volunteers once, sometimes twice a week at a neurology clinic to help care for and support patients and their families because her own family has gone through something similar, even though she already has too much on her plate and can't take on anymore.

Despite her busy schedule, she manages to balance her studies and volunteer work with grace. I often wonder how she does it all, and part of me feels inspired by her unwavering dedication. She has a knack for making everyone around her feel valued.

The day we officially met was a Saturday, at a freshman fraternity party. I usually avoid campus parties, I hadn't been to one before, ever, but that night, I had to go. I needed to see if the beautiful girl I'd spotted earlier, surrounded by butterflies, would be there.

Luckily, she was. While Justin got acquainted with Meghan, Inès and I started talking. We clicked instantly, unraveling bits and pieces of each other's lives. Of course, I had no idea she was only seventeen at the time; that little fact came to light much later.

The more we talked, the more I realized how much I liked her, but I also knew I couldn't lead her on. Any relationship we built would have an expiration date, and I couldn't ignore that. When all is said and done, I have to go back to Quebec and marry someone my parents have already chosen for me.

But how do you sit back and pretend not to want the only person you've ever loved?

"You listen to me," Meghan hisses, pointing an accusatory finger at me. "Inès is a sensitive girl with a big heart, the biggest. The last thing she needs is for you to keep playing with her heart and hurting her."

"Meghan, you know that's the last thing I want."

"Then man up and tell her how you feel before you lose her completely," she whispers, making sure Inès doesn't hear us.

I turn an accusatory glance toward Justin.

He immediately raises his hands in surrender. "Don't give me that look, I didn't tell her," he says.

"He didn't have to. The only person you're fooling with that friend zone bullshit is Inès. I see right through you, King. You've been in love with her since forever, so stop hurting my best friend or I swear to…"

Justin covers her mouth before she can finish her threat. "Alright, okay, woman, he got it."

I can't even be mad about the way she's speaking to me. Normally, no one dares, but she's only looking out for Inès, and I respect her for it.

"If you know about my feelings, why are you encouraging her to go on this date?" I ask her.

"Because she deserves to be happy and a part of me was hoping maybe it'll push you to confess your feelings for her. But until then she is allowed to go on a date with a nice man who isn't afraid to actually ask her out."

"I'll fix it, I promise." I give in with a sigh, and she seems to relax a bit.

"I hope so, because you guys are so perfect for each other, it's ridiculous."

Meghan's words linger in the air. She's right, I can't afford to mess this up, not when it comes to Inès. With a nod, I silently vow to make things right, knowing that nothing less than my all will be enough.

Once we're back at the penthouse Justin and I share, I slump onto the couch, feeling like the weight of the day has finally caught up with me. Justin saunters into the kitchen and pours us both a drink. The soft clink of ice against glass breaks the silence, and I can feel his eyes on me, gauging my mood.

"What are you going to do?" he asks, handing me a glass.

I take a sip, the burn of the whiskey doing little to ease the tight knot in my chest. "I don't know, man. But I can't sit back and watch her date another guy."

"No offense to your dad, you know I love him like my own, but he can't force you to go through with this marriage. You have a choice, frère,"[1] Justin counters, leaning casually against the counter.

"And lose the company?" I snap, running a frustrated hand through my hair. "That's everything I've worked for, and you know it. If I don't marry her, I lose it all."

"I don't think your dad would actually go through with that. You're his only son," he argues, his tone steady but insistent. "Plus, you're smart. You know this company inside and out. Why not work somewhere else? Or better yet, start your own?"

"And go where, J?" I shoot back, my voice rising slightly. "Start from scratch? Watch the company I've poured everything into go to someone else, someone who doesn't care about it the way I do? No, that's not an option. Not for me."

"It's either you stand up to your dad or you let her go, man. This isn't fair to her," he tells me, and he is right, I just wish it was that easy.

"Yeah, well, it's not that simple," I retort, feeling heat rising in my chest. "I can't just throw away everything I've worked for, and I don't want to hurt her."

"Then let her go, frère," he says, and I stay quiet for a while thinking, though not about letting Inès go; I'm too selfish and too far gone for that. She is mine and no one

---

1. Brother.

else's, but maybe I can find a way to get out of this business deal.

I glance at my phone, a sense of urgency prickling at the back of my mind. Maybe it's time to take a leap of faith. But can I risk everything I have ever worked for? What if it's too late? What if I lose her for good?

I decide to send her a quick text. I don't like that she's angry with me, maybe fixing that could be the start of something… anything.

> Hey, butterfly. I'm sorry. You were right, I have no say in what you do with your number. Let me take you out tomorrow so I can properly apologize.

I don't get a response until later in the night as I get ready for bed. She was probably studying and she always has her phone off when she focuses.

My phone dings next to me, and I quickly pick it up, but her response makes me want to throw it across the room.

PAPILLION

Can't, I have a date tomorrow.

That's all she says? She has a date tomorrow? Fuck, fucking fuck of all fucks! The love of my life is going on a date tomorrow with someone who isn't me. If she enjoys herself, she might want to go on more dates, and then what? I lose her forever? Merde![2]

> Don't go.

I hit send before I can think it through. I am so fucked.

---

2. Shit!

INÈS

PASTA, KISSES, AND UNWANTED THOUGHTS

I'm nervous, this is officially my first date. I never dated in high school because, one, my parents were strict, and two, I never really had the time. Between AP classes, honor roll, and extracurriculars, there was barely a moment to breathe, let alone date. I thought college would be different, that I'd finally have the freedom to explore, to experience what everyone else seemed to have already figured out. But no one ever asked me out, not that I wanted them to. The truth is, I only ever wanted one person to ask me out. But Kingsley will never see me as more than a friend, no matter how much I wish otherwise.

I sigh, pushing the thought of him out of my mind. *Stop thinking about him, Inès,* I scold myself. *You're on your way to a date with another man, for God's sake.* Last night, after game night, I was still upset, because Kingsley keeps acting like my brother, protecting me, caring for me, but never in the way I want him to. Honestly, I was more upset with myself for still crushing on him after all this time. It's unhealthy, and

I know it needs to stop. That's why, in a moment of frustration and determination, I texted Nathan back and agreed to go on this date. Maybe I shouldn't use Nathan to get over Kingsley, but that's not all this is. I actually want to go. Nathan is cute, after all. Sure, he seems a bit older than me, but that's not a problem. My dad is fifteen years older than my mom, and they're the happiest couple I know. Not that I'm saying Nathan and I are going to get married, God no, but if things go well tonight, maybe there will be a second date.

The second I park Meghan's car outside the Italian restaurant Nathan chose, Trattoria, my phone rings. I roll my eyes, knowing it's Meghan. She's been more anxious about this date than I am.

"Hey, Meg, I just parked. I'm still alive," I joke.

Meghan doesn't miss a beat. "Make sure you share your location with me and take a picture of the place, so I know where to lead the cops in case he turns out to be a kidnapper, or is it an abductor? I can never tell the difference."

I can't help but laugh, despite my nerves. "Neither, or, it depends on his reason for taking me, but if he does take me and calls to demand a ransom, then you can definitely call him a kidnapper. I shouldn't be the one to explain this to you, you're the one who wants to be a criminal lawyer," I tease, trying to mask my own anxiety with humor. It's not that I'm actually worried Nathan's going to kidnap me, the odds of that are less than one in a million. Statistically, kidnapping typically involves more deliberate planning and criminal motivation than an impulsive abduction. Yes, I did the math. Anyway, my nerves aren't about that. I'm more anxious about the date itself.

"*Bitch*, just make sure you share your location with me the entire time. If I don't hear back from you within an hour, I'm calling the cops."

"Alright, Mom, you got it," I reply with a grin, though her concern is actually comforting.

After we hang up, I do as she asked, sharing my location and snapping a quick selfie in front of the restaurant. The neon sign of Trattoria glows softly in the twilight as I smile in the photo.

Once I step inside, I realize Trattoria is more of a cozy pub than a traditional restaurant. The lighting is warm, with dim amber bulbs casting a soft glow over the rustic wooden tables. It's intimate, with the low hum of conversation and soft music playing in the background. There's a bar area that's full, which makes sense for a Saturday night, and a dining area that feels tucked away, offering a bit more privacy.

I scan the room, and my eyes land on Nathan. He's already standing up, smiling as soon as he sees me. He's definitely handsome, with his clean-cut look and easygoing demeanor. As I make my way over to him, I feel a little of the tension in my shoulders ease.

"Hey, you made it," he says warmly, stepping forward to give me a hug. The scent of his cologne hits me, earthy and leathery. It's surprisingly comforting.

"Hi, yes," I reply, returning the hug. "I'm sorry I'm late. I promise I'm usually on time, but my roommate was fussing over me."

Meghan had been relentless about getting me ready for this date. She straightened my hair, waxed my eyebrows, apparently, I had a unibrow, and did my makeup. The only thing I didn't let her do was pick my outfit. I decided on a navy-blue skirt that falls just above my knees, paired with a simple white shirt and white sneakers. It's the middle of August, and it's still hot out, so I wanted something comfortable but still cute.

"That's all right. You look beautiful."

I blush at his compliment. "Thank you. You don't look bad yourself," I reply as I take a seat across from him. "This place is great. I've never been here."

The restaurant itself is more than thirty minutes away from my apartment.

"Oh, yes. This was the first place I ate at when I moved here," he tells me.

"Oh? You moved here from where?"

"Vermont. I figured as an Italian, the first place I should eat at should be an Italian restaurant." He smiles coyly.

"You're Italian?" I ask just as the waitress arrives to take our drink orders. Nathan orders a beer, and I stick with water.

"Yes, born and raised," he says after the waitress leaves. "I moved to the U.S. with my family when I was fourteen."

"That's so interesting! I'm French. I also moved to the U.S., more specifically Minnesota, with my family, but I was ten," I share, feeling a small connection with him over our similar experiences.

Though I currently live in Boston, my parents still reside in Minnesota while my older sister lives in New York.

"That makes sense now," Nathan says, leaning in slightly. "I've been racking my brain, trying to figure out what your accent sounds like, and now I know, it's French." His eyes, which I now notice are a striking shade of gray, lock onto mine.

"Yeah, I guess I haven't gotten rid of my accent yet," I say with a small laugh.

"I like it. It's cute," he says, his voice softer now, almost as if he's sharing a secret. His eyes bore into mine, and I find myself getting lost in the moment, in the intensity of his gaze. For a split second, everything else fades away.

The waitress returns with our drinks, breaking the spell. We place our food orders before she leaves again.

"Which part of Italy are you from?" I ask, genuinely intrigued.

"A small town called Sorrento. It's right on the coast. The views are breathtaking, especially at sunset. You can see the Amalfi Coast from there." His eyes light up as he speaks, painting a picture of vibrant colors and rich culture.

"I'd love to see that one day," I reply, my imagination drifting to the beauty he describes. "It sounds amazing."

"You should. When you visit, take a boat to Capri and try the limoncello, it's the best you'll ever have. Oh, and don't miss the marina; it's a local favorite for late-night strolls."

"That sounds incredible," I say, smiling at his enthusiasm.

"What about you? What's your favorite thing about France?" He leans back, his interest seeming genuine as he waits for my answer.

I think for a moment, recalling fond memories of my childhood. "The food, definitely. My dad used to make the best ratatouille, actually, he still makes it but somehow it was better back home. And the bakeries! I miss fresh croissants; I used to be obsessed with them!" My mouth waters at the thought. "What about you? What's your favorite Italian dish?"

"That's easy, lasagna! My nonna's[1] recipe is unbeatable. It's layered with love, if that makes sense." He chuckles, and I can't help but smile at his enthusiasm.

"I think I get it. Food made with love always tastes better," I say, feeling a warmth spread in my chest.

As we continue chatting, I learn more about Nathan's family and their traditions. He tells me about Sunday lunch,

---

1. Italian word for: Grandmother.

filled with laughter and an abundance of food, where everyone gathers at the table.

Before long, our food arrives. Nathan's pasta dish looks mouthwatering, and my zucchini noodles with tomato sauce smell heavenly. We dig in, and I savor the flavors, the dish far exceeding my expectations.

"This is so good!" I exclaim, taking another bite.

"Right? I could eat this every day," Nathan agrees, his eyes sparkling.

As we continue eating, the conversation flows effortlessly. We talk about our favorite movies, music, and travel dreams. Eventually, we finish our meals, and the waitress comes by to check on us. I glance at Nathan, who seems content and relaxed. We ask for the bill, and she brings it. Nathan reaches for it, but I stop him.

"I can pay half!" I insist, not wanting him to think I expect him to cover everything.

"No way," he says firmly. "If you pay, then it's not a date."

I open my mouth to protest, but he holds up a hand. "Let me," he says, so I do.

"What? No way you were a stripper! I don't believe you!" I laugh, nearly doubling over as we walk out of the restaurant. I couldn't finish my plate, so they boxed it up for me to take home.

"I was," he insists, glancing at me with a smirk. "When I was twenty, college was expensive, so I danced for two years to pay for classes."

"Well, I guess I'm just going to have to see you dance to

believe it," I tease, smiling as I avert my gaze. I'm practically admitting I want to see him again. The night was surprisingly fun, I wasn't expecting to enjoy myself as much as I did.

"Is that a challenge, Inès?" he asks, his voice dropping an octave. "Challenge accepted," he adds, his eyes twinkling with mischief as we reach my car.

"This is me," I say, pointing to Meghan's old 2005 Hyundai Elantra.

"I had a lot of fun tonight," he tells me, stepping closer. My heart skips a beat. "I hope we can do it again sometime."

"Yes, me too," I reply, my voice almost a whisper. My throat feels dry as he closes the distance between us and gently presses his lips to mine. Oh, this is… this is happening, Nathan is kissing me. And now is the moment my brain decides to wander off to thoughts of Kingsley. Why does it feel like I'm betraying him? *Stop it, Inès. Don't be pathetic. You aren't his girlfriend.* But last night… his message felt like maybe he does have feelings for me. I mean, someone who doesn't care wouldn't beg you not to go on a date, right? Okay, maybe he didn't beg per se, but a girl can dream, right?

"Jesus!" Nathan's voice snaps me back to reality. He looks dazed, and he's smiling at me. Did I just completely zone out while he was kissing me? What is wrong with me? "That was amazing," he says breathlessly.

Not knowing what else to do, I lie. "Yes, amazing." But honestly, I felt nothing, no butterflies, no spark.

"Listen, I totally forgot your cake back at my house… maybe you'd like to come over tonight and get it," he says, not being at all subtle.

I give him a gentle smile. "I'll have to take a raincheck on that. Maybe next time?" I say fidgeting with the car keys. I am not an idiot. I know what he means by going over to his place tonight, and I am nowhere near ready for that.

"Sounds good, have a good night, Inès." He kisses my cheek this time, and I force a smile.

"Night." I open the car door as he takes a step back.

"I'll text you tonight."

"Uh, sure," I mumble, getting into the car. I start the engine and wave at him, I drive off, groaning in frustration. "Oh my God!" I mutter, feeling the overwhelming urge to bang my head on the steering wheel. What can I do to stop thinking about Kingsley? It's as though he has ruined me for any other man, and he hasn't even touched me, not like *that* anyway.

By the time I get home, I'm mentally drained. I spent the entire drive lost in overthinking, as usual. After showering Beau with kisses and checking that his bowls are filled with food and water, I pop my leftovers in the fridge. Then I head straight to Meghan's room, where I find her at her desk, her glasses perched on her nose. She dislikes wearing them, but she needs them to see clearly.

"Hey, so how did it go?" she asks, turning in her chair to face me.

I groan dramatically as I throw myself onto her bed.

"Oh, that bad, huh?" she asks, walking to me and lying down next to me, her concern evident.

"No, it's not that… Everything was going so well. We talked, got to know each other, and I wasn't awkward," I explain, staring at the ceiling.

"Okay, so why do you look like this was the worst date ever?" she asks, sitting up suddenly, alarmed. "Did he do something you didn't want?"

I shake my head, taking her hand. "No, Meg, no. He was a gentleman the entire time. It's just…" I sigh, feeling the weight of the situation pressing down on me. "After dinner, he kissed me…"

"Oh my God, how was it? Is he a good kisser?" she asks. Her excitement is palpable.

"I… I don't know."

"What do you mean you don't know?" Meghan's voice is laced with confusion.

"I… I zoned out and started thinking about Kingsley, so I don't even remember the kiss. God, what is wrong with me?" My voice cracks as tears start to well up.

"Oh, honey," Meghan whispers, pulling me into a warm, comforting embrace.

"I wanted this date to work so badly," I confess. "I thought maybe it would help me stop these feelings. I hate them. I feel so stupid, wanting someone who has made it clear time and time again that he doesn't feel the same."

"Hey, stop that. If there's one thing you are not, Inès, it's stupid. And how many times do I need to tell you that Kingsley is crazy about you?" I snort at her words, though I'm starting to believe her. "Listen, who's to say you can't try with Nathan one more time? If you like him, give yourself another chance. Maybe the kiss will be better next time."

"I guess," I say, getting off the bed. "I have a few assignments due Monday, but if Nathan asks me out again, I'll say yes."

"That's my girl!" Meghan cheers, making me laugh.

I retreat to my room with Beau following me. He makes himself comfortable on my bed as I sit on my desk diving into my assignments for the next three hours. If there's one thing I can always rely on, it's my books. Studying is the only thing that calms me. With each page I turn, each problem I solve, I can escape the chaos of my own mind. Numbers, facts, equations, they never change. They don't hurt. They don't confuse. They just are.

But then I hear it. "I just want to see her." Kingsley's

voice carries from the front door, and it's as if the metaphorical noise cancellation headset I had on was removed by an unknown force and I can hear everything now. A flutter runs through my chest. What is he doing here? My hand freezes over my notes, and suddenly, the tranquility I had wrapped myself in vanishes.

Panic surges through me as I glance around the room, even though it's spotless, neat and organized, as always. But then I look down at myself. I'm in sleep shorts and an old tank top with no bra, my hair thrown up in a messy bun. I look like a complete mess. There's no time to change, no time to make myself presentable. A part of me wants to hide, to pretend I didn't hear him, but another part, a deeper, desperate part, feels drawn to him, no matter how much I try to fight it. I feel like I'm standing on the edge of something dangerous, and the panic mixes with something else, something I don't want to name. Before I can think of what to do, I hear Meghan's voice at the door, softer now.

"Fine, but if she doesn't want to see you, then I'll drag you out," she says. Then there's a brief silence, followed by a knock on my door.

I clear my throat, trying to steady my nerves. "Come in," I say, my voice trembling slightly.

Kingsley walks in, his presence filling the room. He seems almost mythical, too powerful to be real. He's been in my room before, but this feels different. I'm barely dressed, and he looks... determined.

KINGSLEY

EMBERS OF ANGER AND ATTRACTION

As I step into her room, my gaze is immediately drawn to Inès. She's sitting at her desk, immersed in a sea of papers and her laptop. She looks up at me. Her delicate features are framed by the simplicity of a tank top and sleep shorts. The outfit is casual and unassuming, yet it reveals more of her than I've ever seen, her bare thighs, her arms, and… Is she not wearing a bra? The sight catches me off guard, and I feel a rush of heat. I force myself to look away, struggling to maintain my composure. *Jesus, Kingsley, focus. You came here to talk, not to gawk.*

Beau leaps off the bed and runs to me. I crouch down to give him some head scratches and a kiss on the head. "Hi, buddy," I say before he goes back to the bed. I stand to my full height, and my eyes go back to Inès.

"Hi," she says softly, almost shyly, breaking the silence. She's trying to act casual, but I can see the uncertainty in her eyes, the same uncertainty that's been gnawing at me since last night.

"Hi," I manage to reply, my voice rougher than I intended. I take a few steps deeper into the room, trying to focus on anything but how beautiful she looks sitting there. "Meghan isn't my biggest fan at the moment," I add, attempting to lighten the mood.

Inès chuckles, the sound sweet and innocent, completely unaware of the effect it has on me. The thought of corrupting that innocence, of showing her a side of me she's never seen before, is too tempting to ignore. But I have to, at least for now.

"What are you doing here?" she asks, her tone curious but cautious.

"I called and texted you," I explain steadily despite the storm brewing inside me. "I should have known you were studying."

"Yeah, I turn off my phone when I study…" Her gaze shifts back to her computer as if she's trying to distance herself from me.

"I know," I say with a smirk, closing some of the distance between us. The closer I get, the harder it is to keep my composure. "I wanted to check on you, see how you're doing."

She shrugs, her eyes not meeting mine. "I'm fine," she says, the words almost robotic as she pretends to focus on her screen.

The tension between us is almost unbearable, and I can't ignore the way she's shutting me out. It's clear this isn't just about the small disagreement we had last night. I know Inès well enough to recognize that her frustration runs deeper than a simple reprimand.

She's never been one to hold on to resentment this long, especially not over something as trivial as being told what not to do. If anything, I've noticed that her brilliance comes with its own challenges, she tends to carry the weight of the world on her shoulders. But when she trusts someone, she seeks their emotional support, even if she doesn't say it outright.

Determined to bridge the chasm between us, I gently reach down and tilt her chin up with my fingers, compelling her to meet my gaze. Her eyes, a rich, captivating shade of brown, lock onto mine, and in that fleeting moment, everything else fades away. The world outside this room becomes insignificant. Inès has no idea of the effect she has on me, how profoundly I'm affected by her presence. I would go to great lengths and endure any hardships to see her smile again and make sure she's safe.

"Inès," I murmur, my voice low and pleading, "I hate fighting with you, butterfly. I can't sleep knowing you're upset with me." The words spill out, raw and honest. I can't remember the last time I begged anyone for anything, but with her, it's becoming a habit. "Please, say you forgive me."

Finally, she gives me a small smile that stops my heart altogether. I want to bathe in that smile, lose myself in it. If I could spend the rest of my life just making her smile, I would be a very fulfilled man.

"Okay, fine, I forgive you. I can't really stay mad at you," she says, her voice soft and warm, like a favorite song you didn't realize you missed until you hear it again.

"How was your date?" I ask, unable to keep the sneer out of my voice. The words taste bitter on my tongue. I've tried to play it cool today, but the thought of her out there with someone who isn't me was driving me insane. It took everything in me not to track her down and stop her from going.

Whatever spell I had her under breaks, because she yanks her chin out of my grasp, sitting up straight. "It was great, perfect," she says defensively, crossing her arms over her chest. The movement only accentuates her breasts, pushing them up, and I swear this is the sweetest form of torture.

"Does that mean you're planning on going out on another date?" I ask, my voice dripping with disdain. I pronounce the word "date" like it's the worst curse imaginable.

"Yup. We might even make a nightcap out of it, who knows?" she quips, her tone light but her eyes challenging.

"Don't be cute, Inès," I warn, my patience thinning. This isn't how I saw this conversation going.

"Who says I'm being cute?" she teases. At least, I hope she's teasing.

"I wouldn't test me on this," I growl, my control slipping.

Inès narrows her eyes and stands up, her movements deliberate. Jesus, those shorts are even shorter than I thought. My resolve weakens as I force my eyes to stay on her face, which is now closer to mine than I anticipated.

"Why do you care?" she challenges, her voice low and steady. "You realize that you're not my brother, right? Or my dad? I can date whomever I want. Hell, I can even sleep with whoever I want, "

Before she can finish that thought, I grab her and pin her against the wall. Our mouths are inches apart, her breath warm against my lips. Her pupils are dilated, and her breaths come out in short, rapid pants.

"Listen to me, and listen carefully, papillon,"[1] I growl, barely above a whisper, thick with possession. "You won't be going on any more dates, and you sure as fuck won't be sleeping with anyone else. Do you understand me?" I'm so close to her that I can almost taste her. She smells intoxicating, like coconut and cherry, and I want nothing more than to devour her right here, right now.

---

1. Butterfly.

"Why not?" she retorts, her voice dripping with defiance. Jesus, how I crave to bend her over my knee and spank her until she can't see straight. I have to admit, I have a weakness for brats, especially the ones who seem innocent until they reveal their true colors.

I lift my hand and wrap it around her delicate neck, feeling the rapid pulse beneath my fingertips. Her pupils dilate impossibly wide, and she bites her lip, clearly turned on by the possessiveness in my touch. "Because you are mine. You have been mine from the moment I saw you. If you think I'm going to let another man take what's mine, then you've got me all the way fucked up."

In an instant, something shifts in her eyes. She goes from looking completely turned on to absolutely enraged. "No," she spits out, pushing me away with a force that doesn't match the strength of her small frame. But I stay rooted, unwilling to let her push me away completely. "Stop. Let go."

I release her immediately and take a few steps back, giving her the space she demands.

She takes a shaky breath, her cheeks flushed and her eyes blazing with anger. "I am not yours. The only reason you're here saying all of these things I've been dying to hear is because someone else is interested in me. You only want me because someone else is playing with the toy you tossed aside. Well, guess what, asshole? I am not a toy, and I am most definitely not yours."

Tears, which I hate seeing on her, start to fall down her cheeks. Each drop is like a dagger to my heart. I step closer, desperate to fix this, my worst nightmare unfolding before me, her crying because of me. "Butterfly, that's not true…" I try to bridge the distance, but she pushes me away again, her anger giving her strength.

"Yes, it is. Otherwise, you would have tried to claim me a

long time ago. You knew, you knew how I felt about you," she cries. "You've been nothing but confusing, and I'm over it."

"Inès, it's complicated. I can't just… I can't risk our friendship," I say, though the words feel hollow, weighed down by the truth I'm too afraid to admit. Yes, our friendship means everything to me, but it's more than that, I want more. The thought of holding her, of calling her mine, consumes me.

But I know I have no right to feel this way, let alone say it aloud. She deserves better than the mess I'd bring into her life. A part of me even considers risking everything, my business, the wedding, just to have her. But that isn't smart. It's reckless, and it would cost me everything I've worked for.

Inès lets out a sarcastic laugh, the sound ripping through the thick atmosphere. "Then why are you here? Telling me that I belong to you?"

"Because…" The word hangs in the air, and I struggle to find a justification for the possessiveness that consumes me. I want to confess my love, but I know that revealing my true feelings could destroy the fragile bond we share. I'd rather cling to the hope of friendship than risk losing her completely.

"Right," she scoffs, her expression shifting from curiosity to disappointment. "Well, you know what? That's fine. Because someone better came along. And you know what? I don't want to see you again. So, go. Get out. Just go."

Each word she hurls at me feels like a puncture straight through my heart, and I stand there, paralyzed, caught in a storm of conflicting emotions. The thought of losing her, even as a friend, sends a chill down my spine. I want to reach out, to take her hand and pull her close until she calms down, to comfort her and make things right. But I know she needs space, time to process. I give her one last look, hoping it conveys how deeply sorry I am, before turning around and leaving the apartment.

As I walk away, I feel every step like a heavy weight on my chest. The only thing I can think about is how to fix this, how to prove to her that I am committed to her, not just reacting to someone else's interest. The thought of losing her forever is unbearable, and I know I have to do everything in my power to make things right.

INÈS

PROFESSOR X STUDENT

"Hey, how are you feeling?" Meghan asks as she walks into my room while I'm getting ready for school.

I know Meghan's trying to get me to talk about what happened between Kingsley and me the other night, but the truth is, I'd rather not go there. Just thinking about it makes my head throb. Kingsley saying that I was *his*, those words should mean something, right? They should imply that he has feelings for me, but the context feels all wrong. It bothers me, deeply, that he only seemed to realize what he wanted when someone else showed interest in me. That's not okay with me. I deserve more than to be someone's choice out of fear of losing me. And until he understands that, I don't know if I can move past it.

"Aside from the annoying headache I woke up with this morning? Yeah, I'm fine," I say with a smile, beginning to gather my things. "I've got four classes and two tutoring sessions today, so it's going to be a busy one."

Tutoring has become a regular part of my routine. It's not a huge source of income, but it's enough to get by. More than that, I love it. There's something incredibly fulfilling about teaching, breaking down complex ideas and watching that moment when everything finally clicks for someone. It brings me a sense of joy and purpose, and it helps that I'm good at it.

"Inès, you know that's not what I meant…"

"Meg, I'm fine, really. I've just got a lot on my plate today, so whatever boy problem I have can take a back seat. School is my priority," I say, giving her a reassuring smile because I mean it. School has always been my focus, and being a neurologist my goal, and now, more than ever, I need to keep my head in the game.

I'm here on a scholarship, Ashford University was my first choice, but my family couldn't afford it, so I worked hard to earn a full ride, a full ride only 0.05% of applicants received, so there's no room for error. I can't let myself get distracted now, especially not because of boy problems.

"I have to go. I can't be late, we've got a new psychology professor starting today. Please remember to take Beau out before and after work, thank you!" I say. Grabbing my laptop, I head for the door, giving Beau lots of kisses before leaving.

Last week, we got an email from the dean informing us that Professor Raven was retiring for personal reasons and that we'd be getting a new professor. That's all the information we were given, no name, no background, not even whether the new professor is male or female. Honestly, I don't care who they are as long as they are a good professor.

When I arrive at Hawthorne Hall, where the psychology department is located, I have just enough time to stop by Mind Brew Café for a pick-me-up. I order a large vanilla latte with stevia instead of regular sugar. Just one sip of the coffee starts to ease my headache. I head to my usual seat at the front of the room. The new professor hasn't arrived yet, so I take out my old but functional laptop, my notebook, and a pen, preparing for class.

"Good morning, everyone. I apologize for my delay. I give you my word that I won't be a repeat offender!" a voice rings out just as I take another sip of my hot coffee. I choke on my coffee, causing it to spill all over my laptop, my shirt, and my notebook, making a mess.

Oh merde![1]

Merde.

Merde.

Merde.

My heart races at the familiar voice. I know that voice, no, it can't be. There's no way. I lift my head, only to come face-to-face with Nathan's gray eyes. He looks just as surprised to see me as I am to see him. I wish the ground would open up and swallow me whole.

"Miss?" Nathan asks, close enough now that when I look at him, I can see the tightness in his jaw.

"Dubois," I manage to whisper, stunned.

Nathan reaches into his suit pocket and pulls out a hand-kerchief, offering it to me with a look of genuine concern. I take it and notice the psi symbol embroidered on it. I then dab at the coffee stains on my laptop and notebook. Thankfully, my laptop still turns on, I can't afford another one.

"Are you okay, Miss Dubois?" Nathan's voice is soft but filled with an underlying note of concern.

"Yes, I'm sorry. I just… sorry," I stammer, trying to manage the mess and my mounting embarrassment.

"That's all right," he says, stepping back to give me

---

1. Oh shit!

space. "As I was saying, my name is Dr. Nathan Salvatore, but to you, it's Professor or Dr. Salvatore," he adds, writing his name neatly on the whiteboard.

This can't be happening. Am I dreaming? I discreetly pinch myself and wince in pain. No, this is real. What are the odds of meeting a man, going on a date with him, and letting him kiss me, only for him to turn out to be my professor? I do a quick mental calculation.

0.0001 percent.

I close my eyes, trying to will away the new headache that's starting to pound behind my temples.

"Professor? How old are you?" a girl asks, her voice full of a purring curiosity.

Thirty-one.

"That question is not appropriate," he responds firmly. "I am willing to answer any questions as long as they pertain to the course material, not my private life. Now, as I was saying, please clear your desks. This exam will not count towards your grades; it is merely to gauge where everyone stands and how well you've comprehended the lesson plan thus far."

The room fills with groans and complaints as he hands out a four-page exam. I finish it in less than thirty minutes, but I pretend to work on it for the remainder of the time to avoid drawing attention. I can feel Nathan, no, not Nathan, Dr. Salvatore's eyes on me, but I do my best to ignore him. I need to figure out what to do about this mess, and fast.

About another thirty minutes later, students start putting down their pens. As class ends, Dr. Salvatore addresses the room. "Alright, I'll see you all on Thursday. The discussions will be posted on the school website. Remember, class partic- ipation and discussions are 5% of your grade. It might not seem like much, but it helps. My office hours are Mondays and Thursdays, from 2 PM to 4 PM, in room 305. If you have any questions, make an appointment first."

Everyone starts gathering their things and making hasty exits. I try to slip away unnoticed, but Dr. Salvatore's voice stops me in my tracks. "Miss Dubois? My office, please." Then he heads to his office.

Merde.

A few minutes later, I find myself standing outside Dr. Salvatore's office, my nerves frayed as I contemplate knocking on the door. My coffee-stained shirt clings uncomfortably to my skin, and the lingering smell of coffee is the last thing I need as I prepare to face him. With a final, resolute breath, I lift my hand and knock.

"Come in," he calls out.

I push the door open, letting it swing wide as I step inside. "You wanted to see me, Professor?" I ask, my voice betraying a hint of nervousness. Dr. Salvatore is seated behind his desk, his expression unexpectedly warm. I frown slightly, taken aback by his demeanor. I had anticipated a more stern or perhaps even angry reception.

He rises from his seat and walks past me, causing my confusion to deepen. What is he doing? My apprehension grows as he moves to close the door.

"Professor…" I start, but my words are cut off as he suddenly closes the distance between us. Before I can react, his lips are on mine and he's pulling me closer. The kiss is intense and invasive, his tongue pushing into my mouth with a hunger that catches me off guard. I can feel the hard bulge of his erection pressing against me, and my mind races, struggling to process what's happening.

I'm paralyzed, my thoughts colliding in a chaotic swirl. Why do I feel more butterflies when Kingsley is in my room than I do now, while Nathan kisses me? On our date, I thought it was because I was distracted, but now the truth hits me hard, I feel nothing. This kiss, meant to be passionate, leaves me cold and unresponsive.

Desperately, I push him away, shaking my head in disbelief. "No," I say, my voice trembling as I take a step back. "Stop, you can't... we can't."

Dr. Salvatore looks shocked, his eyes widening in confusion. "What do you mean?"

"You're my professor," I explain, trying to steady my breathing. "I'm sorry, but I can't."

He seems taken aback by my reaction. "Inès, I understand this isn't conventional, but as long as we're discreet, we should be fine," he argues, his voice filled with a mix of hurt and frustration.

I frown deeply. Did I miss a conversation about us being something worth being discreet about? As far as I know, we've had one date, and while we've texted and planned another, it's hardly the basis for a secret relationship.

"I... I'm sorry, but I can't risk my scholarship," I say, my voice firm despite my inner turmoil. "And you shouldn't risk your job. What we had was fun while it lasted, but it can't continue. My education means everything to me."

A flicker of hurt and regret crosses his face before he lowers his gaze. "Right, of course. You are absolutely right. I'm sorry for assuming... I just really like you, so..." He offers me a sad smile. Oh God, now I feel bad.

"I'm sorry..."

"I'm a grown man, Inès, please don't pity me. I'm fine. Hopefully, we can stay friends," Nathan says, extending his hand for me to shake. His voice is steady, but there's an undercurrent of hurt that's hard to ignore.

It's on the tip of my tongue to tell him that a friendship between a professor and his student is entirely inappropriate given what just happened between us, but I can see the genuine sadness in his eyes. I don't want to make him feel worse than he already does, so I take his hand and shake it. The gesture feels formal, almost alien, given the intimacy of what just happened.

"Friends," I echo, trying to sound as sincere as possible. I offer a small smile, hoping it conveys my attempt at kindness.

"I… I should go. I have another class," I add awkwardly, gesturing toward the door.

"Right, of course. Hey, I'll see you in class on Thursday," he says.

"Yeah, I'll be there," I say, quickly opening the door and dashing out. God, that was the weirdest situation I have ever been a part of.

Making my way to my probability and statistics class, I try to shove the thoughts of Dr. Salvatore and the lingering awkwardness out of my mind. As I walk, my phone rings unexpectedly, jolting me. I quickly fumble for it, realizing I forgot to turn it off. It's always off during class time, how could I forget? Great, I'm already getting distracted.

Just as I'm about to turn off my phone, Camille's name lights up the screen. My sister, my only sibling, is two years older than me and has always been the dreamer of the family. She's an aspiring ballerina who fought tooth and nail to earn her spot at Juilliard.

It's not an easy life, even though our parents help with tuition she's still juggling part-time jobs to cover rent for the tiny studio apartment she shares with her boyfriend, Avery. But Camille has always been a fighter, pouring her heart into everything she does. We're all rooting for her, because if anyone can turn dreams into reality, it's her.

"Salut, poupée,"[2] she chirps the moment I answer, her voice a joyous melody. She's called me "poupée" since I was a baby. She was convinced I was a doll when our parents first brought me home. I suppose it made sense to her two-year-old mind.

"Hey, Mimi. I can't talk long, I'm about to head to class. How are you?"

"Missing you, as always. But enough about that. You still haven't told me about your date with Nathan. Was it fun?"

I cringe, but then a laugh bubbles up because it's absurd now that I think more about it, but it wasn't a few minutes ago.

"It was fine... until I came to class today and discovered he's my new psychology professor."

She gasps. "Shut up! You're kidding." She's clearly taken aback, but there's a note of amusement in her tone.

"I wish I was. You have no idea how awkward it was."

"I think it's pretty hot," she teases.

"Camille!" I scold, though I'm still laughing.

"Oh, come on. Don't tell me you've never read those professor x student steamy novels."

"I haven't, and even if I did, those are fantasies. This is real life, and I could lose my scholarship," I say with a mix of exasperation and amusement.

"Relax, would you? I'll send you a few of my favorite stories, but don't read them in public," she warns playfully.

I roll my eyes. "You're hopeless. I have to go. I'll call you later. Je t'aime."[3]

"Je t'aime aussi, poupée."[4]

---

2. Doll.
3. I love you.
4. I love you too, doll.

I end the call, shutting off my phone and slipping it into my bag before heading to my next class.

INÈS

BEAU KNOWS BEST

As soon as I slide my key into the lock, I hear growling from the other side of the door. My brow furrows in confusion as I open it, revealing Beau, growling and barking like I've never heard him before. He doesn't settle until he sees me.

"Whoa, hey, what's going on?" I ask, scooping him up when he runs to me. I press a kiss on his head, feeling a little concerned. He never acts like this. "Are you okay, mon amour? [1]Hungry?"

I carry him to the kitchen, but his bowls are still full like someone just refilled them. "Was your aunt Meghan just here?" I question, setting him down. He sniffs around but doesn't touch his food, so hunger isn't the issue. Deciding he might just need some fresh air, I grab his leash and take him out for a run.

An hour later, he's back to his usual self, playful and full

---

1. My love.

of energy. Feeling relieved, I head home. Just as I walk in the door and turn my phone back on, it buzzes with a call from my mom. I answer as I step into my room, already smiling.

"Salut, Maman,"[2] I greet her warmly, my chest tightening with how much I miss everyone. I haven't seen my family since last year, and between school and everything else, a trip back to Minnesota just isn't in the budget right now.

"Mon ange,[3] how are you?"

"I'm fine…" I pause in the middle of my room, glancing back at the dresser I just passed. One of the drawers is slightly open, which is strange because my room is always spotless, and I know I closed that drawer. Maybe Meghan was in my room? Sometimes she borrows things, but that drawer is where I keep my underwear.

"Inès? Are you there?" My mom's voice pulls me back to our conversation.

"Uh, yes, sorry. I think Meghan was in my room."

"How is Meghan?"

"She's fine. I think this semester has been tough on her, but you know Meghan, she'll surprise everyone in the end." I put the call on speaker so I can change and shower.

"She's a very smart girl." It's true. People often underestimate Meghan because of how outgoing and social she is, always the life of the party. But I've seen her pull all-nighters, show up to a test after a night of drinking, and still manage to ace it. She's the only person I know who can pull that off. "Are you coming home for your dad's birthday?" Mom asks over the phone. "Your sister and Avery are coming down, and I was hoping to see you too." Avery is Camille's boyfriend and soon-to-be fiancé. They've been together since high

---

2. Hi, mom.
3. My angel.

school, and last week he called me asking for help picking out a ring and planning the proposal. I smile at the thought, it's exciting, and I know Camille will be over the moon. I just have to keep the secret until then.

My dad's birthday is in November, and this year it falls on Thanksgiving. I really want to be there with my family, but I'm not sure I can afford the flight and my bills. But the thought of missing his birthday, especially with it landing on a holiday, makes my heart sink. But with three months left, maybe I can squeeze in some extra tutoring sessions and save up enough to make it work. It's not impossible, I'll just have to manage my time better. I know how much it would mean to him if I could be there.

"I don't know, Maman. I'll have to check, but I'll let you know." I enter my bathroom, one of the things that sold me on this apartment was that both Meghan and I have our own bathrooms, not to mention the price.

"Papa[4] and I could try to put some money together for you…"

"Maman, non.[5] Don't worry about me; I'll find a way to get there, so I'll see you then." I stop her from offering money they don't have. My mom is a high school French teacher, and my dad is a sous chef. We didn't have much growing up, but I wouldn't change my life for anything. Camille and I grew up happy and loved, even if our parents were a bit strict about school. But I didn't mind that one bit.

"Are you sure, mon ange?"

"Maman."

"Alright, well, I'm going to let you go. Je t'aime, mon

---

4. Dad.
5. Mom, no.

ange.[6] Oh, and don't forget to call your papa, he misses you, and say hi to Beau for me."

"Je le ferai.[7] Love you, too Maman," I say before hanging up. I open my cabinet and pull out a new Dexcom G7, my continuous glucose monitor, along with some alcohol wipes. Laying everything neatly on my bed, I take a deep breath and head to the bathroom to wash my hands. It's time to change my Dexcom again, something I've been doing since I was fourteen. I hate it. Fine, I'm being dramatic, it's not that I hate needles, I've got piercings, so clearly, I can handle those, but changing my Dexcom and taking insulin is what I hate.

You'd think after all these years I'd be used to it, that it would just become routine. But every time, without fail, I find myself tearing up. It's not the pain, really. It's the emotional weight of it, the reminder of what it means to manage my diabetes every single day. It's like clockwork, I tell myself to stay calm, but the moment I sit down to do it, the tears come.

It takes far longer than I'd like to admit getting the new Dexcom inserted and my insulin injected. Every step feels like an ordeal, a test of patience and resolve. By the time I finally finish, I'm completely worn out, crying in the shower, letting the hot water cascade over me. Thankfully I get some puppy love afterward, Beau has been with me for eight months now so as soon as he sees me pulling out my insulin or Dexcom he comes and lies next to me to let me know that he is here for me, and it means the world.

A few hours later, after finally finishing my homework, I'm curled up on my bed, engrossed in one of the books Camille recommended. I had to borrow Meghan's Kindle

---

6. I love you, my angel.
7. I will do it.

since I don't have one of my own, but I'm surprisingly enjoying it, despite how unrealistic the story can be. There's something comforting about getting lost in a world that's far removed from my own reality. The plot might be a bit far-fetched, but that's kind of the point, right? Sometimes, it's nice to escape into a fantastical narrative, even if it's just for a little while.

"Hey, hey, hey!" Meghan sing-songs as she bursts into my room, throwing herself onto my bed. "Today was a long day," she groans, pulling Beau on her lap and petting him.

I glance at the digital clock on my wall and frown. "It's almost ten. Did you have a double shift today?" Meghan works as a waitress at Hooters. She loves the job, especially the tips. Justin hates that she works there, but he knows better than to tell her not to, if anything, it would just make her want to do it more.

"No, I was with J... and King," she says, watching me carefully as if I might combust at the mere mention of his name. And with the way I'm heating up, it feels like a real possibility. "He misses you, you know."

I think I might miss him more, but I don't say that.

When I don't react, Meghan switches gears. "So, have you spoken to Nathan? And when do I finally get to see a picture? You're killing me here, you know I'm a curious and impatient creature. Put me out of my misery."

At the mention of Dr. Salvatore, I start laughing again.

"Ouhh, sounds like something juicy happened. Come on, spill!" She sits up, her eyes wide with curiosity. Having had enough of us, Beau leaves the room.

"You have no idea how juicy," I say, still laughing.

"I'm on the edge of my seat here, Inès. Come on."

"Remember when I told you my psychology professor was retiring, and we were getting a new one?"

Her mouth hangs open at the realization of what I am implying.

"No!" She gasps, amusement all over her face.

"Yep. Turns out Nathan, or should I say, Dr. Salvatore, is my new professor."

"Holy shit! Why am I low-key jealous of you right now?" she says, and I roll my eyes because we both know how happy she is with Justin. "So, did you guys, you know, get it on in his office or something?"

I throw my pillow at her, hitting her square in the face. "You and Camille are too much alike. No, we did not get it on in his office, he's my professor," I say firmly.

"I guess that makes sense."

"But... he kissed me."

Meghan's eyes go wide again. "Wait, was this before or after you told him you couldn't date him?"

"Before. He kind of took me by surprise," I explain.

"And?"

"Well", I sigh, "I expected to feel butterflies, you know, the way you've told me you feel every time Justin kisses you. But I didn't. I feel more with Kingsley than with Nathan, and I haven't even kissed Kingsley." I groan in frustration.

"Okay, this needs to stop. This push-and-pull game you and King have been playing for two years, it's getting old. You like him, and now you know he likes you, too so what's the problem?"

"The problem is that he only realized he likes me when someone else showed interest. And that's not how I want him," I say, contemplating my words. Am I overreacting? Am I just trying to find a reason to push him away because I'm afraid of my feelings for him? It was one thing knowing my feelings were unreciprocated, but now that they are, why am I so scared?

INÈS

LINES THAT BLUR

The clinic hums with antiseptic and quiet murmurs, a background I've grown to find comforting over the year I've spent volunteering here. Each time I walk through these doors, I feel the familiar mix of nerves and excitement. Neurology fascinates me to a degree I can't explain to most people, even though everyone here is caring, genuinely invested in the patients. But my interest? It goes beyond fascination. It's rooted in a history that, no matter how much time passes, feels fresh in my mind, the memory of watching my grandfather slowly fade from the man who told me bedtime stories to someone who struggled to recognize his own family.

As a double major in biology and psychology with a minor in math, I'm used to juggling complex theories and concepts, but this, the human element, is something no textbook can prepare me for.

After a quick change into my scrubs, I grab the patient roster for the day, smiling when I see Mr. Hernandez's name.

He's someone I've come to know well, a retired musician who suffers from moderate Alzheimer's. We have a silent understanding between us, one that allows him to be himself, however fragmented that self has become.

When I enter Mr. Hernandez's room, he is sitting in his wheelchair, looking lost until I say his name. His face lights up at the sound, and he reaches a trembling hand toward me.

"Inès, mi niña,"[1] he says, his voice faint but affectionate.

It's not every day that I'm reminded of my grandfather in this way, but with Mr. Hernandez, it's impossible not to think of him. I squeeze his hand, feeling the frailness of his fingers, and remind myself why I'm here. Alzheimer's is cruel, and more vicious than people realize until they see it up close.

"¿Cómo estás hoy, Mr. Hernandez?"[2] I ask, smiling.

He talks, his voice like a quiet melody, about things half-real and half-remembered, drifting seamlessly from a memory of his wife to an imagined adventure in the Caribbean. As he speaks, I listen intently, leaning in, nodding where needed, letting him feel heard and understood. In some ways, this is my own study, an analysis of what's left when memory disintegrates, the parts of a person that remain.

Afterward, I sit with Mrs. Lawson, a retired teacher who has the sharpest wit and an arsenal of math puzzles she brings out whenever I visit. She struggles with early Parkinson's, so we work on small motor exercises as she goes on about her former students and math theories. She asks me about my studies, pushing me on calculus problems and teasing me about my minor.

"Most kids go to college to avoid math, and here you are, collecting degrees like trophies." She laughs, though her

---

1. Spanish for: Inès, my girl.
2. Spanish for: How are you today, Mr. Hernandez?

smile wavers when her hand trembles and she drops her pencil.

"It's not trophies. It's just… logic," I reply, picking up the pencil and guiding her fingers back around it. "Math, biology, psychology, they're all just pieces of a puzzle that explain us, don't you think?"

"Yes, but how many people are brave enough to look for those answers?" She grins at me, her eyes still bright with intelligence. Her gaze has a way of making me feel seen, her questions always going deeper than surface-level curiosities.

I enjoy talking to her; she's sharp, an academic in her own right. I tell her about a recent paper I read on neuroplasticity, and we discuss the brain's ability to adapt, a fascinating topic to her as a teacher and to me as a student of life itself. She grasps concepts as quickly as I do, and we fall into an easy rhythm, exchanging theories like peers.

As I'm leaving her room, I feel the presence of someone at the far end of the hallway. I glance up, half expecting one of the regular doctors, but my breath catches when I see him, Dr. Salvatore, leaning casually against the wall, a faint, almost calculating smile on his face. I blink in surprise. He's… here? I wasn't aware he worked at the clinic. I have been volunteering here for over a year now and have never seen him. He just moved here, so that might be the reason why, but still it's weird to see him here.

When he catches sight of me, he offers a thin, almost hungry smile and strides over.

"Inès," he greets, his voice smooth, a bit too pleased. "I didn't know you volunteered here."

"I do. Been here over a year now," I reply, hoping my unease isn't obvious. "Do you… work here, too?"

He tilts his head, his eyes fixed on mine, his gaze lingering a little too long. "Occasionally. I consult. There's always something to be learned from this place, don't you agree?"

"Yes, definitely," I say politely. But his stare doesn't waver.

"In fact, I've been keeping an eye on your work," he says, in a low voice. "I'm intrigued by your passion. Few students seem to have the same... hunger."

I blink, unsure if he means it as a compliment or if there's something else lurking behind his words. "Thank you, Dr. Salvatore," I reply, keeping my tone as neutral as possible. "It's a field I'm dedicated to."

"Of course. Listen, I've been meaning to ask you about your IQ?" he asks casually as if he is simply asking about the time or the weather.

I falter because, who asks that to someone they barely know? He must have figured out that I am smarter than average, though I don't understand why he would come to that conclusion given that he's been my professor for less than two weeks and we've never had a one-on-one about anything intellectual.

"Excuse me?" I ask, I don't mention my IQ to many people, in fact, only my family knows, which includes Meghan.

"Down girl, I'm only asking because I am your professor, and it's the type of thing I need to know," he says, and I cringe, did he just say down girl? He seems like a completely different person than the one I went on a date with, which is making me feel uneasy. "How about I make it fair? I have an IQ of 158," he says, smiling, though his smile seems forced.

I wonder if he asked me about my IQ just so he could brag about his own. For a split second, I consider giving him a lower number, something modest, if only to spare his ego. But I push that thought aside. I'm not going to downplay myself for anyone, especially not a man who asked for the truth.

"Mine's 161," I say, letting the number hang in the air.

He goes still, and a flicker of something, surprise, maybe even relief, crosses his face. His gaze sharpens, and there's an odd light in his eyes as he studies me more intensely than before.

"You're even smarter than I realized," he says, voice softer, almost reverent.

That reaction surprises me, and I can't tell if his approval is flattering or unsettling.

"Is that shocking to you?" I ask, trying to keep my tone casual.

His mouth curves in a faint, almost secretive smile. "It confirms what I suspected. You're extraordinary, Inès."

There's a quality to the way he says it, a mix of admiration and an undertone I can't quite name, as if he's seeing through me, beyond me, to a truth only he can grasp.

He steps just a fraction closer, his eyes pinned to mine with unnerving intensity. "Do you know how rare it is to find someone with both intelligence and…" his gaze dips, sweeping over me in a way that feels heavier than it should, "compassion."

Something about his tone makes me think compassion isn't what he truly meant. But I force a smile, playing along.

"I like to think they go hand in hand," I say, folding my arms to create a small barrier between us.

A low, dark chuckle slips from him, and he shakes his head slowly. "Only in the rarest cases," he murmurs. "Most people are driven by one or the other. And most people certainly aren't capable of truly… understanding."

A frown tugs at my brow, and for a moment, I wonder what exactly he's trying to convey. His gaze lingers, drinking in my reaction, holding the silence long enough to unsettle me before he finally takes a step back.

"Well, I won't keep you from your rounds," he says, his voice deceptively casual. "I have a feeling we'll be seeing more of each other soon. It was good to see you again, Inès. I'm glad we'll be... working together."

There's a subtle emphasis in his words, one that suggests this "work" he's referring to extends beyond the clinic, beyond what's appropriate between professor and student. Most men don't take rejection well, I've learned, but I'd expected someone with Dr. Salvatore's intelligence and career success to respect the boundaries implied by our positions. A man like him should recognize the logical dangers: the conflict of interest, the academic consequences, the ethical implications.

But the way he stands too close, the way he seems at ease invading my space, makes me wonder if his awareness of those risks is merely theoretical, something he understands but has chosen to disregard. And it would be one thing if I were interested. But I'm not. I have no desire to complicate my life with a relationship that could jeopardize everything I've worked toward.

As I continue with my work, I catch him glancing at me from time to time, and it's as though his attention lingers like a soft, persistent buzz in the back of my mind, just quiet enough to question, yet not too constant. I could be overanalyzing; I know my mind tends to dissect details in search of patterns, sometimes inventing connections where none exist.

Still, the impression doesn't fade, even after I leave the clinic. I'm logical, rational to a fault, but there's a fine line between analytical and perceptive. And something about Dr. Salvatore's gaze feels too intentional to ignore.

INÈS

THE BUTTERFLY EFFECT

I'm sitting in the back of the lecture hall, struggling to focus on Dr. Salvatore's lecture on cognitive psychology. His voice is a soothing murmur in the background, but my attention keeps drifting. My blood sugar is low, I can feel it even before checking my Dexcom app.

I usually keep an emergency snack with me for situations like this, a granola bar or a pack of glucose tablets, just in case my levels dip too much. Low blood sugar can make me lightheaded, shaky, and irritable, and if it drops too far, it could lead to confusion, fainting, or even more serious complications.

A quick glance at my Dexcom app confirms my suspicion: my levels are at 73. Not dangerously low yet, but if I don't eat something soon, it'll get worse. I usually manage to keep my levels steady, but lately, between tutoring, my own workload, and the stress of planning a trip home for my dad's birthday and Thanksgiving, I've been letting my health slip.

As the class winds down and students begin filing out, I

slip my notebook into my bag, ready to head home. It's my last class of the day, and without any tutoring sessions lined up, I'm looking forward to an evening of uninterrupted study, after I eat something, of course. But as I turn toward the door, I spot Dr. Salvatore weaving through the crowd of students, his gaze already fixed on me.

"Inès," he calls, his voice cutting easily through the noise of the room. "May I speak with you for a moment?"

I pause, weighing his approach. In the last few days, he's managed to not corner me or act overtly inappropriate. In fact, he's been almost entirely professional, a shift I'd consider genuine progress if I didn't still feel his gaze on me during class and at the clinic, like an unspoken presence that's always just a little too near.

I nod, following him out of the lecture hall and down the hallway to his office. The door clicks shut behind us, and I stiffen slightly. The last time I was here, he kissed me, and I hope nothing of the sort happens again.

Dr. Salvatore takes a seat behind his cluttered desk and gestures for me to sit across from him. My heart pounds with anticipation. What could he want to discuss?

"Inès," he begins, his gaze steady and serious, "I've been observing your progress in my class, and I'm quite impressed."

I blink and relax. Oh, he wants to talk about my performance in his class. This is one topic I'm more than willing to discuss with him.

"I have an opportunity I'd like to offer you," Dr. Salvatore continues. "I'm looking for a TA for next semester, and I believe you would be perfect for the role."

My eyebrows shoot up in surprise. It's not that I don't want the opportunity or that I'm not grateful, but it's not something I had considered or worked toward. I'm a bit taken aback that he's offering me the position when I'm only nine-teen. Sure, I'm a junior, but still.

"You look surprised. Do you not believe you deserve it?" he asks, raising an eyebrow.

I sit up straight and put on a composed expression. "No, that's not it at all. I do believe I deserve it. It's just that it's more common for graduate students to be TAs, and I'm only a junior. I was just a bit taken aback, that's all."

"With an IQ as high as yours I'm surprised you haven't been offered the position before," Dr. Salvatore says with a smile. So, this is why he asked for my IQ? "I've been paying close attention to your work. You're more than qualified for the position. In fact, based on your records, you're the only student in my class who fits the bill."

Warmth floods my chest at his words. Recognition from someone of Dr. Salvatore's caliber, it's validating in a way I hadn't anticipated. I'd assumed, admittedly a touch overcon-fidently, that his attention had less to do with my intellect and more to do with his... lingering interest. I mean, with the constant glances, the inexplicable tension, and that odd exchange we had at the clinic, can you blame me for making a calculated assumption?

But maybe I misjudged him. Perhaps his focus has always been academic, and I've read too much into things.

"And as for compensation," Dr. Salvatore adds, reaching for a sheet of paper on his desk, "you would be paid three thousand dollars per semester, plus additional benefits that we can discuss in detail another day."

My eyes widen at his words. Three thousand dollars per semester? That's more than I currently make.

I'd accept the job immediately if it weren't for the fact that my low blood sugar is starting to make me shake. "This is such a generous offer, Dr. Salvatore. But I need some time to think about it," I manage to say.

Dr. Salvatore frowns as if he had expected me to jump with joy and say yes on the spot, but then his expression changes to that of understanding. "Of course, Inès. Take all the time you need. But know that I have every confidence in your abilities. You have a bright future ahead of you."

"Thank you." With a grateful smile, I rise from my chair but sway a little.

"Whoa there, are you okay?" Dr. Salvatore catches me gently. "Is it your blood sugar? Is it low?"

"Yeah, I…" I pause and frown. "How do you know about my blood sugar?" I ask, wary.

"Relax, Inès. I saw your glucometer the other day in class. You should eat something," he says, trying to help me out of his office. The last thing I need is someone to see him holding me and think something inappropriate is going on.

"Yeah, I will. Thank you, I'll be fine." I step out of his grasp.

"Are you sure?"

"Yes, thanks," I say, stepping out of Dr. Salvatore's office with a polite nod. The moment I'm outside, my gaze falls on a sight I know all too well, a sleek, black and gold Bugatti parked front and center. Kingsley is there, leaning against the car with his signature cool indifference, drawing a small crowd of admirers. Typical.

I roll my eyes internally; I'm too drained to summon a real reaction. He's been away on business again, and I haven't seen him since our fight, one that left words unspoken and emotions raw.

Of all the cars Kingsley owns, this one is his prized possession. He doesn't let just anyone ride in it. *He let you in it once*, a little voice in my head reminds me. But that doesn't count. That was only because I had a tutoring session to get to, it was pouring rain, and Meghan was busy. Kingsley just happened to be there, and he offered me a ride, no big deal. At least, that's what I keep telling myself.

"Inès?" Kingsley abandons his group of admirers when he sees me and walks over. His frown deepens as he approaches. "Butterfly, are you okay?"

"King…" I sway again.

"Shit, it's your blood sugar, isn't it? Come here." He wraps his arm around my waist, guiding me to his car. The girls are gone, which is a relief. Kingsley helps me into the passenger seat and then rounds the car to the driver's side. He opens the center console and pulls out a packet. "Here, take this," he says, opening the packet and handing it to me. Seeing what it is makes me want to cry.

"Kingsley? Why do you have glucose paste in your car?" My voice is weak, and not only because of my low blood sugar.

"Swallow it all first, then I'll explain." He uses that authoritative tone, the one I can't help but obey.

I put the small end of the packet in my mouth and suck on it. It tastes as disgusting as you'd imagine. I swallow it and lean back in the seat, knowing it will take about fifteen minutes for my levels to rise.

Kingsley takes the empty packet from me and stows it somewhere out of sight. He leans over to buckle my seatbelt then starts the car and begins to drive. "To answer your question," he says, his voice gentle, "I keep these glucose packets in all of my cars for you, in case you have low blood sugar."

The fact that he thought ahead and bought glucose packets for me in case of emergencies makes me feel over-whelmed. I'm too weak to cry, so I hum in acknowledgment and close my eyes, letting the warmth of his care wash over me.

I wake up to a gentle caress on my cheek. When I open my eyes, I see Kingsley, his dimples showing as he smiles softly at me. "King?" I croak, trying to sit up.

"Yes," he answers as he helps me up.

"Where am I?" I ask, looking around.

"My room. I made you something to eat." He sets a tray on my lap. The tray holds a sandwich made with what looks like multigrain bread, smashed avocado, chicken, and tomatoes, along with a bowl of grapes and a glass of water.

I've never been in Kingsley's room before. I've been to his penthouse, but never his private space. It's cleaner than I expected, masculine and sophisticated. The room is dominated by dark, rich tones: deep, matte charcoal walls contrasted by sleek, polished ebony hardwood floors. A California king-sized bed with a high, upholstered headboard in dark leather takes center stage, dressed in high-thread-count cotton sheets and a plush, charcoal gray duvet.

The furniture is minimalistic yet opulent, black lacquered nightstands with clean lines, each holding a modern lamp with geometric brass accents. A matching dresser displays an array of expensive colognes and accessories, all meticulously organized. Floor-to-ceiling windows are draped with heavy, dark gray curtains.

"Are you allergic to color?" I ask.

He chuckles, a rich, velvety sound that I could listen to forever. "You're more than welcome to add however many colors you want, but first, eat." He gestures toward the tray.

"Bossy."

"You have no idea." He smirks, getting up and walking to what I assume is his bathroom. He returns a moment later and sits next to me on the bed. I try not to feel nervous as I take a bite of the sandwich. I almost moan, it's delicious. I'm so hungry that I devour the sandwich quickly.

"Now, want to tell me what happened?" Kingsley asks, taking a grape and popping it into his mouth.

"What do you mean?"

"You usually have a better handle on your blood sugar levels. What happened today?" He looks at me intently. I bite my lip, suddenly feeling like a kid about to get in trouble. Kingsley gently touches my lips with his thumb, tugging at my bottom lip so I release it. His finger lingers, and I'm tempted to lick it, but he drops his hand.

"I… I've been busy and just forgot to eat, that's all."

His frown doesn't ease, it gets more intense. "You are not one who easily forgets anything, so how about you tell me exactly what happened?"

"Okay, fine," I say, feeling a bit defensive. "I didn't have enough time to eat. I had classes and tutoring sessions this morning, and I thought if I could just make it through my last class, I'd be okay." Seeing the frown on his forehead deepen even more, I add, "I needed to do those tutoring sessions. I need the money, my dad's birthday is coming up, and I want to go home for it."

Kingsley's expression softens as he listens. "I see. I understand why you'd push yourself like that, but from now on, prioritize your health. I understand school and tutoring are important, but you need to put your health first. If you see that you won't have time to eat, call me, and I'll come to you and feed you myself if I have to." His tone is stern, making me sit up straight. God, I'm pathetic.

"You can't tell me what to do; you're not my brother or..." My old argument seems weak even to my ears. I honestly don't know why I'm giving him a hard time when I love it when he tells me what to do.

He grabs my chin and tilts my head up to meet his eyes. "Believe me, butterfly, I'm not telling you this as your brother." His eyes drop to my lips briefly, and I instinctively lick them.

"Then as what?" I ask, my eyes locked on his piercing blue eyes.

He smirks. "How about I take you out on a date tomorrow, and then I can tell you just what I am to you?" He lets go of me. I'm so caught up in his spell that I don't immediately process what he said, but then it hits me, Kingsley asked me out on a date!

"You... you want to take me out on a date?" I ask, sounding dumbfounded.

He smiles. "Yes, if you would allow me. Tomorrow is Saturday, and I thought we could go somewhere and enjoy each other's company."

My smile fades instantly. "Are you saying this just because I went out on a date with someone else? Because if you are..."

"Inès, I promise it's not about that. Please, just give me a chance to show you, it's never been about you going on a date with someone else. Let me take you out because I want to," he says, and as if he wasn't already getting his way he smiles at me, he puts his dimples on full display.

I snort. "Okay, fine. Whatever." I try to act cool, but it only makes him laugh deeply, which is delicious.

"You're adorable," he says, and I blush.

"I should probably go home before Meghan freaks out," I say as he takes the tray off my lap and stands up.

"I already texted Meghan earlier, she's here in Justin's room, but you should shoot her a text, too just to let her know you're okay. Oh, and Beau's here, too he's in his room," he says.

A few days after we adopted Beau, Kingsley turned a small closet that was not so small into the cutest dog room ever. Meghan and I had so much fun decorating it; it was one of those random projects that ended up being way more fun than we expected.

"If you want to stay the night, you're more than welcome," he adds. "I can sleep in my office. You can shower if you want, I set aside a few things for you."

"Wait, what? No. King, I can't ask you to do that, I can sleep in the living room..." I pause, when did I start calling Kingsley King?

"Good thing you didn't ask, I offered. Go take a shower, I'll be back when you're done." With that, he leaves the room, not giving me the chance to say anything else.

I find my phone on the dresser and text Meghan.

> Hey, sorry to have worried you, but I'm fine.

I send the text and climb out of bed. My backpack is on Kingsley's dresser, so I retrieve my insulin bag and set it on the bed before I head into his bathroom.

The space is a luxurious retreat with marble finishes, a walk-in shower featuring a rainfall showerhead, and a deep soaking tub. Everything is pristine and elegant.

My phone buzzes with a message from Meghan.

MEG

Oh, I'm so glad, babe. You can't scare me
like that! King told me he offered you his
bed. Rest up, and I'll see you tomorrow.
Love you 😊

Love you too. See you tomorrow.

I take a quick shower, the hot water easing the tension in my muscles as I reach for Kingsley's body wash. The scent hits me instantly, rich, fresh, and utterly intoxicating. I close my eyes, letting the steam surround me as I breathe it in, momentarily wishing I could stay in this luxurious, fragrant bubble forever. There's something comforting about it, like I'm wrapped in him, even though he's not here.

Once I'm finished, I towel off and step out of the shower, my gaze landing on the clothes he left out for me: a shirt that practically swallows me whole, more like a dress than an actual shirt, and a pair of shorts that are too big. I fold the waistband over to make them work, shaking my head with a soft smile.

But then, something else catches my eye. A small package sits neatly on the counter, the sleek brown wrapping tied with a delicate satin ribbon. My brows furrow as I pick it up, my heart already fluttering in anticipation. I carefully pull at the ribbon and open the package, and the moment I see what's inside, my breath catches.

A bonnet. A *brown* bonnet.

I lift it out, running my fingers over the fabric, smooth, luxurious, softer than anything I've ever felt before. Anything I have. The quality is undeniable; it's thick yet lightweight, made to protect my hair without causing tension or friction.

I press my lips together, trying to keep the overwhelming

emotions at bay. He thought about this. About me. About my *hair*.

Looking around, I spot one of his combs on the counter. I run it through my damp hair, carefully braiding it in to two French braids before slipping the bonnet on, adjusting it over my head, and stare at myself in the mirror. It fits perfectly, securing my hair in a way that feels effortless. I swallow the lump in my throat as warmth spreads through my chest.

Kingsley never stops making me fall for him more.

Less than a minute after I head back to the room, there's a soft knock on the door.

"Come in," I call out, and Kingsley peeks his head inside.

"Did you find everything okay?" he asks, stepping fully into the room with Beau nestled in his arms, the puppy already half-asleep against his chest.

"Yes…" My eyes stay on him, watching him carefully. "You got me a bonnet."

His gaze flicks to my head, and the faintest hint of a smile tugs at his lips. "It looks good on you."

I shake my head slightly, still processing it. "King, you got me a *bonnet*."

To some people, it might not seem like a big deal. But to me, as a Black woman? This *is* a big deal.

"I got you a few more," he says casually, like it's nothing. "They're all in my closet."

My lips part slightly in surprise. "*Why*?"

He shrugs, and for the first time since I met him, he looks almost boyish, like a man caught doing something thoughtful but not entirely sure how to explain it.

"I always see you wear one when you're home," he says simply. "And I know how important it is for your hair, so I got a few extras. Just in case." His voice softens as he adds, "What's important to you is important to me."

My heart clenches at his words, a slow, sweet ache settling deep in my chest.

"Thank you," I whisper, my voice barely more than a breath, but he hears it.

He gives a small nod, his eyes locked onto mine, the weight of unspoken things stretching between us. We just *stand there*, caught in the kind of silence that isn't empty, but heavy, thick with longing, with questions neither of us is ready to ask, with emotions neither of us knows how to name.

His gaze dips to my lips, and I swear I see something flicker there, something raw, something that makes my breath catch. My fingers twitch at my sides, aching to reach for him, to close the space between us.

And then,

Beau sneezes.

The tiny, dramatic *achoo* startles both of us, shattering the moment like glass. Kingsley blinks, straightens, running a hand over his jaw as if shaking off whatever had just passed between us.

"Come here, baby!" I say quickly, reaching for Beau as he wiggles free from Kingsley's arms, leaping straight into mine. I press a kiss to his head as his tiny tail wags furiously, his warm tongue flicking against my cheek.

Kingsley watches for a moment before asking gently, "Before I leave you for the night, do you need any help with your insulin?" His concern is written all over his face.

"Actually, yes. I hate doing it, and it takes me too long when I have to do it myself," I admit as I walk closer to the bed, I take a seat and put Beau on my lap.

"Of course. Let me wash my hands first." He heads into his bathroom. While he's gone, I prepare everything and lie back on the bed with Beau on the other side of me with his head on my chest to offer me comfort. I lift Kingsley's shirt just enough to expose my stomach. When he returns, I explain the process.

"Just do it. Don't tell me when, okay? Just…" I start, my voice trembling. I cover my face with one hand while the other caresses Beau, feeling tears welling up. "I'm ready."

"I've got you," Kingsley reassures me. I feel a brief sting as he administers the injection. I stiffen, a sob catching in my throat. Somehow feeling my pain, Beau whimpers, snuggling closer to me. "There, all done," Kingsley says softly, removing the needle.

I keep my eyes covered as tears silently fall.

"You did so well," he says in a soothing voice. I feel his gentle kisses on my stomach, sending shivers and butterflies through me.

Kingsley carefully tucks me and Beau in and presses a soft kiss to my forehead. "Bonne nuit, papillon,"[1] he whispers tenderly.

"King?" I call out just before he leaves the room.

"Yes, Queen?" Oh my God, he just called me Queen!

"Would you mind staying with me tonight?" I ask, my voice barely a whisper in the dark.

"Are you sure?"

"Yes, please. Just hold me." Sometimes the loneliness of dealing with this illness daily is just too much.

There's a pause, and then I hear him closing the door and moving toward the bed. The mattress dips as he settles in beside me. He wraps his strong arms around me, pulling me close. I pull Beau to us, too. My back presses against Kingsley's chest, and I've never felt so safe and cherished.

Kingsley's presence feels like a warm cocoon of security as he wraps his arms around me. His body against mine is a

1. Goodnight, butterfly.

comforting weight. The softness of his touch and the gentle rise and fall of his chest create a sense of peace I've never experienced.

"Is this all right?" he asks softly, his voice a low murmur against my ear.

"Yes," I reply, snuggling closer to both of my boys. "This is perfect."

He lets out a contented sigh and tightens his hold slightly as if to say he's just as comfortable as I am. The darkness of the room is soothing, and the occasional rustle of the sheets is the only sound that breaks the silence. I can feel his heart beating steadily beneath my ear, and it lulls me into a state of tranquility.

"Bonne nuit, papillon," he whispers again, his breath warm against my neck. "Sleep well."

INÈS

*VERY DEMURE, VERY CUTESY, VERY
MINDFUL*

As the first light of dawn creeps through the curtains, Kingsley's warm, possessive arm tightens around me, pulling me closer. His breath is steady and calm against my neck, a stark contrast to the raw intensity he usually exudes. His scent, woodsy with a hint of something darker, wraps around me, cocooning me in a sense of safety I've never felt before.

I slowly open my eyes, blinking away the remnants of sleep. Kingsley is still asleep, his face relaxed and peaceful, looking more beautiful than I ever imagined. Beau is not in bed, so he must have left at some point in the night. I've dreamed of waking up in Kingsley's arms but never thought it would actually happen. Gently, so as not to wake him, I hover my hand over his face, tracing each of his features. His thick, dark eyebrows and sharp jawline are captivating, and I can't resist the urge to admire him.

But as I shift slightly to continue my exploration, I freeze. Something hard is pressing against my inner thigh, and it keeps growing. My eyes widen, and I quickly cover my mouth to stifle a gasp as my cheeks burn with realization. Oh my God! It's his erection, or at least, I think it is. Curiosity gets the better of me. I've always loved research, and this feels like the kind of "research" I need to do. Slowly, I drag my thigh against it, and it twitches in response. Holy... I do it again, and again, each movement intensifying the ache between my legs.

I glance up at Kingsley to make sure he's still asleep, but he's already awake, those piercing eyes locked onto me with an unwavering focus that makes my heart race. My blood turns cold as I squeak, caught in the act.

"I hope you know what you're doing," he murmurs, his voice a deep, gravelly rumble that sends shivers down my spine. His hand, big and strong, gently caresses my cheek, and I melt under his touch. "Morning, butterfly," he says, his gaze roaming over my features and lingering on my lips.

"Morning," I whisper back, my voice barely audible as my heart pounds in my chest.

He shifts, leaning in to kiss the top of my head before untangling himself from me and standing up. I can't help but let my eyes drop to the enormous erection tenting his pajama pants. "Come on, let's brush our teeth and get some break-fast," he says, taking my hand and pulling me out of bed. Whether he noticed my ogling or chose to ignore it, I'm not sure, but I follow him to the bathroom in a daze.

In the bathroom, I find a new toothbrush and toothpaste laid out for me by one of the sinks. Kingsley goes to the other side, and we start brushing as if we've done this a thousand times. I steal glances at him, noticing the tattoos on his arms peeking out from under his shirt. One in particular catches my eye, a pair of fists bumping on his forearm, a tattoo I know Justin has in the exact same spot. It's endearing to see this side of him, the side that's deeply connected to those he cares about. His body is sculpted to perfection: tall, lean, and muscular. Even the way his shirt clings to him feels unfairly attractive.

"You can't leave this room like that," Kingsley says once we finish brushing.

I frown. "What's wrong with it?" I snap, a little more defensive than I intended. I like wearing his shirt; I'd spend the whole day in it if I could.

Kingsley raises a perfect eyebrow at me, a silent admonishment that makes me feel like a scolded child.

"Sorry," I mumble.

"As much as I love seeing you in my shirt, I don't want anyone else to see you like this," he says, his tone soft. "I'm going to see if Meghan left some spare clothes here you can borrow. I think it'd be a good idea to keep some of your things here too, just in case." He leaves with a kiss on my forehead, and I stand there, stunned.

Did he just suggest I leave some of my things here? The idea of spending more nights in his arms fills me with giddy excitement I can hardly contain.

A few minutes later, he returns with one of Meghan's handbags and hands it to me. "She said she brought a few things from your apartment last night."

"Thank you." I take the bag.

"Let me change out of these quickly before you change," he says pointing at his pajama set before heading to his closet.

I rummage through the bag, relieved to find a pair of jeans, a nice shirt, and underwear, thankfully, because I've been going commando all night. Meghan even packed my hair kit, I can't survive without shea butter.

Kingsley emerges from his closet, looking effortlessly

handsome in a navy-blue half-zip sweater over a crisp white undershirt and khaki pants. The combination makes him look polished, though I can't help but think he looks even better with his hair tousled in that just-woken-up way I secretly prefer.

"Take your time," he says softly, leaning in to place a gentle kiss on the top of my head. "I'll get started on breakfast."

As he leaves the room, I can't help but smile, the memories of last night rushing back. He took care of me, he asked me out on a date! We slept in the same bed, and now, he keeps kissing me on the head like it's the most natural thing in the world. Am I dreaming? Because this feels like a dream, and if it is, I never want to wake up. The man I've had an almost unhealthy crush on for years is treating me the way I've always imagined, always wished, he would. It's everything I wanted, and while I couldn't be happier, part of me knows I need to calm down. It all feels too perfect, like it's happening too easily, except I know it hasn't been easy at all and this has been building for so long.

I take my time getting ready, making sure every detail is perfect. My curls are carefully defined, and I take extra care moisturizing my skin before slipping into the outfit Meghan brought me. When I finally leave the room, I head to Beau's room, which is right next to King's. I peek my head in to see that he's resting so I leave him be and make my way downstairs, hearing the familiar sounds of laughter and conversation. I've been here enough times to know the way to the kitchen, so I head there, feeling a mix of nerves and excitement.

The penthouse is nothing short of breathtaking. Perched atop one of Boston's most prestigious high-rises, it's a masterpiece of luxury and modern design. As you step off the private elevator, you're greeted by a double-height foyer with gleaming marble floors and a grand chandelier that casts shimmering light throughout the space. The open-concept living area is an expanse of elegance, with floor-to-ceiling windows offering stunning views of the city skyline. Plush, designer furnishings in neutral tones are arranged around a sleek, custom-built fireplace, and contemporary art pieces adorn the walls, adding a touch of sophistication.

"There she is," Justin says when I walk into the kitchen. Kingsley is behind the stove, focused on whatever he's cooking, while Justin and Meghan are seated on the bar stools at the island, enjoying their breakfast. When Meghan sees me, she jumps up and hugs me tightly.

"Hi, babe, how are you feeling?" she asks, her voice full of concern.

"I'm fine, honestly. I just forgot to eat, that's all," I reply, trying to reassure her.

Kingsley turns around, his gaze locking onto mine. "Yes, and we agreed that she won't do that again, didn't we, butterfly?"

I nod and roll my eyes as I take a seat next to Meghan. Almost immediately, Kingsley places a bowl of oatmeal with cut-up apples and crunchy walnuts in front of me. "Thank you, King," I say shyly, warmth spreading through me at how attentive he is.

"You're welcome, Queen," he replies, his voice softening as he meets my gaze.

"Aww, you guys are too cute, I can't!" Meghan exclaims, and then, with a dramatic gasp, she adds, "Oh my God, Inès! We can finally check 'spending the night with a guy' off your list!"

I choke on my oatmeal, panic setting in. *Oh no.*

"List? What list?" Kingsley asks while I start shaking my head furiously.

"Meg!" I wheeze, still coughing.

Without missing a beat, Kingsley places a glass of water in front of me, which I gratefully take.

"Oh yeah, she didn't tell you?" she says with a teasing grin. Why, Meghan, why on Earth would I tell my crush about a silly bucket list we made in high school? I internally roll my eyes, praying she doesn't go into too much detail. "So, in high school, we wrote each other a bucket list to finish before we turn thirty. Inès wrote five for me, and I wrote five for her. Here's hers," Meghan says, handing Kingsley her phone.

"Meghan!" I exclaim, mortified.

"Oh, hush. We're all friends here," she says, winking at me.

"Yeah, butterfly, we're all friends here," Kingsley repeats, a mischievous glint in his eyes as he looks down at the phone. His expression shifts from curiosity to amusement to shock, and his eyes drop to my chest before he smirks. Oh. My. God. I'm dying inside, because I know exactly what he's reading.

> Sneak a guy into your room (at your parents' house).
> * Get a nipple piercing (both nipples).
> Lose your V-card (preferably before college).
> * Go to five college parties with me (have at least one beer).
> Spend a night with a guy (in the same bed).

It was Meghan's way of making sure I had some fun, since she always thought I was too serious for my age. I don't mind it; I've even completed numbers two, four, and now five. But still, having Kingsley read it is beyond embarrassing.

Meghan's list, in contrast, was all about making sure she took life a little more seriously:

Graduate with at least a B average (I'll help you study).

Get into Ashford University with me (please!).

No more sneaking guys into your parents' house (you know better).

Date someone for more than two months (don't just sleep around).

Pass the bar! (And we'll celebrate however you want).

"Interesting. Do you mind sending me that, Meghan?" Kingsley asks, and I groan, sinking lower in my barstool.

"Wait, I want to see," Justin says, earning a glare from Kingsley.

"Don't even dare. That list is for my eyes only," Kingsley warns, leaving no room for argument, and I can't help but smile at his protectiveness.

"Sent!" Meghan beams, clearly proud of herself.

"Thank you, Meghan," Kingsley says, a satisfied smile on his lips.

"You are most welcome," she replies, grinning at me. I mouth "I hate you" at her, but she just blows me a kiss in return.

"So, what are we doing today? I don't want to be cooped up in the house all day," Justin says as he gets up and pulls Meghan into his arms, kissing her.

"Oh, I know! We can go clubbing," Meghan says, grinding playfully against Justin.

"We have a date later tonight, but maybe we can go clubbing afterward," Kingsley says as he takes my dirty bowl to the sink. For a moment, there's silence, and then Meghan squeals so loudly I'm sure they can hear her two floors down.

"You guys are going on a date? Like, for real?" she asks, hugging me so tightly I can barely breathe.

"Yes, we are," I say, smiling.

"I'm so happy for you two! See, King, finally asking her out is very demure, very cutesy, very mindful," she says then whirls on her boyfriend and yells, "Pay up, sucker!"

I frown, mirroring the confusion on Kingsley's face. Clearly, we're both lost.

Justin grumbles, "Damn it, guys. I mean, I'm happy King finally got his head out of his ass and made it happen, but y'all couldn't have waited just a couple more months?" He pulls out his wallet and hands Meghan a dollar, which she takes with a smug grin.

"Wait, hold on. You guys bet on us?" Kingsley asks, a mix of disbelief and amusement in his voice. I'm trying not to laugh, because of course they did.

"Uh, yeah," Meghan replies, kissing her dollar bill. "I told J that you guys would go on a date before the end of this semester, and he said you didn't have the balls."

That does it, I can't hold it in anymore and burst out laughing.

"Good job, Meg," I say, holding out my hand for a high five.

"Thanks, babe."

Kingsley shakes his head, a playful smirk on his lips. "I'll have you know I have balls bigger than yours, you asshole.

Plus, you're my best friend, shouldn't you have been betting for me rather than against me?"

Meghan and I laugh harder as Kingsley and Justin go back and forth, their banter lightening the mood.

"I have to go. I have to volunteer at the clinic," I say a few minutes later.

Kingsley steps closer, his presence commanding as always. "What time will you be done?" he asks, his voice low and caring.

"I'm just doing five hours today."

"Okay, take my Jeep," he says, his tone leaving no room for argument. When I start to protest, he adds, "I'm not taking no for an answer, butterfly."

"Fine. Thank you," I reply, giving in with a small smile. Kingsley walks away to grab his car keys, and I quickly hug Meghan and Justin before following him out.

KINGSLEY

THE KING'S WINTER WONDERLAND

I struggle to focus as my father's voice fills the room, discussing the intricacies of the upcoming Tokyo deal over the phone. Normally, I'd be locked in, eager to prove myself, to strategize our next move. But today, my thoughts keep drifting back to Inès.

The way she looked this morning, her eyes wide with realization after she'd been caught dragging her thigh over my hard cock. I had been awake for hours, just watching her sleep, lost in how peaceful she seemed. I was going to say something when she woke up, but as soon as she stirred awake, I closed my eyes. I don't know why, maybe because I thought she might freak out and want to sneak out, instead she just lay there, watching me. It was adorable.

When she felt my erection, instead of pulling away or getting uncomfortable, exactly what I thought she'd do, and she'd have every right to, she surprised me by exploring. She was hesitant at first, like she wasn't sure if she should continue, but then my brave girl kept drawing her thigh over my erection. A part of me wanted to see how far she'd take it. But then reality set in. I had just asked her out. We've been friends for over two years. I know enough to know that she's innocent, and the last thing I want is to rush this, to hurt her by moving too fast. She deserves more than that.

"Kingsley?" my dad calls, snapping me back to reality.

"Yes... I, uhh... I've been thinking about an alternative arrangement we could propose since they weren't too keen on those incentives we initially offered," I say, forcing myself to refocus on the task at hand. It's a good thing I'm good at what I do.

"Go on, I'm listening," my father replies. I can picture him leaning forward, the familiar intensity in his voice. He's never been one to hand us anything on a silver platter. I started working in our company when I was fifteen, and my sister, though still young at sixteen, has already begun her journey the same way. While EcoTech Innovations is set to be mine when Dad retires, Ashford Airlines will go to her once she graduates. It's how we've been raised, earning everything we have, step by step.

EcoTech Innovations is a leading global technology firm specializing in sustainable energy solutions, advanced robotics, and artificial intelligence. Founded in the early '30s by my great, great grandfather, it has grown into a multi-billion-dollar enterprise, recognized for its innovative approach to solving some of the world's most pressing challenges, such as climate change and resource scarcity.

"Given the changing regulatory landscape in Japan, we could pivot towards a more localized strategy," I suggest. "Highlight the adaptability of our technology to suit their evolving needs."

"Interesting. But how can we make this more appealing to

them?" he asks, knowing full well that I have the answer. It's his way of pushing me, making sure I'm always on top of my game. I can feel the eyes of the board members on me even though they're not physically present, all of them evaluating my every word, every move.

"And because Japan is heavily invested in sustainability goals," I continue, "we could emphasize how our technology aligns with their long-term environmental targets, making it a strategic partnership."

"That's a solid point. But remember, they still want to see direct benefits from our technology," my father responds, his tone slightly more approving. It's a subtle acknowledgment, but one that speaks volumes. He knows I'm ready to take on more responsibility, to lead EcoTech Innovations into its next phase. I want to be the one to secure this deal; it'll further prove how ready I am.

As my dad and I keep talking about the deal, there's a knock at my door. My focus shifts entirely the moment I see Inès at the door, her beautiful face peeking through with a shy smile. My father's voice fades into the background as I motion for her to come in.

"Let's make sure we have everything in place before the meeting. I want this deal wrapped up neatly," my father says and my attention shifts briefly back to him.

"Of course. I'll finalize the adjustments and send them over for your review," I reply. "I'll talk with you later." I hang up before he can protest. All my focus needs to be on the beauty that invades my dreams.

She steps into the room, hesitantly standing by the door. "Are you busy?" she asks, her voice soft and almost uncertain. The sound of it sends a rush of heat straight to my dick, and I have to mentally rein myself in.

"I'm not," I reply, my voice betraying the need I feel, the urgency to have her close. "Come here."

When she's close enough, I pull her into my lap, feeling her warmth against me. She wiggles slightly, trying to get comfortable, and I have to bite back a groan as her ass brushes against my already eager cock. Fuck, I need to think about something else before she realizes just how much I want her.

"How was it?" I ask, trying to focus on her instead of my rapidly deteriorating self-control. I knew Inès was innocent, but the bucket list Meghan shared with me today showed me just how innocent she is. Fuck, thinking about the list makes me think about how number two was checked off, which would mean that my little sweet innocent butterfly has her nipples pierced. My mouth waters at the thought.

"King?" she calls out.

"Shit, I'm sorry, Queen. Got distracted. What were you saying?" I murmur, wrapping my arms around her and pressing a soft kiss to her cheek.

"I like it when you call me Queen," she whispers.

I chuckle, my breath brushing against her skin. "I love it when you call me King." Ever since she first called me King yesterday, it felt different, special. I knew right then that no one else was allowed to call me that but her. Because every King needs his Queen, and Inès... well, she's the only one for me.

"I'm sorry for zoning out, really. Tell me how your tutoring session went," I prompt again, resting my head on her chest. The scent of coconuts and something purely her fills my lungs. I could drown in it, hell, my body's already reacting, and I love it as much as I hate how much control she has over me.

"It went well. We did some memory exercises and a workshop, today was an easy day," she says with a soft laugh, her voice carrying a warmth that settles in my chest. Her hand lifts slowly, almost hesitantly, fingers brushing through my hair with a gentleness that feels both unexpected and intimate. The sensation of her touch, a light, delicate stroke, sends warmth flooding through me, igniting something deep and undeniable.

My heart picks up, each beat a reminder of just how much this moment means, how much her simple, affectionate touch dismantles the calm I'd convinced myself I had.

"Mhmm." I groan something unintelligible. I don't want her to stop what she is doing. This is everything, her in my arms, her fingers in my hair, it's better than anything I could've imagined, it's better than sex.

"You big baby," she teases, and I can't resist swatting her ass lightly in response. Her laughter is contagious, filling the room with warmth and light.

"Who are you calling a baby?" I challenge, flipping us over so she's lying on the couch beneath me. Her laughter rings out again, carefree and pure, and I realize it's my favorite sound in the world. I start tickling her, enjoying the way she writhes beneath me, tears of laughter rolling down her cheeks as she begs me to stop.

When I finally relent, she's still laughing, her eyes sparkling as she looks up at me.

"You want to try that again?" I ask, my hands hovering over her sides.

"I was only going to say you big… strong man." She giggles, her smile so wide and genuine that it makes my heart ache.

As I hover over her, the weight of my feelings becomes

undeniable. I love her. I've loved her for two years. It's not news to me, I've always known that what I feel for Inès goes far beyond friendship or simple desire. But I hadn't realized just how much those feelings had grown, how deeply they've taken root, how profoundly she had woven herself into my heart.

The realization crashes over me like a freight train, an unstoppable force that I can no longer ignore. I can't let my father's plan to marry me off to his friend's daughter become my only option. He is only making me do this to save his friend's company. I need to find a smarter solution, one that preserves everything I've fought for my entire life, because I can't stand the mere thought of a future without her, of waking up every day without her by my side.

Her laughter fades, and she looks up at me with those big, beautiful brown eyes that seem to hold the entire world in them. "King?" she whispers softly, her voice wrapping around my name like a melody meant just for me. My heart stumbles, and every instinct screams to tell her, to let the words spill out of me, that she's it for me, the one I didn't know I was searching for until I found her.

But I can't. Not yet. If I say it now, I might scare her away, or worse, I might not be enough for the weight of those words just yet. Instead, I lean down and press the gentlest kiss to her forehead, lingering just long enough to let my touch speak the words I'm too afraid to say out loud. *I see you. I care for you. You mean more to me than you know.*

Someday soon, when the moment is right, I'll tell her. I'll give her the words and everything else she deserves, my heart, my soul, my everything. But for now, I'm happy just being here, wrapped up in this moment, holding her close, and letting her laughter echo in the quiet spaces of my heart. Because with her, even silence feels like a love song.

"Ready for our date?" I murmur as I gaze into her eyes. Her smile in response is a gentle caress to my soul, and she nods with eager anticipation.

"Yes, but should I go back to my apartment to change?" she asks as I help her up, my hand lingering on her waist for just a moment longer than necessary. Her outfit, a simple pair of leggings and a shirt, somehow looks effortlessly perfect on her.

"Do you have a coat?" I ask, knowing it's still warm out, it is only September after all, but where we're headed, it'll get cold.

She nods.

"Good," I say, flashing her a grin. "Then you don't need to change a thing. Let's go."

With her hand in mine, I lead her out the door, my grip gentle but firm, like I never want to let go.

As we drive through the city, Inès glances around, her curiosity lighting up her face. It's cute, really, how she's trying to piece together the surprise, not realizing that whatever she's imagining won't even come close to the reality I've planned for her. She has no idea what's waiting for her, but seeing the excitement in her eyes makes it all worth it.

When we arrive at Boston Common, which I've had transformed into a winter wonderland, her eyes widen in disbelief. The Frog Pond, usually not open for skating until mid-November, has been frozen over, bathed in the glow of twinkling lights. I wanted this night to be magical, something so special that she'd one day tell our kids about it. *Jesus, Kingsley, focus, this is just your first date.*

I step out of the car and quickly make my way to her door, opening it with a flourish and offering her my hand. She takes it, her smile warmer than any fire, and as she steps out, bundled up in an oversize sweater and those boots she loves, I can't help but think how breathtakingly beautiful she looks.

She gasps. "Oh my God! King, this is amazing." Her is voice filled with awe and delight.

"I thought we could go ice skating," I say, retrieving the custom skates I bought last week from the trunk. I wanted tonight to be perfect for her.

She hesitates for a moment. "I can't skate," she admits, though her eyes betray her excitement. "But I've always wanted to learn. I've always envied the people who skate effortlessly."

"Don't worry," I say softly, squeezing her hand reassuringly. "I'll hold your hand the whole time, and I won't let go."

As we walk toward the rink, she looks around, noticing the emptiness. "Why is it so empty? I thought this place usually gets packed."

"I… uh, rented out the place for the day. So, it's just going to be us," I confess, leading her to the building where we lace up our skates.

"But… that must have cost a fortune…" she protests, looking up at me with those wide, sincere eyes.

"Don't worry about it," I reply, brushing a strand of hair from her face. "I wanted to do something special for you. Plus, it was nothing compared to seeing you smile like this."

When we step onto the ice, she wobbles at first, but I'm right there, holding her hand firmly, guiding her until her nervous laughter turns into something more, something pure and infectious that echoes in the crisp air. As we skate hand in hand, the world narrows down to just the two of us.

"This is perfect," she breathes after a few laps, her cheeks flushed from the cold and the excitement. The sun is beginning to set, casting a golden glow over the winter landscape, and I can't resist the urge to make this moment even more special.

"Dance with me," I suggest, offering her my hand with a soft smile.

She chuckles, glancing around. "But there's no…" Her words trail off as she places her hand in mine, and right on cue, "Endless Love" by Diana Ross and Lionel Richie begins to play through the speakers.

"King!" she gasps, her smile so full of warmth and affection that it makes my chest tighten. I pull her into my arms, and we begin to sway to the slow, melodic tune, the rest of the world fading away.

"I'm not usually one for romance," I confess, my voice low as I lean in closer. "But I wanted this day to be perfect for you, butterfly. I want every day with me to be perfect because you deserve nothing less."

She tilts her head back, her eyes searching mine. "You say you're not one for romance," she teases gently, making a point to glance around at the magical setting. "Could've fooled me."

"Just for you, butterfly, only for you," I murmur in a husky whisper.

"Why did you start calling me butterfly? It felt like it came out of nowhere, but I never had the courage to ask," she says, looking up at me with those beautiful brown eyes that never fail to draw me in.

"The very first day I saw you," I begin, my hand brushing over her shoulder as I recall the memory, "you were by the garden on campus, literally smelling the roses. Then a butterfly appeared and landed on your shoulder, right here." I touch her left shoulder gently, feeling the warmth of her beneath my fingertips. "Another one landed in your hair, and soon there were at least five of them, all surrounding you as if they were protecting you."

Her eyes widen in recognition. "I remember that day... it was my freshman year, right before classes started. I thought the first time we met was at that frat party."

"No," I say, my voice soft as I shake my head slowly. "I went to that party because I wanted to see you again, to get to know you. I didn't normally go to frat parties, or any campus parties, really. But that night... I couldn't stay away. I know I acted like I wasn't interested, but that was only because I thought you deserved someone better... I still think that. Yet I'm selfish enough to want you anyway, to make you mine despite it all."

Her breath hitches, the space between us almost non-existent as her eyes search mine, desperate for the truth. "I really didn't think you liked me that way," she whispers, her voice trembling as she gazes at me, her breath warm against my lips.

"Inès... you've been all I can think about since the moment we met. You've invaded my thoughts, my dreams... my..." I stop myself in time before I say something that may ruin the moment; she's not ready to hear how much my heart belongs to her. "I've grown to care for you in ways I never thought possible. You're everything, Inès. Everything."

The last words escape me in a seductive whisper, my eyes fixed on her parted lips, so soft, so tempting. She licks them slowly, and that small, innocent gesture is all the invitation I need.

"King," she breathes, her voice tinged with anticipation and raw need, just before I close the distance between us. My lips find hers in a kiss that starts slow, deliberate, a perfect blend of tenderness and command. With every movement, I pour my soul into it, hoping she can feel the depth of my love, the certainty that with every press of our lips, she's claimed a piece of my heart forever.

Her body responds in kind, molding against mine as her hands begin a journey of exploration. Every touch ignites a trail of desire, fueling the urgency between us. I pull her closer, lifting her off her feet with ease as I lick her lips, urging her to let me in which she does. We both groan at the first swipe of my tongue against hers. What began as a sweet and gentle kiss quickly deepens into something more frantic, more consuming, as if we can't get close enough, can't kiss hard enough to satisfy the growing need within us.

When we finally pull back, both of us are breathless, our foreheads resting together. I gently set her back on her feet. Just then, soft snowflakes begin to fall around us. She gasps in wonder, her eyes wide as she looks up at the sky.

"You made it snow!" she exclaims, turning to look around, momentarily forgetting that we're still on the ice. She wobbles, and I quickly grab her, pulling her close to steady her.

"Be careful," I murmur, my voice still thick with the remnants of our kiss.

Before I can lean in to kiss her again, because I didn't get enough, and I'll never get enough, her phone rings. She pulls it out and sees Meghan's name, but dismisses it, tucking it back into her pocket. "I'll call her back later," she says with a smile.

But then, my phone rings too. I frown as I see Justin's name on the screen and show it to her. Her smile fades, replaced by concern.

"It might be an emergency," she says softly, urging me to pick up.

"J…" I answer, but Justin's voice is frantic on the other end.

"You guys need to get back to the girls' apartment, now," he says, urgency clear in his tone.

"What's going on?" I ask, frowning.

"Someone broke in."

"We'll be right there." My mind immediately shifts gears. I take Inès's hand, the magical moment we shared still lingering in the air, and quickly lead her toward the car.

INÈS

CAUGHT BETWEEN INK AND INTRIGUE

We rush back to the apartment, my heart pounding in my chest. As soon as I step inside, the sight before me is like a punch to the gut. Our place, our little sanctuary, has been trashed. It's as if someone took a baseball bat to everything we own. The TV is shattered, our photos are scattered and torn, and the furniture we painstakingly collected from Goodwill is now a pile of debris on the floor. I gasp, covering my mouth, my eyes stinging with tears that I can no longer hold back.

Meghan is at my side in an instant, her arms wrapping around me tightly. "Oh my God, you're okay," she says, her voice trembling as she hugs me. I hold her just as tightly, feeling the tears spill down my cheeks.

"I'm fine," I manage to say, though my voice betrays me with a crack. I pull away slightly, my heart racing as I scan her face. "Meg, are you okay?"

"I'm fine," she says softly, but her wide, terrified eyes

mirror my own. "I just came back to grab a few things before we headed out to the club... and found this."

"Beau?" My chest tightens with panic.

"Still at the penthouse," she reassures me, soothing the rising fear in my throat.

I exhale shakily, but my mind is still spinning. "Who would do this? Who would break into our home?" My voice trembles as I take in the wreckage of what was once our living room. "Did they take anything?"

"That was my first thought, too," Justin says from the corner of the room. I hadn't even noticed he was here. "But you should take a look at your room."

Panic rising, I rush to my bedroom, and what I see there steals the breath from my lungs. It's even worse than the living room, everything is destroyed. My bed is slashed, my clothes thrown everywhere, my bookshelves knocked over. I stumble into the bathroom, and that's when I see it. Written in bold, red lipstick on the mirror is one word: *meretrix*.

"We don't know what it means, " Meghan starts, but I cut her off.

"It means prostitute," I say, my voice hollow with confusion. It doesn't make sense. Why would someone write that on my mirror? I barely interact with anyone outside of the people in this room.

"What the hell is that supposed to mean?" Justin asks, frustration edging his voice.

"I think they meant slut, but the word doesn't exist in Latin. So meretrix is the closest they could get," I whisper, the realization dawning on me that whoever did this must know that I read Latin. I've been self-taught since high school.

"Butterfly," Kingsley says softly, pulling me into his

arms. My whole body is trembling now, and I don't know how to stop it. Who would do this? And why?

"I don't understand…" I cry into his chest, his arms the only thing grounding me as the world tilts on its axis.

"Shh, we'll figure this out. It's going to be okay," he soothes, his hand gently stroking my hair.

"They ruined everything, King. And I don't know what they mean by meretrix."

"We'll replace everything, alright? Justin's already called the cops, and they're on their way. Baby, look at me," he says, his voice taking on that commanding tone that never fails to steady me. I force myself to meet his gaze, my breath hitching. "Breathe for me, Inès."

I take a shaky breath, then another.

"Good girl. Let me handle this."

"We shouldn't touch anything until the cops have done what they need to do," Justin adds. "But once they're done, you two need to pack up. You're staying with us until further notice."

"And that's not up for debate," Kingsley says firmly, his protective streak flaring up as he tightens his hold on me.

"We need to let the landlord know what happened," Meghan says, trying to keep her voice steady, but I notice Kingsley stiffen slightly at her words.

"Should we tell them?" Justin asks in French, causing a ripple of tension to go through me. I look up at Kingsley, catching his eyes as they meet mine, filled with something I can't decipher.

"Tell us what?" I ask, my voice sharp as I switch to French, not liking the secrecy.

"Hey, guys, American here, please stick to English," Meghan interjects, trying to cut through the tension.

Kingsley sighs, his eyes never leaving mine. "We own the

building," he says, switching back to English. The revelation hangs in the air, heavy and unexpected.

"When we found out you were looking for an apartment and couldn't find one within your budget, we bought this building to make sure you were somewhere safe and close to campus," Justin explains.

The room falls into a heavy silence as the reality of what they've done sinks in. It's overwhelming, the lengths they went to, the sheer magnitude of their care. They bought an entire building for us so we wouldn't have to worry about bills or safety, leaving us free to focus solely on school. My mind races, trying to process this, but before I can say anything, a loud knock echoes through the apartment, shattering the quiet. I flinch at the sudden noise.

"That must be the police," Meghan says, her voice steady despite the shock still lingering in her eyes. She turns to Justin, pointing a finger at him. "We are so not done with this conversation."

Without waiting for a response, she leaves my room to answer the door, and we follow close behind.

The police ask us plenty of questions, meticulously taking our statements. They inform us that we can't touch anything yet because their forensic team needs to gather evidence, fingerprints, and photos. It all feels surreal, like a nightmare I can't wake up from. They mention that a report will be filed documenting the break-in.

"Wait, I can't take anything at all?" Meghan asks, her frustration palpable.

"I'm afraid not right now, but once we've gathered enough evidence, we'll let you know."

By the time we are done, I'm utterly drained. Kingsley wraps his arms around me, his presence comforting, grounding me when I feel like I might drift away.

"If you don't need anything else from us, we'd like to take the girls home. It's been a long day," Kingsley says, his voice firm yet respectful as he shakes Officer Riggs's hand.

"Yes, I've got everyone's contact. We'll be in touch," Officer Riggs replies, offering a sympathetic nod.

"What a clusterfuck," Meghan sighs, collapsing onto the sofa. We've been back at the penthouse for about thirty minutes. The first thing I did was check on Beau, smothering him with kisses before hopping into the shower while King took him outside. The hot water washed away the grime, fear, and lingering sense of violation that still clings to me.

"Yeah," I murmur, sitting down beside her. King and Justin are in the kitchen, probably discussing what to do next.

"What are we going to do about the apartment? Because I don't feel safe going back there," Meghan says, her voice wavering as I reach out to squeeze her hand.

"We might have a solution to that," Justin says as he and King join us, sitting down beside us.

"We think it'll be best if you two move in with us until this is all figured out," Kingsley suggests. I frown, looking between them, unsure of how to respond.

"Please hear us out," Justin adds, drawing my attention to him. "We feel responsible. It's our building, and we should have had better security. We assumed it was safe because of the neighborhood, and we didn't want to invade your personal space with cameras since you didn't know we were the owners."

King picks up where Justin leaves off. "We've been saving all the rent you two have been paying since you moved in. The money is yours, and once things settle down and they catch whoever is behind this, you can use that money to get a new place if that's what you want."

Meghan and I exchange a look before turning back to them. "Absolutely not," we say in unison, causing their brows to knit in confusion.

"We're eternally grateful to you for buying the building, but we don't want that money back," Meghan insists. "It was rent, cheap as it was, but that money is yours."

"And please don't think what happened is your fault. It's not. You've both been so caring, even when we didn't realize it, but…" I trail off, turning to Kingsley. "I can't ask you to let me move in here until things settle. It's too much. Plus, we just went on our first date, I don't want to make things awkward by moving in the same night."

Kingsley reaches up, cupping my cheek with a tenderness that makes my heart ache. "It's cute you think staying here until things are resolved was a choice. It's not. I understand the intimate part of our relationship is new, but don't forget we have a two-year friendship behind us. I assure you; things won't be awkward. I'll barely be home anyway, you know how much I travel."

He's right. We've been friends for a while, and he does travel a lot. Plus, where else would I go? "Okay, fine," I relent, but I add firmly, "But we definitely don't want that money back."

King and Justin share a look I can't quite decipher before shrugging. "Okay," they say in unison, a bit too easily, but Meghan and I decide to let it go.

After we eat and hang out for a bit, it's time for my insulin. Kingsley and I go upstairs, where he once again helps me with the injection. He kisses my stomach after- ward, calling me a good girl and praising me for my bravery.

His words warm me, making the discomfort of the injection fade.

"I can stay in my office," he offers once everything is cleaned up. "I know we just had our first date today, so if you feel like sharing a room is too much, I'll be more than happy to sleep in my office."

"No, I'll take your office or the couch. I can't…"

"Inès." My name comes out firm and authoritative, making me press my lips together instinctively. There's something about the way he says my name that always makes me react, something that's been there since the moment we met. "You will have my bed, and that's final."

"But, "

"No buts. Now, get in the bed and have a good night."

I stand there, eyeing him defiantly until he raises an eyebrow and takes a step toward me. I run and get into the bed so fast you'd think he lit a fire under me. But honestly, what would he have done if I pushed him just a little more? The thought makes my heart race. I've never tried before, but I'm truly curious, would he throw me over his knee and spank me like in the romance novels Camille sends me? The mere image makes me clench my thighs together.

He chuckles when I get under the covers. "That's what I thought."

"Well, maybe we can share the bed. I mean, it's big enough for five people, and I like it when you hold me at night," I admit, feeling my cheeks burn.

He stands there for a long moment, debating my offer. Just as I'm about to rescind it, feeling stupid and too eager, he speaks. "Only if you're sure."

"I am," I say, nodding.

"Scoot over." He starts removing his shirt but then hesitates.

"I don't mind if you… take your shirt off… you know, if it's uncomfortable to sleep in," I say, trying not to sound too eager. I've been dying to see him without a shirt. Hell, I want to see him naked. God, I feel like a creep, but I'm curious. I've never seen a man naked, other than in porn, and I have a feeling none of those men could hold a candle to Kingsley.

King pauses a second too long, debating what to do. I start to feel self-conscious again. Oh my God, what if he just doesn't want me to see him naked? Or maybe he isn't ready for that. I mean, we just had our first date today, of course he is not ready for that, just like I'm not ready for him to see me naked tonight. "B… but if you aren't comfortable, you don't have to… I didn't mean…"

"It's not that. It's… okay, I want to show you something, but I don't want you to freak out," he says, and I frown.

"Why would I freak out?" I ask, confused. If he's self-conscious, he really doesn't need to be, because even with the shirt on, I can tell he has a great body.

"Alexa, turn on the overhead lights," he commands, and I realize I didn't even know he had an Alexa. The overhead lights turn on, illuminating the room. I look up to see Kingsley staring down at me intently, his blue eyes even more striking under the light. He smirks, showing me a dimple. "Ready?"

I roll my eyes. "Just show me already," I say impatiently.

He chuckles and slowly takes his shirt off. A sound escapes me, I can't begin to understand what sound exactly but oh my God this man is beautiful; he is a man everywhere. "Mon Dieu, que tu es beau,"[1] I whisper, not realizing I'd spoken until the words are out.

---

1. My God, you're so handsome.

Kingsley just chuckles. "Merci.[2] I'm glad you like what you see."

Oh, I like it. I like it so much that I feel a flush of heat between my legs. Kingsley's body is perfection, perfectly sculpted muscles, a defined six-pack, and tattoos that make my mouth water. There's a snake, a compass, a skull, and a massive lion on his biceps, which I assume is for the university mascot. But then I see something that makes my heart stop.

"King!" I say, scrambling to my knees on the bed to get a closer look. My name is tattooed on his left pec, surrounded by delicate butterflies. Let me say that again: *my name* is tattooed on his left pec! "Is that… is that real?"

"Yes, it's real," he confirms, laughing when I lick my thumb and rub the area to check if it'll smudge.

It doesn't.

"You have my name tattooed on your skin… as in, it's really there, permanently?" I say, my voice barely a whisper as I stare at the inked letters, my heart racing.

"Are you upset?" he asks calmly, yet there's a trace of something vulnerable in his eyes.

"No, not upset… just, why?" My words tumble out, full of curiosity and disbelief.

He doesn't answer right away, instead, he leans in, capturing my lips in a kiss that steals my breath and melts away my questions. I'm left dizzy, clinging to him as he gently guides me down onto the bed, his strong body following mine. He turns me around and cuddles me. I feel the warmth of him, the solidity of his chest pressing against my back as he wraps his arms around me, holding me close.

"Ask me again in a few weeks," he murmurs against my

---

2. Thank you.

ear, his voice a soothing promise that makes my heart flutter even as exhaustion pulls at me.

"But, King, " I start to protest, the need for answers still gnawing at me, but he hushes me softly.

"Shh... You've had a long day. Sleep now. We'll talk about everything later," he soothes, his hand stroking my hair in slow, comforting motions.

I can't fight the yawn that escapes, the weight of the day finally crashing down on me. "Fine... but we will talk about this later, got it?"

His chuckle vibrates through his chest, a low, comforting sound. "Got it. Good night, papillon."[3]

"Night, King," I murmur, already drifting off.

---

3. Butterfly.

INÈS

YES, KING: THE BEGINNING

I startle at the sound of a knock on the door, pulling me out of the world of research papers and deadlines. I've been holed up in Kingsley's office since I got home from school, savoring the quiet as I worked on my ten-page research paper due next month.

It's been a week since the break-in, and the police still have no leads. They mentioned that officers were keeping an eye on the building, but so far, nothing suspicious has been spotted.

"Yes?" I call out.

The door opens, and Kingsley steps into the office, looking effortlessly handsome in casual wear, a fitted black V-neck shirt that clings to his broad shoulders and chest, paired with dark jeans that sit perfectly on his lean hips. His hair is slightly tousled, giving him that relaxed yet polished look that only he can pull off, and his sleeves are pushed up just enough to reveal the strong, sinewy lines of his forearms.

His blue eyes find mine, a soft smile playing on his lips as he closes the distance between us. "How long have you been in here, papillon?" he asks, concern lacing his voice.

"I…" I glance at the time on my computer screen and my eyes widen. "Oh wow, I guess I lost track of time." I chuckle softly, realizing it's already seven in the evening. I've been in here since ten this morning. Right after my early class ended, Meghan told me that she would take care of Beau, so I turned my phone off and focused.

Kingsley's smile fades as he steps closer, his gaze sweeping over me as if he's assessing my well-being. "When was the last time you ate?" he asks, his tone firm yet gentle.

I bite my lip, glancing around the office as if food might magically appear. "I'm fine, my blood sugar is, "

"When was the last time you ate?" he repeats, his voice now carrying a reprimanding edge as he scowls at me.

"Breakfast," I mumble, feeling small under his intense scrutiny. "I really did lose track of time. You know how I get when I'm focused on my schoolwork."

He sighs, the sound heavy with both frustration and care. "I thought we talked about this, butterfly…" He doesn't sound angry, but there's a hint of disappointment that tugs at my heartstrings. The way he cares for me, for my well-being, is so endearing it almost brings tears to my eyes.

"I know, I'm sorry…" I say, standing up, though it does little to bridge the height difference between us. He still towers over me, making me feel like a child in comparison.

"Come on, you need to eat, and then we need to talk."

His words make me freeze. *We need to talk?* The phrase sends a chill down my spine. *We need to talk* is universal code for *I'm about to break up with you*, or at least that's what my anxious mind tells me. I've barely had time to enjoy him, and now he wants to end what's barely begun? We've only been on two dates, and although we've shared some heated kisses and slept in the same bed, we haven't officially defined what we are. All throughout the week, he has been busy and so have I so we've not seen each other much.

Tears prick at the corners of my eyes at the thought of him not wanting to continue whatever it is we've started. The idea of losing him, of being reduced back to just friends, feels unbearable.

"Hey, whoa, whoa, it's not what you're thinking at all. Don't cry," he says quickly, pulling me into a sweet, reassuring kiss. "It's never that, so please don't think like that, okay?" He kisses me again then places light pecks on my lips, my chin, my cheek, and finally my nose.

"Okay," I whisper, a small, nervous chuckle escaping my lips.

"Let's get you some food," he says, taking my hand and leading me out of the office and downstairs. But instead of guiding me to the kitchen, where we usually eat, he takes me to the formal dining room, a place I've never been before.

When he opens the door and steps inside with me, my steps falter, and I freeze for the second time today, though this time for an entirely different reason.

The dining room, which is larger than I thought, is decorated with balloons. Red flower petals are scattered on the floor and across the table, where a massive bouquet of red roses sits as the centerpiece. The lights are dim, casting a soft, romantic glow over the entire room. I'm officially confused, because my birthday isn't for a few months, and this can't possibly be a proposal… right?

"King?" I call out, my voice wavering as I try to make sense of the scene before me. *Please don't tell me he's about to get down on one knee.*

"I may have gone a bit overboard," he admits, a slight blush creeping up his cheeks. "I've never done this before, so please, bear with me." He takes my trembling hands in his, his touch grounding me.

"Oh God…"

"I had to ask Meghan to help me out. That's where I've been all day, shopping with her. I hope you like this… otherwise, this is going to be very awkward." He chuckles nervously.

Meghan knew about this and didn't warn me? She knows marriage and kids aren't on my radar right now. *What was she thinking?*

"I know we've only been on two dates, and we haven't discussed anything concerning us, but I want to make it clear that you are mine, and I don't share," he says, his voice deepening with possessiveness as he reaches for a plate I hadn't noticed. He turns it to face me, revealing an elegant arrangement of small desserts, some topped with fresh strawberry slices, others with a delicate pink mousse. But what steals my breath is the message written in chocolate: "Will you be my girlfriend?" The words are written in a stylish, cursive script, clear and beautiful.

"King?" I whisper, my voice shaky as tears fill my eyes. This man, this God of a man, who claimed he didn't do romance, who I thought might never feel the same way I do, has done nothing but spoil me and take care of me.

"Say you'll be my girlfriend, Queen. I need to hear you say you'll be mine." He turns me to face him, his blue eyes filled with a raw, desperate need.

"Yes, King. I'm yours," I breathe out, watching as he visibly relaxes at my words.

He wraps his hand possessively around the back of my neck and pulls me closer to him. "Good. Now I don't have to lock you up in here for life," he says with a smirk, just as I laugh. Then he slams his lips onto mine, kissing me hard and possessively, licking and biting my lips, claiming me in the process. "I want to fucking devour you, butterfly," he whispers, his breath hot against my ear as he lightly sucks on my earlobe, sending shivers down my spine.

"Please," I moan, desperate for more, but just as quickly as the fire ignited between us, he pulls away.

"You need to eat," he says, pulling out a chair for me with a stern look that dares me to argue.

I scowl at him but take a seat. That's when I notice the small, black velvet box in front of me. Inside, nested in soft velvet, are the most delicate gold earrings and a matching necklace. The necklace is thin and elegant, with a single-letter pendant, *K*.

"Oh my God, King, this is beautiful!" I whisper, overwhelmed with emotion.

"I'm glad you like it," he replies softly as he watches me with those piercing blue eyes that I could drown in.

A moment later, someone I don't recognize enters the room, carrying two plates of spaghetti with perfectly squashed meatballs. The aroma is mouthwatering, and I waste no time digging in. The meal is simple but delicious, and the comfort of sharing it with Kingsley after the past moments' emotional rollercoaster makes it even better.

After dinner, we head up to our room. I take a hot shower, letting the water wash away the remnants of the day. When I'm done, I braid my hair, slip into one of Kingsley's shirts that's soft and oversize on me, and then carefully put on my new necklace and earrings. The gold glints perfectly against my skin.

When I walk out of the bathroom, King is sitting on the bed, shirtless, his toned body illuminated by the soft glow of the bedside lamp. He's scrolling through his phone, but the moment he sees me, he sets it down on the nightstand and reaches out his hand, beckoning me to come closer. I don't hesitate.

He takes my hand and pulls me in, guiding me between his legs so I'm standing right in front of him. His eyes roam over me, filled with a mixture of admiration and desire. "You are the most beautiful woman I have ever seen," he murmurs, his voice thick with sincerity.

A blush creeps up my cheeks at the intensity of his compliment.

"Come here," he demands softly, grabbing the back of my neck and pulling me down into a deep, searing kiss. Even though he's sitting and I'm standing, we're nearly the same height, our lips perfectly aligned.

But before I can fully lose myself in the kiss, Kingsley's hand slides between us, and he wraps his large hand around my neck. He pulls back slightly, breaking the kiss, and smirks down at me, his thumb gently stroking the pulse point in my neck. "If we're going to do this, butterfly, if we're going to be exclusive, there's something you need to know."

My heart flutters at his words, the possessiveness in his tone sending a thrill through me. "What is it?"

"I want to practice something called domestic discipline with you," he says, his voice low and controlled, but there's an intensity in his eyes that I can't ignore.

"Domestic discipline?" I echo, frowning slightly as I try to understand what he means.

"It means I'll have rules for you to follow," he explains, his hand still resting lightly on my neck. "Rules that we'll discuss and agree upon ahead of time, of course."

"And if I break these rules?" I ask, my voice barely above a whisper.

His grip tightens ever so slightly, pulling me closer until our faces are just inches apart. "Then I'll punish you."

The thought of Kingsley taking control in this way sends a wave of heat straight to my core. I may be inexperienced, but I'm not naïve. I know enough about BDSM to understand the general concept, and Meghan made sure I watched *Fifty Shades of Grey* more times than I can count. Plus, I've dabbled in a few online videos, and I won't pretend I wasn't intrigued by what I saw.

He smirks, clearly reading the desire in my eyes. "I see you like that, don't you?" he asks in a seductive purr.

I nod, feeling my cheeks heat up again.

"Use your words, butterfly," he commands softly, his gaze never leaving mine.

"Yes," I breathe out, my voice trembling slightly. "I like the idea of it, but I've never… well, been a part of something like this before," I admit, the honesty in my words making me feel vulnerable.

Kingsley releases his hold on my neck, his expression softening as he takes my hands in his. "That's why we need to talk seriously about it. Sit," he instructs, and I immediately obey, sitting down on the bed beside him.

"Good girl," he praises, his voice warm with approval. The words send a thrill through me, and I can't help the smile that spreads across my face.

INÈS

HIS BUTTERFLY, HIS RULES

"So, domestic discipline, or DD, is a lifestyle where one partner takes on a dominant role, guiding and disciplining the other, who's usually the submissive partner," Kingsley begins, his tone calm but firm. I'm sitting on the bed while he's on a chair he pulled over. He insisted we don't touch while we talk about this, so I'm not swayed by physical affection. He wants me to have a clear head, and though I agree, I can't help but feel a bit uneasy.

"So… do I have to start calling you 'Sir'?" I ask, half-joking, but genuinely curious.

"No," he replies with a small smile. "You can if you want, but it's not necessary. My name or any nickname you choose is fine. This isn't a BDSM relationship, so I'm not a 'Sir,' but if that's something you're interested in, I'd be open to exploring it with you."

"Oh, okay." I nod, trying to take it all in. "I'd like to know more about this DD lifestyle."

"Of course," he says, leaning forward slightly. "In this

dynamic, I'd be the Head of Household or HoH. I'll give you a list of rules that I expect you to follow, and if you don't, there will be consequences, like spanking. I could use my hand, a paddle, or even a belt. Sometimes, you might lose a privilege. Or I could find something you hate to do, like exercise, and make that a punishment." He pauses to let that sink in. "This isn't meant to break you, trust me, that's not what I want. It's meant to safely discipline you and keep you safe. You'll have a safe word, and I'll need your explicit consent before we move forward. That's why I want you to take a few days, if not weeks, to think about it and do your research. We'll have clear boundaries and regular check-ins. The last thing I want is to hurt you, physically, emotionally, or mentally."

"Okay," I reply, nodding again. "I'll definitely do my research. So… you said you have rules?"

"Yes, I have a few rules, and I take them very seriously," he says. "First and foremost, your health is my top priority, as well as yours. You should never go too long without eating. Your blood sugar levels shouldn't drop because you forgot to eat or got too busy, nor should they spike because you couldn't resist those chocolates you love so much." He adds the last part with a knowing look, and I roll my eyes internally, of course, he'd mention that.

"Second, I want you to share your burdens with me. I'll never underestimate the trust you place in me, and I promise to respect and honor that trust. Third, honesty is crucial. I won't tolerate lying, respect for each other demands full transparency. Fourth, respect is essential. As the Head of this relationship, I expect you to respect my role and the decisions I make. And finally, communication is key. If there's an issue with you or our relationship, I need you to talk to me about it. I'm not a mind reader, and while I might make mistakes, as long as we keep the lines of communication open and respect each other's feelings, nothing can come between us.

"These are just the initial rules. As we get to know each other better, there might be more, but I'll always discuss them with you first."

I'm surprised, pleasantly so. I don't know what I expected, but this isn't it. His rules aren't about control for the sake of control; they're about keeping me safe. For some reason, I thought he'd ask me to cook, clean, or kneel by his feet, things I would've flatly refused. When I heard "domestic," that's what came to mind. But none of what he's said is humiliating or designed to make him feel superior.

"Okay," I say with a genuine smile. "I'll take some time to think about it and do my research." So far, being with Kingsley has only made me feel protected, spoiled, and cared for, I'm comfortable with where we are and where we are headed.

"Good," he says, a small smile tugging at the corners of his mouth. "There's one more thing." He pauses. "Your father's birthday, I know you've been working extra hours to afford a ticket home, but you don't need to. I'll arrange for you to use my private jet so you can see your family."

My eyes widen in disbelief. "What? Wait, really? You'd do that?" I ask, trying, and failing, to hold back tears. After the break-in, I'd resigned myself to not going home, planning to use the little I'd saved to replace what was broken.

"Of course, butterfly. And if Meghan wants to head home, too, she's more than welcome. There's plenty of room."

Unable to resist, I climb onto his lap, wrapping my arms around his neck and letting his warmth envelop me. Then something hits me.

"Oh God, I can't bring Beau with me, my mom is highly

allergic," I admit. I have always wanted a dog, but I couldn't because of my mom's allergy.

"He can stay with me. You forget I'm his other parent," he says, and something about the way he claims that role makes my heart race. My ovaries might even be screaming, despite the fact that I do not want kids any time soon.

"Actually, I was thinking of asking if you'd like to meet my family. Maybe we could check out the Mall of America together for the first time?" I say, teasing him with a sing-song lilt at the end.

He chuckles, the sound deep and rich. "You do know I've been to Minnesota more times than I can count, right? And I've been to the mall plenty of times. But sure, baby, if you want me to go, we can. There's a dog hotel here in Boston we can visit, check it out, and if you like it, he'll stay there while we are in Minnesota."

I pout at the thought of not being with Beau for several days. That's my baby, my little shadow, and we've never been apart this long. The idea makes my heart ache. I don't think I can do it.

"Breathe, he'll be fine. I promise they will take good care of him. You'll get a chance to look at the facilities, and if you don't like a single thing, we'll find a different option," Kingsley reassures me, his warm hand gently cupping my cheek. "Just think of Beau," he murmurs softly, brushing a stray hair from my forehead. "He'll have a great time, and you can spoil him with extra cuddles when we get back."

I sigh, my heart still heavy. "Fine, we'll take a look." I force a smile, but I don't think it reaches my eyes.

"If you're not comfortable with someone else watching him, I can, "

"No, I want you to come," I interrupt. I want him to meet my family.

"Are you sure? I don't want you to feel like you have to invite me just because I offered the jet," he says, concern etching his features.

"What? No, of course not. Believe me, my family is dying to meet you." I can't help but smile at the thought.

Kingsley raises an eyebrow, a smirk dancing on his lips. "You've been talking about me to your parents, butterfly?" he teases, and I shove him playfully, feeling a rush of warmth in my cheeks.

"Don't flatter yourself. Meghan's the one who told them about you. Ever since my dad found out you speak French, he's been eager to meet you," I explain, chuckling at the thought of my dad's excitement.

"Well, if that's the case, I'll be honored," he replies, his smile disarming.

In one effortless motion, Kingsley lifts me into his arms as if I weigh nothing at all. He walks us to the bed and gently lays me down, hovering over me, our faces just inches apart. My heart races as his deep blue eyes lock onto mine, his intense gaze making my breath hitch. The world fades away, and all I can focus on is the warmth of his body, the safety of his presence, and the comfort that comes from knowing he's by my side.

"King," I whisper as his thumb brushes over my lower lip, and I part my lips, inviting his touch. A knowing smirk lifts the corner of his mouth before he leans down and captures my mouth with his. The kiss is slow, almost languid, but it holds a delicious promise.

"Queen," he murmurs against my lips, a low growl that sends shivers down my spine.

"Please," I whisper, not entirely sure what I'm begging for, but my core aches, and I hope he can fix it.

He smirks before kissing me deeply again, a possessive

force of nature, every inch of him radiating power and desire. I shiver, not from fear, but from the anticipation that coils through my body like a tightly wound spring.

Breaking the kiss long enough for me to breathe, his hand cups my face with a gentleness that contrasts with the raw hunger in his eyes. "You need me to make you feel better? Hmm? Is that pretty pussy weeping for me?" he asks as I rock my pelvis against his to alleviate some much-needed pressure.

I nod, words escaping me as his hands trail down my neck, fingers brushing over the pulse that beats wildly beneath my skin. He tugs at my shirt, lifting it over my head in one swift motion, leaving me completely exposed to his hungry gaze. I feel vulnerable but also powerful, knowing that I can unravel this strong, controlling man with just a look.

He growls when he sees my naked body for the first time. "Fuck me, you have the most perfect tits I've ever seen. And these piercings, fuck!" He grunts before lowering his hot mouth to my nipples, causing my hips to buck. The sensation feels incredible.

"King!" I moan as he sucks on my nipple and nips at it. He stops, giving the other nipple the same treatment. My breasts are small and almost fit in his mouth.

"Tell me what you like," he whispers, but I'm too turned on to focus.

"What are you into?" he asks as he keeps abusing my nipples. "Would you like me to call you my good girl?"

I hum, needing him to touch me like he means it, because everything hurts and only he can make me feel better. "Or would you prefer I call you my good little slut?"

"Oh God, King, please." I moan louder as I feel more wetness seeping out of me.

"Oh, so you want to be my little slut. You want me to use you like my plaything?" A few days ago, if you'd asked me if being called a slut would make me impossibly needy, I would've called you a liar. But now? With King? I love it.

He chuckles darkly. "Always so perfect, always so good. But in here, you want to be my cum bucket." He tweaks my nipples, making me gasp.

"King..." I moan, my body trembling with need.

Leaving my breasts, he hooks his fingers in the waistband of my cotton underwear and begins removing it, and I straighten my legs up in order to help him. Once the underwear is off, I lower my legs but don't spread them.

He lowers his head and presses a kiss on both of my knees, his eyes never leaving mine. "Spread your legs for me, butterfly," he commands, his voice wrapping around me like a velvet caress.

I obey, my legs trembling slightly as I open myself more to him.

"Jesus... look at you, so fucking perfect," he growls as his hands trail up my thighs, leaving a burning path. He positions himself between my legs and places gentle kisses down my navel, causing butterflies to swarm in my belly. His hands slide down my sides to rest on my hips, his touch possessive, reminding me who's in control. He looks up at me, and the intensity in his eyes makes my knees weak.

He presses a kiss to the inside of my thigh, so close to where I need him, yet not nearly close enough. I gasp, fingers tangling in his hair, silently begging for more.

"Patience, papillon," he whispers, his breath hot against my skin. "I'll take care of you."

With agonizing slowness, he inches closer, his mouth hovering just above my aching core. The anticipation is almost too much to bear. He blows air against my clit, and I whimper, my hips instinctively arching towards him. He chuckles a deep, sinful sound that vibrates through me.

"Look at you," he murmurs, possessiveness dripping from his voice. "So needy, so desperate for me, aren't you, slut?"

"Yes," I gasp, the words tumbling out before I can think. "King…"

He grips my hips harder, his fingers probably leaving bruises. "Beg for it, Queen. Beg for my mouth."

"Please," I whimper, my voice trembling. "Please, King, I need you."

"What do you need?"

"Your mouth, please."

He smirks, finally lowering his mouth to my core. His tongue flicks out to taste me, and I cry out, hands tightening in his hair. He groans against me, the vibration sending shockwaves of pleasure through my body. His tongue moves with practiced strokes, each one driving me closer to the edge.

"You taste so fucking good," he growls, his voice muffled against me. He doesn't let up, his tongue and lips working me with relentless precision. My hips buck against him, but he holds me firm, controlling every movement.

"King," I gasp. "Please…"

He doesn't answer, but his movements increase in intensity. His hands grip my hips, holding me steady as his tongue explores every inch of me. The pleasure coils tighter and tighter in my core until I feel like I might snap.

Just when I think I can't take anymore, he pulls back slightly, his lips brushing against my sensitive skin. "Not yet, Inès," he murmurs, his voice rough with desire. "You don't get to come until I say so."

I whimper in frustration, my body aching for release. He laughs, his fingers tracing circles over my throbbing clit. The pleasure is almost unbearable, and I feel myself teetering on the edge again, only for him to stop once more.

"Please, King," I beg, barely even whispering. "I need to come…"

He looks up at me, a cruel smile playing on his lips. "You'll come when I allow it," he says, dripping with authority. "Until then, you're mine to play with."

He resumes his torturous ministrations, his mouth driving me to the brink once more. My entire body tenses, ready to shatter into a million pieces, but once again, he pulls back just in time.

Tears of frustration prick at my eyes as I struggle to hold back a sob. He holds himself over me, his free hand gripping my face as he forces me to look into his eyes. "Do you understand who's in control here, Inès?" he demands in a low growl.

"Yes," I manage to choke out, my body trembling with need. "I never doubted it."

"Good girl," he murmurs, his lips brushing against mine in a teasing kiss. "Come for me like a good little whore," he commands. "Scream my name."

With that, he slides back down, his mouth returning to my aching core with renewed intensity. This time, he doesn't hold back, his tongue working hard to push me over the edge. The release is explosive, and I cry out his name just as he demanded, my body shaking as wave after wave of pleasure crashes over me. He doesn't stop, drawing out every last bit of my climax. I can feel him smiling against me with the satisfaction of knowing he's undone me completely.

As I come down from the high, he stands and heads to the bathroom. He comes back with a small towel and gently cleans me up. I can clearly see his erection, and I lick my lips.

I've never given a blow job before, nor had anyone touch me the way King just did, but I want to reciprocate.

"Don't even think about it. Tonight was about you," he says gently.

"But… you're hard," I point out.

"A state I will always be in when you're with me. Just ignore it," he replies softly, continuing to clean me with a tender unhurried touch.

"But I want to reciprocate…" I murmur, feeling the strong desire to please him as intensely as he pleased me.

"That's not how this works, Inès," he says, his tone softening as he looks deeply into my eyes. "Just because I do something for you doesn't mean you have to reciprocate. Do you understand me? There will be times when all I want is to taste you, to make you come undone in my arms. Your pleasure is my reward. An erection isn't going to kill me, okay?"

"Okay," I whisper, my heart swelling with affection and gratitude.

He smiles, pressing a tender kiss to my forehead before heading back to the bathroom. When he returns moments later, he slides into bed beside me, wrapping me in his embrace. His arms envelop me, strong and protective, yet gentle as if he's afraid I might slip away.

I can still feel his erection pressing against me, but he doesn't push for more. Instead, he just holds me, his breath warm against my ear as he murmurs, "Sleep, my Queen. I've got you."

His words soothe me more than any lullaby ever could. I surrender to the peaceful slumber that his presence brings, knowing that in his arms, I am truly home.

KINGSLEY

THE KING'S BIRTHDAY TREAT

I wake up to an empty bed.

The warmth of her body, usually pressed close against mine, is gone, and my arm instinctively reaches out to her side, finding nothing but cool sheets. Irritation prickles at the edges of my mind. Inès isn't in bed. My chest tightens, a strange, possessive reaction, but it's become routine. Waking up without her doesn't sit well with me.

Where is she?

I swing my legs over the edge of the bed, stretch, and scrub a hand through my hair. My gaze flicks toward the bathroom. Might as well get the morning routine out of the way. As I stand in front of the mirror, brushing my teeth, my mind wanders to Inès. The thought of her sends a pulse racing through me that has nothing to do with the crisp morning air. She's soft, warm, mine. Having her and Beau living with me is the best feeling, and I wouldn't trade it for anything.

The scent hits me as soon as I open the bedroom door and

step into the hallway, burnt sugar, something acrid. My gut tightens. That can't be right. *Inès*.

I take the stairs two at a time, and the smell intensifies. As I near the kitchen, I hear her voice. Quiet curses, followed by the scraping of a spatula against a pan. I stop in the doorway, crossing my arms, taking her in. Inès is standing at the counter, wrestling with what looks like a disaster of a cake. It's burnt around the edges, the frosting slipping off the sides, and she's so focused on trying to salvage it that she doesn't even notice me at first.

Beau spots me before she does. He barks, tail wagging furiously, then bolts toward me. I crouch down and scoop him up, pressing a quick kiss to his furry head, his enthusiasm infectious.

"Papillon,"[1] I say, unable to keep the amusement from my voice. "What the hell happened here?"

She spins around, eyes wide like I've caught her red-handed. Her cheeks flush that gorgeous pink, and it takes all my willpower not to cross the room and kiss her right there.

"You were supposed to stay in bed!" she scolds, pouting adorably. "I was going to bring this up to you. It's… supposed to be your birthday cake."

I grin, taking in the chaos around her. The cake is a disaster, but she, with her messy hair, oversize shirt, and flustered expression, is perfection. She crosses her arms, her lips forming the cutest little pout, then whispers, "Happy birthday, King. I'm sorry I burned your cake…"

My heart softens instantly, and I set Beau down before striding over to her. The moment I'm close enough, I pull her into my arms, tipping her chin up so I can look into her eyes. She fits perfectly against me, and I have to resist the urge to

---

1. Butterfly.

bend her over the counter right here, cake be damned. "I love it. I'll eat an entire slice."

Her eyes widen in horror. "King, no! You don't have to do that. It's awful. You'll…"

"Hush," I say, leaning down to press my lips to hers in a soft, lingering kiss. She melts into me for a moment, her body relaxing before she pulls back slightly to protest again.

"You really don't have to…"

I grab a plate before she can stop me, cutting a slice of the burnt cake and dropping it onto the dish. I take a seat on the island, fork in hand, and take a bite. The taste hits me, and for a second, I struggle to keep my expression neutral. It's… bad. But I can't help the grin tugging at the corner of my mouth as I chew and swallow.

"Kingsley…" she groans, reaching for the plate. "Seriously, don't eat that. You'll get sick. I didn't mean for it to…"

I hold the plate out of her reach, raising a brow. "Hands off my cake. You made it for me. I'm eating it."

She gapes at me, torn between exasperation and laughter. Eventually, she crosses her arms again, giving me a look like I'm the most ridiculous man on the planet. "You're impossible," she mutters.

After choking down a few more bites, each worse than the last, I set the plate aside and stand. I pull her back into my arms, my hands sliding down her waist, squeezing her hips. "That was the best birthday gift I've ever had," I tell her, my voice low and teasing.

She snorts, rolling her eyes. "Yeah, right."

"Now," I murmur, my lips brushing the shell of her ear. "I want another present."

Before she can respond, I hoist her over my shoulder in one smooth motion, her squeal echoing through the kitchen as

I head back upstairs. Her hands slap at my back in mock protest, but I can hear the laughter in her voice.

"King! Put me down!"

"Not a chance." I push open the bedroom door with my foot, walking us in before setting her down on the edge of the bed. She's breathless, eyes sparkling, but before I can kiss her, she holds up a hand.

"Wait. You just ate burnt cake."

I narrow my eyes, leaning in to nip at her neck. "You'll wait for me," I say. "Naked."

I push off the bed and walk to the bathroom, rinsing my mouth out quickly. I then head into our closet and retrieve the new toy I bought for her, something I've been dying to try on her. Grinning to myself, I grab the Rose toy, two ties, and head back into the bedroom.

When I step into the room, toy in hand, Inès is sitting on the bed, legs crossed, completely naked, just as I asked her. I can't help but give her an appreciative smile.

"King? What is that?"

"On your back. Now," I command, my voice rougher now, darker.

She complies immediately, eyes filled with excitement, nerves, and something darker, something needier.

I set the toy aside and walk to her with the ties. "Do you trust me?" I ask, and she nods immediately.

"Use your words, Queen."

"I trust you, King," she says breathlessly.

"Good girl. I'm going to tie your hands together with one of these." I show her the ties. "And I'll also blindfold you." Her eyes widen, but not in fear, in lust. "If you ever want me to stop for whatever reason, just say stop. Do you understand me?"

"Yes, King."

"Good." I crawl onto the bed, positioning myself between her thighs. "You've been so good, trying to bake me a cake. Now, it's my turn to spoil you," I say as I take her hands and tie them above her head against the headboard. "I'm going to make you scream my name," I say while blindfolding her; her breaths come out in short pants. "You look so pretty bound and at my mercy," I whisper against her ear, and she shivers, turning her head toward my mouth, wanting to kiss me, but I move out of the way just in time, chuckling darkly.

She whines and wiggles her hands to test the restraints, but they're sturdy. "King?" she calls out when I get off the bed.

"I'm still here, butterfly," I tell her as I take my pajama pants off. My dick is so hard it hurts; I wrap my hand around my shaft and squeeze to alleviate the pressure.

"Please, King, I... I need to touch you," she tells me. She once told me that physical touch is her love language, and I believe it. When she has a long day, my mere touch can make her feel better in an instant. She told me mine is gift-giving, and I told her my love language is her, but she just laughed it off. I was dead serious.

"I know, Queen. Soon," I tell her, grabbing the toy.

I crawl between her thighs, pressing her knees apart, spreading her wide for me. I can see the slick glistening between her folds, and fuck, it takes all my control not to bury my face in her right there. But I've got plans.

I turn the toy on, and her breath catches, her hips already twitching. But I don't press the toy where she's expecting it; instead, I press it against her already hard nipples. She gasps and nearly bucks off the bed, but I hold her down. "K... King!" she moans.

"Yes, Queen?" I taunt as I remove the toy, only to press it against the other nipple. Then I press my lips to hers, swallowing her cries as I press my bottom half against her core. She gasps when she feels my dick against her pussy. Immediately, she starts grinding against me, and fuck… fuck me, she's so warm and slick. I only meant to tease her; I'm not actually planning to fuck her, she's not ready for that, but fuck, she feels too good, and I'm not even inside her.

"Fuck!" I groan against her lips. "You feel fucking fantastic," I say as she continues to grind against me.

"I'm close… I'm so close," she moans, her voice thick with desire, but I refuse to let her tip over the edge. I disengage our hips just in time, and her protest is a sweet cry in the air.

"No… what are you doing?" she begs, squirming against her restraints.

I say nothing; instead, I remove the toy from her nipple and lower myself between her legs. The intoxicating scent of her arousal fills my senses, and I inhale deeply, almost getting lost in her.

As I blow cool air against her clit, she squirms, her body a canvas of anticipation. "You have the prettiest cunt I've ever seen," I murmur before latching on to her, my tongue flicking and teasing.

"Oh God!" she screams, her back arching as I pull away, lightly tapping her sensitive clit with my fingers.

"Never mention another man in my bed. Now, what's my name?" I demand. When she hesitates, I spank her pussy harder, the sound echoing in the room, a mix of pleasure and pain. "What. Is. My. Name?"

"King… King, please," she begs, and a smirk curls my lips.

"That's my good fucking slut."

Her breath hitches as I press the toy to her clit, the soft, pulsing suction drawing gasps from her lips. I watch her intently, every twitch of her body, every desperate sound she makes, she's utterly beautiful and so responsive to the vibrations.

"Kingsley," she gasps, wiggling against her restraints. "I, I need to come, please!"

I remove the toy and relish the tremble that runs through her. "Not yet," I tease, my voice low and taunting.

"W-Why are you being so mean?" she cries, her frustration dripping with sweetness.

"I can be meaner; is that what you want?" I challenge, hovering over her, watching her body language.

"No! I just want to come, please!" she pleads, her desperation showing.

"I know you do, baby. But if you hold it, it'll feel ten times better, I promise." I align my cock against her wetness, rubbing it teasingly, feeling her heat against me.

"Please take these off so I can see you," she begs, a note of desperation creeping into her voice. She's never seen me like this, and that's by design.

"Not a chance."

"Ugh, I hate you," she huffs, trying to sound fierce, but it's too cute.

"Hmm, you hate me? Is that why you're soaking the sheets right now?" I smirk, leaning in for a deep kiss. She bites my lip hard, and I groan in surprise.

"Oh no, I'm so sorry, King! I don't know why I did that!" she gasps.

I chuckle, both amused and turned on. "You can bite me whenever you want, Queen." I lower myself back to her pussy, and the moment the toy touches her, her body jerks in response. The suction is soft at first, but I gradually turn it up, watching as her moans fill the room.

"Don't you dare close your legs," I growl, my hands

firmly spreading her thighs. I lean down, kissing her inner thighs, my breath hot against her skin. "Tell me how badly you need to come."

Her response is a choked whimper, and I growl, pressing the toy harder against her clit. "Tell me."

"I… I need it," she gasps, her voice breaking with need. "Please… please, Kingsley, I need it so bad."

"Good girl." My fingers dig into her thighs, holding her steady as the toy works her over. Her hips buck, moans becoming desperate whimpers that fuel my own arousal.

As I keep the toy pressed against her, her body starts to shatter under the pressure. "That's it," I murmur, my voice thick with satisfaction. "Come for me."

"I… I can't! It's… oh… I'm scared."

"Yes, you can," I whisper, flicking the toy to a higher setting. She cries out, her back arching off the bed. "Let go for me, Inès. I want to watch you come."

Her moans fill the room, her body trembling as the sensation builds. When she finally shatters, her scream echoes off the walls, her entire body convulsing with pleasure. I keep the toy pressed against her, watching her writhe, her thighs clamping down around my hand, but I hold her steady.

As the pleasure washes over her, I wrap my hand around my cock and stroke hard and fast, the sight of her in ecstasy driving me wild. "Fuck!" I groan, my breath ragged, as I near my own climax. With a few more strokes, I spill myself, painting her skin with my release, a primal satisfaction coursing through me.

Breathing heavily, I crawl up her body, pressing a soft kiss to her lips. "Happy birthday to me," I murmur, and she laughs breathlessly, a sound that fills me with warmth.

"You're insufferable," she whispers.

I get off the bed, slipping on my pants before returning to her, untie her hands, and remove the blindfold.

Her eyes blink in the soft light, and I brush a strand of hair from her face, my fingers lingering on her cheek. "You did so well, Inès. How do you feel?"

"I feel… amazing," she breathes, still coming down from the high, and I can't help but smile at her. She looks down at me and frowns. "I can't believe you didn't let me see you," she complains, making me smile. "Please tell me you don't have another tattoo of my name on your…"

This time, I throw my head back and laugh. "You are just too cute, let me go get your bath ready."

"You haven't answered my question, King," she says, sounding serious, and it only makes me laugh harder.

"No, I do not have your name tattooed on my dick, but now I'm thinking about it," I say as I make my way to the bathroom.

"Not funny," she yells from the room, and I just continue to laugh. Of course, I won't get a dick tattoo, but a part of me is thinking of getting a fake one just to see Inès's reaction.

KINGSLEY

*WATCH OUT, PROFESSOR, KING'S GOT HIS
EYE ON YOU*

I've been sitting at the back of the lecture hall in Inès's psychology class for the past thirty minutes, a bouquet of roses in my hand. She knows I'm here, but I'm content to wait. The plan is to take her out to lunch before I have to travel to Tokyo for business. It pains me that I won't see her for a few days, but as much as I want to bring her with me everywhere, I know how important her education is to her. It's something I've known since the moment I met her, and I would never come between her and her dreams. That's why I'm currently tucked away at the back of the room, not wanting to be a distraction.

I have to admit that this class is intriguing. Dr. Salvatore's lecture has everyone captivated as he speaks of Freud and Jung, cognitive dissonance, and behavioral conditioning. His passion breathes life into each concept, making them more than just academic theories.

His gaze sweeps across the room, locking onto each student momentarily, as if assessing their potential. "Psychology is not merely an academic subject," he continues, his voice dropping to a more intimate tone, "It is the study of us, our fears, our desires, and the intricate dance between them."

From where I sit, I can see Inès taking notes, her focus unbreakable. She's so adorable when she's deep in thought. The fact that I can finally call her mine is more than I ever hoped for.

It's been two weeks since the burglary, and the police are still no closer to catching whoever did it. A couple of days ago, Justin and I went to the apartment and packed up the remainder of the girls' essentials since they are staying with us until the cops catch the person who broke in.

Every night, I share a bed with Inès, and most nights, I make her come with my mouth. It's a test of my control, a battle I face repeatedly, especially as Inès grows bolder, teasing me relentlessly. She wears my thinnest shirts to bed, with no bra, her nipple piercings always visible, driving me to the edge. She loves pressing her ass against my erection every night, a constant temptation. Of course, I'm aching to take her virginity, I'm not a saint, but I'm determined to wait until she's ready.

Midway through the lecture, Dr. Salvatore pauses, his eyes narrowing thoughtfully. "Let's conduct a little experiment, shall we?" He steps away from the lectern, moving closer to the students. "Who here believes they can read another person's mind?"

A few hands tentatively rise, and Dr. Salvatore's lips curve into a knowing smile. "Miss Dubois?" he calls, his voice gentle. "Would you do me the honor and join me up here."

I smile as Inès stands and walks to the front of the room. When her eyes find mine almost immediately, I give her a small nod, and she visibly relaxes.

"Imagine a scenario," Dr. Salvatore instructs. "You are walking down a dark alley, and you see someone approaching. What do you feel?"

"Fear," Inès replies after a moment, her French accent adding an irresistible charm to the word.

"Interesting," Dr. Salvatore murmurs, his eyes never leaving hers.

I stiffen, narrowing my eyes. There's something in the way he looks at her that sets me on edge. *Relax, King. He's her professor, not someone who wants your girl. You're just being a jealous fucker.* "Now, why do you feel fear? Is it the darkness? The unknown figure? Or perhaps something deeper within you?"

Inès hesitates, clearly unsure of how to respond.

Dr. Salvatore turns back to the class, finally taking his eyes off my girl. "You see, our reactions are often rooted in deeper psychological constructs. It's not just the external stimuli but our internal narratives that shape our perceptions. This experiment illustrates how our minds create fear based on context and past experiences, not merely on the immediate situation."

He places a hand on Inès's shoulder, and I grit my teeth. "Fear is a primal emotion, an evolutionary response to danger. But what constitutes 'danger' is not always clear-cut. Our brains interpret signals based on learned experiences, cultural context, and personal history."

Dr. Salvatore's voice grows more intense, drawing the class into his explanation. His hand remains on her shoulder but then drops to the small of her back; my vision threatens to go red. Why the fuck is he being so familiar with her? Am I the only one seeing this? "Thank you. You may return," he finally says, and Inès returns to her seat.

As the lecture draws to a close, Dr. Salvatore's voice

softens, taking on a more personal tone. "This course will not be easy. It will challenge you; it will frustrate you, and it will force you to confront uncomfortable truths. But if you stay with me, I promise you, it will also transform you."

He pauses, letting his words sink in. "Class dismissed."

I stand, ready to go to my girl, when I notice Dr. Salvatore walking over to her desk, saying something I can't hear. As I try to make my way down to her, I am stopped by a few people I don't know. They greet me, and I greet them back absentmindedly. My sole focus is on Inès, who looks back at me, guilt written all over her face.

"I'm glad you decided to take the opportunity. I believe it will be good for your future," I hear the professor say as I approach them.

"I am grateful for the opportunity..." They both turn to me when they notice my presence. "Hi," Inès says, her smile almost forced.

I hand her the bouquet I brought and kiss the top of her head. "Hey, butterfly," I say softly. When I glance back at the professor, his features are tight, his jaw clenched. Yeah, this motherfucker wants my woman.

"Oh, I'm sorry, uh, King, this is Dr. Salvatore, my professor. Dr. Salvatore, this is my boyfriend..."

"Kingsley Ashford," the professor interjects, extending his hand to me. "I've heard that the great-grandson of Alexander Ashford graduated last semester. It's interesting that you choose to stick around on campus." His smile is fake, and I return it in kind. When we shake hands, we both apply pressure, trying to outdo the other, but I've got inches, muscles, and strength on him. He grits his teeth in pain and yanks his hand away.

"What's this I heard about an opportunity?" I ask, my

eyes landing on Inès, who is nervously biting her bottom lip, her tell when she's anxious.

"Miss Dubois here is going to be my new TA next semester. She will be the youngest TA this university has ever had," Dr. Salvatore says, a triumphant smile playing on his lips, one I desperately want to wipe off. But this is Inès's education, and as much as I hate that she'll be forced to spend more time with this prick, being a TA is an incredible opportunity for her.

I glance back at Inès and feel a genuine smile spread across my face. "Is that so? Then we definitely need to celebrate!" I say, my voice warm as I take in her excitement. "Let's head out; we wouldn't want to be late for our reservations."

"Oh yes, I'm ready," she replies, her eyes lighting up. I take her backpack from her, leaving her free to hold the bouquet of roses.

As we turn to leave, Dr. Salvatore's voice cuts through. "I'll see you at the clinic tomorrow, Miss Dubois, and it was a pleasure meeting you, Mr. Ashford."

"See you, Dr. Salvatore," Inès says politely, slipping her hand into mine. I don't bother acknowledging him. Yes, I'm that petty, sue me.

Once we're in the car, heading toward one of my favorite restaurants in the city, I can't shake the unease gnawing at me. I glance over at Inès, trying to sound casual. "So, Dr. Salvatore seems pretty familiar with you." I try to mask the bitterness in my tone, but it's there. I can't help it, I'm a jealous bastard when it comes to her.

She looks down at the bouquet, avoiding my gaze. "Did he? I don't think so. That's just who he is," she says softly, almost dismissively.

"Inès?" I press.

"Yes, King?"

"Is there something going on that I should know?" I ask, my eyes flicking between the road and her. I hate the doubt gnawing at me, but I can't shake the feeling that something's off.

"No, I promise nothing is going on." Her words are quick, almost too quick.

I want to believe her. I do. But something doesn't sit right with me. Still, she's never given me a reason not to trust her, and I owe her that trust now, no matter what my instincts are telling me.

"Alright," I say, my tone softening as I reach over to gently squeeze her hand.

As we sit in the private dining room of Luxe, the soft glow of the lights casts a gentle radiance across Inès's face, high-lighting the delicate curve of her jawline. My God, she's beautiful. Every time I look at her, I'm reminded of how lucky I am.

The waiter pours our wine, takes our food order, and quietly leaves us in our private world. I reach across the table, taking her hand in mine. Her fingers are warm and soft, and when she looks at me with that sweet smile, I feel a swell of pride that's almost overwhelming. "I'm so proud of you, Inès. Being chosen as a TA is incredible." She's worked so hard to get here, and I couldn't be prouder to simply exist by her side.

"Thank you, King," she says, her smile turning shy, a slight blush tinting her cheeks.

"Had I known ahead of time, I would've gotten you

something special to celebrate. But luckily, I picked this up today." I pull out her personal Amex card and hand it to her.

She blinks in surprise, her gaze shifting from the card to me. "Uh… is this what I think it is?" she asks, her eyes narrowing in curiosity.

"It's yours to use whenever you want. No budget." I say it with all seriousness, watching as she laughs then stops when she realizes I'm not joking.

"Oh, you're serious?"

"I am."

"Thank you, I really appreciate it, but no thank you." She firmly pushes the card back toward me, and I frown at it like it's personally offended me. Before I can argue, the waiter returns with our food, interrupting the moment.

"Oh my God, that smells amazing. I'm starving." Inès claps her hands, her mood instantly lightening as she digs into her meal, completely unbothered by the earlier exchange.

We eat in comfortable silence for a few minutes before she looks up at me, her expression thoughtful. "I wanted to talk to you about what we discussed a few days ago," she begins, sounding soft yet determined. "You know, the domestic discipline lifestyle."

"Yeah?" My curiosity sharpens, wondering where this conversation is headed. Of course, if she's not comfortable with it, I'll respect her wishes, I'm more than capable of having a "normal" relationship. But deep down, a part of me hopes she's open to at least exploring the idea.

As I sit there, waiting for her to elaborate, my mind drifts. I've never really unpacked where my interest in DD comes from. Maybe it's because I grew up in a household where control was absolute. My father was always a commanding presence, decisive, authoritative, the kind of man who expected things to run smoothly, both at home and in business. He wasn't cruel, but he demanded respect and structure, and that shaped a lot of who I am today. My mother, on the other hand, has always been more distant, physically and emotionally. She was there, but not *present*, if that makes sense.

But DD isn't about control for the sake of power, at least not for me. It's about structure, trust, and a kind of intimacy that feels stabilizing. I guess, in some way, it gives me the balance I never had growing up. My father controlled everything to feel powerful; for me, this lifestyle is about creating a space where both people feel seen, secure, and respected.

Inès nods, her eyes meeting mine with a mix of determination and vulnerability. "I've done a lot of research, read countless articles, and watched videos. And I want this, King. I want to live this lifestyle with you, to follow and respect you as the man of our relationship."

Hearing those words from her sends a rush of emotions through me, a potent blend of pride, responsibility, and desire. "Are you sure this is what you want? That you don't feel pressured or coerced?"

She reaches out, holding my hand tightly. "I'm sure. I want to at least give it a try, and I know if I ever tell you it's not for me, you'll stop everything." Her smile is reassuring, and I can see the trust she's placing in me.

I lean back in my chair, studying her face, the way her eyes flicker with anticipation and a touch of anxiety. "We'll take it slow, and we'll always communicate about how we're feeling. But there's one thing we need to establish right from the start, a safe word. Something you can use if things ever get too intense or if you're not comfortable."

"Right, yes. I've thought of one, frisson," she says softly, the word rolling off her tongue with a hint of her French accent.

"Frisson," I repeat, letting the word linger on my lips. It means shiver or thrill. I smile, reaching over to tuck a strand of hair behind her ear. "It's perfect."

"Thank you," she murmurs, a small smile playing on her lips as she returns to her meal. After a moment, she looks back up at me, curiosity in her eyes. "So, what now?"

I take the Amex card that's meant for her and slide it back across the table. Her eyes land on it before she meets my gaze. "Take the card," I say, raising an eyebrow when she starts to protest.

"Fine," she grumbles like a petulant child, finally taking the card and slipping it into her bag.

"Good girl," I say with a smile, knowing tomorrow will be very interesting indeed.

I have Inès's hand in mine while Justin holds Meghan's.

"This better be good, J. You know I hate surprises," Meghan complains, making Inès laugh softly beside me.

"She really does," Inès adds with a knowing smile.

We've got the girls blindfolded as we ride the elevator down to the underground parking garage, I can't wait to see the look on Inès's face when she sees what we've planned.

"Woman, would you relax? You'll love this," Justin reassures Meghan just as the elevator doors slide open. We carefully guide the girls out, their steps tentative but trusting.

"Okay, we're here. Ready?" I ask, my voice filled with anticipation.

"Yes!" they both exclaim in unison.

Justin and I remove their blindfolds simultaneously. It takes a moment for their eyes to adjust to the light, but when they finally see the two Range Rovers, one black and one white, parked in front of them with big red bows on top, Meghan lets out a shriek so loud I wince.

"You got us matching cars!" she cries out, bouncing up and down with uncontainable excitement.

Inès, on the other hand, is quieter, her eyes wide as she stares at the cars in disbelief. "You got us matching cars?" she whispers, almost as if she can't believe it.

"Well, technically we just helped pay for them. We used the money you two paid in rent and added to it to get these," I explain, carefully watching Inès's reaction.

"Oh my God, oh my God, J!" Meghan continues her excited dance, practically throwing herself at Justin. But Inès remains still, blinking at the car as if it might vanish if she moves too suddenly.

"What's wrong? You don't like it? I can return it and get you something else. We just thought you'd like matching cars," I say, a hint of concern creeping into my voice.

"No." Inès finally turns to look at me, her expression softening. "It's not that. I love it. It's just... it's too much, King. I can't take this. You've already done so much for me. I feel like I'm taking advantage of you."

I step closer, cupping her cheeks and forcing her to meet my gaze. "Listen to me, you are not taking advantage of me. I want to take care of you, Inès. Let me. It's my way of showing you that I... care about you," I say, my voice dipping as I nearly confess my love. I catch myself just in time. "Let me spoil you."

Justin's voice cuts through the moment. "Wanna guess which one's yours?" he asks Meghan with a grin.

"Uh, the black one is mine, obviously," Meghan says confidently, and Justin hands her the keys.

"And the white one is mine," Inès says, her smile finally

breaking through the shock, lighting up her entire face. Relief washes over me as I pull out the key and hand it to her. We'd known what color each of them wanted long before we got the cars, I needed to be sure Inès would love it. "I can't thank you enough, King," she whispers, her voice soft and sincere.

I don't hesitate. Wrapping my arms around her waist, I pull her close, so close I can feel her heartbeat against my chest. "Just kiss me, and we'll call it even," I murmur, my voice low and commanding.

Her eyes sparkle with a playful challenge as she grins. "I can do that," she replies, sliding her arms around my neck. She rises on her tiptoes, her lips meeting mine in a kiss that starts off sweet and gentle, a tantalizing taste of her that has me craving more. But I'm not one to hold back. I deepen the kiss, my tongue sliding into her mouth, claiming her in the way only I can. She moans softly, the sound vibrating through me, igniting a fire that's impossible to ignore. I pull away before I lose control, my breathing heavy, my heart racing.

"How about a ride in your new car?" I ask, trying to focus on something other than the way she makes me ache.

"Yes!" she says, her excitement bubbling over, and I can't help but smile at how happy she is.

I take a moment, clenching my jaw, trying to calm the surge of desire still coursing through me. Three days without her? I don't know how I'm going to survive.

INÈS

VIRGINITY IS A SOCIAL CONSTRUCT

I'm in our room, well, Kingsley's room, but when did I start thinking of it as ours? He left for Tokyo yesterday for work, and he's supposed to be back tomorrow. Ever since he left, I've been restless. Last night, I tossed and turned, because apparently, I can't sleep without him wrapped around me. The lack of sleep made me grumpy, and even now I'm supposed to be studying for an upcoming exam, but all I can think about is Kingsley.

It's unsettling. I'm usually good at blocking out distractions when I study, but lately, he's all I can focus on. And the fact that I don't want to go back to my apartment, even after they catch whoever broke into it, because I love living with Kingsley, it worries me.

Kingsley has been nothing but a gentleman. He hasn't pushed for more than kissing or making me come with his mouth. Don't get me wrong, I love the orgasms, but I want more. I ache for him so much it's almost painful. I know he's trying to be considerate, especially since he found out I'm a virgin, but I hate the wait. All I want is for him to take me, to ravish me like an animal, because this need for him is consuming me.

Beau is on my lap taking a nap as I pretend to focus on whatever is on my screen when the door to the bedroom opens and Meghan walks in. "Meg, what are you doing? You know I don't like being disturbed when I'm studying," I say, trying to sound stern.

"Oh please, we both know that door would have been locked if you were actually focused. Anyway, I need you, it's important." She looks scared, which immediately makes me close my laptop and get up with Beau. I gently set him on the bed before she takes my hand, leading me to the bathroom without another word.

"Meg, what's going on, " I start, but I'm cut off when she places a box of pregnancy tests on the counter. My eyes widen, and when I look at her, I notice her red, puffy eyes. She's been crying. "Meg?" I call out, and she breaks down, crying even harder.

"I haven't had my period in two months, and I've been feeling sick and tired… I haven't taken the test yet, because I'm scared, Inès…" she sobs.

I instantly pull her into my arms. "Hey, hey. It's okay, Meg. Everything's going to be okay," I soothe her. "How about we take the test first before jumping to conclusions?"

She nods, sniffling.

I gently let go of her and open the box, reading the instructions before telling her what to do. "I'll be right outside, okay?"

She doesn't respond, just sniffles again. I leave the bathroom to give her some privacy, my heart heavy with concern.

After a few moments, she comes out and hands me the

pregnancy test, her hands trembling. "I can't look," she says, her voice small.

I nod. "Would you like me to?" I ask, and she nods.

I flip the test over, and my heart sinks when I see the two pink lines. My throat tightens as I glance over at Meghan, who's standing by the bed, nervously wringing her hands. I know this isn't what she wanted, definitely not now, not like this. She's been so focused on law school, working toward her dream of becoming a criminal lawyer. But life doesn't always go according to plan.

"It says you're pregnant," I say softly, my voice barely above a whisper, as if speaking louder might make it more real.

Her eyes widen with panic, and she stares at the test in my hand for what feels like forever. Slowly, she crumples, her knees buckling beneath her as she sinks to the floor.

I'm by her side in an instant, wrapping my arms around her tightly as she collapses into me, her sobs shaking both of our bodies. "It's okay," I whisper, rubbing soothing circles on her back. "I've got you, Meg. We'll figure this out together."

Beau, sensing the tension, trots over from his spot on the bed, his little face full of concern. He noses his way between us, determined to help in whatever way he can. Without hesitation, he presses his soft body into Meghan's side, his tail wagging faintly as if trying to say, *I'm here, too.* Meghan lets out a shaky breath and, with a tear-streaked face, wraps one hand around Beau, pulling him closer. Beau lets out a little whine, snuggling in even tighter as if trying to absorb some of her pain.

"What am I going to do, Inès?" Meghan's voice cracks as she clings to both me and Beau. "I can't be a mother. I don't know how… My own mother was barely in my life." Her words come out in a rush like she's been holding them back for too long. "And what about school? I have *years* left before I can even think about becoming a lawyer."

I hug her tighter, resting my chin on top of her head as she continues to cry. "I know you're scared," I murmur, "but it's going to be okay. Whatever choice you make, I'll stand by you." I pull back just enough to cradle her head, making sure she looks at me. "If you choose not to go through with this, I'll hold your hand at the hospital. And if you choose to keep the baby, I'll be there every step of the way. You won't quit school, because I know how much you want to be a lawyer and how hard you've worked to get where you are. I'll help you study if that's what you need. Okay? You are not alone, Meg; you have a man who is crazy about you, and I know he will support you in whatever decision you choose." I stroke her hair gently, glancing down at Beau, who's now resting his head on her lap, looking up at her with those big brown eyes full of unconditional love.

Meghan sniffles, running her fingers through Beau's fur absentmindedly. "But what if I mess it up?" she whispers in a fragile voice. "What if I end up like my mom?"

"You are *not* your mom, Meghan. You're so much more than that. You're strong, determined, and caring. But you don't have to make any decisions right now, okay? We'll take this one step at a time."

She bites her lip, her eyes still red and swollen from crying, but I can see a flicker of hope there, like maybe, just maybe, she's starting to believe me.

Meghan manages a smile, small but genuine, as she rests her head on my shoulder. "Thank you, Inès," she whispers, quieter now, like she's finding her way back to herself. "I love you, you know that, right?"

"I love you, too," I tell her, resting my cheek on the top of her head. "I'm always here, no matter what."

The three of us sit there on the floor for a while, me, Meghan, and Beau, wrapped in a little bubble of quiet support. Eventually, Meghan's sobs fade into soft breaths, and the tension in her body relaxes. Beau is already dozing off, his little form still snuggled up against her.

"Talk to me. Distract me so I'm not thinking about the mess in my life right now," Meghan says, pulling back from my embrace. She wipes a stray tear, trying to collect herself, her shoulders squared as if readying herself for battle.

I hesitate, unsure of what to say, then, without thinking, I blurt out, "Well... when Kingsley gets back from Tokyo, I'm going to ask him to have sex with me."

Her head snaps toward me, eyes wide in disbelief. "What? Seriously? You're actually going to ask him?" she asks loudly, making Beau get up from her lap and make his way back to the bed.

I nod, trying to project a confidence I don't feel. "Yeah. I mean... I haven't exactly figured out how I'm going to convince him yet, though. He's done everything possible to avoid it. I know he wants to take things slow, to be sure it's what I want, but... part of me wonders if maybe it's something else."

Meghan's brows furrow, her attention fully on me now. "What do you mean?"

"I mean... maybe he just doesn't see me that way. You know, sexually." The words come out in a rush, and I cringe as I say them. "I'm not exactly like the girls he used to date. They were all... bold, confident, sexy. And me? I feel like a walking contradiction. One minute I'm witty and sure of myself, the next I'm tripping over my own feet or making dumb jokes. I don't know how to be that kind of girl, overtly sexy. It makes me wonder if I'm what he really wants in that way."

Meghan's expression softens as she places a hand on mine. "Hey, stop that. There's no doubt he wants you like that, babe. Trust me, have you *seen* yourself? Even when you're being a total dork, you're still sexy." She squeezes my hand, her voice turning gentle. "Kingsley's not pulling back because he's not attracted to you. He's probably just trying to be careful, to respect your boundaries. The guy worships the ground you walk on."

I sigh, leaning back against the wall. "I don't know... I guess I'm just afraid that maybe I'm not enough for him."

Meghan shakes her head with a knowing smile. "Oh, trust me, if Kingsley wasn't into you, you'd know. Guys don't fake that kind of restraint for no reason." She pauses, tilting her head thoughtfully. "Are you really ready for that step, though? This isn't just about wanting it. Are *you* ready?"

I shrug. "I think so. I'm not expecting some grand moment, but I want to feel connected to him in that way. It's just..." I sigh, running my fingers through my hair. "It's hard not to overthink it, you know? Especially with all those stories of people saying your virginity is this big deal."

Meghan rolls her eyes. "I'm not going to lecture you about saving yourself for marriage or any of that crap. Virginity is a social construct anyway. What matters is what *you* feel, and what *you* want. If you're ready, and you trust him, that's all that matters."

I smile, appreciating her honesty. "Thanks. I just... I want it to be special, but I don't want to put too much pressure on it, you know? Kingsley means a lot to me, and I know he's waiting for the right moment, but I think I'm ready for that moment to be now. Or... well, when he gets back."

"Then go for it," Meghan encourages. "Just be honest with him. You two already have something real, something special. The rest will follow when you're both ready."

"Thank you, Meg," I say.

"Of course! But I want details when you do lose your virginity," she teases, causing me to laugh.

"Not happening, weirdo," I reply, even though I know I'll probably tell her.

She smirks, clearly reading my mind. "You know you're going to tell me everything. You always do." With a playful kiss on my cheek, she stands up. "I'm going to talk to Justin about… you know…" She gestures toward her stomach, her expression softening.

I nod, understanding, and she adds, "But let's go out for dinner later. I want to dress up and just… get out for a bit."

"Dinner sounds great. Let me know where you want to go and what the vibe is," I say, smiling at her.

She nods, giving me one last glance before leaving the room.

KINGSLEY

I'm jolted awake by my phone ringing. Glancing at the screen, I see it's Inès calling. I answer with a yawn. "Butterfly?"

"Oh my God, were you sleeping? I forgot to check the time difference between Tokyo and Boston."

"It's thirteen hours. It's currently…" I check the time on my phone. "Six a.m. here."

"I'm sorry! I'll call you later; please go back to sleep."

"No, it's fine. I have to get up anyway. What's up?" I say, sitting up in bed.

"Nothing… I just missed you, that's all," she says nervously, and it takes everything in me not to jump back on the private jet, fly back to Boston, and kiss her until she's begging for more.

"I miss you, too baby. I'll be home soon, I promise," I tell her. "Let's switch to FaceTime so I can see your beautiful face." I switch the call, eager to see her.

Her pretty face fills the screen, and I can't help but smile. "There you are. How was your day?" I ask as I get out of bed and head into the bathroom. My body's already reacting to just the sound of her voice.

"It was fine. I had two tutoring sessions today. I also called my parents and told them I'd be coming for Papa's[1] birthday and that I'm bringing you. Everyone's excited to meet you," she says, and I prop my phone up against the wall as I start my morning routine.

"I'm excited to meet them, too. Have you eaten today?" I ask, but when she doesn't respond, I glance at the screen. The look she's giving me makes me grin. I'm standing there in nothing but my black boxer briefs and there's no hiding my erection. She's biting her lip, staring at my chest, my tattoos, and definitely at my hard-on. Seeing her react like this only makes me harder.

"Can I… um, can I see your…" She blushes. God, she's going to be the death of me.

"My cock?" I smile, flexing a bit, making my dick twitch in my pants.

"Yes," she breathes then hides her face in embarrassment.

"Say it," I demand, my voice low and raspy, her desire fueling my own.

---

1. Dad.

"Can I see your cock?" she asks. Her voice is shy but laced with longing.

"No," I reply, nearly laughing at the look on her face. She looks like I've just denied her the world.

"What do you mean no?" she pouts.

"When I get home, you can see my cock whenever you want." I chuckle at her frustration.

"Ugh, I hate you," she huffs.

"Sure, you do," I tease, winking at her. "You look good in our room," I add, hoping she's starting to see it as *our* space, not just mine.

"Thanks," she says, trying to hide her smile, but I catch the subtle curve of her lips. It's those little moments, moments where she's relaxed, happy, that make me feel like the luckiest man alive.

"I have go. Meg and I are going out for dinner."

"Okay, have a good dinner. I'll call you later," I say, not wanting to keep her.

"Okay, bye." She hangs up, leaving me staring at the screen, my chest tight with the words I didn't say. *I love you, butterfly.*

I've been thinking those words more and more lately, but saying them feels dangerous, like admitting them aloud will make the tangled web of my life even harder to navigate. Because the truth is, my love for her only complicates everything else.

The arranged marriage is always at the back of my mind, pressing on me like a weight I can't shake. My father's ultimatum was clear: marry the woman they chose for me, or lose the position I've spent my life preparing for. And for the longest time, I thought there wasn't a choice. My family, the company, my future, it's all tied to their expectations.

But now? Now there's Inès. She's changed everything. I can't imagine a life without her in it.

I've been trying to come up with a plan, a way to have both: to keep the company and hold on to her.

Still, I don't have a solid Plan B yet. And that terrifies me. What if my father calls my bluff? What if he really does strip me of everything? Could I walk away from it all for her?

I run a hand through my hair, frustration bubbling up. I want to tell her everything, to let her in on this mess I'm in, but I don't want to burden her with my problems. She deserves better than a man who comes with this kind of baggage.

But one thing is clear: I'm running out of time.

INÈS

THERE'S NO WAY THAT'S GOING TO FIT

I gather my things, preparing to leave as Sean, a senior I've been tutoring for over a year, thanks me once again. "Thank you so much, Inès. Seriously, I'm graduating at the end of this semester because of you," he says. Even though we were never really friends, I'll miss these sessions.

I smile at him. "No need to thank me. You put in the work and gave yourself a fighting chance. I was just here to guide you, and it's been an honor. You'll ace your final, I'm sure of it." When we first started, he was more interested in getting me to do his work than in learning. The only reason he began taking me seriously was because I threatened to report him for trying to pay me to take his exams. After that, he buckled down and put in the effort.

"You know, I definitely would have asked you out if it weren't for Kingsley threatening me to not even think about it. You're just the type. My dad would love for me to bring home," he says boldly, grabbing my arm as I prepare to leave the student lounge we usually reserve for our sessions, his blond curls bouncing on his forehead. I smile again, gently removing my hand from his grip and taking a step back.

"Good luck on your exam, Sean," I say, walking away.

"Oh, so it's like that?" He chuckles, but I ignore him and keep walking.

Sean is my only session on Sundays. Tutoring has always been something I love, but today, I could hardly focus. Every time I tried to explain a math problem or guide Sean through an essay, my thoughts would drift back to him.

Kingsley.

It's only been three days since he left for his work trip to Tokyo, and I've been counting down the days, the hours, the minutes until he's back. I miss everything about him, the sound of his voice, the way he looks at me like I'm the only woman in the world, and the warmth of his arms around me, making me feel safe and cherished.

I'm ready for more with King, and I know how badly he wants me, too. I feel it poking me every night and every morning. I haven't even seen him completely naked yet. I may be a virgin, but I know what I want, and that's to give him my virginity because I trust King wholeheartedly.

"Inès?" a familiar voice calls out, snapping me out of my thoughts. I look up to see Dr. Salvatore walking toward me with a smile on his face.

"Dr. Salvatore, hi," I greet him, my fingers nervously fidgeting with my car key. It's not that he makes me uncomfortable exactly; it's just…awkward. Standing here in the middle of the parking lot, just the two of us, feels strange, especially with the weight of the lie I told King about him still hanging over me.

Guilt churns in my stomach. I know I only lied to avoid unnecessary drama. There's nothing inappropriate between Dr. Salvatore and me, nothing King needs to worry about. But if King ever finds out that we went on a date, even if it was a single, uneventful outing, my lie might not look like an attempt to keep the peace. It might look like I was hiding something worse.

That thought unsettles me more than I'd like to admit.

"What did I say about that? Please, call me Nathan."

"What are you doing here on a Sunday?" I ask, ignoring his request. I don't think it's appropriate for me to call him Nathan when everyone else calls him Professor or Dr. Salvatore.

He sighs as he falls in step with me. "I was here grading some late submissions. I can't wait for your help next semester. Then I won't be the only one here on Sundays grading papers." He chuckles.

"Right," is all I say as awkward silence falls upon us before he breaks it.

"Oh, I've been meaning to ask you, I heard your apartment was broken into a few weeks ago. How are you doing? I hope nobody was hurt." He asks, genuine concern lining his voice.

"Yes, thankfully nobody was hurt. Thank you for asking," I reply with a small nod, feeling a flicker of gratitude for the concern.

He shifts slightly, a touch of irritation creeping into his tone. "Did the police catch the person who broke in? Or are they at least close to getting them?"

I let out a sigh, brushing a loose strand of hair behind my ear as we continue toward my car. "No, they didn't. It's still an ongoing investigation," I explain, feeling the weight of it all settle over me again.

"Well," he says with a sudden intensity, "since it's clearly not safe at your apartment, I have a spare bedroom. You're welcome to stay there until you can find another place, or the police catch her."

I falter, taken aback for two reasons. First, the sheer inappropriateness of his offer, it would be highly unprofessional for me to stay in my professor's home, and I'm certain he knows it. But more unsettling is the second reason, the small detail that I can't ignore.

"Why do you assume it's a female?" I ask, my brows pulling together. The shift in his expression is immediate, as though I've caught him off guard.

"Excuse me?" he replies, indignant.

"You said, 'until they catch *her*.' Her, as if you already know it was a woman who broke into my apartment."

He hesitates, but then a sly, almost smug smile tugs at his lips. "Given that you're involved with a man who's rather popular with the female population here at school, it's not unreasonable to assume that one of them might be... jealous. It's the sort of thing you wouldn't have to worry about if you were with me, Inès."

I stop mid-step, gaping at his audacity, the sheer arrogance dripping from his words. "Dr. Salvatore, that was completely out of line and wildly inappropriate." My voice is firm, and I meet his gaze with a level stare, anger flaring up in my chest.

I take a steadying breath, my mind shifting quickly through the implications of his words and the boundaries he's just crossed. "Dr. Salvatore, let's be clear. Your comment wasn't only presumptive, it was a baseless assumption, one that overlooks both the facts of the investigation and the ethical boundaries of our relationship. Not only is it unprofessional to imply that I would be safer with you, but it's also entirely inappropriate to suggest any ownership over my personal life. I'd expect someone with your experience to know better."

He opens his mouth to respond, but I don't let him.

"And as for this hypothetical 'jealous ex' scenario, let's also consider the lack of logic there. You have no evidence or even reason to believe this is true, beyond a convenient assumption. In truth, you've projected a very personal opinion onto a professional situation, which is not only misguided but disappointing from someone of your caliber."

His expression shifts from surprise to something more subdued, his gaze dropping as he listens to the weight of my words. A moment passes, and he clears his throat, his voice softer than I've heard it before.

"Inès," he says, visibly uncomfortable, "you're absolutely right. That was entirely inappropriate, and I should never have presumed to make assumptions about your personal life or... anything else." He hesitates, looking at me with what I can only describe as genuine regret. "I apologize. I crossed a line, and I'm sorry if I made you feel uncomfortable. That was never my intention."

"Don't let it happen again."

"You have my word," he says, and we continue our walk in silence.

"This is me," I say, relieved to have reached my car. His eyes widen when he sees my brand-new Range Rover. Even I'm still shocked that this is my car.

"Wow, I see you've upgraded," he says, frowning in question. "This isn't the car you had on our date." This causes me to look around to see if anyone overheard him. The last thing I want is for rumors about him and me to start.

"Yeah, well, that car wasn't mine, and this one is new," I say, not wanting to give him more than that. "Well, I should go... I'll see you in class tomorrow." I open my car and put my backpack inside. He looks like he wants to say something, but instead, he smiles and nods.

"Drive safe," he says. I return his smile before getting into my car and driving out of the parking lot.

The entire drive home, my thoughts circle around Dr. Salvatore, a puzzle that seems to shift with each encounter. One day, he's the charming, attentive professor, his gaze warm and inviting. Then, he flips to being perfectly professional, barely sparing me a second glance, as if he's pulled a wall up between us and I'm just another face in the classroom. And then there are days like today, where he crosses boundaries without hesitation, his words laced with an intensity that feels... off.

It's like there are layers to him, charming, distant, and then something else entirely, something unpredictable. I can't shake the feeling that there's something more to it. He always seems calculating, as if he's not just interested in me as a student or even a person, but as a puzzle he's trying to solve. And no matter how much I try to make sense of it, every new conversation leaves me feeling like I'm only scratching the surface of who he really is.

When I get to the penthouse, it's quiet, which is expected. Justin is at the gym, and Meghan told me she was taking Beau to the park, and Kingsley returns tonight. Speaking of, I take out my phone and power it on as I walk upstairs so I can call him, but I freeze when I enter the room to find Kingsley coming out of the shower in nothing but a towel around his waist.

For a moment, I just stand there, my breath catching in my throat. He's home. I bite my lip, my pulse pounding in my ears. The muscles in his shoulders ripple as he runs a hand through his wet hair. A small towel hangs low on his hips, barely covering him, and my eyes immediately drop lower, tracing the lines of his body. His skin is still damp, the water glistening on his tattooed chest and arms, and the sight takes my breath away.

He's beautiful, perfect, really. Every inch of him is a masterpiece, from the broad expanse of his chest to the defined ridges of his abs, all the way down to the prominent V that disappears beneath the towel. I can't stop staring, my eyes locked on the way the towel clings to his hips, leaving little to the imagination.

My gaze travels lower, and I catch a glimpse of the bulge beneath the towel. The way it strains against the fabric, it's impossible to ignore. My mouth goes dry, and I feel a rush of heat between my legs at the thought of him inside me, filling me in a way I've never been filled before.

"Inès." His voice pierces through my daze, pulling me from the whirlwind of my thoughts. I look up to find him standing there, his smirk both teasing and predatory. "You're home."

I nod, words failing me as he steps closer, the towel around his waist shifting slightly, revealing more of his sculpted hips. He's so close now, the air between us thick with tension, crackling like a live wire ready to spark.

"You're staring," he murmurs, his voice low and dripping with amusement as he closes the distance between us.

"I… I didn't expect you to be home yet," I manage to say, my voice barely a whisper.

"I got in less than an hour ago," he replies, his gaze darkening as it rakes over me. "I couldn't wait to see you."

My heart skips at his words, a flush creeping up my cheeks. I can barely think with him this close, his presence overwhelming, intoxicating.

"Tu ma manqué,"[1] I admit, my voice trembling.

His smile softens, and he reaches out, cupping my cheek, his thumb tracing delicate circles on my skin. "I missed you, too papillon," he murmurs tenderly, yet edged with a roughness that sends shivers down my spine. "Every damn second."

I lean into his touch, my eyes fluttering closed as I savor the warmth of his hand. But as much as I crave this tenderness, there's a fire kindling inside me, a desperate, gnawing need that refuses to be ignored. I want more, I want him to claim me completely.

"Stop looking at me like that." His voice is almost a warning, but it only stokes the heat pooling between my thighs.

"How am I looking at you?" I whisper, my breath hitching.

"Like you want me to rip your clothes off and fuck you," he growls, the crude edge to his words making my pulse race. God, I love how blunt he is, how he knows exactly how to get under my skin.

"And what if that's exactly what I want?"

"You don't know what you're asking," he warns, his face so close now that I can feel the heat of his breath against my lips.

I frown, not backing down. "Don't do that, King. I'm a big girl, and when I tell you I want something, believe that I'm not just saying it." I speak with all the sincerity I can muster. "King," I whisper, my voice barely audible. "I'm ready."

His hand stills on my cheek, his eyes narrowing slightly as he studies me, searching my face for any sign of doubt.

---

1. I missed you.

"Are you sure?" he asks, his voice gentle but laced with an intensity that makes my pulse quicken.

"Yes," I breathe, locking my gaze with his. "I'm sure."

For a moment, he just looks at me, his eyes so intense it feels like he's peeling back every layer of my soul. Then, with a low groan, he dips his head, capturing my lips in a kiss that makes my knees buckle. It starts slow and gentle, but quickly deepens, his tongue tangling with mine as he pulls me closer. The heat of his body presses into mine, the hard planes of his chest igniting something primal within me.

He kisses me like he's been starving and I'm the only thing that can sate his hunger. His hands slide up my back, pulling me impossibly closer as his lips continue to claim mine, possessive and demanding. My head spins from the sheer intensity, and I cling to him, my fingers digging into his shoulders as if he's the only thing keeping me grounded.

His hands move to my waist, gripping me tightly as he guides us backward toward the bed. I can feel the heat radiating from his body through the thin fabric of my clothes, and I arch into him, desperate to feel more, to feel everything.

When the back of my legs hits the edge of the bed, he lifts me effortlessly, laying me down with a gentleness that contrasts with the fierce desire in his kiss. He pulls back just enough to gaze down at me, his eyes dark with lust as they drink in the sight of me beneath him.

"You're so beautiful," he murmurs. "So fucking beautiful."

I blush under his intense gaze, my body trembling with anticipation as he reaches for the hem of my shirt. He tugs it up and over my head, tossing it aside before his hands move to the button of my jeans. A thrill of excitement rushes through me as he undoes the button and slides the zipper down with agonizing slowness, his fingers grazing my skin as he pulls the denim down my legs.

He steps back for a moment, his eyes roaming over my body as I lie before him in just my bra and panties. The way he looks at me like I'm the most precious thing in the world makes my heart swell. "Do you know what you do to me, Inès?" he asks, his voice thick with desire as he reaches for the clasp of my bra.

I shake my head, breathless, unable to speak.

"You make me crazy," he growls. "All I can think about is being inside you, filling you up, making you mine in every way."

I shiver at his words, my pulse racing as he unclasps my bra, sliding the straps down my arms. My breasts are bared to him, and though we've been here before, today feels different. I can't help the flicker of self-consciousness that surfaces, but the look in his eyes obliterates any doubts. He's staring at me like I'm the only woman in the world, and the intensity of his gaze makes my breath catch.

"Perfect," he murmurs, his hands cupping my breasts as he leans down to press a kiss to my collarbone. "Every inch of you is perfect."

I moan softly as his lips trail down my neck, leaving a searing path in their wake. His mouth moves lower, kissing across my chest before his tongue flicks out to tease my nipple. I gasp at the sensation, my body arching into his touch as he lavishes attention on my breasts, his tongue and teeth driving me wild.

The heat between my legs intensifies, the ache becoming almost unbearable as he continues his sensual assault. I can feel the wetness pooling in my panties, my body desperate for his touch, for the release I know only he can give me.

"King," I moan, my hips lifting off the bed as he switches to my other breast, giving it the same devotion.

He hums against my skin, the vibration sending a jolt of pleasure straight to my core. "I love hearing you say my name like that," he murmurs, his breath hot against me. "So desperate, so needy," he says as he helps me out of my panties.

His kisses trail lower, past my navel. Anticipation coils tight within me. He spreads my legs, placing an open-mouthed kiss right where I crave him most.

"Oh... God!" I cry out, my hands fisting the sheets beneath me.

He chuckles darkly, his fingers circling my clit in slow, deliberate strokes that push me closer to the edge. "You're so fucking desperate for it, aren't you?" he growls with a raw mix of desire and dominance. "Such a needy slut."

I moan in response, my body trembling as he continues to tease me, his fingers sliding lower, parting my slick folds before pushing one inside me. I gasp at the intrusion, my body tensing, but he's patient, working me open with slow, deliberate strokes.

"Relax, baby," he murmurs, his voice soothing despite the sinful intent. "I need to stretch you out if you want to take my cock."

I force myself to relax, my body slowly adjusting to the delicious pressure. When he adds a second finger, I clamp up again. "I... I can't, it's too much," I try to close my legs.

"Yes, you can, open those legs and take my fingers like the good slut I know you are," he growls. "I think you can take one more," he tells me while his other hand caresses my thigh. I will my body to relax as he inserts a third finger and I'm at my limit.

"That's my good fucking girl, I'm so proud of you," he

praises. My hips move instinctively, seeking more as he curls his fingers inside me, brushing that perfect spot while his mouth lavishes attention on my clit. The pleasure builds, a coil tightening inside me, wound so tight I feel like I'm about to snap.

"King! I'm going to, " The words spill from my lips as I shatter, coming hard on his fingers and tongue.

"Good girl," he murmurs, pulling his fingers free only to find my clit again, the sensation so intense it's electric. I cry out, my hips bucking against his hand, desperate for more, desperate for him.

"Fuck, you're so wet for me," he groans, his voice thick with need. "I could play with you all night, make you come over and over until you're begging me to stop."

"Please, King. I want you. Please."

"I got you, papillon,"[2] he says, finally undoing his towel, letting it fall to the floor. My breath catches as I take in the sight of him, thick, long, veiny, and already leaking with desire.

I am both needy and terrified, my body trembling with anticipation. There's no way that's going to fit.

---

2. Butterfly.

KINGSLEY

APPARENTLY IT DID

Inès sits up, her nervousness clear in those wide, beautiful eyes, and it takes everything in me to stay calm, to remind myself that I need to be gentle, careful with her. I cup her face, pressing soft kisses to her forehead, her nose, and finally her lips.

"King…" she whispers, and damn if my heart doesn't skip a beat hearing her say my name like that.

"We'll make it fit," I murmur, deepening the kiss, "but if you don't want this, it's okay. We don't have to do more." The last thing I want is to push her into something she's not ready for.

"I want it, I promise. I'm just nervous about the unknown," she admits, her voice trembling slightly.

I brush a strand of curly hair behind her ear. "Trust me to take care of you. It might hurt a little at first, but I swear I'll make it feel good for you."

"Will you… teach me? You know, how to give you a

blow job?" she asks, her shyness endearing, making me want to protect her even more.

"You want to give me a blow job?" My dick throbs at the thought of her mouth on me.

"I do."

"Off the bed and on your knees," I command.

She smiles, almost skipping off the bed as I get off as well. I stand in front of her, naked with my dick in hand. She gracefully kneels, looking up at me with so much enthusiasm in her eyes that I can't help but lean forward and kiss her passionately before standing back up.

"Let's see if that pretty mouth of yours can take me," I murmur.

Her eyes flick up to meet mine, wide and trusting.

"Touch me, Queen," I grunt, feeling as if I'll die if she doesn't. She reaches out slowly. The second her hand wraps around me, I can't help but hiss at the contact. I have waited for this for so long it's pitiful. Her touch is soft and tentative, and it drives me wild.

She flinches at my hiss and begins to remove her hand. "I'm… I'm sorry," she says, and fuck me her innocence is too much of a turn-on, why is it so much of a turn-on?!

"No, don't…" I sound wounded because I am wounded, her small delicate hand is no longer on me, she needs to touch me now, now, now, now. "I'm fine, Queen, touch me," I grunt, and when she does I feel like I can both breathe again and pass out. "Tighter, papillon. You won't hurt me," I encourage her, even though her grip already feels like heaven. When she tightens her hold, I groan, the pleasure almost unbearable. "Fuck, just like that. See? It won't hurt you. I promise."

She smiles beautifully as she opens her mouth. The warmth of her mouth envelops me as she takes me in, inch by inch. I can feel her trying to accommodate my size, and when she doesn't gag, I'm both surprised and insanely turned on.

"Fuck, Inès... fuck! You're perfect," I groan, my hand tangling in her hair as she takes me deeper. The sight of her, lips stretched around me, eyes locked onto mine, is nearly enough to make me lose control. She's eager, and that lack of a gag reflex is a fucking blessing. She begins to bob her head, sucking harder, and I can't help but thrust slightly into her mouth, each motion driving me closer to the edge.

When she swallows around me, I pull back before I lose it, needing more, needing to be inside her. "Jesus... I need you, now," I mutter, pulling her back up and crashing my lips to hers, kissing her hungrily as I back her up until we reach the bed. I lay her down and crawl on top of her, spreading her legs with one hand, the other wrapping around my heavy erection.

"Tell me you're on birth control, because I want nothing between us," I say, needing to hear it, needing to know I can have all of her.

"Yes, I'm on birth control. I want nothing between us either." Her words send a thrill through me, and I can't resist dragging my cock over her folds, coating myself with her wetness, teasing her entrance.

When she stiffens, I stop. "I need you to relax, Inès. Can you do that for me?" I ask gently.

"I'll try," she says, her voice a little steadier now.

"Good girl," I praise, pressing a deep kiss to her lips until I feel her body soften beneath me.

"King..." she gasps as I start pushing in, the tightness of her body almost too much. I grit my teeth, fighting for control as I slide deeper into her warmth.

Then I feel it, that slight resistance that further solidifies that she's never done this before. My heart pounds, a possessive surge of pride and something far darker washing over me. She's mine. All mine.

As I press forward, breaking through, her body tenses beneath me. I pause, my breath hitching as I glance down. The sight of her blood coating me, marking me as the first and only one to ever claim her like this, sends a primal surge through my veins. My vision blurs with a possessive rage so intense it threatens to make me go feral.

"Fuck…" I grit out, barely holding onto the last shreds of my control. "Inès… fuuck."

Her eyes are wide, filled with pain and trust. Her gaze grounds me and reminds me that I need to be gentle, to take care of her. "How are you doing?" I ask, even though I've barely got the tip inside.

"It's a little painful, but I'm fine. Put more in," she pleads, and damn if that doesn't send a jolt of desire through me.

"You're doing so good, butterfly. Look how well you're stretching to take me," I whisper, pressing my thumb to her clit, rubbing slow circles as I push further inside her. She's tight, so tight, and it's a battle not to just plunge into her all at once. "Halfway in… putain,[1] you're so fucking tight and sexy. I'm so in love with you," I blurt out, the words slipping out before I can stop them.

Her eyes shoot open, staring at me in shock. "You… what?" she asks, her voice choked with emotion.

I can't hold it back anymore. "I love you," I say, thrusting into her to the hilt, filling her completely.

"King!" she gasps, her body arching under mine.

"Fuck!" I roar, holding still to give her time to adjust. "You make me fucking crazy," I admit, bending down to capture her lips in a passionate kiss. "I've been in love with

---

1. Fuck.

you since the moment I laid eyes on you. I love you so much it physically hurts," I confess, my voice raw with emotion.

Tears fill her eyes, and all she can do is cry, her hand cradling my cheek as she kisses me tenderly.

"Are you ready for me to move?" I ask.

"Yes, please move. Make love to me," she whispers, and it's all the permission I need.

"I'm going to slide almost all the way out and then back in, okay?" I explain, my voice strained as I start to move, pulling out and then sinking back into her heat, over and over. Each thrust is a claim, a promise, as I murmur praises into her ear, telling her how brave she is, how perfect, how much I love her.

Pain seems to give way to pleasure, her body finally relaxing, and I can feel her walls tightening around me, driving me closer to the edge. "I'm close, King. I'm so close!" she cries out, her voice trembling with need.

"Come for me," I murmur in a low, possessive purr as I watch her teeter on the edge.

The instant those words leave my mouth, I feel her unravel beneath me. The coil of tension inside her seems to snap, sending her spiraling into a mind-shattering orgasm. She screams my name, her entire body trembling as wave after wave of pleasure crashes over her. I keep thrusting into her, deep and slow, drawing out every last bit of her ecstasy until I've wrung her dry and there's nothing left but the aftermath of bliss.

It's the most beautiful thing I've ever seen, her completely undone because of me. And it's more than I can take.

A few more thrusts and I'm there, too, groaning her name as I spill inside her. The force of my release rocks through me, leaving me trembling, my muscles quivering as I empty myself into her warmth.

For a moment, I just collapse against her, letting us both catch our breath. Our bodies are tangled together, hearts pounding in sync. I can feel her soft, rapid breaths against my chest, and it's like I just ran a marathon. But this... this is the best kind of exhaustion.

Slowly, I pull out of her, careful not to hurt her. As I move, I feel an overwhelming feeling of gratefulness and humbleness surge through me at seeing the streak of blood on her and my dick, proof of what she just gave me. I will make sure I was worth it for the rest of my life... our life.

I get out of bed and grab a small towel, wetting it with warm water. Returning to her side, I gently and slowly clean her, my heart swelling with the need to take care of her, to show her that she's everything to me. Her body is swollen, and the sight of that small streak of blood makes me want to protect her from the world even more. Once I've finished cleaning her, I head back to the bathroom to clean myself.

When I return to the bed, I gather her into my arms, needing to feel her close, needing to know that she's okay. I press a soft kiss to her forehead, my fingers threading through her hair, brushing it back in gentle strokes.

"Are you okay?" I ask, my voice softer than usual, a hint of concern lacing my tone.

She nods, snuggling into my chest, and I can't help but tighten my arms around her, holding her as close as I can. "I'm more than okay," she whispers, her voice trembling with the lingering emotion. "That was... amazing."

I let out a low chuckle, relief and pride swelling in my chest. "I'm glad you think so," I murmur, pressing another kiss to her forehead. "Because I plan on doing that to you every chance I get."

She gives me a small laugh, I can feel the exhaustion

taking over her body. As she closes her eyes, I keep her close, my hands moving in soothing circles along her back.

I watch her drift off to sleep, her breaths becoming soft and steady. The warmth of her body against mine, the rhythm of her heartbeat, it's a symphony that soothes my soul.

I know without a doubt that she has ruined me for anyone else. Inès Dubois is the only woman who will ever own my heart. I am completely, irrevocably, and arrogantly in love with her, and there's no going back. Every part of me belongs to her, and I wouldn't have it any other way.

INÈS

DON'T THREATEN ME WITH A GOOD TIME

ALMOST TWO MONTHS LATER...

"Holy... how rich are you exactly?" Meghan asks, gaping at the private jet in front of us, emblazoned with the name *Ashford* across its sleek exterior.

We're all heading to Minnesota, because Meghan wants Justin to meet her family, too. She and Justin have decided to keep the baby, and I'm genuinely happy for them, even though I can't see myself in their position. Kingsley and I haven't really talked about the future yet. I mean, we're still new. When he told me he loved me, I thought it was just a heat of the moment talking, but then the next day, when he brought me breakfast, he kissed me and said it again. I haven't said those words to him, I don't think I'm quite there yet.

"Yeah... what she said," I echo, still in awe. We knew

Kingsley's family had a private jet, and I think Justin's family does as well, but I wasn't expecting something so... big.

Justin chuckles. "You girls have no idea," he says, taking Meghan's hand and leading her into the jet.

We decided to send Beau to a dog hotel. I visited beforehand and saw how luxurious it was, decked out with plush beds, daily massages, and even a private dog park. Beau seemed to love it the moment we walked in, his tail wagging furiously as he sniffed around and explored. Still, my nerves wouldn't settle. The idea of leaving him there, even for a few days, tugged at my heart in ways I wasn't prepared for.

They reassured me I could call to check on him every night before bed, which gave me some peace of mind, but I couldn't stop the tears when it was time to leave. King had to practically drag me out of there, rolling his eyes but smiling as I clung to the doorframe one last time, trying to catch another glimpse of Beau's fluffy black tail.

"You're acting like we're abandoning him in the woods," King teased, rubbing my back as I sniffled into my sleeve.

"I know," I mumbled, wiping away my tears, "but what if he thinks we aren't coming back?"

"He'll be fine, baby. He probably won't even notice we're gone with all the pampering he's about to get," he said with a chuckle, but I wasn't convinced.

"Don't say that!" I cried; I didn't want him to forget me.

"You're right, I'm sorry."

"I'm still calling them every night," I insisted.

King just smiled and kissed the top of my head. "Of course, you are."

As we drove away, I peeked out the window one last time, my heart aching. Beau was in dog heaven, but that didn't stop me from missing him already.

"Hey," Kingsley calls, bringing me back to the present.

He turns me around to face him. "Are you okay? Have you eaten?" His concern is clear as he wraps his hand around my neck, gently massaging my pulse point. It's something he does often, whether it's my wrist or my neck, whenever we talk, he has to touch it. I think it's his way of making sure my pulse doesn't spike because of something he says.

"Yeah, I'm fine. I had toast this morning," I reply, taking his hand and kissing his palm.

"You were up late last night. Did you have an assignment you were finishing up?" Thank God I took his hand away from my neck, because my pulse actually spikes.

Last night, Dr. Salvatore emailed me all the details about the TA position, responsibilities, scheduling, everything I'd need to prepare. Since I was still up, I replied, and our exchange was friendly, professional. It's almost a relief, the way he's been handling himself lately. After that uncomfortable moment, he's kept to himself, and most of our interactions are brief and to the point. Sometimes, I even catch him looking a bit ashamed, as if he's aware he crossed a line. He's been careful, almost tentative, only speaking to me when absolutely necessary, until last night's email, which came in a little late.

The one part of his message that stands out, though, is his insistence that I call him Nathan, not Dr. Salvatore. He's been consistent about it, almost casually pressing, as if he's eager to erase the boundaries that make me feel better about our interactions. But I keep the formality, calling him Dr. Salvatore in both emails and in class.

I haven't told Kingsley that Dr. Salvatore was the man I went on a date with. Telling him would mean overreactions and lectures, neither of which I want. I haven't even told Meghan about the TA position either. Don't get me wrong, I adore her, but subtlety isn't exactly her strong suit, and if I confided in her, it'd only be a matter of time before she "accidentally" let it slip to King.

"Yeah, it was just a last-minute assignment I forgot to turn in," I say, looking away.

"Okay. Come on, let's get inside," he says, taking my hand and gently leading me toward the jet. His touch is warm and comforting, but the guilt gnaws at me, twisting in my chest. I feel horrible for lying to him, for getting tangled in this web of half-truths.

I don't want to lie, especially not to him, not to my boyfriend. But how do I even begin to untangle this mess I started?

The inside of the private jet is all about comfort and style. Soft, ambient lighting sets a relaxed mood, highlighting the sleek, dark wood accents and polished metal finishes.

"Whoa!" I exclaim as soon as I walk in.

"That's exactly what I said!" Meghan chimes in, grinning.

We all settle into our seats, and then the plane takes off. Meghan falls asleep almost immediately, while Justin is absorbed in his work on his computer. I'm sitting on King's lap as he goes through his emails on his phone. We're less than an hour into the flight, and I'm already bored. The plane jostles slightly, causing me to shift on King's lap, and he grunts.

I realize he's hard. Smirking, I begin to move my hips in a slow, circular motion, eliciting a groan from him. He tightens his grip on my waist, leaning in close to my ear, and whispers, "Behave, before you get fucked like a slut."

I moan at his words, feeling a thrill of excitement, and grind on him again. Kingsley stands up quickly, tossing me over his shoulder before delivering a sharp spank that makes me squeal as he strides to the back of the plane.

Justin glances up from his laptop and just shakes his head

at us, a knowing smile on his lips. In the back, there's a private bedroom with a king-sized bed covered in luxurious linens, and an en suite bathroom with a spacious shower, marble countertops, and premium toiletries.

Kingsley sets me gently on my feet, his touch sending shivers down my spine. He doesn't waste a moment, crashing his lips onto mine with a hunger that ignites a fire within me. I eagerly respond to his passionate kiss, feeling the heat between us intensify.

"Clothes off," he commands in a husky voice, his eyes dark with desire as he steps back and starts to undress. I don't hesitate, feeling a rush of excitement as I quickly shed my sweatpants and hoodie. Standing there, naked before him, I can't help but admire the sight of Kingsley. He's not just perfection; he's my desire incarnate.

The anticipation has me nearly trembling with excitement as I watch Kingsley, his strong frame moving confidently toward the bed. The room is bathed in a warm, soft glow from the bedside lamps, casting an intimate ambiance that makes everything feel electric. His tattooed skin is flawless under the light, every inch of him a testament to the man he is, powerful, commanding, and entirely irresistible.

He lies back on the bed, completely naked, and starts to stroke himself with a slow, deliberate rhythm. His eyes are locked on mine, filled with a smoldering hunger that sends a shiver down my spine. I can't help but watch, my breath catching in my throat at the sight of him, his dark eyes boring into me.

"Come here," he growls, a thick, primal command.

My body responds instinctively, moving toward him as if drawn by an invisible force. I straddle him, my knees pressing into the mattress on either side of him. The heat radiating from his body is almost overwhelming, and I can feel the throbbing tension in the air, a palpable charge that makes my skin tingle.

I look down at him, and the sight of his dark eyes, burning with desire, makes my heart race. Kingsley's lips curl into a predatory smile, and in one fluid motion, he flips me around as if I weigh nothing. I frown in confusion, my body suddenly facing away from him. I thought we were about to have sex, but now I'm left wondering what he has in mind.

"You know what to do, Queen," he murmurs, his voice sending vibrations through my skin. No, I don't know what to do. "Get on my face and give me that sweet pussy of yours. Let me taste you while you choke on my dick." If that's what he wanted, why flip me... oh, oh gosh I'm an idiot.

My heart pounds as I slowly shift backward, positioning myself over his mouth. The sheer filthiness of the moment has my head spinning, and my body trembling with anticipation. The thought of him tasting me while I pleasure him sends a rush of heat between my legs, and I bite my lip, trying to contain the moan that wants to escape.

Kingsley's grip tightens on my thighs, and with a quick, almost impatient tug, he pulls me down on his mouth. His tongue immediately delves into my folds with a greedy hunger that makes me cry out. The pleasure crashes over me like a tidal wave, relentless and all-consuming. There's no teasing, no hesitation, just Kingsley's mouth on me, devouring me like I'm the most exquisite meal he's ever tasted.

"Fuck, you taste so good," he groans against me, his voice muffled but still dripping with lust. "Such a good slut, giving me everything I want."

His filthy words make my head spin, the mix of degradation and praise making my body burn with need. I can't help but grind against him, riding his face as his tongue works me over, sending jolts of pleasure through my body with every flick and swirl.

The sensation of his tongue on me is overwhelming. I gasp when I feel a sharp sting on my ass.

"Get my cock in that pretty little mouth of yours," he growls, leaving no room for argument.

I scramble forward, my hands trembling as I reach for his cock. It's hard, pulsing with need, and the feeling of his thick length in my hand makes my mouth water. I lower my head, taking him into my mouth, savoring the taste of him as I start to suck him with slow, deliberate strokes.

Kingsley groans against me, the sound vibrating through my core as his hands grip my hips, guiding my movements. The dual sensations of his tongue inside me and his cock in my mouth are overwhelming, and I can't hold back the moans that spill from my lips as I take him deeper. The taste of him drives me wild, each movement sending electric jolts through my body.

"That's it, papillon," he growls, a low rumble against my skin. "Suck my cock like the dirty slut you are. You're going to make me come in that pretty mouth of yours, and you're going to swallow every drop."

I moan around his length, the vibrations making him groan in pleasure. I want to please him, to make him lose control just as much as he makes me. I quicken my pace, taking him deeper into my throat, feeling the way his body tenses beneath me.

Kingsley's mouth doesn't relent, his tongue working me with an intensity that makes my body tremble. He knows exactly how to push me to the edge, how to keep me teetering on the brink of release without letting me fall over. It's a game we play, and he always wins. But tonight, I'm determined to match him.

I hollow my cheeks, sucking him harder just like he taught me, my hand pumping his length in time with the bob of my head. Kingsley's hips jerk upward, and I know he's close. His hands dig into my flesh, his growls vibrating through me as he devours me with a ferocity that leaves me gasping.

"Come on, baby," he orders, his voice rough with lust. "Come on my tongue, and I'll fill that pretty mouth of yours. And don't you dare waste a fucking drop."

The command is all I need. My body obeys without question, the tension inside me snapping as I come apart on his face. My cries are muffled by the thickness of his cock in my mouth, the pleasure blinding and overwhelming. I hold onto him to keep from falling, wave after wave of ecstasy crashing through me.

Kingsley doesn't stop. His tongue is relentless, drinking in every drop of my release, his growls of satisfaction sending shivers through me. And then, just as I'm coming down from the high, he thrusts into my mouth one last time, groaning loudly as he finds his own release.

I feel the hot rush of his seed hit the back of my throat, and I swallow greedily, not wanting to waste a single drop.

"Fuck! Fuck, fuck!" he roars, using one of his legs to hold me in place as he rides out his orgasm. The sound of his pleasure fills the room, raw and unrestrained.

When it's over, I turn around, collapsing against him. Both of us are panting, spent from the intensity of what we've just shared. Kingsley's hands are gentle now, his touch soothing as he strokes my back, holding me close. The weight of our passion settles between us, an intimate bond that feels both comforting and exhilarating.

"You did so good, butterfly," he murmurs softly and full of praise. "My perfect little slut."

His words make me smile, a warmth spreading through my chest at the satisfaction in his tone. I may be his to command, but the way he looks at me, the way he touches me, makes me feel like I'm cherished in every way.

I shift slightly, turning my head to press a tender kiss to his chest. The taste of him still lingers on my tongue, a reminder of the intense connection we've shared. Kingsley's arms wrap around me, holding me close, and for a moment, we just lie there in silence.

"I love you," he whispers, his lips brushing against mine in a lingering, soft kiss. The words, so tender and genuine, make my heart swell with emotion. He doesn't wait for my response, he just holds me tightly.

We landed in Minnesota forty minutes ago and are just pulling up to my parents' two-story house in Saint Paul. It's the cozy, four-bedroom, three-bath home where my parents raised me and my sister.

We drove in separate cars, since Meghan and Justin are staying the night at Meghan's place. Meghan decided to visit my parents first, because she gets along so well with them.

As we approach the house, I notice the door is already ajar. I walk in with Kingsley, Meghan, and Justin, greeted immediately by the delicious aroma of my dad's cooking. I'm home! My dad is the chef of the family, having trained professionally, while the rest of us can't cook to save our lives.

We head straight to the kitchen where I know everyone would be. The moment they see me, their faces light up. Camille screams and rushes toward me with open arms.

"Poupée![1] You made it! I've missed you so much," she exclaims, enveloping me in a tight hug. "And guess what? We're getting married!" she says, flashing her engagement ring.

"Stop! Really?" I gasp, taking her hand to admire the ring. "Let me see that rock! WOW." It's a simple, elegant princess cut, just as I knew she'd love.

"Oh hush, I already know you helped him pick it out," Camille says with a teasing grin, and I hug her again.

"I'm so happy for you, Mimi." I smile.

"Where's my hug?" my mom asks after finishing her embrace with Meghan. I go to her and let her envelop me in a warm hug. "Mon ange,[2] let me look at you!" she says, kissing me and holding me close.

"I missed you, too Maman." But then I'm swept off my feet in a bear hug, and I know exactly who it is. "Avery! Oh my God, put me down, you caveman!" Avery, who's been like a brother to me since he started dating Camille, is loud and rough but endearing in his own way.

"Avery, if you're going to break her, let me get my hug in first." My dad's strong accent fills the room.

"It's good to see you, little one!" Avery says, tousling my hair before heading into the kitchen to, no doubt, steal some of Dad's cooking.

"Mon cœur!"[3]

"Papa!"[4] I hug my dad tightly. Okay, yes, I'm a daddy's girl, sue me. "Everyone, I'd like you to meet my boyfriend, Kingsley."

---

1. Doll.
2. My angel.
3. My heart.
4. Dad.

"Enchanté,"[5] Kingsley says with a smile that shows off his dimples.

"Welcome to the family, King," Camille says with a grin as she gives Kingsley a hug.

"Oh, Camille, Kingsley doesn't like being called 'King' anymore. Ever since his precious *Inès* started calling him that, it's only reserved for her," Meghan says, rummaging through the fridge.

"No, it's not," I protest, but when I glance at Kingsley, he has a smug look on his face. "Oh my God, did you really start telling people not to call you 'King' anymore?"

"I did," he replies nonchalantly, just as my mom embraces him.

"Welcome to the family, Kingsley. That's a very beautiful name," my mom says in French.

"Thank you," Kingsley responds in French, and my heart warms at their interaction.

"Welcome, Kingsley. How about you and I talk?" my dad suggests, and I groan.

"Yes, sir," Kingsley says with a nod.

"Maman,[6] can you please not let him do this?" I ask.

"He did it with me, twice. I didn't hear you complain," Avery says, rolling his eyes.

"Everyone out of my kitchen, please," my dad announces in his authoritative dad voice, which he thinks carries weight. My dad is a big teddy bear; it's my mom who we fear most. "I promise not to embarrass you, mon cœur.[7] The sooner you leave, the sooner I'll be done."

"I'm okay, butterfly, I promise," Kingsley says, and I

---

5. Nice to meet you.
6. Mom.
7. My heart.

reluctantly leave the kitchen, hoping I'll still have a boyfriend after their "conversation."

KINGSLEY

FORBIDDEN ESCAPADES

"Kingsley, right?" Jonathan says in French, turning away from the stove where a pot of something deliciously aromatic bubbles away. His voice is deep, steady, and kind. He looks more like Inès's sister, whereas Inès takes after her mother.

Their home is a cozy mix of modern appliances and homey touches, a place that feels lived-in and loved.

"Yes, sir, " I reply in French.

"Make yourself comfortable," he says, gesturing to a wooden chair at the kitchen table. I take a seat, feeling the weight of the moment settle in. I've never met a girlfriend's parents before, and I definitely have never had a conversation with their dad. This is all new to me.

"So, Kingsley, what do you do for a living?" Jonathan asks, leaning against the counter with his arms crossed.

"I work for my family's business, Eco Tech Innovations," I explain, aiming to sound impressive. "We're at the forefront of sustainable technology and infrastructure."

Jonathan raises an eyebrow. "That's impressive. But do you have a passion for it?"

I chuckle nervously. "I do, sir. I've been learning the ropes for years, it's what I am passionate about."

"Hmm." he nods, clearly not entirely convinced. "What about the future? Where do you see yourself in five years?"

"In five years, I see myself helping the business expand and thrive. And, of course, I want to build a life with Inès. I want to make sure she's happy and well taken care of," I say, looking him directly in the eyes.

Jonathan's expression softens slightly, but only slightly. "You love my daughter, don't you?"

"Very much, sir," I say earnestly. "Inès means the world to me. All I want to do is take care of her."

He leans in, his gaze intense. "And how do you plan to take care of her? Emotionally, I mean. It's not just about money, you know. My daughters are very special to me, and I want to make sure whoever they choose to date, or maybe marry, truly has their best interests at heart. Kingsley, you are the only man she's ever brought home. Inès has always been focused on studying and making a future for herself. I want to make sure you are here to make her life better, not worse."

I meet Jonathan's intense gaze and take a deep breath. "Mr. Dubois, I understand your concerns. Inès is incredible, and I'm honored to be the first man she's brought home. I want to assure you that I'm here for the right reasons. Emotionally, I plan to support her dreams and ambitions, to stand by her side through the ups and downs. I'm not perfect, but I'm committed to making her life better, not worse. I care deeply about her, and I'm dedicated to being someone she can always rely on."

Jonathan strokes his beard thoughtfully. "Alright, let's get down to the important stuff. Can you cook?"

I blink, caught off guard. Then I laugh. "Cook?"

"In case you haven't realized, Inès can't cook. None of my girls can." He too laughs.

"Oh, I know, Mr. Dubois," I say thinking about the disastrous cake his daughter made for my birthday. I can still taste it sometimes, that's how bad it was. "I can cook, sir; our house manager taught me from a very young age."

Jonathan bursts out laughing, a deep, hearty laugh that fills the kitchen. "House manager... I like you, Kingsley, and please, call me Jonathan," he says, going back to English. "How about you come help me with dinner?"

I stand up. "I'll be honored," I say and make my way around the kitchen island.

A few minutes later, Inès walks into the kitchen, a curious look on her face. "How's it going in here?"

Jonathan and I look up.

I smile. "Everything is fine, your dad was telling me that your grandmother is actually American," I say, kissing her forehead when she gets closer to me.

She chuckles. "Yeah, she moved to France for college, fell in love, and never left again."

"Are we talking about my mom?" Hélène, Inès's mother, asks, walking in with Camille.

"Justin and Meghan had to leave, but they said they will be here tomorrow," Inès says when she sees me looking past everyone.

I smile and nod.

"Where are you staying, dear?" Hélène asks.

"I was planning on staying at the Blackwood Hotel," I reply, feeling Inès's gaze on me. She wanted me to stay here with her, but I didn't want to overstep.

"Nonsense, you are more than welcome to stay here. Of

course, it's not a five-star hotel, but it's cozy, and you are family," Hélène insists warmly.

"Of course, we would ask that you stay in the room in the basement... No funny business," Jonathan warns with a mischievous grin, prompting laughter from everyone except Inès, who looks like she wants to disappear.

"Papa!" she exclaims, her eyes wide.

"If you're sure it's not too much trouble," I say, trying to keep a straight face but failing as I catch Inès's embarrassed expression.

"Absolutely not," Hélène says. "We insist. Make yourself at home."

"In the basement," Jonathan adds, emphasizing the word with a dramatic pause.

"Oh my God," Inès groans, burying her face in her hands while the rest of us dissolve into laughter.

It's close to midnight, and I'm up trying to catch up on some work. The basement is as cozy as the rest of the house, with only one room and one bathroom. When you first come down, you see a worn-out couch and an old TV, with neat containers stacked against one wall.

The bedroom's focal point is a large wooden desk, cluttered with papers and notebooks. There's also a full-sized bed and a small closet, everything I need for a late-night work session.

My phone rings, interrupting my thoughts. I frown, wondering who would be calling me at this hour. When I see it's Inès, my mood instantly lightens. "Butterfly?" I answer, my voice soft.

"Hi," she whispers, trying not to wake anyone.

"Hi," I respond, smiling.

"I didn't think you'd be up. What are you doing?" she asks, her voice filled with warmth.

"I couldn't sleep, so I decided to catch up on some work. What about you? Why are you up?" I ask, abandoning my emails completely.

"I couldn't sleep either... I miss you," she admits softly, her vulnerability making my heart ache.

"I miss, you too," I reply, wishing I could hold her right now.

"I... I was thinking. Remember that bucket list Meghan sent you?" she asks, her voice tinged with mischief.

My smirk deepens as I recall the list. "How could I forget? It's safely stored in my phone and my brain."

"Well, um... I was thinking maybe we could cross off number one tonight..."

"Are you asking me to sneak into your room, butterfly?" I ask as I get up, already putting on a shirt in case I bump into someone.

"Maybe... please," she begs, her voice dripping with sweetness.

"I'm on my way, baby. Which room is yours?" I don't want to accidentally stumble into the wrong one.

"It's the first room to the left, right next to the stairs."

"I'll see you soon," I say before hanging up.

The house is dark and quiet as I move through the kitchen hallway, making my way up the stairs. The hallway is empty, and I quietly open the first door, slipping inside where the soft glow of a nightlight guides me.

As soon as I close the door behind me, Inès jumps into my arms, wrapping her legs and arms around me. She's so small she fits perfectly against me. I wrap my hand in her hair, fisting it to position her head the way I want before slamming my lips onto hers. She moans, her hands cupping my face as I slip my tongue into her mouth. Blindly, I navigate toward what I hope is her bed. When my leg bumps the bed frame, I gently lower her onto the mattress, hovering over her.

"You know I love you, right?" I whisper against her skin as I kiss her neck. I feel her nod. "Good, because I have every intention of fucking you like I don't."

"Yes! Please," she moans, louder than I anticipated. I claim her lips again, sucking on them until she's a writhing mess beneath me. I bite down on her bottom lip, not too hard but enough to make her whimper.

"You're going to be quiet for me, aren't you? Hmm? I'm sure you don't want Mommy and Daddy to know you snuck a man into your room just so you could get fucked like the slut you are," I murmur as I strip off her silky pajama shirt. My mouth finds her perfectly puckered nipple, and I suck it, playing with the piercing.

"Oh God," she moans again, louder this time, and I hover over her, pinning her with my gaze.

"Butterfly, if you don't keep quiet, I'm going to gag that pretty mouth of yours and fuck you without letting you come. Do you understand?" I ask, my tone firm.

"Yes," she pants, her breath quickening.

I find her neck and wrap my large hand around it, squeezing just a little. "Yes, what?"

"Yes, I understand. I'm sorry, please," she begs, bucking her hips, desperate for friction.

"That's my good little slut," I hum as I lower my mouth to her other nipple, giving it the same attention before sliding down. I hook my fingers into the waistband of her shorts and panties, dragging them down. I hate that there isn't enough light to fully appreciate her perfect cunt, but I lower my face anyway, inhaling deeply.

"Oh my God, King," she whispers, her voice heavy with need.

"You smell so fucking good," I murmur before lowering my mouth onto her pussy, immediately sucking on her clit. Inès bucks hard, her hand flying to cover her mouth as she lets out a muffled moan. I continue to lick and suck on her little nub, savoring the sweet, feminine taste of her, a mix of coconut and berry that drives me wild.

Spreading her legs wider, I dive into her, devouring her sweet cunt with a hunger that borders on obsession. Inès's free hand claws into my hair, tugging so fiercely I wouldn't be surprised if I ended up with a bald spot... not that I'd care. The way she trembles beneath me, the muffled sounds she makes growing louder, tells me she's close, so damn close.

I pull back just enough to slip my ring and middle finger into her mouth, locking eyes with her. "Suck," I order. "And if you need to, bite as hard as you want." The thought of her teeth sinking into my flesh sends a dark thrill through me. I don't give a damn if she bites my fingers off.

Inès eagerly wraps her lips around my fingers, sucking on them with such a filthy enthusiasm that precum leaks from my cock, soaking my boxer briefs. Just the sight of her, the knowledge of what that mouth is capable of, nearly drives me to the edge. But I'm not done with her yet.

I return to her clit, sucking and nipping at the swollen nub, my free hand sliding down to find her entrance. I thrust two fingers into her tight, wet heat, curling them just right. She bites down on my fingers hard, a sharp pain that only fuels the fire burning inside me as she comes undone beautifully for me.

Her entire body shakes as the waves of her orgasm crash

over her, her grip on my hair finally loosening. I lift myself up, my chest heaving as I tug down my pants just enough to free my aching cock. I don't waste any time, I fist myself, aligning my thick length with her tight entrance before leaning down to capture her lips in a bruising kiss, and then I slam into her.

She gasps, her body arching up to meet mine, and I can feel every inch of her wrapped around me, hot and tight. I don't hold back, I pound into her with everything I've got, claiming her in the most primal, possessive way possible, though my movements are measured to avoid making the bed frame bang against the wall. My thrusts are slow but powerful, each one sending shivers through her.

"King…" she whispers against my lips, breathy and desperate. She places her hand between us, trying to slow me down. But I don't slow down. Instead, I tighten my grip on her hips, pulling her closer as I grind into her, making sure she feels every inch of me.

"This is what you wanted, so take it. Take every inch," I growl, not relenting.

"King… oh God. King, it's too much. I… I feel you everywhere. It hurts," she whimpers, even as she tries to match my thrusts.

Grabbing both of her wrists, I pin them above her head, locking them in one hand while my other hand finds her clit again, fingers rubbing circles around the sensitive bundle of nerves as I continue to thrust into her. She shakes, muscles tightening around me as she gets closer to another orgasm. "Good. I want you to feel me for days. Now be a good little slut and come for me," I order, my lips brushing against her ear. "Now, Inès."

"King…" she starts, but she's too loud, so I slam my lips onto hers, swallowing her cries as she comes undone beneath me, her cunt squeezing me so tightly that I lose control. My thrusts become more erratic as I chase my release, the intensity of it ripping through me as I spill into her.

"Fucking... fuck," I snarl against her lips, my breath ragged as I finally pull out, leaving her drenched and trembling beneath me. But I'm not done yet. My need to claim her, to mark every inch of her, burns hotter than ever.

"Give me your phone," I order, voice thick with the remnants of lust. She doesn't hesitate, handing it to me with those trusting eyes that drive me insane. I turn on the flashlight, illuminating the mess we've made. My cum oozes out of her, glistening on her swollen, used cunt. The sight makes me harder, my cock throbbing with renewed hunger.

"What are you doing?" she breathes out, a shiver of anticipation in her voice.

Ignoring her question, I dip my fingers into the slick mixture of our fluids, gathering the thick cum that's leaking out of her. Her gasp is sharp as I push it back inside her, my fingers spreading her open as I fuck my seed deeper into her.

"It needs to stay in there," I murmur, my voice softening as I gently fuck my cum back into her. "I want you dripping with me, soaked in every fucking drop."

Her body quivers, her pussy clenching around my fingers as I relentlessly stuff her full, making sure she takes everything I've given her. Her moans turn desperate, her hips lifting to meet my hand, hungry for more even as she's overwhelmed by the filthy, raw need I'm pouring into her.

I lean down, kissing her softly, her lips pliant and sweet beneath mine. "One more time," I whisper against her mouth, sliding back into her slowly, savoring the way she feels. "I need you again, just a little more."

She moans softly, wrapping her legs around me, and we move together in a rhythm that's slow, tender, and infinitely more intense than before. This time, it's not about the raw hunger, but about the closeness, the connection that makes every touch feel like a promise.

When we finally collapse together once I clean us up with some tissue, our bodies are spent and satisfied. I hold her close, brushing a kiss against her forehead. "I love you, butterfly," I whisper, not expecting her to say it back, I know she's not ready, and that's fine by me. She finds my lips and kisses me softly, sensually.

"Will you hold me until I fall asleep?" she asks in that adorable voice of hers.

Unable to resist, I kiss her again. "Of course, butterfly. Are you sore? I know I was rough…"

"I loved it. I'm a little sore, but that's how I like it," she assures me.

We stay quiet for a long time as I contemplate telling her what's been on my mind, something that's been eating at me since I first asked her out.

"Hey, I know it's a few weeks away, but I need to go to Canada. I have… a problem I need to take care of," I tell her, shifting slightly in the dimly lit room.

"Is everything okay?" she asks, concerned.

I take a deep breath. "It will be. I just need to handle something, but I want you to come with me. I'll be working a lot, but Meghan will be there, too, J is going to ask her this week."

What the fuck are you doing, King? This might be the worst idea you've ever had.

"Really?" I hear the excitement in her voice, but then it fades. "But I have school. I can't miss school." Her mention of school reminds me of that psychology professor who was way too familiar with her, but I push the thought aside.

"Well, it's going to be around winter break. I want you to

meet my grandma, plus, my family hosts a New Year's gala every year, well, technically, my mom does, but that's beside the point. I'd love it if you were my date." *For the love of all that's holy, King, shut the fuck up.*

"Oh my God, a gala? That sounds so sophisticated. I don't think I have a dress for that."

"Good thing you have your own Amex card. I'm sure Meghan would love to go shopping with you," I say, pressing my lips to the top of her head, her curly hair tickling my nose.

"I don't know... I feel weird using your money to buy a dress..." she starts, but my hand finds her ass, and I spank it hard.

"Ow!"

"That card is not a decoration. It was given to you to use, and I expect you to do exactly that. Understood?"

She giggles. "Yes, King."

INÈS

*BREAK THE RULES, FACE THE
CONSEQUENCES*

T he next day, Meghan, Camille, my mom, and I head
to the mall to find the perfect gift for my dad while
he and the guys are busy in the kitchen. Despite our
insistence that he shouldn't cook on his birthday and that we
could simply order food, he took offense and decided to cook
anyway.

As we walk through the Mall of America I wrap my arms
around Meghan. "So, how did they take the news about the
pregnancy?"

She sighs. "My dad was supportive, but my mom… well,
she made it about herself. She even cried until she found out
Justin is rich. Don't ask me how she discovered that; I think
in the middle of her tantrum about my pregnancy, she
researched Justin. Once she knew, she was thrilled and even
tried to convince me to make him pay child support, as if I
would ever." The pain in her voice is palpable. Meghan and
her mom have never got along.

Meghan always felt like her mom was competing with

her. I personally can't stand that woman; she's obsessed with being liked and, I believe, jealous of Meghan because she's younger and prettier. Plus, Meghan's dad loves her. Her mom did nothing but degrade her, making her feel worthless. Meghan believed her, thinking she was stupid and destined to fail. But then she met me. I made sure Meghan knew just how smart she was, especially when she applied herself.

Gritting my teeth, I squeeze her arm and stop walking as my mom and Camille go into a store. "Listen to me, Meg," I say, cupping her face. "Do not let her ruin this for you. Do not let her plant any weird ideas in your head, do you understand me? If she's not happy or supportive, that's her prerogative. I support you, and so do J, King, your dad, and my entire family. You have so many supporters, and we won't let you go through anything alone. Got it?"

"What would I do without you?" She hugs me. I waste no time hugging her back.

"It's a good thing we'll never find out," I say.

Thirty minutes later, just as we're finally leaving the mall, Meghan is a few steps ahead, walking beside my mom. The two of them are deep in conversation about something I can't quite hear, when Camille catches up to me.

Camille and I look alike, but there are differences. She's a little taller, for one. And then there are her eyes, one a warm, familiar brown like mine, the other a striking green that doesn't feel like it belongs to either of us. That green eye came from our maternal grandmother.

We share the same wild, curly hair, the same light brown skin, and the same smile when we're trying not to laugh.

"It's always the quiet ones who surprise you," Camille remarks with a knowing look.

I blink, then blink again. I pride myself on being a smart

young woman, but I'm ashamed to admit it takes me a moment to grasp what she's implying.

"King... please!" she mock-moans, her voice dripping with playful exaggeration.

I gasp and turn to her, feeling my cheeks burn. "Mimi!" I hiss, mortified.

She laughs, clearly enjoying my discomfort. "What? It sounded like you were having fun," she teases, her grin widening.

"No, nope! I am not talking about my... you know, with my sister!" I whisper-shout, glancing around to make sure no one else is within earshot.

"Why not? I want to know everything," she continues, trying to tickle me.

"Stop that! How did you even hear me? I thought I was being quiet," I mutter, squirming away from her grasp.

"We share a wall, poupée.[1] So... I'm guessing that wasn't your first time. Tell me, when and how was it?" She loops her arm through mine, her curiosity relentless.

I roll my eyes playfully, but in the end, I can't resist her prodding. I give her a very censored version of my first time, carefully omitting the more explicit details.

An hour later, we're all gathered at the dining table, enjoying the meal the men prepared. We're leaving for Boston tonight, I have an early class tomorrow, and so does Meg.

"Poupée, what happened to that TA position you mentioned the last time we talked?" Camille asks casually, and I choke on my water. I start shaking my head immediately.

We're all gathered around the dinner table, having

---

1. Doll.

finished dinner and sung "Happy Birthday" to my dad. Now, we're enjoying the cake together.

"Oh my God, you got offered a TA position and didn't tell me?" Meghan exclaims, and before I can protest, everyone starts congratulating me.

"No, no, it's not like that…" I stammer.

"Oh, don't be so modest, butterfly," King interjects, sounding genuinely proud. "Her psychology professor asked her to be his TA next semester, and she agreed. I'm so proud of you." King is seated across from me looking as handsome as ever. I like him here with my family, and I love that he gets along with everyone. But I cringe, knowing what's coming.

"Wait, your psychology professor?" Meghan asks, her voice tinged with curiosity.

"Oh, look at the time…" I say, trying to escape.

"As in the same guy you went on a date with?" Camille adds, and the room falls deadly silent. I'm too afraid to look at King.

"Hold on, you went on a date with your professor?" my mom asks, her tone disbelieving.

"In my defense, I didn't know he was my professor at the time. When I found out, we obviously decided not to pursue anything," I explain, swallowing hard as I sit back down. I risk a glance at King and instantly regret it.

King's eyes are locked on mine, burning with barely concealed fury. All I want to do is rush to him and explain myself.

"Still, that's inappropriate," my dad adds, his voice stern.

"I don't think so," I say, my voice wavering. "We went on one date that wasn't going anywhere, and we've moved on. I wish everyone would do the same and stop talking about it… please." My eyes drop to my plate, and the room falls into a hushed silence.

The tension lingers until Meghan finally breaks it. "Well, I have news," she begins, her voice steady. "I know I'm not blood-related to any of you, but I consider you all family. I've spent more time in this house than I did in my own, which is why I wanted to tell you all that... I'm pregnant!" Her announcement hangs in the air, the weight of it slowly sinking in before the room erupts into a flurry of congratulations and hugs.

I sneak another glance at King, but he's no longer looking at me. Even though he's smiling, I know I'm in for it when we're alone.

Two hours later, after we've said our goodbyes, Camille pulls me aside. "Hey, are you okay? I hope we didn't make things awkward for you and Kingsley."

I chuckle softly. "No, you just signed me up for my punishment."

"Excuse me?" she asks, her eyebrows shooting up. "What do you mean by punishment? He won't hurt you, will he?"

"Oh God, no, not at all..." I say, reaching out to squeeze her hand. "Well, not in the way you're thinking."

"Explain before I have to go over there and break his legs," she says, pointing to where King is seated in the car on his phone.

"I, uh.. we... God, how do I explain this? Our relationship is not a regular one. I'm in a domestic discipline relationship with him."

Camille's expression shifts from furious to curious. "A what now?"

"It means he's the dominant one in our relationship, and he has rules for me. If I break them, he punishes me. And, well... I broke one," I explain.

Camille stays quiet for a long time. "And you consented to this? It's what you want?"

"Yes, I did a lot of research, and it intrigued me. We haven't done the whole punishment thing yet because, well, I hadn't broken any rules until now... But you know me, Camille. I wouldn't do anything I didn't want to. And if it turns out it's not for me, I'll tell him. I know for a fact he would stop immediately."

Camille studies me for a moment before sighing. "My God, I've learned a lot about my little sister today," she says, pulling me into a warm hug. "I trust your judgment, and he seems like a good guy. Just promise me you'll always stand up for yourself and call me if anything ever feels wrong, okay?"

"I promise, Mimi. I trust Kingsley, he'd never do anything to hurt me," I reply, feeling a comforting sense of relief wash over me.

As soon as I get in the car, Kingsley pulls out of the driveway, his eyes fixed on the road. His jaw is clenched tight, and the tension is unbearable.

"King..." I start, my voice small.

"Not now, Queen." The fact that he's still calling me Queen is a good sign, but his tone sends a shiver down my spine.

"But..."

"I don't want to hear a peep from you until we get to the private jet, understood?" he commands, his voice low and dangerous. King has always been sweet to me, spoiling me so much that I forgot for a moment how scary he can be when he's angry. I've seen glimpses of his controlling side before, but nothing like this. He seems like a different person, and it's terrifying.

So why are my panties so wet right now?

"Yes, King," I whisper, knowing better than to push him further.

We drive for a while before Kingsley pulls into a CVS parking lot. Without a word, he gives a single command: "Stay." I roll my eyes, knowing he can't see me, and watch as he disappears into the store. When he returns, he's carrying a small bag, and though I'm dying to know what's inside, I bite my tongue and keep quiet.

He resumes driving, not stopping until we reach the airport. Inside the jet, Meghan and Justin are already settled, having arrived before us. I barely have time to greet Meghan before Kingsley leans in close, his voice a low growl. "Go to the room and sit on the bed. I'll deal with you in a moment." His command sends a shiver down my spine, making me want to both flee and squeeze my thighs together at the same time. I nod quickly and rush to the room, my heart racing.

Minutes stretch into what feels like an eternity before Kingsley finally enters the room. The moment he does, I leap to my feet and start rambling.

"I know you're upset, but like I told my family, we only went on one date. Just one. And when I realized he was my new professor, we both agreed it wasn't appropriate..." My words come out in a frantic rush, and I realize I'm repeating myself. "Besides, you can't really be mad. You and I weren't together then..." I'm trying to dance around the real issue, but I know exactly why he's angry.

"Are you finished?" Kingsley asks, his tone low and measured. He stands tall, feet planted firmly apart, arms crossed over his chest, exuding power.

I swallow hard. "I... yes." My shoulders sag under his gaze.

"I have one question," he says, his voice carrying the weight of authority. "When you were up in the middle of the night the other day, I asked what you were doing. You told me you were turning in a last-minute assignment. What were you really doing? And let me remind you, you're already in enough trouble, so make sure whatever you say is the truth."

Oh, crap. "I... King, I was... I was emailing Dr. Salvatore about the TA position," I admit, lowering my head. I can't believe I lied to him. What's wrong with me?

He nods slowly, his hand dropping to his jeans as he unbuckles his belt. "Strip," he commands, sliding the belt from the loops and folding it in his hand. My whole body trembles at the sight.

Oh. God.

Fear and arousal wage a war inside me, and I'm torn between the two. What the hell is wrong with me? Why do I find this both terrifying and unbearably sexy?

"King?" I call out in a seductive tone, licking my lips. Yes, I'm trying to flirt my way out of this. "I'm sorry I lied to you, but maybe because this is my first offense, you could just let me off with a warning. I need you, please, King. Maybe we can skip the punishment and go straight to, you know..." I let my voice drip with seduction, hoping it'll work.

But he grits his teeth so hard I can almost hear it. Then, without warning, he cups the back of my neck and crashes his lips onto mine, kissing me so fiercely that I nearly lose my balance. If he weren't holding me so tightly, I'd fall.

When he finally breaks the kiss, he pulls back slightly, his voice rough. "Cute." His eyes darken. "Now strip before I do it for you."

I huff, frustrated that my seduction didn't work on him, though it certainly worked on me. Slowly, oh so slowly, I begin to undress, taking my time to fold each piece of clothing, even my underwear.

Kingsley is patient, watching me without a hint of irritation. Finally, I'm standing completely naked while he remains fully clothed, and there's something about the contrast that's so intensely sexy.

He gives me a once-over, his nostrils flaring. "Fucking beautiful," he mutters as if my beauty offends him. "Put your hands flat on the desk and don't move them until I say otherwise."

I turn and spot a desk I hadn't noticed before, tucked away in the corner. Biting my lip, I obey, placing my hands flat on the surface as instructed.

INÈS

A MASOCHIST IN HER OWN RIGHT

The moment King's finger whispers across my back, goosebumps spread over my skin, and I'm certain he can feel them too.

"So soft," he murmurs right by my ear, making me shiver. He steps away, and I immediately miss the comfort of his touch. "Safe word?" he asks, his voice steady and calm.

"Frisson,"[1] I reply, my voice barely a breath, trembling already even though the punishment hasn't started yet.

"That's my perfect girl." His praise is like a drug, one I'm hopelessly addicted to. "Now, tell me why you're being punished."

"B-Because I lied to you... although, in my defense, it was only because I knew you'd make a big deal out of it," I add, letting a little sass slip into my tone.

His chuckle is deep and warm, sending a thrill through me. "Are you sure you want to be a brat right now? I was

---

1. Shriver.

going to spank you ten times, but I can easily make it fifteen." His words make my eyes widen in alarm.

"Ten?" I gasp, nearly lifting my hands off the desk but stopping just in time, remembering his command. "But King... ten is just..." I stammer, the realization of what's about to happen sinking in. I've never been spanked before, my parents were strict with Camille, but I was the good girl who never talked back or broke the rules. And now, here I am, about to be spanked by my boyfriend. The mix of fear and arousal is dizzying, and the humiliation only makes it worse. "Maybe you could just do five this time? Please?"

"No," he says firmly. "You're getting ten, and you don't need to worry about counting, I'll keep track. Understood?"

I swallow hard, my voice shaky. "Yes, King."

"Good. Now, let's try that again. Why are you being punished, Inès?"

"Because I lied to you," I reply, my voice small and ashamed.

"That's right. And why is it important that you don't lie to me?"

"Because it breaks our trust," I say, the words tasting bitter in my mouth.

"Exactly. And trust is everything between us."

Before I can prepare myself, the belt comes down on my bare ass. "Ow!" I whimper, the sound pathetic even to my own ears, as I sniffle softly.

"That wasn't a real one, and you know it. Stop acting like a baby and hold still." He's right, it didn't hurt much, but I can't help the mood I'm in.

"But it hurts," I pout, turning to him with wide, pleading eyes.

"Don't even try that pouting shit with me. This is happening." His tone leaves no room for argument, and I know there's no escape from what's coming.

The sound of the belt slicing through the air reaches my ears before I feel the sharp sting on my ass. The pain radiates through my body, catching me off guard. I gasp, sucking in air as the burning sensation spreads, it hurts so much more than I ever imagined.

Before I can even process the first strike, King delivers two more blows to my already heated flesh. He doesn't pause, methodically laying down a series of firm, deliberate smacks. Each one sears into my skin, punctuating the lesson he's determined to teach me.

The heat builds, the sharp sting transforming into a deep, throbbing ache. Tears prick at my eyes as the pain intensifies.

"Oh my God..." I cry out, my voice trembling. "King, I'm sorry! I'm so sorry, I won't lie to you again, I promise!" Tears spill down my cheeks, mingling with an overwhelming mix of pain and regret.

"Good," he growls, low and commanding. Without warning, he lands four more swift spanks in rapid succession. The room fills with a chorus of sounds, my desperate cries, his determined grunts, and the unmistakable thwack of leather meeting flesh. *Thwack, thwack, thwack, thwack.*

Panic sets in as I remember that Justin and Meghan are just outside. Yes, I told Meg about the DD lifestyle, but this is embarrassing. "Jesus, King, please..." I sob. "They'll hear, they'll hear everything."

He drops to his knees, his lips pressing against my burning skin, soothing the sting for a brief moment before he trails down, finding my throbbing clit I'm ashamed that this is turning me on even when it hurts so bad. When did I turn into a masochist? "Good. Let them hear you sing for me,

Queen," he murmurs, sending a shiver through me as he buries his face between my legs, licking my slit before sliding two fingers inside me.

"Look at you, such a desperate little slut for me, aren't you? Already soaked for me, and I've barely even touched you." His words, oh God, his words are going to be my undoing.

A moan escapes me as my hips begin moving on their own, chasing the pleasure he's so expertly giving. But all too soon, his fingers slip away, leaving me empty, and I can't help the whimper that follows. The way King handles me when I'm out of line truly does make me a slut for him. But don't get me wrong, the pain is real and intense, and I'll definitely be on my best behavior to avoid his belt again.

He stands again, and I'm teetering on the edge, so close to release, and when he resumes spanking me, the building tension inside me reaches a fever pitch. And then, just as suddenly, he stops and drags his fingers to my clit. With one stroke, I come undone, the orgasm crashing over me with such force that it steals my breath away.

"That's it, good girl," he praises, his voice rough with desire. Before I can even process what's happening, King is there, his cock already probing my entrance. When did he even free himself? In one harsh thrust, he's buried deep inside me, stretching my walls to their limit. His groan vibrates in my ear, primal and possessive. "Holy fucking fuck... fuck, Inès. You're perfect. So fucking perfect, baby," he murmurs, giving me a moment to adjust to the overwhelming fullness.

His lips latch onto my neck, sucking and licking with abandon, undoubtedly leaving marks that I'll wear with pride. "Your cunt opens up at my praises, baby," he whispers, and then he begins to move, deep and hard, each thrust forcing the air from my lungs. "Fuck! That little gasp you make when

I'm deep inside you? It's going to haunt me," he grunts as he keeps thrusting, drawing more gasps from me.

"More, please, I want more," I cry out, my body surrendering to the relentless rhythm. He's so deep inside me that it feels like he's touching my very soul.

"That's it! That's my good slut. Christ, you're so fucking gorgeous like this, taking my cock like the good girl you are. Come for me, baby." His hand finds my nipples, squeezing them just right, and I shatter around him, my vision blurring with the intensity of my orgasm.

"Yes, Queen. Fuck, you're so beautiful when you come around my dick. Give me one more, papillon, come on," he demands, dripping with command and confidence.

I shake my head, my body trembling. "I can't... too weak," I gasp, barely able to hold myself up. But he doesn't relent. Without pulling out, he maneuvers me to the edge of the bed and throws me onto my stomach. Grabbing a fistful of my hair, he yanks me back, lifting me slightly off the mattress.

"Touch yourself and give me one more," he growls in my ear, and I can't deny him. My hand moves between my legs, rubbing my oversensitive clit as he continues to pound into me with relentless force. To my surprise, the pleasure builds quickly, coiling tight in my core.

"That's it, baby girl. Come hard for me again. I want to feel you on my cock."

His words push me over the edge, and I come with a force that leaves me trembling and breathless. My walls clamp down around him, milking him for everything he has. I feel him swell even more inside me, the pressure intense, and then an animalistic growl rumbles from his chest as he finds his release, spilling his warmth deep inside me.

The sensation is overwhelming, the heat of his cum filling

me to the point that it starts to drip out, mixing with my own arousal on the bed beneath us. We stay like that for a moment, our bodies intertwined, our breaths mingling, before he finally collapses beside me, pulling me close.

That was the most intense sex we've ever had. I lie on the bed, utterly spent, feeling like my bones have turned to jelly. I'm completely out of it, but I feel King slide in next to me, pulling me into his arms. He kisses me softly, whispering sweet praises about how well I took his belt and how in love with me he is. His words are a balm to my sore body, and I bask in his affection.

After a while, he gets up and lifts me effortlessly into his arms, carrying me to the bathroom. He turns on the shower, waiting until the water reaches the perfect temperature before stepping in with me. He sets me down gently, and my legs wobble beneath me. King laughs, holding me steady.

"It's not funny," I say, swatting at him, but I can't help laughing, too.

"I know, my love. I'm proud of you," he whispers, his lips brushing against mine in a tender kiss.

"I'm sorry I lied, King," I say, my voice wavering as tears sting my eyes.

"Shh, I know. It's over and forgotten," he reassures me, squeezing body wash into his hands and lathering it over my skin. He's so gentle now, treating me like a delicate porcelain doll, a stark contrast to the way he was with me earlier. "How are you feeling? This was your first punishment, and even though you didn't use your safe word, I want to make sure you're okay and still want to continue with the DD lifestyle." His voice is sincere, full of concern.

I tilt my head up to meet his gaze. "I'm fine. I liked and hated it at the same time. It hurt more than I expected."

"Well, it's supposed to, it's a punishment." He chuckles.

"Yeah, well, I'm never going to do something to earn your belt again," I say, and he laughs.

"Does that mean you're okay with the lifestyle?"

"Yes, I am. I like that you're in charge and that if I do something I'm not supposed to, you'll hold me accountable, even if I hate the punishment itself." I smile, a sense of peace washing over me.

"Fair enough."

"I trust you, King, with my life," I tell him honestly, and his face lights up with a beautiful smile, those irresistible dimples appearing. "I want to do something I've wanted to do since you first smiled at me over two years ago." He frowns slightly, cocking his head in curiosity. "Just give me the biggest smile you can."

His frown deepens, but he indulges me, giving me a wide, albeit forced, smile that showcases his dimples. I stand on my tiptoes, cradle his face, and lick his cheek before dipping my tongue into one of his dimples, wiggling it playfully. He bursts out laughing. "Alright, you weirdo," he says through his laughter, making me laugh, too.

After our shower, we head back to the room, and King pulls out the small bag from CVS. "Drop the towel and lay on your stomach," he commands. I do as I'm told, turning my head to see what he's doing. He pulls out a small tube of Aquaphor, so that's what he got from CVS. He leans over my ass, gently caressing it, and I hiss at the contact. He then applies a small amount of the ointment to his fingers and carefully spreads it over my sore skin. Once he's done, we get dressed and prepare to face the others.

My face burns with embarrassment when I see Meghan and Justin, knowing they heard everything.

Kingsley grabs a pillow and places it on the seat next to Meghan. I nearly die of embarrassment. "Sit, I'll be right back," he says, kissing my forehead before leaving me to face them.

Justin gives me a knowing smile. "Don't be embarrassed. I've known Kingsley since we were babies. I wouldn't have expected anything less." His smile is genuine, without a hint of judgment.

Meghan taps the pillow. "Yeah, we know you guys are kinky as fuck. No big deal. Sit with me."

I smile, but the sting on my ass makes me wince as I sit down. I'm definitely going to feel this for days.

Justin gives Meghan a strange look that makes me frown, and she awkwardly stands up, rubbing her belly. "Well, I'm off to the bathroom because, you know... pregnant and all, which means I pee every five seconds." She offers a quick, nervous laugh before hurrying off, leaving just me and Justin.

I chuckle, watching her disappear. "Uh, what was that?" I ask, raising an eyebrow at Justin, whose eyes are now focused on me.

"That," he chuckles, "was your best friend not knowing how to act normal."

I laugh, but before I can say more, his expression shifts to something more serious.

"I wanted to talk to you."

"Me? I hope everything's okay."

"That's for you to tell me," he says, making me even more confused. "Look, I know I'm Kingsley's best friend, but I need you to know that I'm here for you too. I understand this domestic discipline lifestyle is new for you, and it takes a lot of trust to let someone lead like that. I can vouch for Kingsley, he'd never intentionally hurt you. But I also care about *you*, and I want you to think of me as your... safeguard.

If he ever steps out of bounds or does something that makes you uncomfortable, I want you to come to me. I'm serious, I'll kick his ass if I have to. You're like a little sister to me, and I need you to know I'm here to hold him accountable."

His words catch me off guard, and the sincerity in his eyes makes my heart swell with gratitude. I smile at him, touched. "Thank you so much, J. You have no idea how much that means to me."

He gives me a soft smile, but I can't resist adding, "Though, if King ever hurt me in a way that's malicious or crossed a line, I'd probably kill him myself first. Then I'd come to you so you could help me bury the body."

Justin's eyes widen in surprise, clearly not expecting *that* from me. I guess my quiet, innocent vibe throws people off. But then he grins, looking almost proud. "Attagirl."

Just then, Meghan and Kingsley return. King looks between me and Justin, his brow furrowing slightly. "Everything good here?"

Justin and I exchange a glance, smiling like we're sharing a secret. "Oh, everything's great," Justin says, his grin widening even more.

Kingsley raises an eyebrow, clearly suspicious, but instead of asking more, he hands me a bottle of ibuprofen and water, pressing a kiss to my forehead. "Take two. We'll be landing in a few."

I look at him, my heart swelling with warmth and love. In that moment, I realize just how deeply I love Kingsley. His care, his thoughtfulness, and his protectiveness mean the world to me. It's not just the way he takes control but also the way he looks after me, making sure I'm okay even when he's being dominant. Kingsley understands me like no one else, always knowing exactly what I need, whether it's a moment of intense passion or a simple act of kindness. His kisses, his touch, and his words all convey a deep, unwavering affection that makes me feel cherished and adored.

As I gaze into his eyes, I see the man who has become my rock, my confidant, and my lover. I'm not just in love with Kingsley; I am completely, irrevocably his.

KINGSLEY

TIS THE SEASON

I wake up to the soft sound of Christmas tunes playing through the Alexa speaker, a sure sign of Inès's handiwork. I smile to myself as I stretch in bed, knowing how much she loves this season. It's one of the many things about her that make me fall more in love with her each day, her ability to embrace the magic of life, even in the simplest moments.

Inès's usual quiet and serious demeanor disappears during Christmas. Her whole personality shifts into this festive, holiday-obsessed mode, where everything becomes about twinkling lights, cinnamon-scented candles, and ugly sweaters. And despite how ridiculous it can seem at times, I can't help but be charmed by it. Her excitement is contagious, and, God, if it doesn't make me love her more than I already do.

I stagger out of bed, my body still heavy with sleep, but drawn to the sound of her humming coming from the bathroom. There she is, standing in front of the mirror, brushing her hair. The sight of her reflection is enough to wake me up fully. She's wearing those leggings that hug her curves in all the right ways, paired with what has to be the ugliest Christmas sweater I've ever seen, one I'm sure she got for me as well. The sight of her makes my heart ache with how deeply I care for her.

Unable to resist, I walk up behind her and wrap my arms around her waist, pressing my chest to her back. "Merry Christmas, love," I murmur into her ear, my lips brushing against her skin.

She turns in my arms, her eyes sparkling with joy. "Merry Christmas, King!" she squeals, throwing her arms around my neck and pressing a quick kiss to my lips. "We have so much to do today! You need to shower, and then we can do presents." Her excitement is so pure and infectious, I can't help but smile. She's like a little kid when it comes to Christmas.

"You're adorable, you know that?" I say, bopping her nose lightly with my finger, making her giggle.

Just then, Beau trots into the bathroom, his little tail wagging as if he senses the festive energy in the air. He nudges Inès with his wet nose, his big brown eyes full of love.

"Look who's ready for Christmas!" I chuckle, leaning down to scratch behind his ears. Beau responds by rolling over, wanting belly rubs.

"Alright, you little furball, you'll get your Christmas treats soon," Inès promises, leaning down to give him some love. "But first, coffee and presents!"

Reluctantly, I let go of her and head to the shower. The hot water clears the last bit of grogginess from my mind, but it also gives me a moment to reflect. Every day with Inès feels like a gift, but there's something about this holiday season, about the idea of waking up next to her on Christmas morning, that makes me want to savor every second. I don't know how I got so lucky, but I'm determined to keep making her smile like she did just now.

After getting dressed, I pull on the matching ugly sweater she picked out for me. It's just as hideous as I expected, but the thought of making her happy overrides any reservations I might have about wearing it. As I step out of the room, I run into Justin, who's wearing an equally horrendous sweater. We exchange a knowing look, and it's all we can do not to burst out laughing.

"Pas possible,"[1] Justin chuckles, shaking his head. "When did we lose control?"

"I don't think we ever had control," I reply with a laugh. "They've had us wrapped around their fingers from day one."

We both laugh, but there's truth in what I said. Inès and Meghan have a way of making us do anything just to see them happy. Not that I mind, seeing Inès smile is worth every ugly sweater in the world.

As we head downstairs, Justin catches my arm, his expression turning serious. "Hey, we're leaving for home tomorrow. Are you sure it's a good idea for Inès to come? She won't be happy about it."

I let out a sigh, rubbing the back of my neck. "I know. But I can't ask her to stay behind when Meghan is coming. Plus, I've already asked her to meet Grams."

Justin gives me a sympathetic smile then squeezes my shoulder. "T'es mort,"[2] he says with a grin.

"Ouais, va te faire foutre,"[3] I reply light-heartedly, giving him a gentle shove as we head downstairs together.

----

1. No way.
2. You're dead.
3. Yeah, go fuck yourself.

Beau dashes ahead of us, his little paws pattering against the hardwood floors. He skids to a halt at the bottom of the staircase, his tail wagging furiously as he watches us approach, ready to burst into action.

"Hey, buddy! Ready for some Christmas fun?" I call out, and Beau responds by bouncing in place, clearly excited for whatever mischief he has planned today.

The penthouse smells like Christmas, cinnamon, pine, and cookies. The tree is already glowing with lights and ornaments, and Meghan and Inès are waiting for us by the fireplace, their faces lighting up when they see us.

"Aww, you guys are adorable!" Meghan coos, giving Justin a quick kiss on the lips. Her baby bump is more noticeable now, and it only makes her glow more.

Inès practically bounces on her toes in excitement. "Present time!"

We gather around the tree, passing around gifts. Laughter fills the room as we take turns unwrapping presents, each one more thoughtful than the last. I watch as Inès opens her gifts, her eyes lighting up with every little thing. It's moments like these that remind me how much she means to me, how much I want to give her the world.

I pull the last envelope from my pocket, feeling a thrill of anticipation. "I have one more gift for you," I say, extending it to her.

Her eyes go wide with surprise, a spark of excitement she tries to hide. "King, you've already given me so much," she protests softly, but her curiosity wins out as she carefully opens it.

When she sees what's inside, her face transforms, lighting up in pure, unguarded joy. "VIP tickets... to the largest neurology conference in the world?! Are you serious?" Her voice is filled with awe, and I can tell she's already imagining it.

"Not just that," I add, my voice low, watching her face closely. "It's a completely personalized experience. You'll get to arrange private meetings with the top neurologists and researchers, one-on-one discussions where you can ask anything you want. And there's an exclusive lab tour lined up just for you."

Her eyes glisten, and before I can say another word, she throws her arms around me, holding me so tight I almost lose my breath. "King, this is... incredible. You don't know how much this means to me." Her voice cracks a little, and she buries her face against my shoulder, holding on as though she'll never let go.

"You're welcome, butterfly," I murmur, gently brushing a tear from her cheek as she pulls back to look at me. Her eyes, full of so much love and gratitude, make my chest ache in the best way possible. She's the only woman who's ever made me feel like this, like there's no place I'd rather be than by her side, sharing every moment.

She sniffs and then pouts, playful again. "Now my gift totally sucks compared to yours," she says, a touch of self-consciousness in her voice.

I laugh, shaking my head. "Hey, I love my homemade coupon gifts, and I can't wait to cash them in. Each one is personal. And you know I meant it when I told you you didn't need to get me anything," I remind her, because what do you give a billionaire anyway?

Beau barks, playing with wrapping paper, and I reach down to ruffle his fur. "Hey, buddy! You ready for your gifts?"

Inès laughs, her eyes sparkling. "Oh yes, he is going to love it!" She grabs the gifts we got him. "From Mommy and

SAFFRON BROOKS

Daddy!" she declares, and I can hardly contain my excitement as I help her unwrap it.

Inside is a plush dog bed with a note that reads, *For our favorite pup, may you dream of chasing squirrels!* Beau sniffs at the bed then jumps up, his tail wagging even faster. He curls up on it, looking utterly content, and I can't help but laugh at how he immediately makes himself at home.

"And this is from your aunty and uncle!" Meghan says, handing us a box, this one containing a luxurious, hand-crocheted sweater, complete with tiny reindeer patterns. "He needed something stylish for the holidays!" she says, and Inès gently puts the sweater on him. Beau prances around, showing off his new look, and I swear he poses as if he knows he's the star of the show.

"Look at you, Beau! You're the cutest little holiday pup around!" Inès says, cheering him on.

"We actually have one more gift for both of you," Justin says, getting our attention.

Inès pulls away from me, curiosity piqued. "What is it?"

Meghan hands her a small, wrapped box. "Open it."

Inside is a single blue baby bootie, and Inès's eyes widen as she looks between Meghan and Justin.

"We're having a boy," Justin announces proudly. "And we were hoping you two would be the Godparents."

Inès's face breaks into a joyful smile, her eyes brimming with tears. "Oh my God, yes! Of course! We would be honored," she says, her voice choked with emotion.

I pull my childhood best friend into a heartfelt embrace. "That's not something you even needed to ask, man! But I'm honored. Thank you," I tell him, my voice thick with emotion.

Meghan and Inès share a tight, tearful hug, both of them

overwhelmed with happiness. I have no doubt that Justin and Meghan will be amazing parents.

INÈS

HELLO, QUEBEC

As we touch down in Quebec, the cold hits us immediately, a stark contrast to the warmth inside the jet. I shiver despite the heavy coat Kingsley insisted I wear, and he wraps one arm around me while his other hand holds Beau's leash. Beau bounces excitedly on his feet, it's his first time on a plane, and it seems like he's already eager for his next adventure.

"Ready, buddy?" Kingsley chuckles as Beau whines softly, his nose pressed to the window, watching as we head toward a sleek black SUV parked nearby. A burly man who looks like he could be straight out of a Russian mafia movie stands beside the car, his muscular frame towering over us.

"Welcome home, Mr. Ashford, Mr. Williams," the man greets Kingsley and Justin with a firm nod.

"Thank you, Silas. It's good to be back," Kingsley replies. "This is my girlfriend, Inès," he introduces me, and Silas gives me a respectful nod.

"And this is my girlfriend, Meghan," Justin says as Silas shakes Meghan's hand.

"And this little guy is Beau," Kingsley adds, scratching behind Beau's ears, causing him to wag his tail even faster.

"Nice to meet you all. Let's get you out of the cold." Silas opens the car door, and we all pile into the spacious vehicle, Beau hopping in first and immediately settling on my lap as if this whole trip was planned for his comfort. His little body radiates warmth, and I can't help but smile as he curls up, resting his head on my coat.

As the car pulls away, I rest my head against Kingsley's shoulder, feeling his fingers stroke my back while the others chat. Beau, now content, lets out a happy sigh as he nestles deeper into my lap, his fur soft against my gloves.

"Babe, wake up, we're here," Kingsley whispers, his fingers gently brushing my cheek. I blink, realizing I must have dozed off during the ride. Beau stirs in my lap, stretching lazily before hopping down to the car floor. Kingsley helps me out of the SUV, and as I step out, the sight before me takes my breath away.

A sprawling mansion stretches across acres of snow-covered land, its sheer size making it feel like something out of a dream. The driveway alone seems endless, but despite the heavy snowfall, it's perfectly dry.

Kingsley must notice my wide-eyed awe, because he answers my unspoken question with a casual, "The driveway is heated."

"Of course it is," I murmur, half to myself.

Beau, ever curious, sniffs the ground, his small paws leaving little imprints in the freshly fallen snow.

"This is… wow," I whisper, still trying to take it all in.

Kingsley chuckles, pointing to a distant house. "That's Justin's place, just over there."

"You have no close neighbors?" I ask, still mesmerized by the vastness of it all.

"Not for miles," he replies as we head toward the front door.

As soon as we open the door, a girl comes bounding toward us. "Oh my God, you're here!" she exclaims, her excitement palpable as she leaps into Kingsley's arms. Thanks to the pictures King has shown me, I can tell she's his sister.

She's blonde and very pretty, and with their shared features, the family resemblance is unmistakable, though she looks much younger.

"I told you I would be, Pay! Do you doubt my word now?" Kingsley asks, setting her down. His tone is affectionate, and it makes me smile to see how sweet and loving he is with his sister.

"I don't doubt you. It's just… I didn't think you'd come…"

Kingsley cups her cheeks gently. "Of course, I'm here. And hey, I told you, any time you need me, just call and I'll be there," he reassures her with a smile.

Beau barks excitedly, sensing the energy, and runs around us in circles, clearly wanting some attention.

"And who's this little cutie?" Paisley asks, crouching down to pet Beau. He immediately rolls onto his back, exposing his belly for rubs.

"This is Beau, our fur baby," Kingsley introduces.

"Oh my God, you are so domestic now, I love it," Paisley

teases. "And you are just too adorable," Paisley coos, scratching Beau's belly before standing up to hug Kingsley again. "I'm glad you're home."

After one more hug, Paisley turns to me. "So, you're Inès. Kingsley talks about you all the time. I'm Pay." She grins widely and pulls me into a warm embrace before I even have a chance to react.

"It's nice to meet you, Pay," I say, smiling back at her.

"Oh, you're going to love it here! Come on inside, we should totally grab lunch sometime," she gushes, practically bouncing with excitement.

Kingsley pulls me back, shaking his head with a chuckle.

"Let's get Inès settled in first, Pay," Kingsley says. "But we'll catch up before I head back to Boston, alright?"

Pay nods. Just as we're about to leave, she calls out, "Kingsley?"

"Yeah?"

"Where's J? I thought he was coming with you," she asks with a hint of impatience as she glances around. King rolls his eyes, his annoyance barely concealed.

"I thought we talked about this, Pay," he says firmly.

She scoffs, folding her arms across her chest. "What? I'm just asking if he's home so I can go say hi. He's my friend, too, you know," she retorts, her voice a little sharper than before.

King chuckles, a deep, knowing sound that makes my curiosity spike. I stand there, watching the exchange, feeling a bit lost as they go back and forth.

"Yeah, he's home, but if I were you, I'd think twice before heading over there. Don't say I didn't warn you," King says, placing a kiss on top of his sister's head before turning to me. His hand finds mine, his grip warm and reassuring as he guides me up the stairs toward the house. Beau follows us closely, trotting along, his nose twitching at the new scents. As we pass through the front entrance, I'm struck by the lavish decorations inside, the sparkling chandeliers, the rich mahogany furniture, and three massive Christmas trees standing proudly in the living room, each one glistening with lights and ornaments.

"This is my wing of the house," Kingsley explains as we walk through a hallway lined with doors. "My parents and Pay have their own, so you won't have to worry about bumping into anyone unexpectedly."

"Wow," I whisper, glancing around. Beau darts ahead, his little paws slipping slightly on the polished floors as he explores.

When we finally reach Kingsley's room, I'm stunned again. It's more like a luxurious mini-apartment, clean, organized, and masculine, with modern décor and dark wood furniture. A king-sized bed sits in the center, flanked by floor-to-ceiling windows that offer a panoramic view of the snowy landscape. Beau hops onto the bed without hesitation, making himself right at home.

"You like it, buddy?" Kingsley asks, amused as Beau spins in a circle before settling down on the plush blankets.

I laugh softly, shaking my head. "Looks like he's claiming the bed already."

Kingsley turns to me with a grin. "Beau always knows how to make himself comfortable. But the bed is ours. I'll make sure he gets his own cozy spot," he says as he reaches out to pull me into his arms.

"This is beautiful, King. I'm almost afraid to breathe and mess anything up," I say. "But seriously, are you allergic to color?" Before I can react, King sweeps me off my feet, literally, lifting me effortlessly and laying me down on the bed.

Beau huffs and leaps off the bed and goes to lie down by the window.

King hovers over me with that playful smile that makes my heart race. I can't help but giggle as his lips brush against mine. "You're more than welcome to change anything you want here. What's mine is yours, remember?" he whispers before kissing me, the softness of his lips making me melt.

"What was that downstairs with Pay?" I ask, curiosity getting the better of me as he begins to remove my shoes.

He laughs softly but then tries to scowl. "It's not funny," he says, though the corner of his mouth twitches like he's fighting off a grin. "Pay has had a crush on Justin since she was a kid. It's only gotten worse over the years, but Justin just ignores her," he explains, his hands now sliding my coat off with practiced ease. "But I'm sure she's about to get a dose of reality very soon when she sees Meghan." He chuckles, and as he starts to remove my yoga pants, I can't help but smirk.

Whatever we were talking about slips from my mind as his touch distracts me, drawing me deeper into his world, one piece of clothing at a time. Once I'm left in nothing but my underwear, I get on my knees on the bed, expecting King to take the hint and strip me bare. But instead, he quietly walks into a different room, leaving me in a state of confusion.

When he returns, it's with a shirt in hand, a shirt he slips over my head, much to my disappointment. I pout, feeling the sting of unmet anticipation. This isn't where I thought this was going at all. Determined not to let him take the lead this time, I reach out, wrapping my arms around him and pulling him down toward me. He towers over me, his presence both commanding and intoxicating.

I slant my lips to his, moaning softly as I try to take control. I know he hates it when I do this, when I challenge his authority. He never lets me. Just as I'm about to thrust my tongue into his mouth, his hand wraps around my neck, gently but firmly pushing me back. I whimper in protest, but he's quick to assert himself.

"You need to rest, papillon.[1] Dinner's in", he glances at his watch, "four hours."

"But I'm not tired... I need..." My words falter as his grip tightens around my neck, sending a shiver down my spine. So much for taking control.

"You didn't sleep on the flight here, and you dozed off in the car. That tells me you need to rest, even if it's just for an hour, butterfly," he says. His voice is gentle but leaves no room for argument.

I roll my eyes, annoyed by his overprotectiveness. "I said,"

My words are cut short when his eyes narrow danger-ously, that intense, frightening, yet undeniably sexy look crossing his face. His grip tightens further, pulling me closer to him.

"Unless this is your way of begging for punishment, which I'd be more than happy to hand out, I suggest you quit being a brat and lay down," he warns, his tone sending a ripple of fear and undeniable arousal through me.

I resist the urge to roll my eyes again, biting my lip instead.

"Yes, King," I say, my voice small but obedient.

"Good girl," he murmurs, leaning in to kiss me deeply, his lips claiming mine with a passion that leaves me breathless. When he finally pulls away, he gently lays me down on the bed, tucking me in with a tenderness that contrasts with the

---

1. Butterfly.

authority in his voice. A moment later, Beau comes and cuddles with me, and before long, I fall asleep.

KINGSLEY

OPEN WIDER AND RELAX

Once Inès and Beau settle into bed, she falls asleep almost immediately, so much for not being tired. I head to my home office, where I check Inès's glucose levels on my phone. Her levels look good, slightly elevated, but I'll make sure her dinner is carb-free.

My love for Inès grows stronger each day. I'd marry her today if she'd let me, but I understand that her studies are her priority. She's made it clear that kids and marriage are not in her near future, and I respect her decision. I'm a patient man. After an hour of responding to emails, I get the call I knew I'd get. He just can't resist.

"Son." My father's voice comes through the phone when I answer.

My dad and I used to be close. In many ways, we still are, but one issue has driven a significant wedge between us, his insistence that I marry his friend's daughter. He's not just suggesting it; he's using the company I've poured my heart and soul into as leverage. Growing up, he was my role model, the one who taught me the difference between right and wrong and shared his business acumen. We were a team, and I admired him deeply. But that changed when he made it clear that securing my future with the company, EcoTech Innovations, came with strings attached. Now, our relationship feels more like a transactional partnership than a father-son bond. He holds the keys to everything I've worked for, and while I respect him, it's hard not to feel resentment when the stakes are so personal.

"Father," I respond curtly, returning to my emails.

"I assume you'll be coming into the office now that you're home?" It sounds like a question, but it's a command. I don't take kindly to being told what to do. I clench my teeth. I haven't been back to Canada in two years, which means I haven't set foot in our headquarters, much to the board's displeasure. Even though I was technically a student, the agreement was to visit at least twice a year.

"You could have asked me that at dinner in a few hours," I reply.

"Why wait when I can ask you now? I heard you brought a girl home." There it is, his real reason for his call. "Son, I hope…"

"I'll be in the office tomorrow," I cut him off. But like a dog with a bone, he won't let it go.

"Is it serious? This is the first girl you're introducing to your grandmother." I anticipated this question. My grandmother means the world to me, and I'd never bring a girl I don't see a future with to meet her. But Inès is different; Inès *is* my future.

"Listen, Dad, I have another meeting to get to," I lie wanting to end the call. "See you at dinner."

"Son?" he calls out before I can hang up. When he realizes I'm not going to respond, he adds, "It's good to have you home." And before I can reply, he hangs up. He always has to have the last word.

"Fuck," I mutter to myself. Things are about to get dramatic.

I decide it's time to stop working. I head back to my room to find Inès and Beau still asleep. Not wanting to disturb her, I head to the bathroom for a quick shower. A few minutes later, Inès walks in, naked and absolutely stunning.

"Mind if I join you?" she asks in that sultry voice that drives me absolutely insane.

"Shoot me in the face the day I say no to that."

"But I love your face," she murmurs as she steps into the shower, her voice a seductive whisper.

I pull her close, capturing her lips in a heated kiss that makes her melt against me.

"Where's Beau?" I whisper against her lips.

"Your sister just asked to let her take him out, so I did," she explains before boldly wrapping her fingers around my throbbing erection, her touch making me inhale sharply.

"Inès," I warn, my voice strained with the intensity of my desire. Since the night I used my belt on her, she's become bolder, and I'm certainly not complaining.

With a mischievous glint in her eyes, she gives my erection one last squeeze before rising on her tiptoes. Her lips brush against my shoulder, and she bites down hard enough to leave a mark. My body responds instinctively, knowing exactly what she wants. Groaning, I grip her neck, applying just the right pressure to make her shiver. "Butterfly," I warn again, pulling her closer until our mouths touch.

She looks at me with a feigned innocence that only heightens my desire. "I'm not doing anything, King," she pouts, her expression a perfect mix of defiance and seduction. The urge to fuck her is overwhelming.

"On your knees!" I command, releasing her neck. She smiles and gracefully drops to her knees, water cascading over her, I adjust to shield her from the shower head. My dick is so hard it's almost painful. "Open your mouth and stick out your tongue." Her compliance is instant, and watching her eager obedience fuels my hunger even more. "Lick," I demand. She reaches up to take my cock, but I grab her hands and pin them above her head against the shower wall. "Little whores don't need to use their hands. Now lick me." I see her try to suppress her smile, but it breaks free.

With her tongue out, she licks me as best as she can. I groan. "Good girl." Loving the praise, Inès licks me again and again like I'm her favorite lollipop. "Suck!" I order, and she does without missing a beat. "Fuck," I moan, loving the feel of her tongue gliding up and down under my shaft. I let go of her hand and hold her head with my hands. "Pinch if it gets to be too much, understand?" She quickly nods. I curse under my breath, loving how perfectly she submits to me.

I start slowly fucking her mouth. "Open wider and relax," is the only warning I give her before I force myself down my throat. "Just like that," I grunt. I love that she has no gag reflex. "Take it all, Queen."

I fuck her mouth savagely, hitting the back of her throat again and again. "Fuck, you are unreal!" I growl when she swallows around my tip. "Keep your eyes on me, butterfly, look at me while I fuck your throat," I demand as my voice becomes breathier. I'm going to come, but I don't want to come in her mouth today.

I slide out of her mouth, my cock glistening with her saliva. She looks up at me, lips swollen, eyes glazed with lust, and it's enough to make me nearly lose control. Grabbing her arm, I urge her to stand up. I push her against the wall, lift one of her legs over my forearm, and crash my lips into hers.

The kiss is bruising and desperate as I line myself up with her entrance.

With one powerful thrust, I'm buried deep inside her, and she whimpers into my mouth, her nails digging into my shoulders as she clings to me. The heat, the slickness, it's all too much. I start moving, each stroke deeper and more intense than the last, and she meets me thrust for thrust, her breath hitching with every movement.

"King... I'm going to come..."

"Come for me, Inès," I growl into her ear, and I feel her body tense around me, the telltale signs of her climax building. I don't let up, don't slow down, driving her over the edge with each powerful thrust until she's shaking in my arms, crying out my name as she comes.

It's too much for me. Her tight, convulsing walls milk me, and with a few final thrusts, I'm coming, too, spilling everything I have inside her.

INÈS

"I thought we were having dinner here?" I ask when he picks out one of my formal dresses. After the shower, he got dressed while I took my time applying lotion and doing my hair. He had promised to dress me, and the idea had made me smile, he enjoys taking care of me, and I love letting him.

"It is, but dinner at the Ashford's' is always a formal occasion," he says, gently guiding me into my black lace thong. The way his hands move, confident but tender, makes me feel exposed, not just physically, but emotionally.

I tense, trying to hide my nerves, but I know he can feel it.

"You don't need to be nervous," he assures me, his voice soft as he fastens my bra. "There are only three people whose opinions matter to me. One already loves you, and I'm confident the other two will too."

"Your parents?" I ask.

"No, my grandma and our house manager," he replies, with a small, amused smile.

"House manager?" I echo, puzzled.

"Yes, well… she's more like a mother, really. Her name is Josephine, but you can call her Josie. She oversees the house, manages the staff, cleaners, gardeners, all that, and she practically raised me and my sister. She even taught us how to cook and clean for ourselves," he explains, grabbing the dress to help me slip it on. There's something intimate in the way he adjusts it over my shoulders as if he's setting the final touches on something precious. He kneels down to help me with my heels, and even in them, I still feel small next to him.

"I know she'll love you." He looks up at me with an intensity that makes my heart skip. "My God, you are beautiful," he whispers, leaning in for a kiss. I melt into it, feeling the tension ease away. "Are you ready?" he asks, his eyes warm.

"I thought we still had time," I reply, glancing at the clock.

"We do, but we're going to see Josie first," he says, opening the door and guiding me through the house with a gentle hand on the small of my back.

"Daronne,"[1] he beams as we step into an office. The woman standing before us is a stunning Black woman.

---

1. Mom.

"Kingsley? Oh my goodness, come here!" Josie, I presume, exclaims as she rises from her desk. She appears to be somewhere in her forties and is truly beautiful. She's dressed in an elegant, off-white sleeveless high-neck blouse paired with high-waisted charcoal trousers. Her high heels elongate her figure, and her braids are swept back into a high ponytail, giving her a poised, polished look. As they embrace, I take in the room.

The office is a masterclass in modern luxury and classic elegance. A sleek, matte-black desk dominates the center, flanked by sculptural armchairs that blend comfort with contemporary style. A polished marble coffee table with a curved metal base adds a touch of movement and refinement. Tall arched windows flood the space with natural light, casting shadows that highlight intricate baroque plasterwork on the ceiling. There's built-in shelves, illuminated by recessed lighting, and house-curated books and decor. I'm struck by how impressive it is, especially for a house manager. My attention shifts just in time to see Josie smack King on the back of his head. I widen my eyes, bracing for his reaction, but he merely winces, rubbing the spot she hit.

"Ow! What was that for?"

"Two years, King. Two years! You leave for college, don't call, refuse to answer when we reach out, and don't come home for two whole years?" Her voice is sharp, but there's a deep concern beneath the scolding. I'm caught off guard by the familiarity between them. Then again, King did mention that she raised him.

He sighs. "I was upset…"

"I understand that a lot happened, but you still need to stay in touch, not just with your father. Do you have any idea how much we missed you? Especially your grandmother. She's been worried sick."

King's shoulders slump slightly. "You're right. I'm sorry. But... can we move on? Please, Mom?" He flashes a smile, kissing her on the cheek, seemingly unfazed by her reprimand.

They both turn to look at me, and I straighten my posture, feeling suddenly exposed. I don't fully understand their relationship, but from what I've seen so far, she's incredibly important to King. That means I need her to like me.

"This is Inès," King introduces me with a warm smile, "my girlfriend."

Josie snaps her head toward him, her expression unreadable. They exchange a silent conversation, one I'm not privy to. Unease twists in my gut, but I force a smile and extend my hand.

"It's very nice to meet you," I say, trying to sound confident despite my nerves.

Josephine approaches me, eyes me up and down for a moment, and then completely dismisses my offered handshake. Instead, she pulls me into a warm, motherly hug. "Oh, hon, you are stunning," she says, cupping my face in her hands. I can't help but relax a bit under her kind gaze. She smells amazing, something sweet and just heavenly. "It's lovely to meet you. Come, let's sit and chat." She takes my hand, gently leading me to one of the armchairs.

King just stands nearby, looking like a bodyguard, which makes me stifle a smile.

"So, Inès, that's a French name. I'm guessing you or someone in your family is French?"

"Yes," I reply, settling into the plush chair. "I was born and raised in France until I was ten."

"Oh? And how are you liking the U.S. so far?" she asks, with a friendly, curious glint in her eyes.

"Though I miss home a lot, I love the U.S."

"And you go to Ashford University, I assume?" she continues, glancing over at King, who gives her a subtle nod.

"Yes! I'm in my third year."

"That's wonderful. And how's King treating you? He better be on his best behavior," she says with a wink.

I grin. "Oh, he's been perfect. So perfect, in fact, I've been hoping to hear something at least a little embarrassing about him. You know, to prove he is human," I add with a playful glint in my eye.

Josephine's eyes sparkle mischievously. "Oh, honey, I have plenty of embarrassing stories. Buckle up."

King, sensing where this is going, raises an eyebrow. "Uh, butterfly, maybe I can give you the house tour now," he says, trying to divert the conversation. But the smile tugging at the corner of his lips betrays him.

"In a minute." I wave him off, my curiosity now fully piqued.

Josie grins. "Well, let me tell you about the time Kingsley decided he was a rockstar."

"Really? That's the story you're going with?" King asks, but his face shows he's already resigned to his fate.

"Oh, unless you'd prefer something more embarrassing?" Josephine teases, raising her eyebrows.

King immediately throws his hands up in surrender. "Nope, that's fine. Rockstar it is."

I lean in, excited.

"So," Josephine begins, eyes twinkling, "when King was about fourteen, he signed up for the school talent show. He'd been learning guitar and thought he was going to blow everyone away with his performance. Practiced for weeks."

I giggle, already sensing where this is going.

"The night of the show comes, and he's so nervous he can barely hold the guitar, but he's determined. He gets up on stage, ready to rock. Starts playing, and for a few seconds, it's all going fine." I glance at King, who is just amused. "But then", Josephine pauses for effect, "he totally forgets the chords. Just freezes in front of the entire school."

I burst into laughter, covering my mouth as I picture it. King shakes his head but can't help smiling.

"Instead of stopping or trying to start over, Kingsley decides to improvise. He starts singing a completely made-up song about how 'forgetting the chords is just part of the show.' The lyrics were hilarious, and he ended up dancing around the stage like a maniac, trying to distract everyone from his mistakes."

"Oh my God, I would have loved to see that." I laugh.

"I recorded everything. I'll let you watch it later, but it gets better," Josie continues with a mischievous smile. "At one point, he tripped over the microphone cable and fell flat on his back. The whole auditorium erupted in laughter, but Kingsley just laid there, strumming his guitar and singing his ridiculous song. He got a standing ovation, not because he was good, but because it was the funniest thing anyone had ever seen."

I gasp between giggles, clutching my stomach. "I can't believe you did that! You really know how to put on a show."

King groans playfully, stepping closer and taking my hand. He gently pulls me to my feet, pressing a soft kiss to my forehead. "I'm glad my embarrassment brings you so much joy," he says with mock exasperation. "But I think we've had enough stories for now."

"Oh no, I want more!" I insist with a grin. Sure, the story was funny, but it didn't quite shake the image of his near perfection. I need more dirt.

"Maybe later," King replies, a teasing smirk on his lips.

"Right now, we have to go downstairs. Dinner is about to start."

"Don't worry, Inès," Josephine adds, standing and pulling me into another warm hug. "I've got plenty more stories where that came from." She turns to King, giving him a peck on the cheek. "And I've uploaded the dietary restrictions to the MansionSync, so the kitchen made adjustments accordingly." I'm sure that was for me, and I feel a little warmth at the thought.

"Merci, la Daronne.[2] I'll see you later," King says affectionately.

"Of course, my love. Oh, and Inès, I heard you brought your dog with you?"

"It's actually our dog. We share custody," King corrects.

"Good to know. I'll have one of the house staff take care of him, get him his dinner, and take him out. And tomorrow, if you'd like, I can have someone take him to an indoor dog recreation center. He'll love it, there's so much to do there. I'll also give your number to the staff member so she can send you plenty of pictures and videos," she says, picking up her iPad and jotting down notes.

I look at King, stunned. He's just smiling and nodding, as if this is completely normal.

"Oh my God, that's... I don't even know what to say. Thank you so much! He'll definitely love that."

"Excellent! Well, I hope to see you soon. It was so lovely meeting you." She smiles warmly.

After we exchange goodbyes and step into the hallway, I finally ask the question that's been nagging me. "So... you call your house manager Daronne?"

"I do," King replies with a soft chuckle. "I used to call her

---

2. Thanks, mom.

'Mom' when I was little, and honestly, I still do sometimes. But my mother wasn't exactly thrilled about that, it almost caused a huge problem. Eventually, my dad told me to call Josephine Daronne instead, because I just couldn't call her 'Josephine.' She was more of a mother to me than my own mom ever was."

"But… Daronne and Mom mean the same thing," I point out with a laugh.

"Yeah, I know. For some reason, my mom was okay with Daronne, so we stuck with that. Even Pay calls her that now." Before I can ask about how his dad felt about the whole thing, we reach the stairs, and a tall, elegant blonde woman stands waiting. The air shifts immediately, and I can tell without a doubt that this is King's mother. Not because they look alike, they don't, but her words give it away.

"I should have known you'd go see her first. Like father, like son," she says, her tone dripping with disdain. "What's the point of giving birth if your child chooses another woman to be his mother?" The venom in her voice makes me raise my eyebrows, and I feel King stiffen next to me. Still, he leans forward, kissing her cheeks politely.

"Hello, Mother. I knew I'd see you at dinner," he says, his voice even but tense. He squeezes my hand before turning to me. "Mom, this is Inès. Inès, this is my mother."

I force a warm smile, extending my hand. "It's very nice to meet you, Mrs. Ashford."

She looks at my hand as though I've smeared it with something vile, her eyes narrowing. "Hmm, same," she mutters, not bothering to take my hand.

My smile falters as I quickly glance at my hand, wondering if something's wrong with it. What the heck?

"Mom," King grits out through clenched teeth, clearly holding back frustration.

"Well, we should head to the dining room," she says, ignoring his tone completely. "Your grandmother has been waiting." Without waiting for us, she turns and walks off, her posture rigid. King is practically vibrating with anger, while I'm left standing there in shock.

"This is going to be interesting," I murmur under my breath as we follow her.

INÈS

SECOND BEST ISN'T SO BAD

We walk to the dining room in silence. Kingsley still seems upset, but I hold his hand to let him know I'm fine and can take care of myself. I didn't expect his mom to like me immediately, I'm a stranger in her home, but as long as everyone is respectful, we won't have a problem. If there's one thing my mother taught me, it's to never let anyone who thinks they're better than me disrespect me. I know my worth.

As soon as we enter the dining room, the first person I see is Paisley. When she sees us, she gets up and hugs me warmly, and I can't help but smile. Then she hugs her brother, but before letting go, she whispers, "She's in a mood today." I don't need to ask to know that the "she" Paisley is referring to is their mom.

Kingsley nods then looks to his left, and his face lights up. I follow his gaze and see a petite older woman standing by his mom. I'm guessing that's his grandmother. When she sees Kingsley, she smiles brightly. With his hand in mine,

Kingsley walks directly toward her. He lets go of me and hugs his grandmother tightly as she pats his back.

"My sweet boy," she says, pulling away just enough to cup his cheeks. Kingsley has to bend down so she can reach his head without stretching out her arms.

"I missed you, Grams," Kingsley whispers, and my heart warms. "I'm sorry I haven't come down to see you. I've been really busy with school."

"It's okay, I understand! And who is this pretty young lady?" she asks, looking at me with a sweet smile, which I return.

"This is Inès. Inès, this is my grandmother."

"It's a pleasure to meet you. Your grandson has told me a lot about you," I say, gently shaking her hand. Her grip is firm as she pulls me into a hug.

"It's very nice to meet you. You are beautiful, dear," she says, making me blush.

"Thank you," I reply as we let go of each other.

"Son!" a deep voice calls, causing me to look behind me, and oh my God, it's like looking at an older version of Kingsley. This must be his dad. The resemblance is uncanny except for his salt and pepper hair.

Kingsley grabs my hand, and I don't miss how he stands a bit taller, as if trying to prove something. They're both tall, but his dad is just a few inches taller and a bit broader, making me feel like a kid standing next to them.

"Dad." I can tell something's off by the way Kingsley stiffens. I want to ask, but I keep quiet as Mr. Ashford's blue eyes land on me.

"You must be Inès. It's a pleasure; I'm Atticus," he says, showing me his dimples. Jesus, this family is beautiful. Atticus holds out his hand for me to shake, and thank God

Kingsley is holding my left hand, because I don't think he would have let go.

I clear my throat because, yeah, now I'm nervous. Something tells me if there's anyone I should be nervous around, it's Atticus. "The pleasure is mine, sir," I say, shaking his hand. I almost yelp when Kingsley squeezes my left hand hard. Okay, so he doesn't like me calling his dad 'sir'? Got it!

His dad chuckles. "Please, Atticus is fine. Shall we sit? I'm starving." Atticus moves back to the other side of the table, next to his wife. Kingsley and I sit next to his grandmother, and Paisley sits almost in the middle.

The staff serves us smoked salmon and avocado tartare, which is delicious.

"So, Inès, I heard you're French?" Atticus asks once the food is served and the staff leaves.

Kingsley has his hand placed on my thigh, almost protectively, but who is he protecting me from? I get that his mom doesn't like me, but his dad seems chill.

"Yes, sir, Atticus," I choke out. "We migrated to the United States when I was ten," I explain.

"That must not have been easy, leaving your home at that age," Grams says next to me with a gentle look in her eyes.

"It wasn't at first, and I miss home, but my family tries to go back for vacation whenever we can," I say as Kingsley's gentle hand strokes my thigh, letting me know he's here.

"Where in France are you from?" Paisley asks.

I smile. "Marseille."

"We used to go to Marseille a lot when we were kids. I always loved it there," Paisley says. I miss my home, that's for sure.

"It's a beautiful city," I say, and we fall into easy conversation, with even Kingsley participating here and there. The only one who's quiet is his mom, but I don't mind. The rest of the family seems nice, so I begin to relax. That is, until the main course is brought out: beef tenderloin with red wine reduction.

Everything is going so well, but then Kingsley's mom says: "I can't believe you would bring one of the many girls you sleep with into my house." Though she tried to make it sound like she was murmuring, it's clear she meant for me to hear it.

The dining room falls into an uncomfortable silence. Kingsley stiffens beside me, and I can feel the tension radiating off him. I take a deep breath, gently setting my fork down, refusing to give his mother the reaction she clearly wants.

Kingsley stands up, likely intending to confront his mom, but before he can speak, his dad intervenes. "Enough. That was completely uncalled for." The firmness in Atticus's voice catches me off guard. I didn't expect him to come to my defense, and judging by the look on Kingsley's face, neither did he.

"What? I just think it's disrespectful to his, "

"Thank you for dinner. Always a pleasure, Mother," Kingsley interrupts coldly as he reaches for my hand.

"Oh, don't go," Kingsley's grandmother pleads, and I feel a pang of guilt.

Kingsley bends down and kisses the top of her head. "Don't worry, Grams. I'm not leaving Canada. I'll make some time for you tomorrow, how does that sound?" His tone softens when he speaks to her, momentarily making me forget my anger.

"Sounds good, my boy. You take care of her, alright?" She smiles warmly at me, and I return the gesture, my heart swelling at her kindness.

"Planning on it. I love you."

"I love you, too," she says to him, and I give her a quick hug before Kingsley guides me toward the door.

"Son," his father calls out.

"I'll see you at work tomorrow," Kingsley replies, kissing Paisley's head before leading me out of the room.

Once we're outside the dining room, away from prying eyes, Kingsley turns and kisses me, deeply, passionately, leaving me breathless. It's the kind of kiss that makes the world disappear, if only for a moment. When he pulls back, he searches my eyes. "Are you okay?"

Am I okay? "With a kiss like that, how could I not be? Are you okay?"

"I need to punch something," he mutters, his jaw tight as he guides me down the hallway. We reach a door, and when he opens it, it reveals a large garage filled with cars. Without hesitation, he grabs two jackets hanging on a hook, slipping one onto my shoulders. I don't care whose it is, it smells like him, and that's all that matters.

"Where are we going?" I ask as he grabs a random set of keys and unlocks the nearest car, a sleek black SUV. He opens the passenger door and helps me in, his movements almost too calm.

"To Justin's," he says, shutting my door before rounding the vehicle and getting in. He starts the engine, the low rumble filling the garage.

"Please tell me you're not planning on punching Justin," I half-joke, eyeing him nervously.

He glances at me, a small chuckle escaping his lips. "You're cute," he says, shifting the car into reverse and backing out of the garage.

"Wait, I need to get Beau," I tell him.

"He is being taken care of, I promise," he tells me, but that's not enough for me.

"No, I don't feel comfortable leaving him here alone with people he doesn't know."

He softens a little. "I'll have someone drop him off, how about that?"

"Thank you," I say, and he rushes over to squeeze my hand.

As we drive away, I can feel the tension still lingering in the air, but feeling his hand on mine grounds me.

"What a bitch!" Meghan practically shouts, her voice thick with anger.

We're at Justin's house now, and when I asked King if he was planning to punch Justin earlier, I swear I was joking. Yet here we are, in the basement that's been transformed into a boxing gym. Justin's house is impressive, maybe not as grand as the Ashford estate, but it's definitely up there. I mean, they've got a full-on boxing ring down here, where Justin and Kingsley are going at it like they're in some underground fight club. I know Justin owns a gym in Boston, I've even been there a few times, but I've never seen them spar like this.

They're brutal with each other, but they avoid hitting each other in the face because King's got meetings tomorrow, and when Justin jokingly called him "uppity" King responded with a gut punch so hard Meghan and I gasped. But Justin didn't let up, he returned the punch with twice the force, and I'm sure Kingsley's going to be bruised all over by the end of this. I couldn't watch any longer, so I turned to Meghan and told her about dinner, trying to distract myself.

A few minutes after we got here, someone came by and dropped Beau off. As soon as I had him in my arms, a wave of comfort washed over me. There's something grounding about his soft fur and wagging tail. Now, he's happily running around the basement, investigating every corner and pawing at things that catch his curiosity.

I return my attention to Meghan, who still looks just as angry. "I just can't believe her audacity!" she exclaims, her voice echoing in the expansive basement.

"It's fine," I say, keeping my tone calm, though I can still feel the sting of King's mother's words. "She's looking for a reaction, and I'm not giving her one."

"Still, fuck her," Meghan snaps, her eyes flashing with indignation. "You don't deserve to be treated like that."

Her loyalty makes me smile despite the situation. Meghan has always been fiercely protective, and seeing her so outraged on my behalf makes me feel loved. In the background, Justin and King are still sparring in the boxing ring, trading blows with the kind of intensity that makes me wince every time a punch lands.

Though I'm upset about Kingsley's mom's attitude, I've decided not to let it consume me. "I'm fine, Meg. I'm a big girl. I get that some people are just… wired that way." I pause, taking a deep breath. "As long as she doesn't push it further."

"Doesn't give her the right to be a bitch about it," Meghan says firmly. Her protective streak is coming out strong, and I decide to change the subject before she decides to confront Kingsley's mom herself.

"What about you? How are you getting along with Justin's parents?" I ask, steering the conversation to safer ground. When we arrived earlier, Justin's parents seemed genuinely warm and welcoming, and, frankly, stunning. What is it with rich people just looking effortlessly beautiful?

Justin's mom is gorgeous with beautiful dark skin, brown eyes, and curly hair. His dad is just as handsome and very nice. The first thing I noticed was his teeth, they're so white and beautiful against his dark skin.

"They love me," Meghan admits, her voice tinged with emotion. "His mom is so sweet, she does everything to make sure I'm comfortable. It's not something I'm used to with my own mom, and it made me cry a little."

"I'm glad, Meg. You deserve that love. You deserve to be cherished."

She smiles, but then her expression shifts. "Well, except… I met Kingsley's sister earlier today, and she looked like she hated me. She came over when I was the only one downstairs, so I answered the door. At first, she was sweet, introduced herself as Kingsley's sister, and said she wanted to talk to Justin. But when I introduced myself, she gave me this disgusted once-over, rolled her eyes, and just walked off. I was flabbergasted, how old is she, fourteen?"

I suppress a laugh. "She's sixteen," I correct.

"You know something," Meghan says, narrowing her eyes. "Spill."

"And have you go all Meghan about it? No way." This time I can't stop the laughter.

"Go all Meghan about it?" she echoes, feigning offense.

"You know, get all dramatic over the smallest thing. Don't deny it; you know you do."

She glares at me playfully. "No, I don't." But then she laughs.

"It's honestly harmless, she just apparently has a crush on Justin. She thought they'd get married."

Meghan's eyes widen a little. "Aw, bless her heart," she says, and I give her a look.

"Just be nice. I know how you get about J, but she's just a kid," I warn, causing her to roll her eyes.

"Of course, I'll be nice. I'm not actually threatened by a sixteen-year-old."

"Good, because you shouldn't be," I reply, just as my phone buzzes with a notification. I glance at the screen and see it's an email from Nathan. A frown tugs at my lips as I open it. It's late, and he seems all too comfortable sending me emails well into the evening.

From: nathan.salvatore@ashford.edu

    To: ines.dubois@ashford.edu

    Subject: Excited for Next Semester

Hi Inès,

I hope this email finds you well. I wanted to follow up on the TA position you've accepted for next semester. I trust you've had a chance to review the welcome packet, but please don't hesitate to reach out if you have any questions or need clarification on any of the details.

Just as a reminder, the position will involve assisting with lectures, grading assignments, and holding office hours for students. You'll also be expected to lead discussion groups and potentially help with research projects. I'm confident it will be a rewarding experience, and I'm happy to help guide you through the transition into the role.

If you'd like to meet before the semester kicks off to go over anything or discuss expectations further, I'm more than happy to find time for that.

Looking forward to hearing from you.

Best regards,
>   Nathan Salvatore
>   Department of Psychology
>   Ashford University

My frown deepens as I read through the email, there's nothing new here. It's definitely unnecessary, so I decide to ignore it.

"Everything okay?" Meghan asks, glancing over.

"Yeah, just an email about school, that's all," I reply, brushing it off.

We continue to talk for a while longer until we've had enough of watching our men beat the crap out of each other. Finally, we tell them to knock it off, and they stop immediately. King takes my hand and leads me to the bedroom next to Justin's.

"We'll stay here tonight," he announces, peeling off his sweaty gym clothes.

"But I don't have anything to wear," I protest, glancing down at the dress I'd worn to dinner.

He doesn't respond, just walks over to what appears to be a walk-in closet, moving with a quiet confidence that makes my pulse quicken. Every step he takes seems deliberate, muscles rippling beneath his skin, drawing my gaze like a magnet. The inked lines of his tattoos trace the story of him, each one a piece of the man I've fallen in love with, but it's the one with my name, etched near his heart, that always makes my stomach flip.

He returns with a shirt in hand. "Wear this, and nothing else."

I take the shirt, a man's large, and look up at him. "Uh, no offense to Justin, but I'm not wearing his shirt to bed." I wrinkle my nose, knowing it's a boundary I won't cross.

King's mouth twitches into a smile, clearly amused. "I love you for that, but this is actually mine. This is my room, Justin has his own room at my place."

I finally take a proper look around the room. It's decorated in dark, masculine colors, just like King's style. There's a king-sized bed, a dresser, two nightstands, and a small TV. Photos line the walls, pictures of Justin and Kingsley from when they were younger and some from college, standing in front of Justin's gym.

I roll my eyes. "Are you sure you two aren't in love or something?"

"The sooner you accept it, the better. What, you jealous?" he teases, his eyes sparkling with mischief.

"How could I not be? Meghan and I are clearly playing second fiddle here." I strip off my clothes, even my thong, and put on his shirt. It smells just like him, clean, masculine, comforting.

"Second best isn't so bad." He winks, heading into the en suite bathroom.

When Kingsley comes back out, freshly showered and only wearing boxer briefs, he looks as delicious as ever. He lies down on the bed, and I straddle him, my eyes tracing the bruises already forming on his torso.

"Why do you do this to yourself?" I ask, my fingers lightly brushing over the bruises, careful not to hurt him.

"I needed a release," he admits, his voice softer now. "I had so much pent-up anger, and I needed to get it out somehow." When I don't respond, just keep staring at his battered abs, he hooks a finger under my chin, lifting my gaze to meet his. "Papillon? [1] I'm fine. This is what we've done since we were kids. We do it safely, I promise."

---

1. Butterfly.

"I know," I whisper, my voice trembling with the weight of emotions I can no longer contain. "I just... I love you so much, King. I couldn't bear it if something happened to you."

He stills completely, as if time itself has frozen. His breath catches, his body unmoving, before his eyes slowly come alive, like dawn breaking through the darkest night. A slow, radiant smile stretches across his face, full of unrestrained joy, as if he's just heard the most beautiful words in existence.

"What did you just say?" His voice is rough, almost disbelieving.

I laugh, even as my heart pounds in my chest, exposed in a way I've never allowed before. "Shut up, you knew this already." I shove him lightly, careful to avoid his bruises, but he barely seems to notice.

"Yes, but I didn't think I'd hear it anytime soon." He exhales sharply, like a man who has just been given oxygen after suffocating. "Fuck, Inès, I need to hear you say it again, maybe in both English and French." His hands cradle my face, his touch reverent, as if I'm something sacred, something he's terrified of losing.

I hold his gaze, my soul unraveling at the way he looks at me, like I'm his entire world. "I love you, Kingsley Ashford," I whisper, the words tasting like forever. "Please don't break my heart."

His thumb strokes my cheek, his voice steady, a vow carved in stone. "I promise you, Inès, I will never break your heart. Because it belongs to me. Just as I belong to you."

Then his lips crash onto mine, fierce, claiming, desperate. He tastes of devotion, of longing, of a love too big for words. I kiss him back with everything I have, as if I can pour every ounce of love, every unspoken promise, into him.

Breaking away, I trail kisses along his jaw, savoring the

rough stubble that tickles my lips, down to his neck where his pulse thrums wildly beneath my touch. Then lower, to the bruises on his torso. I press my lips to each one, a silent vow, a prayer, worshiping every wound as if my love can heal them.

"Je t'aime, I love you, je t'aime..."[2] I murmur between kisses, my voice soft, reverent. I want him to feel it, to absorb it into his very bones, to know that he is loved, deeply, completely, unconditionally.

His breath stutters, his fingers threading through my hair, pulling me back up until our foreheads touch. His eyes burn with something raw, something infinite.

"Je ne pense pas que tu réalises à quel point tu me possèdes, Inès."[3]

His hands trail down my spine, holding me as if I'm something precious, something irreplaceable. His voice is thick with emotion, his accent curling around the words like silk.

"You are my breath, my fever, my fire." His voice is raw, unguarded. "Without you, I am nothing but a shadow, a man lost in a colorless world. But with you, my love, I am whole."

His thumb grazes my lips, his gaze softening, turning tender. "Do you know why I call you Queen?"

I blink up at him, my lips curling into a small, teasing smile. "Because your nickname is King?"

He chuckles, shaking his head. "Well, yes, but there's more to it." His expression turns serious, his grip tightening ever so slightly.

"I call you Queen because no other word is worthy. Not 'princess,' not 'Goddess,' nothing else holds the weight of

---

2. I love you.
3. I don't think you realize just how much you own me, Inès.

257

what you are to me. You don't just rule my heart, you own it. Every glance, every smile, every moment you breathe in my presence, you leave me powerless. You walk into a room, and the world rearranges itself around you, like even the universe knows who reigns here."

His lips brush against mine, a whisper of a kiss, but it holds a world of meaning.

"Mon amour, ma vie, ma Reine… Je suis à toi. Maintenant, demain, pour toujours."[4]

Tears sting my eyes, but I don't let them fall. Instead, I kiss him, slow and deep, pouring every ounce of love, every silent promise, every forever into him. And he takes it all, drinking me in like I'm the only thing keeping him alive.

"Et moi, je suis à toi," I whisper against his lips. "Toujours."[5]

---

4. My love, my life, my Queen… I am yours. Now, tomorrow, forever.
5. And I am yours. Always.

INÈS

THE REDHEAD BEHIND FROSTED GLASS

Today is Monday, and since King is working, he decided to bring me to his office. I am seated quietly on the plush leather couch in the corner, watching him move with quiet authority. There's something mesmerizing about the way he carries himself, so self-assured, so effortlessly in control. I marvel at how grown-up he is, how natural it feels for him to not only own his space but seemingly command the world around him with ease.

Behind him, the floor-to-ceiling windows offer a stunning view of the city skyline, made even more magical by the heavy snow falling softly outside, turning the city into a winter wonderland.

The office is nearly empty, it's the day before New Year's Eve, and the building feels hushed, almost intimate. It's just the two of us in this vast, impressive space, and for a moment, it feels like we're the only two people in the world.

We've been here for a little over an hour, and he hasn't stopped working. I'm glad I brought some schoolwork with me, hoping it would keep me occupied and prevent me from distracting him. But no matter how hard I try, my mind keeps wandering. This morning, on our way to the office, he mentioned that once he becomes the official COO, his responsibilities will increase significantly. It's something I've known all along, but hearing it out loud has hit me harder than I expected. It could mean he'll have to move back to Canada, and the thought of that sends a wave of panic through me. I can't just pick up and move here, not now, at least. My family is in the U.S., and with at least eight more years of school ahead of me, there's no way I can leave.

I'm not sure how to bring up the conversation with him, but it's been nagging at me for over an hour. I can't ask him to give up his dreams and responsibilities for me, just as I wouldn't want him to ask me to give up mine. Becoming a neurologist has always been my passion. My grandfather suffered from Alzheimer's, and watching him gradually lose his memories and sense of self left a lasting impact on me, and on my entire family. I was young, but I understood what was happening. I saw how helpless he was, and the heart-breaking reality that there was no cure. That's why I chose to pursue neurology, to unravel the mysteries of the brain and, hopefully, help families like mine who are lost and heartbroken. I want to dedicate my career to finding better treatments.

"Queen?" King's voice pulls me from my thoughts. I glance up, meeting his gaze. He looks so polished, so professional in his suit, a sight I'm not used to. I'm pretty sure this is the first time I've ever seen him dressed like this and, God, does it look good on him. There's something about the way the tailored fabric clings to his frame that makes him seem even more sexy.

"Yes?" I smile back at him as he shows me those irresistible dimples.

"Come here." He gestures for me to join him. I close my book, setting it aside as I get up and make my way to him. He moves slightly from his desk to allow me to sit on his lap. "What's bothering you? You looked like you were deep in thought over there," he says, running his fingers through my hair. "Is it your blood sugar? I checked it thirty minutes ago, and it was at normal levels."

King has the same app on his phone that I use for my Dexcom, so he always has access to my glucose levels. He's never casual about it, when it comes to my diabetes, he's all business. He takes it seriously, sometimes even more than I do, and there's a certain comfort in knowing he's always keeping an eye on me.

I take a deep breath, laying my head on his chest. "It's not that. My levels are fine…"

"Talk to me."

"It's just… I was thinking about what it would mean for us, for our relationship, if you move back here once you become the COO," I say softly, as uncertainty coils in my chest. "Are we going to try long distance? Because logically, I don't think it'll work. But I also don't want to lose you. I understand that work is important…"

Before I can say more, he hooks a finger under my chin, tilting my face up until our eyes meet. His gaze is steady, unwavering. "Not as important as you, Inès."

My breath catches. He can't mean that.

Last night, so much was said, words I had longed to hear, emotions laid bare. When I told him I loved him, he didn't hesitate, didn't run. He gave me *everything*. But this… this is different. This is his career, the thing he's built since he was fifteen, the dream he's sacrificed so much for. How can I possibly compare?

"King…" I say, needing to *understand*.

He exhales, running a hand down my arm before threading his fingers through mine. "I love my job. I've worked hard to get where I am, and I'm damn proud of that." He pauses, squeezing my hand like he's grounding himself. Then his voice drops to something softer, something *unshakable*. "But I love you more."

The weight of his words sinks in, thick and undeniable.

"I'm meeting with my father and the board before we leave Canada," he continues, cupping my face with both hands, his thumbs stroking my cheeks. "I want to discuss plans to open a new office. We need one in the States anyway. And Boston…" He smiles like he's already made his decision. "Boston is where my heart is."

I barely have time to process before his lips crash into mine, claiming me in a kiss so deep, so *consuming*, I feel it in every nerve ending. I melt into him, moaning softly as his hands slide into my hair, holding me like he never wants to let go. But I break the kiss resting my forehead against his.

"Are you sure? I'm not exactly easy to love," I say, my voice soft but serious. "I have diabetes, I can't cook, and I'm obsessed with school in a way that most people don't get. Speaking of school, I still have years left to go. And marriage? Kids? I don't want any of that, not yet, not anytime soon." I pause, letting my words sink in, hoping he understands the weight of what I'm saying.

"I've known all of this about you long before I asked you out," he says, his voice steady, eyes locking with mine. "I'm a patient man, Queen, and for you, I'd wait an eternity." He pauses as if choosing his next words carefully. "There's just one small thing I need to handle before we head back to Boston. But, baby, I love you, all of you, and I'll keep loving you until my dying days. I'd follow you anywhere, not because I have to, but because home is wherever you are."

"I love you, too. So much," I say before crashing my lips onto his. We kiss until my lips feel numb. Then there's a knock at the door. We both chuckle at the same time. I pull away, but he pulls me back for one more kiss.

"I'm sorry, butterfly, that's my meeting. Otherwise, I would have taken you back to the house and shown you just how much I love you."

I smile and give him another peck. "It's okay. You can make it up to me later. I need to go anyway, I promised Meg mani-pedis."

"Okay, the driver will drop you off. Be careful and text me as soon as you're with Meghan," he says as I get off his lap and gather my stuff.

"I will," I tell him as he gets up and adjusts his pants.

"Alright, baby. I love you."

"Love you, too," I say, giving him one last kiss before he opens the door, revealing a beautiful redhead who has to be around my age, if not younger. She's gorgeous and smiles at me with a genuine sweetness. I smile back.

"Inès, this is Emma. She's a family friend. Emma, this is my girlfriend, Inès."

I extend my hand to her, and she shakes it warmly. "It's nice to meet you," I say with a smile.

"It's nice to meet you, too." Her voice is sweet, almost angelic.

"Well, I'll let you get to your meeting. King, I'll text you," I say before turning to leave. But as I walk away, I can't help glancing back at them. King's office is surrounded by clear glass, which he showed me can be frosted for privacy. Right now, it's not, and I can see him pull her into a warm familiar hug, his hand splayed on the small of her back. I've never been the jealous type, I've always prided myself on being more level-headed than that.

And, well, let's be honest, King is my first boyfriend so I've never really needed to be jealous. But the way she smiles up at him, the ease with which they're so close, makes my skin crawl.

My frown deepens when King presses a button on a remote, frosting the glass. It might be my jealousy speaking, but I can't shake the feeling that this isn't right! Or am I just reading too much into the situation?

"Okay, what's going on?" Meghan asks. We're currently in the sitting room of Justin's house, fresh from getting our nails done for the New Year's Eve party tomorrow. Meghan is indulging in the weirdest food I've ever seen, a peanut butter and jelly sandwich dipped in pickle juice. Yes, this psychopath is *dipping* the sandwich in pickle juice before eating it. Every time she does, I swear I gag a little.

"Nothing, I'm fine." I shrug, looking back out the window at Justin and Beau playing fetch in the snow. It's very cute; they're both covered in snow.

"You forget I know you. You've been quiet all day today. Seriously, Inès, what's wrong?" she asks. I glance back at her, instantly regretting it as she takes another bite of her soggy sandwich and then washes it down with a sip of pickle juice. Ugh.

"Maybe it's what you're eating, Meg. Maybe that's what's got me all quiet. I mean, seriously, that's disgusting."

"Hey, don't knock it until you try it! This stuff is fantastic. I could eat ten more of these, and I'm not even exaggerating. I would let you try some, but I don't want to share. Sorry." She licks her fingers, grinning.

"Oh darn, I really wanted to try some," I reply with heavy sarcasm.

She rolls her eyes. "Whatever, hater. Anyway, what happened? Is it Kingsley? Did you two have a fight?"

"No, we actually had a pretty perfect morning."

"But?"

"I wouldn't say something bad happened… it's just… I'm overreacting, seeing things that aren't there," I explain, and she frowns.

"How about I be the judge of whether you're overreacting or not?"

I have no idea where King is right now. He was supposed to come pick me up for dinner, but I haven't heard from him. I don't want to call and seem, I don't know, desperate. I guess I'm completely overthinking everything. Normally, I'm pretty secure in our relationship.

"When I was leaving King's office, he introduced me to this gorgeous girl he was about to have a meeting with. As I was leaving, he was… embracing her, and they just seemed so comfortable with each other…" I sigh, running my hands over my face. "I guess I just feel a little insecure, though I have no reason to be. King has never given me a reason to feel insecure… Tell me I'm crazy, M."

"Oh, babe, you are not crazy. Not at all. You're feeling a little insecure, most of us do at times. What you need to do is talk to your man. Tell him how you feel," she says, but I immediately start shaking my head.

"No, that's not necessary. There's no need to turn something so insignificant into something big. I'm fine," I assure her.

I'm fine.

It's fine.

Everything is fine.

KINGSLEY

IS IT A BOARD MEETING OR A SOAP OPERA?

"She's really pretty, Kingsley. You two look good together. I'm happy for you," Emma says softly as I hand her a bottle of water.

"Thanks." I exhale heavily, sinking into the couch across from her. "Let's just hope this meeting goes well, or I might not have a girlfriend anymore."

Emma frowns as she takes a sip of water. "You haven't told her about the arrangement?"

"I was hoping I wouldn't have to tell her until I came up with a better solution. This whole thing is ridiculous," I mutter, and the look in Emma's eyes turns somber. For a second, I feel like an ass. "I'm sorry. I know this isn't easy for you, or your dad."

"It's fine," she says, though the sadness lingers in her voice. "Trust me, I don't want this marriage either. You're like my cousin." She wrinkles her nose, her attempt at levity making me chuckle.

Emma's father, Mr. Whitmore, is currently in the hospital,

fighting cancer. His condition has taken a turn for the worse, and time is no longer on our side. He's always been one of my dad's closest friends, a business ally, and a man who, to me, seemed invincible growing up. Now, watching him face the end makes everything even more complicated.

"How's he doing?" I ask, breaking the silence that had settled over us.

Emma stays quiet for a moment, staring at the floor, lost in her thoughts. Finally, she shakes her head, her eyes glistening with unshed tears.

"The doctors gave him six months." Her voice is barely a whisper.

I rise from the couch and grab the box of tissues on my desk and hand it to her before I sit beside her. Pulling her gently into my arms, I hold her close. "I'm so sorry, Emma."

She wipes her tears, trying to steady herself. "I'm fine," she murmurs, clearing her throat. "I just wish I didn't have to go through all of this just to get the company. I wish it could already be mine."

"It *is* yours," I say firmly, letting go of her as I pour myself a glass of whiskey. "And trust me, my plan will work. Just follow my lead."

Emma chuckles lightly, though there's doubt in her eyes. "I doubt that. Uncle Atticus is ruthless. Remember when we tried to say no to this two years ago? He didn't even let us speak. I'm low-key terrified of him. And to think he used to play princess with me when I was little." She shakes her head, a soft laugh escaping her lips.

I grin at the memory. She's right. My dad can be terrifying when it comes to business, uncompromising and relentless. But this time, I've got a trick up my sleeve.

"Don't worry. Today will be different," I assure her, sipping my whiskey.

"How?" she asks, skeptical.

"Have you ever heard the saying, 'Every monster has their monster'?" I smirk, watching the confusion spread across her face.

"What are you talking about?" Just then, there's a knock at the office door, and my smirk widens.

"Watch and learn," I tell her then call out, "Come in."

The door swings open, and the energy in the room shifts instantly as Josie walks in with the kind of confidence only she possesses. Her stride is purposeful, and when she spots me, her face lights up with that warm, tender look she always reserves just for me.

There's something about Josie, there always has been. The relationship between her and my parents is… complicated. My mom has always hated her, and I still can't figure out why. It's not like Josie and my dad interact much. The only time they're in the same room is when it concerns me and Pay. In those moments, they act more like co-parents than anything else, but outside of that, there's very little interaction between them.

Still, I've noticed something over the years: If I ever wanted something and my dad was dead set against it, or if my mom and dad did something I didn't like when I was younger, all I had to do was mention it to Josie. And like magic, the next day, my dad would apologize or change his stance. The thing is, my dad *doesn't* apologize. Ever. But Josie has this strange pull over him, one that even my mother can't match.

"Hi, King," Josie greets, wrapping me in a hug. She feels so small now. I remember when she towered over me when I was ten, that was the last time she ever did.

"Hey, Mom, thanks for coming."

"I told you, whenever you need me," she says, kissing my

cheek. She lets go and strides toward Emma. "Hi, sweet girl. Look at you, so beautiful, you look just like your mom." They hug, and I can see Emma relax slightly under her warmth.

"Thank you, Josie," Emma says softly. Before she can say more, the door swings open, of course, my dad doesn't knock. He freezes when he sees Josie, clearly caught off guard, and his jaw clenches in that way that used to make me nervous as a kid.

"I thought this was a business meeting?" he asks, still standing by the door, hands buried in his pockets, pretending to act casual. In my peripheral vision, I catch Josie casually walking over to the bar, pouring herself a drink.

"It is," I say, mirroring his posture, hands in my pockets, too.

"Then why is our house manager here?" He can't conceal his irritation, but before I can respond, Josie slams the whiskey bottle down on the table. Not hard enough to break it, but enough to command attention. She turns, locking eyes with my dad.

"Atticus, have a seat," she demands, her voice cool and firm.

They stand there, locked in some sort of silent showdown, and that's when I see it. For the first time in my life, maybe because I was too young before or maybe they were just that good at hiding it, the tension between them is so thick, it practically hums in the air. Holy shit. What the actual fuck?

My dad sits down on the sofa, his eyes never leaving hers. Josie follows suit, sitting directly across from him. The way he looks at her... it's the way I look at Inès. I've never seen him look at my mom like that. The shock hits me so hard it takes me a moment to realize I'm the only one still standing. I close my mouth and sit down next to Josie.

"I'm listening," my father finally says, tearing his gaze away from Josie to look at me.

I force myself to focus. "I can't marry Emma," I say, my heart pounding in my chest. "I'm in love with Inès."

The silence that follows is thick, charged. My father stays quiet, studying me with that same calm intensity only he seems to master, measured, calculating, unreadable.

Finally, he speaks. "We've already talked about this. You know your options. The only way you get the title of COO is if you marry Emma. This is something you've known for two years now, so I don't understand why you would put yourself in a position to fall for another woman. But that's not my problem. So if we're done here…" He moves to stand.

I grit my teeth so hard it's a wonder they don't crack. I glance at Josie, and for a split second, I feel like a kid again, complaining to my mother that Dad is being unfair. But I have no other choice.

Josie gives me a reassuring nod, and it's all I need.

I straighten, lift my chin. "I am not finished."

My voice is exactly what I want it to be, commanding. It stops my father in his tracks. He frowns at me, his expression unreadable, but I don't falter.

"This is as much my company as it is yours. I know it inside and out. If you think for a second that I'm not willing to walk away and build something of my own, you're sorely mistaken. And believe me, most, if not all, of our clients will follow me. So when I tell you Inès is the only woman I will ever marry, I'd sit and listen if I were you. Because you can't afford to have me as your competition."

A part of me is bluffing. But a much bigger part of me is daring him to test me. I will walk out right now if I have to.

I see the exact moment my father shifts from shocked to proud to *furious*, his expression tightening, his jaw clenching.

It's like looking into a mirror. He steps toward me, slow and deliberate, but just as he's about to breach my personal space, Josie moves between us, arms crossed.

"That's enough," she says coolly.

My father's anger dissipates in an instant. He smirks, his focus shifting entirely. "So this is why you're here?" he asks Josie, as if Emma and I have vanished from the room.

"I'm here to make sure you don't bully him into doing something he doesn't want."

My father scoffs. "Bully? Please. You raised him to be as dramatic as you."

"No," Josie counters, her voice sharp. "I raised him to be a man with morals. And his morals won't allow him to marry someone he doesn't love. That's something *you* do."

The second the words leave her lips, I see it. The flicker of something, guilt, pain, maybe both. My father stiffens, his posture rigid, as if she physically shoved him.

He exhales slowly. "I see," he says, his voice measured. There's no longer anger in his tone, only resolve and something else, something more difficult to place. He turns his attention to Emma, the only one still seated, then looks back at me. After a beat, he lowers himself back into his chair. "So, what's the plan?"

The air in the room shifts, lighter now. I exhale, clearing my throat before taking a seat as well. "Thank you," I say.

"Don't thank me yet. I need to hear this plan of yours before I decide whether or not you still have a job."

I want to tell him that he *can't* fire me, that I'm irreplaceable, but I hold my tongue. It's not enough to walk away from this engagement; there are responsibilities tied to it.

Emma was meant to take over her father's company, *Whitmore Opulence*, when she turns twenty-one. With her father's health in rapid decline, everyone assumed *I* would step in to manage the company in the interim, ensuring its stability until she was ready. But that won't work for me.

"Instead of me taking over Whitmore Opulence outright, we propose forming a trustee board," I explain. "It would consist of trusted executives from both EcoTech Innovations and Whitmore Opulence. This way, they can oversee the company's day-to-day operations and strategic decisions until Emma turns twenty-one."

My father's eyes narrow slightly. "A trustee board?" he repeats, his tone neutral. He isn't dismissing the idea outright, but he isn't sold on it either.

I hold his gaze. "Yes. That way, Whitmore Opulence remains stable, Emma gets the time she needs to prepare for her role, and I don't have to sacrifice my personal life for a business deal. It's a win-win."

For a long moment, my father doesn't say anything. Then with his fingers steepled beneath his chin, he says. "Convince me," we've got his attention, good.

"The board would ensure the company remains stable and prosperous in the meantime. I would take on the role of interim CEO, but it would be temporary, with a clear end date when Emma turns twenty-one. During that time, I'd focus on maintaining the company's success, implementing sustainable practices, and ensuring a smooth transition of power to Emma."

Emma speaks up, calm but determined. "I'd be actively involved in the company's operations, working under the guidance of you, Kingsley, and the trustee board. It would serve as hands-on training for me so that when I take over, I'll be fully prepared." She pauses for a moment, looking directly at my dad. "I know I don't have the same experience running a company like Kingsley or Pay, but I want to learn.

This way, I can step into my father's shoes when the time is right."

My dad leans back in his chair, his expression thoughtful. It's clear he hadn't expected this level of preparation from us. For a long time, the only plan had been for me to take over, and no one had questioned it until now.

"I'll admit," my dad says finally, "it's a good plan. One I didn't see coming." He turns to me with a sharp nod. "I'll speak to Declan about it."

This was easier than I expected. "Thanks, Dad," I say, and he offers a rare smile.

"Inès is a beautiful girl. Make sure you treat her well," he adds, his voice firm but approving.

I smile and nod in response.

Then his tone shifts. "Emma and Kingsley, would you give us the room?" Before I can move, Josie stands up.

"That won't be necessary," she says, but my dad doesn't back down.

"The room. Now." He repeats himself, and this time Emma quickly exits. I stay put, unsure of what's happening as Josie begins to walk away.

But before she reaches the door, my dad's voice cuts through the tension. "Gem, sit down." The command is sharp, and Josie freezes. What the hell is going on?

She turns back, looking livid, an expression I've only seen once, when I got wasted at a party and tried drugs. She ripped into me for an hour and made me work in the garden for a week. She's ruthless when she's angry, and right now, she's just as furious.

"You don't tell me…" Josie starts, her voice low with anger, but he interrupts.

"Sit. Down," he growls.

"Dad, maybe…" I try to step in, but Josie raises a hand to stop me.

"It's okay, King." She leans in, kissing my cheek softly. "I'm fine. Your dad and I just need to… talk." She makes her way back to the couch, her face still tense.

"Are you sure?" I hesitate, feeling uneasy. "I don't feel comfortable leaving."

Josie gives me a reassuring smile, but there's a strange tension behind it. "Trust me, I'm fine."

The way they're staring at each other, though, says otherwise. Either they're about to kill each other, or… No, I'm not even going to go there, there's no way that Josie and my dad are having an affair. I know my parents don't love each other, I have known it for a while now, but I can't possibly imagine he'd cheat on his wife with the woman who runs our home and raised us… Oh, God. No. I cringe, face scrunching in disgust, and quickly leave the room. Please, for the love of everything, don't let this be what I think it is. No kid should ever have to find out their parents still… do that.

INÈS

THE ART OF DECEPTION

B y the time King arrived at the Williams' house, it was too late for dinner. He apologized, saying his meeting ran later than anticipated. We didn't discuss why his meeting lasted past ten, nor did we address how weird it felt seeing him hug another person the way he did Emma.

We went back to his family home, where he helped with my insulin and held me through the night. He left again this morning, and I haven't heard from him. I thought he'd be free today since the gala is tonight, but it seems not. He promised he'd come back in time to get ready with me for the gala. Things are strange right now because we're normally very good at communicating, and the silence is unsettling.

Since the gala is from seven to midnight, Meghan and I started on our hair and makeup around five-thirty. Beau is with Pay who insisted on spending some time with him since she wasn't coming to the gala. Poor Beau, I think she's taking a million pictures of him as we speak.

"He'll be here. Don't worry," Meghan reassures me as I keep glancing at my phone. We're at Justin's house, having just finished our makeup.

"I know, but I can't shake this feeling in my stomach like something is going to go wrong," I explain, fidgeting as Meghan straightens my hair. I normally wear my hair curly, but tonight, I opted for straight.

"Nothing is going to happen. I'm sure if you ask him, he'll tell you the truth. King wouldn't lie to you," she says, and she's right. But I'm not sure tonight is the best time to have this conversation.

"You're right…" I concede.

"Of course, I am. I'm always right," Meghan says, making me laugh despite the tension.

A few minutes later, we hear a knock on the door. My heart skips a beat, knowing it has to be Kingsley.

"Come in," Meghan calls out, and when Kingsley opens the door and steps in, I breathe a sigh of relief. Seeing him feels like a balm to my anxiety, and I have to resist the urge to wrap my arms around him immediately.

"Hi."

"Hi," I respond shyly.

"Hi," Meghan mocks, and we both look at her. "What? I thought we were all saying hi."

"Hey, Meg, Justin was asking for you," Kingsley says, his gaze fixed on me.

"Right!" Meghan says, giving Kingsley a suspicious look. "Don't ruin her makeup," she warns, pointing a finger at him as she heads out.

Kingsley puts his hands up in surrender. "I'll try my best," he says with a grin then locks the door behind her. My heart races and my body tingles as he approaches. He sets down his suit and a small bag, which I hadn't noticed before, and draws closer to me.

"Come here," he demands softly, taking my hand and pulling me toward him. When our bodies press together, he cups my ass and lifts me up. I instinctively wrap my legs and arms around him, giggling.

"Hi," I repeat as he buries his face in the crook of my neck, inhaling deeply.

"Hi. I missed you," he says, making me want to cry.

I hug him tighter. "I missed you more."

"I know things have been weird. Don't think I haven't noticed, but we'll talk after tonight, alright? Whatever is wrong, I'll fix it, I am fixing it," he assures me, looking into my eyes. I fully believe that if something's wrong, he'll make it right, even if I'm not sure what it is yet.

Not knowing what else to say, I nod as he sets me on my feet.

"You are so fucking beautiful," he whispers, his fingers gently tracing my bottom lip. "Fuck." Then he kisses me, his lips crashing onto mine roughly, smudging my lip gloss. I moan into his mouth, and he deepens the kiss, thrusting his tongue inside. He wraps one hand around my neck and uses the other to pull me against his hard body, ensuring I feel how much he wants me.

"King," I gasp, my voice breaking with desperation. The intensity of his kiss makes my head spin, and when he bites my bottom lip, the sharp pleasure makes me moan.

"I feel like I haven't fucked you in weeks, butterfly," he murmurs breathlessly, his lips barely leaving mine.

"Please, please," I beg, my voice filled with longing.

"Fuck… baby, don't tempt me. We need to get ready," he says, pressing a final kiss to my lips before gently pulling away.

I pout, feeling the weight of his absence already. How has he managed to turn me into this craving mess?

"Don't pout. Just a few more hours, okay?" he says, stroking my cheek.

I nod, trying to contain my impatience.

"I got something for you." He reaches for the small bag he left on the bed. "Turn around."

I comply, and a few seconds later I feel the cool metal of a necklace as he fastens it around my neck. My hands instinctively touch it, eager to see it fully. When I turn to face him, my smile is wide.

"May I?" I ask, my excitement palpable.

"Of course," he replies with a smile, and I rush to the bathroom. My breath catches as I see the diamond tennis necklace sparkling under the light.

"It's beautiful," I exclaim, admiring the gift. "Thank you." I turn and give him a heartfelt kiss.

"You're welcome. I have one more gift for you," he says, placing a dark box on the counter. My curiosity piques as he opens it, revealing a silver butt plug with a jewel at the base.

"King…" I begin, my voice trembling with nervousness.

"Don't be scared. I'll go slow, I need you to be ready for tonight," he reassures me.

"Wait, you're planning on putting your… in my…" I chuckle nervously. "King, you're too big. You'll split me in half."

"I promise you I won't, and whenever you want me to stop just say your safe word and I will," he says. "Do you trust me?"

"Of course," I respond without hesitation.

"Good girl. Now, lower your panties to your ankles and bend over the counter. Hold on tight for me, Queen," he commands gently.

I swallow hard, but I obey, feeling a mixture of anticipation and nervousness as I follow his instructions.

I bend over the counter, gripping it tightly. The cool marble contrasts with the heat of my flushed skin. My breath quickens, a combination of nervousness and maybe a little excitement making my heart race.

Kingsley's voice is a low, possessive murmur as he speaks. "Good girl." The intensity in his tone sends a thrill through me, mixing with the anticipation crackling between us.

He goes to wash the plug first before walking behind me.

His hands are warm as they trail over my hips, spreading my legs slowly. I shiver at his touch, my body responding eagerly to his every movement. "Fucking beautiful," he murmurs before retrieving lube from the small bag he brought with him and coating the plug generously, making sure it will slide in smoothly.

"Relax for me," he says softly, his breath warm against my ear. "I promise I'll be gentle."

I nod, trying to steady my breathing as he positions the tip of the plug at my entrance. The cool sensation of the metal is startling, sending a jolt through me. Kingsley's hands are steady and reassuring as he guides the plug in slowly, allowing my body to adjust with each inch.

"Just breathe, papillon.[1] I'm right here," he whispers, his hands soothing my back.

As the plug slips fully inside, I gasp, feeling a mix of fullness and pressure. Kingsley's hand rests lightly on my lower back, his touch grounding me. He leans in and presses a soft kiss to the small of my back.

---

1. Butterfly.

"Good girl. You took that perfectly. How does it feel?" His voice is filled with concern and affection.

"It's… different. But good," I say as I take a step and feel the plug move as well. It's going to be an interesting evening.

"Perfect," he replies, his smile evident in his tone. "You look stunning." He helps me stand and turns me gently to face him. His eyes roam over me with admiration before he kisses me passionately.

"You're breathtaking," Kingsley says, his eyes filled with love and desire. "Let's finish getting ready so we can enjoy the evening together."

I nod, feeling a rush of affection. Kingsley showers quickly while I slip into my dress. The brown silk gown hugs my figure perfectly, with a plunging neckline. The fitted waist and voluminous silk organza skirt create a dramatic effect, complemented by the lace-appliquéd train and a thigh high slit. It feels bold and sophisticated.

By the time I'm done, Kingsley steps out of the shower, quickly dressing in his tailored suit. Between buttoning his shirt and adjusting his tie, he steals kisses every few moments, making me laugh at his ridiculousness. But I love it, the playful, carefree side of him that always manages to surface, even in the middle of his rush.

Eventually, we make it downstairs to meet Justin and Meghan. Meghan is radiant in her midnight-blue silk satin evening gown, featuring off-the-shoulder straps, intricate lace detailing, and subtle sequins. The flowing skirt cascades into a slight train. Justin and Kingsley both look sharp in their three-piece suits, their ties matching our dresses.

We all pile into the car, with Kingsley at the wheel, Justin in the passenger seat, and Meghan and me in the back. Kingsley drives with one hand while the other is twisted at an awkward angle just so he can rest it on my leg. It's as though he can't go a minute without being close to me, and it makes my heart flutter.

As we approach the gala venue, both Justin and Kingsley get out and open the doors for us. Kingsley hands the valet his car key and receives a card in return, slipping it into his suit pocket.

"Holy shit," Meghan says, looking up at the imposing structure before us.

"Wow," I echo, hooking my arm through Kingsley's as I gaze at the grand castle perched on the hill. The weathered stone edifice, complete with turreted towers and a grand entrance flanked by moss-covered statues, is awe-inspiring. The driveway is lined with luxury cars, many elegant guests arriving.

"Let's get you ladies inside," Justin says, taking Meghan's hand. The cold is biting, with snow scattered across the grass but not on the driveway, perhaps due to an under-surface heating system.

We enter the castle without issue. The doorman recognizes Kingsley and lets us in with a smile. Inside, the vaulted great hall, adorned with ancient tapestries, leads to hidden chambers with panoramic views. The surrounding gardens and reflective moat add to the castle's timeless allure. I have to commend Kingsley's mom for organizing such a breath-taking event.

The hall is buzzing with a mix of people. Justin spots his parents and goes to greet them with Meghan. Kingsley places a hand on the small of my back, guiding me to the bar. He orders a whiskey for himself while I decline a drink. We start to make our way to our table, but he stops midway.

"Here, I want to introduce you to some people," he says, leading me through the crowd.

We stop in front of three striking individuals: a handsome

Black man with a well-groomed beard, a stunning blonde woman, and a muscular white man a few inches taller than Kingsley. All three appear to be in their mid-thirties.

"Kingsley, my man, how the hell are you? I haven't seen you at poker in months," the white man says, pulling Kingsley into a hearty hug.

"I've been good but busy. I promise the second I'm back in Boston, we'll get together," Kingsley responds, returning the hug.

"You better. I miss taking all your money, man," the Black man says, grinning.

"Fuck off, you cheat like your life depends on it. Guys, this is Inès, my girlfriend," Kingsley introduces, wrapping an arm around my waist. "Inès, this is Calvin. He owns the biggest architecture company in Boston."

"Hello," I say, offering a polite smile and shaking his hand. Calvin returns the smile warmly.

"And this is Desmond, his brother. He owns, what, four restaurants across the U.S.?" Kingsley continues.

"Three, working on the fourth one," Desmond says, extending his hand for me to shake, and I do.

"Nice to meet you," I say.

"You finally grew some balls I see. Inès, let me tell you something, this man has been talking about you nonstop for over a year. I'm glad he finally got the courage to do something about it," Desmond says with a wink, making my cheeks flush.

"Me, too," I reply, smiling shyly.

"We should talk about how much you all love talking about my balls; it's becoming worrisome," Kingsley says, making everyone laugh.

The woman next to Calvin clears her throat, drawing our attention.

"Oh shit, excuse my manners. Kingsley, this is Abigail, my fiancée," Calvin introduces. Kingsley looks momentarily surprised but recovers quickly, shaking Abigail's hand.

"Abigail, it's nice to meet you. This is my girlfriend, Inès," Kingsley says.

"It's nice to meet you all," Abigail says sweetly, shaking our hands.

"We definitely need to get together once we're in the States. If you'll excuse us, it was good seeing you two again, and Abigail, it was lovely meeting you," Kingsley says, guiding me away.

As we continue mingling, my feet start to ache from the heels, and the cold is creeping in. Kingsley notices and drapes his suit jacket around me. His attentiveness to my comfort is one of the things I love about him. When he senses something is wrong, he does whatever he can to make it right.

A few moments later, I decide to freshen up in the bathroom, needing to pee. As I return from the bathroom, the warmth of the grand hall contrasts sharply with the chill that's settled over me. I scan the crowd for Kingsley, my heart sinking when I spot him with the same redhead from his office. She looks stunning in her sleeveless dress. I frown when I notice Kingsley's hand on her lower back as he leans in to hear something she is saying, her mouth right by his ear. They look cozy, too cozy. I feel that same familiar feeling running through me: jealousy, ugly jealousy. Why does he need to be that close to her, especially in front of everyone he just introduced me to as his girlfriend?

"Don't they look cute together?" a voice says beside me. I turn to see Kingsley's mom, her smile icy and insincere. My heart races, I'm already on edge from the scene I just witnessed.

"Excuse me?" I manage to ask. My voice is shaky despite my best efforts to stay strong.

"Oh, he didn't tell you? Oh dear, that's Kingsley's fiancée," she says with a condescending tone that makes me clench my fists. Her words pierce through me, but I try to hold my composure. There's no way Kingsley would be engaged without telling me. "Yes, it's been two years now. We were just waiting for Kingsley to finish college and come back home to marry the girl of his dreams."

Her words strike a painful chord. Despite my resolve, part of me believes her. But I won't let her have the satisfaction. I turn to confront Kingsley, only to have her grip my arm with a bruising hold.

"What, you think just because he fucks you and pays for expensive dresses that you're worthy of my son? No, you're just a whore, a gold-digging whore here for him to have a little fun with before he settles down with a sophisticated girl," she sneers, poking me in the chest. "Oh, and I'd get out of my house if I were you."

The insults hit hard. I've never been spoken to so cruelly. Her words make me feel small and worthless, and as much as I try to remind myself of my worth, I can't do it. I look back at Kingsley and the redhead; they do look cute together.

I'm not one for conflict. I avoid aggression and arguing because I find it pointless. I usually steer clear of cursing, Meghan and Camille handle that sort of thing, but Evelyn's blatant disrespect has pushed me to my limit. I can't leave without saying something. "Écoute-moi, espèce de connasse,"[2] I snap, my French a harsh contrast to the prim atmosphere.

Evelyn's eyes widen in shock. She might be American,

---

2. Listen to me, you fucking bitch.

but Kingsley told me that she has been in Quebec for twenty-three years, so she understood everything I just said. "Excuse me, you can't talk to me like that!" Her scandalized look might have been amusing under different circumstances, but I'm too angry to find it funny.

"Why not? It seems like it's a fitting name for you since you've been nothing but a bitch towards me since we met. Let this be the only time you ever fix your mouth to speak to me like that or touch me. Next time, I'll shove my foot so far up your ass, it'll knock out whatever sense you've got left! Got it? Espèce d'andouille!"[3] I spit out, turning on my heel and walking away before anyone can see me further humiliate myself.

Tears pour down my face uncontrollably as I flee the scene. I had a sinking feeling about Kingsley and the redhead, but I had tried to convince myself otherwise. Now, the reality is undeniable.

I remember that I'm wearing Kingsley's coat and approach the valet. I retrieve the card he was given and hand it over. A few minutes later, the car pulls up. I drop the coat on the ground and get in, driving away with a heavy heart.

The roads are clear of snow, but I drive cautiously, wiping my tears as I go. I need to get away from this pain as quickly as possible.

My phone rings, and I see it's Kingsley. I ignore the call, though I know I'm being childish. I should talk to him, but the hurt is too fresh. Meghan's call comes through next, and I decide to answer to tell her I'm leaving tonight.

"Inès?" Kingsley's angry voice comes through the phone, and my heart wrenches at his tone. "Why aren't you answering my calls? And where are you?"

---

3. You idiot!

"Fuck you, Kingsley. You don't need to worry about where I am anymore. We are done," I cry, my voice breaking.

"Ex... excuse you?" His shock is palpable, and it only makes my resolve stronger. I've never cursed at him before; respect has always been a cornerstone of our relationship. But he didn't respect me enough to be honest about his engagement.

"Are you engaged?" I demand, needing to know the truth.

There's a long, exasperated sigh on his end before he mutters, "Inès..."

Wrong answer. I hang up before he can finish. He said he loved me and would never hurt me. Clearly, that was a lie.

I deserve better than this.

KINGSLEY

WE WILL NEVER BE DONE

"F uck!" I curse, seething with frustration. How the fuck did I mess things up so badly? I should have told her. I should have explained. I was an idiot to think I could have her here and fix my problem without it getting back to her.

"Kingsley?" Meghan calls, her voice breaking through my turmoil.

"I need to go get her. I need a car," I say, storming back inside. When I find Inès, I swear I'll attach her to my fucking hip and never let her go.

"Oh, Kingsley, there you are. I think your dad is ready to announce you as the new COO of EcoTech," my mother says, reaching for my hand.

I snatch it away. "I can't right now, Mom, I need to go find Inès," I say, pushing past her.

"Don't tell me she's still here. Let me tell you, Kingsley, she is very rude."

I freeze and slowly turn to face her with my brows raised

in question. "What do you mean, still here? What did you do, Mother?" I ask, already knowing the answer to my question.

"Well, she saw you all cuddled up with Emma. And can I just say, you two looked very good together. I told her you were engaged and it's unbecoming for her to whore around with men about to be married." She laughs, as if anything about this is funny. "But then she insulted me. Can you believe that?"

A high-pitched ringing drowns out the sounds around me, making it nearly impossible to focus on anything else. I can't remember when my mother turned into this bitter, spiteful person, and for the longest time, I just accepted it. Truth be told, I didn't care, until now. I never thought she'd go this far, that she'd treat someone I love, someone I brought home, with such cruelty. My jaw clenches so tight it aches, and I can't stand to meet her eyes any longer. I turn away, unable to bear it.

"Oh, honey, don't…"

"I wouldn't do that if I were you." I hear Justin speak to my mother. I don't have to look to know he just stopped her from touching me, which I am grateful for. I am too angry and too on edge for her to even try to touch me, the only person who could calm me down is running from me, thinking I betrayed her after I promised never to hurt her.

"Son, here, take my car and go. People are staring." My dad's heavy voice rings out behind me as he places a hand on my shoulder.

I turn and grab the valet card he is offering me. "Deal with your wife before I do." I warn then walk out. I hand the valet the card while I keep trying to call Inès, but she keeps sending me straight to voicemail. Fireworks begin, signaling midnight and the start of a new year, and the love of my life is running away from me.

Meghan stands next to me, her arms crossed, looking concerned but staying quiet as I stare at my phone.

"I'm driving," Justin says when the valet brings my dad's car. I don't protest; as long as he gets me to my girl, that's all that matters. "Any idea where she would be?" Justin asks as I stare at my eight unread messages. Fuck.

"I don't..." Then I remember that there's one person in this car who would know, the only person Inès wouldn't do anything without warning. My eyes flick to Meghan, who is also on her phone typing a mile a minute. "Meg? If you know where she is, please tell me."

"What makes you think I know where she is?" With the amount of sass radiating from her, I figure she not only knows where Inès is, but she knows exactly why Inès is upset.

"Meg, come on, please, that's the woman I love."

She snorts. And though we are driving to what looks like the airport I know we are wasting precious time. "What you did was fucked up. Engaged? Really, Kingsley? If you were only interested in playing with her heart, you should have just stayed the fuck away from her. That girl is too sweet and deli-cate for you and your bitch ass mother to treat her like this, and yes, I said it, bitch, and if you or anyone got a problem with that, I invite you to call my number at 617- go-fuck-yourselves."

"Alright, enough with that," J warns.

"And you, did you know? Did you know he was engaged?" she asks Justin, whose face says it all.

This is exactly why I never wanted to start anything with Inès in the first place. I wanted to fix everything, to have my life in order before I brought her into it. But nothing went as I planned. I was weak for her, and I couldn't wait another second. Now, here we are, caught in a mess of emotions, with no way out.

Meghan sighs in disappointment, her voice laced with disbelief. "You've gotta be kidding me."

"It's not what you think, alright?" I say, my voice strained.

"You know Kingsley, and he would never purposely hurt Inès. We all know how much he loves her, so just cut him some slack, baby."

But deep down, I know the truth. Nobody except me knows how deeply I'm in love with her. How close I came to throwing everything away, my company, my family's expectations, everything I've worked for since I was fifteen, for her.

Meghan's expression softens slightly, her guarded stance wavering as she listens. I take a deep breath, knowing how crucial this moment is.

"Let me fix this, Meghan. Please, let me get my girl back." The plea in my voice is raw and heartfelt. The fact that I'm here, begging someone else to help me reach Inès, speaks volumes about how deeply I care for her.

After holding my gaze for what feels like damn near an hour, she finally sighs. "She's back at the house packing."

Justin does a U-turn when it's safe and gets us to my parents, house in record time. I'm out of the car before it comes to a complete stop. I rip off my tie, feeling the constriction around my neck easing as I storm up the stairs two at a time. Reaching my room, I find it locked. There's a digital keypad next to the door, but even after I input the code, the door remains closed. She locked it from the inside. I wouldn't be surprised if Meghan had sent a heads-up to Inès, warning her that I'm on my way.

"Open the door, butterfly." I knock firmly, but there's no

sound from the other side. "Inès, baby, let me explain," I call out, but still, nothing.

"Fuck," I mutter under my breath, frustration rising. "You've got five seconds to open this door before I break it down," I warn, my voice low and serious. Before I even reach five, I hear the soft click of the lock turning. She knows I'm serious.

I step inside and find her standing in the middle of the room, her suitcase is open on the bed. She's still in her gown, still beautiful, despite the redness circling her eyes. Her mouth, usually soft and inviting, is now twisted into an angry sneer. She looks both stunning and shattered. The space between us, the distance she's put up, feels unbearable. Her anger is justified, I know that, but she has no right to run from me. Not like this.

"Kingsley..." she starts. I have never hated my name more than in this moment. I prefer King to come out of those sinful lips. I shut her up by kissing her harshly, angrily.

"Don't," she says, pushing me away. "Just don't. You can't just..." she cries.

I seal our lips again and then whisper against them, "If you ever leave me like that again, I swear to fuck, Inès, I'll lock you up with me and throw away the key. Do you understand me?" She has no idea the panic, the fear, that coursed through my whole being when I realized that she left me.

"No, I'm done. I told you we are done." Her voice wavers, but her resolve is clear as she tries to push me away. It's a futile effort, her strength can't match mine.

I grip her chin firmly, forcing her to meet my eyes. "We will never be done. Do you hear me? Never," I say, my voice a low growl of desperation and determination. "You are mine, and that's final."

"So, what, I'm just supposed to be your mistress? Your

whore? No, thank you. I deserve more, I deserve better." She cries, and I hate her tears, most importantly, I hate that I caused them.

"You deserve everything, Queen, and no one is allowed to give it to you but me. I'm yours, Inès. I was never going to marry her. It was a business deal my parents arranged two years ago. My father insisted I marry her before he'd make me COO of the company."

I keep our foreheads pressed together, our noses brushing as I hold her face in my hands. I refuse to give her even a fraction of space. The forty-six minutes between realizing she left me and walking into this room felt like an eternity, an eternity I never want to relive. Trust and believe that this is the last time I'm ever allowing that to happen again.

"Why didn't you just tell me?" she whispers. "Why lie?"

"I needed time to find a better deal to present to my dad and tell him I didn't want to marry his Goddaughter and not lose the company I have worked for since I was a kid. I don't want her, baby, I never did. She's like a little sister to me. I just want you. I will never want anyone else, just you." She relaxes a bit, her forehead resting against mine. "And I kept something from you, true, but I did not lie."

"It's the same thing," she says, pulling away to look at me. "And I thought lying was a big no in our relationship. Your rules, remember?"

"I never lied, butterfly. If you'd asked me directly whether I was engaged to someone I had no intention of marrying, I would have told you the truth." I can see the wheels turning as she absorbs this, even as she rolls her eyes, wiping a stray tear away.

"That's a technicality, and you know it," she counters, her voice steady but edged with hurt. "I understand that the engagement wasn't your choice. I get that, to you, it wasn't real. What I can't grasp is why you felt the need to keep it from me. We were friends before anything else, weren't we? Yet somehow, this massive detail never came up."

She pauses, her eyes piercing as she lays out her thoughts, each one sharp and deliberate. "I think you knew you would eventually date me or sleep with me, and you didn't want anything to stop you. Because had I known you were engaged, fake or not, I would have never…"

She steps back from me, a physical distance that feels like a chasm, and the hurt in her eyes cuts me deeper than any knife. My heart feels like it's being ripped apart, and I can't stand the look she's giving me.

"Inès?" I plead, my voice softening as I take a cautious step toward her.

But she holds out her hand, shaking her head.

"I need a minute," she says, her voice breaking as she continues to retreat.

"No," I grit out, feeling panic surge within me. "There's no distance between us. There will never be…"

"Stop, please, just stop walking… frisson." Her voice quivers as she utters her safe word, and I freeze mid-step, my heart plummeting. The moment those words leave her lips, I feel a crushing weight settle in my chest. She's serious. I blink back tears, my vision blurring.

"D-don't do this, please," I beg, desperation clawing at my throat.

"I'm sorry, but I need time. For my own sanity, I need time away from you to think things through." She starts closing her suitcase, each zip echoing like a countdown in my mind.

"How… how long?" I ask, feeling the tears spill over and track down my cheeks.

"I don't know. But please, give me at least a few days

before you start calling." Her words are heavy, and I feel them settle like lead in my heart.

"Is there anything I can say to make you stay?" I ask in the barest whisper.

She shakes her head, her bottom lip trembling as if holding back everything she feels. "No. I think we both need the space."

I want to scream that I don't need space from her, not for a single second, but I know *she* needs this time.

"I'm going to go get Beau and call a cab…" she says.

"Let my driver take you," I manage to say, my voice heavy with emotion. "You can take the jet anywhere you'd like, on me."

"Happy New Year, King," she says without looking back, and it feels like she's taking my heart with her, piece by piece. I stand there, frozen in disbelief, before I whirl around in a blind rage. Grabbing the mounted seventy-inch TV off the wall, I yank it free, the drywall crumbling beneath my hands as it crashes to the ground with a deafening thud.

"Fuck!" I scream, the sound ripping from my throat. I didn't realize losing her would hurt this much. The sharp sting of heartbreak courses through me, leaving me feeling hollow, lost. My mind races, but all I can think about is how much I want her back, how I would do anything to undo the past.

INÈS

AWAY FROM THE STORM

The winter wind cuts through my coat as I step onto the tarmac. Beau tugs at his leash beside me, his small paws skidding over the slick snow-covered ground. I don't look back as I climb the steps to the private jet, the door closing behind me with a soft hiss.

Once inside, I head straight for the bedroom to change out of my dress. The most humiliating part of this process is removing the butt plug. It's uncomfortable and awkward, a reminder of the evening's intensity that I would rather forget. Afterward, I rush to the bathroom to clean it up thoroughly before tucking it away in my suitcase, as if hiding a piece of my own shame.

Settling into the soft leather seat of the jet, I feel Beau curl up on my lap, his warm body offering a fleeting sense of comfort amidst my turmoil. Just as I begin to breathe a little easier, my phone buzzes with a call from Meghan. I hesitate before picking it up, but I'm relieved to find it's just her.

"Hey, babe! Where are you?" she asks, her voice bright but laced with concern.

"On the jet," I reply, gently petting Beau's soft fur as I try to ground myself.

"What do you mean, the jet? Where are you going?" Her tone shifts, curiosity piqued.

"If I tell you, do you promise not to tell him?" I ask, knowing full well that the pilot probably reported my destination to Kingsley the moment I stepped aboard.

"I'm sorry I told him where you were earlier. He looked so broken, but I promise not to tell him where you're headed."

"It's okay. I'm going to Minnesota for a few days before the semester starts. I just need some time away from him to think. I don't trust myself to make the best decision for me when he's right next to me."

"You should have told me. I would have been on that plane with you."

"I know, Meg, but I need to do this alone. Plus, you came here to get to know Justin's parents. I'm not taking that away from you. I'll text you as soon as I land, okay?"

"Okay. Are you sure you're okay?"

"I'm fine, Meg, I promise. I have to go. I'll talk to you later."

"Okay. Love you."

"I love you, too."

As I hang up, I sink back into my seat, feeling a mix of gratitude for Meghan's support and the weight of loneliness creeping back in. I close my eyes, trying to silence the whirlwind of thoughts in my mind.

We land in Minnesota at four in the morning, the air sharp and cold, carrying the familiar scent of pine. The crisp winter breeze feels like a bittersweet embrace, grounding me for a fleeting moment. As much as I want to go to my parents' house, I know I can't, Mom's allergic to dogs, plus I don't really want to bother them so early in the morning.

Instead, I opt for a hotel. The Blackwood Hotel in downtown Minneapolis seems perfect, and without hesitation, I book their most expensive suite, charging it to Kingsley's card. Petty, maybe, but it feels like the least I can do after the emotional wreckage I've been through.

Once I get to my room, I strip out of my clothes and step into the shower, letting the hot water cascade over me. The scalding heat feels harsh against my skin, but I welcome it, it's the only sensation that makes sense in this whirlwind of emotions. My tears mingle with the water, indistinguishable now, but the tightness in my chest remains. The ache doesn't wash away as easily as the grime of the day.

How did we even get here? I trusted him. I *chose* to trust him. The betrayal, no matter how justified or unintentional it might seem to him, cuts deeper than I ever thought possible. Lying was always a hard limit for him, so why would he choose to lie to me?

After the shower, I order room service, though I can't remember what I picked. When it arrives, the food is a blur, just something to stop my stomach from twisting in on itself. I eat mechanically, tasting nothing. Fuel, that's all it is. My eyes drift to Beau, who's lying by my feet, his loyal gaze a tiny anchor in this storm. The hotel has a dog daycare, so tomorrow I'll drop him off before heading to my parents' house.

But what will I say to them? My dad, always protective, will surely sense that something is wrong. My mom will press for answers, and I'll have none to give.

Tonight... tonight, all I want is sleep. I crawl into bed, curling up with Beau nestled beside me, his warmth a fragile comfort against the emptiness that's threatening to swallow me whole. The silence of the suite is deafening. Yet, as exhausted as I am, my mind refuses to quiet.

The next morning, I wake up to Beau bouncing around the bed, his playful energy impossible to ignore. His small paws tap against my legs, and I groan, rubbing my eyes.

"Alright, alright, I'm up." I yawn, sitting up and stretching my stiff limbs. "Let me just put something on and I'll take you out." I grab the nearest warm clothes, pulling them on quickly before attaching his leash and grabbing a doggy bag.

The Blackwood Hotel, of course, has a designated dog area, so fancy I can hardly believe it. Beau prances around as we head to the pet-friendly courtyard, where he happily does his business. His innocence is a small joy amid the chaos of my thoughts.

Once he's done, we head back to the suite and I fix him breakfast before calling room service for myself. Minutes later, the scent of fresh pastries and coffee fills the room, but as I dig in, everything tastes a little... bland. My mind is somewhere else, and then my phone rings. I glance down, frowning as I see who's calling. Reluctantly, I pick it up.

"Dr. Salvatore?" I ask, my frown deepening.

"Yes, Inès. How are you?" His voice is strained, almost out of breath.

I pause, an unease creeping in. "Uh... how can I help you?"

"I was hoping we could meet," he says, barely pausing. "I

know it's the holidays, but I have something important to discuss with you."

"I'm not in Boston right now," I say, wariness building. Lately, his behavior has made me uncomfortable. I've been planning to mention it to someone when I get back to campus. Maybe he doesn't mean to sound or act so unsettling, but that's definitely how it's coming across.

"Oh, that's right, Canada, right?" His casual knowledge of my whereabouts sends a chill down my spine, and instinctively, I glance around the room.

I hesitate, choosing my words carefully. "Dr. Salvatore… how did you know I was in Canada?"

"Your friend Meghan loves posting everything on social media," he responds, his tone shifting, becoming less familiar and more… invasive.

I feel a wave of discomfort. I don't use social media, finding it mostly a distraction, so I have no idea what Meghan might have shared.

Taking a steadying breath, I say, "I don't feel comfortable continuing any interactions with you outside of a strictly professional setting. I think it's best if we keep things as professor and student, and I don't feel comfortable being your TA next semester. I hope you'll understand and find a suitable replacement." Before he can reply, I add, "Please don't contact me again."

Right as I'm about to hang up, I hear his voice, tense and slightly raised, calling my name with an edge of anger that sends a shiver down my spine. I press End Call and let out a breath I hadn't realized I was holding, feeling the weight of unease settle heavily in my chest.

After Beau's fed, I send him to the daycare. I've got to pull myself together before I visit my parents.

Back in the suite, I shower, the hot water soothing but not

quite enough to wash away the mess swirling inside me. I choose something clean and simple to wear, something that won't trigger Mom's allergies, and call an Uber.

Thirty-five minutes later, I'm standing in front of my parents' door, heart pounding as I ring the doorbell. The door opens, and my mom is the first to see me. Her eyes widen in surprise, her mouth dropping open slightly.

"Salut, Maman," [1] I greet softly, forcing a smile.

"Mon ange?"[2] she gasps. "What, ? Come in, come in, it's freezing outside!" She quickly ushers me in, wrapping me in a tight, warm hug the moment I step inside. The smell of her perfume, the comfort of her arms, it's almost enough to break me completely.

"Who is it?" My dad's voice drifts from the living room, but he freezes when he sees me standing there. His eyes darken, instantly knowing why I've come. "Where is he? I'm going to kill him!" His voice is hard, anger rolling off him in waves.

"Papa!"[3] I gasp as he strides toward me, pulling me into a hug and kissing my cheeks. His protective energy would normally make me smile, but today, it only deepens the weight in my chest.

"How did you even know this is about him?" I ask, my voice cracking a little.

He gives me a sad look, shaking his head. "It's written all over your face, mon cœur. [4]Now, where is he?"

"Jonathan…" my mom warns gently, placing a hand on his arm.

---

1. Hi, mom.
2. My angel?
3. Dad!
4. My heart.

"What? He gave me his word!" My dad's frustration is palpable.

"How about we all sit down?" my mom interjects, steady and calm. "Would you like some tea, mon ange?"

I nod, my throat too tight to speak. We sit down in the living room, the warmth of their home enveloping me, though I feel anything but warm on the inside. I watch my mom move around the kitchen as my dad sits next to me, his hand on my shoulder. I explain everything that happened with Kingsley.

"Oh, honey. I am so sorry," my mom says gently, her hand reaching out to rub my arm.

"He better not show his face anywhere around here or, " my dad starts, his voice rising in that all-too-familiar protective growl.

"Jonathan," my mom warns, a soft reprimand, pulling him back before he can go off the rails. Then she turns her full attention to me, her gaze tender. "Listen, mon ange, I'm proud of you for walking away, for taking a minute to yourself. But, honey, I get that you're frustrated right now, just don't forget, he loves you, and we're all human. We make mistakes. Isn't that right, Papa?" she says, turning her eyes toward my dad.

And then they do that thing only parents can, have an entire conversation with just their eyes, an exchange that seems to happen in less than thirty seconds but feels like a lifetime. My dad's shoulders sag in reluctant agreement.

He sighs dramatically before cupping my face with both hands. "Maman's right, ma fille.[5] We all make mistakes. But we're proud of you for standing up for yourself."

"Thank you," I whisper, my chest tightening with

---

5. My daughter.

emotion. "I just needed time to think. Everything's so... over-whelming."

"You've come to the right place for that." My mom's voice is soothing, as if she's wrapping me in a warm blanket. "Where's your bag, sweetheart?"

"At the hotel," I reply, taking a deep breath. "I came with Beau."

"Oh, okay. But where is he right now?"

"I left him at the daycare at the hotel. He's being taken care of."

"Good. Well," she says, her tone brightening just a bit, "your papa and I have a fundraiser tonight in Minneapolis for Alzheimer's research. You're welcome to come with us if you'd like."

I pause for a moment. Maybe going out would be good for me, a distraction from everything swirling in my head. "Sure," I say softly, feeling a small flicker of hope. Maybe getting out of my own mind for a while will help me see things more clearly.

KINGSLEY

THIS ISN'T AMERICA

"What's the meaning of this?" my mother demands, storming into my father's office where she was summoned. My dad sits at his desk with me by his side.

Yesterday was the longest night of my life. Not a single ounce of sleep. All I could think about was Inès, whether she was okay, whether she'd eaten. I can still see her glucose levels on my phone, a cold comfort that tells me she's physically fine. But it's not enough. I want more. I want to hear her voice, know what's going through her mind, and most of all, I need to know how long she needs space, because every second without her feels like a slow death.

The unknown is crushing me, the silence from her end deafening. I'm left with nothing but this gnawing emptiness, my thoughts spiraling. Does she miss me? Or is she trying to convince herself she's better off without me?

Every second away from her is agony, like my heart is tearing apart bit by bit. I keep replaying every word, every look from last night, searching for some sign, some clue that I could fix this if I just tried harder. But the truth is, I have no idea what she's thinking. And that's the part that's killing me the most, feeling helpless when the one person I love more than anything is slipping away.

"Have a seat, Evelyn," my dad says, bringing me back to the present. He sounds calm, even though what he's about to do is anything but.

"Listen, I don't have time for this. I have a meeting soon, and if this is about that girl…" Her eyes narrow at me with disdain. I grit my teeth but let it slide. I don't know much about my parents' history, how they met, why they stayed together, but for years, one thing has been painfully clear: They don't love each other, they never did. For the longest time, I convinced myself that my mother loved me and my sister, even if she didn't know how to show it. But now? I'm not so sure. It's not that she hates us, but I can see it in her eyes, she blames me for ruining her life, for making her give up the dream of becoming the international model she always wanted to be. And the more I think about it, the more I realize that my mother doesn't have a single motherly bone in her body. One thing I know for certain is that she loves money more than she loves us. That truth cuts deep, especially for Pay, who's still so young, so naive about all of this.

"We're well aware of your 'meetings' with André Morin, your lover," my dad says calmly, turning his laptop around to show her footage of her and her lover in bed. I didn't want to watch it, but my dad already filled me in, and I'm not an idiot. She's been cheating on my dad for years, and apparently my dad has known all along, just waiting for the right moment to confront her. Apparently, her pissing me off was all he needed.

She slams the laptop shut so hard I'll be surprised if it isn't cracked. "You've been spying on me?" she seethes.

"No, Evelyn. You're just not as smart as you'd like to think, and you got sloppy." Dad's voice is so calm it's almost chilling. I know he hasn't loved my mom in years, but he sounds almost relieved.

Mom lets out a bitter laugh. "You've got some nerve. No, really, you do. You don't get to judge me. You don't get to sit on your freaking high horse and judge me. Not after everything. I did what I had to, to not wake up one morning with the utmost urge to eat a fucking bullet. Do you have any idea what it's like knowing your husband never loved you? In fact, you hated me, hated me for ruining your precious plans, isn't that right?" Her voice rises, sharp and raw. "And then you and your mother had the audacity to hire her in my house. You gave her so much power, over me, over everything, I had to sit back and watch my kids adore her and my husband love her. Twenty-three years, Atticus, we've been married for twenty-three years, and not once have you ever looked at me the way you look at her."

My eyes widen as I glance at my father, but he's laser-focused on my mom, silent and stone-faced.

"I was faithful to you and this family," my father says, his voice low but firm. "Yes, I worked long hours, and missed things I shouldn't have, but I was dedicated. I'm not perfect, but I love my family. I love our kids, even if I wasn't always there the way I should've been."

Mom scoffs, shaking her head. "I love our kids, too. I was always busy, just like you."

"Doing what? You're a stay-at-home mom, but you were never home. You didn't show them affection or love." Dad raises his voice slightly, revealing the pain this truth brings him.

"I am not going to sit here and have a man shame me on how I mother. I'm guessing there are divorce papers somewhere here? Let's just get this over with." Her indifference stings more than her anger would have. I thought she'd fight for her family, but she's too selfish for that.

My dad opens his desk drawer and hands her the divorce papers. In silence, they sign, as if the last twenty-three years meant nothing.

"Get ready for court," my mom says, her voice low but dripping with venom. "I'll bleed you dry. Do you think you can just toss me aside? I'll take everything you own. I might even take half of this company. Let's see who gets the last laugh." She smiles triumphantly as if she hasn't just threatened to take the company I've worked for since I was fifteen, the company that's supposed to be mine one day.

My dad stands up slowly, a smirk spreading across his face. "You forget a few things, Evelyn. This isn't America, and you signed a prenup. The most you'll get from me is alimony, and trust me, hon, that won't even make a dent in Paisley's bank account, let alone mine. And let this be the last time you ever threaten me. You know I don't take kindly to threats." His voice is so chilling, so calm, it makes my skin crawl. And from the look on my mom's face, she's even more terrified than I am.

"You know what? Keep your damn money," she snaps, standing up abruptly. Then she turns her glare on me. "I can't believe I raised a son who'd choose a whore over his own mother."

My blood boils as I step toward her until I'm right in her face. "You didn't raise me. Josephine did. And if you ever speak about Inès like that again, I'll ruin you, and whatever little reputation you have left."

She huffs in disbelief before turning to leave.

"One more thing," my dad says, as he presses a button on his desk phone. "Bring them in." The doors open, and our security team enters. I wonder why, since it seemed like she was already leaving.

"What is this?"

"You know that money you've been stashing in the overseas account? The money you've been stealing from me? Yeah, I took that back. Good luck, Evelyn." That finally sets her off. The reaction I expected when she saw the divorce papers comes out now, triggered by losing the money.

"You can't do that! That's my fucking money, you prick!" she screams, lunging at us, but a security guard blocks her path.

"Get her out of my sight," my dad orders, sitting back down.

"I'm going to kill you!" she yells as they drag her away. Jesus, that was intense.

"Are you okay?" I ask my dad, taking the seat my mother just vacated.

"I'm fine, son. Just a lot of work to get through, that's all. Are you planning to see your grandmother before you head out tonight?" He deflects the tension with practiced ease.

"Yes, I am. And I'll be back at least once a month to check on her." We sit in silence for a moment, the air thick with unspoken thoughts. I finally break it, even though I already know the answer. "The woman Mom was talking about, it's Daronne,[1] isn't it?"

After the other day in my office, I started to suspect that there is much to my dad and Josie's relationship.

My dad sighs, running a hand through his hair, a rare gesture of vulnerability. "Josie and I grew up together. Her

---

1. Mom.

mother worked for your grandparents, and… I've loved her since I was fourteen." That's surprising. I know she's been working for my family a while but to hear that she not only grew up with dad, but he apparently loved her since he was fourteen is crazy.

"What happened?" I ask, already bracing for the answer.

He hesitates then says quietly, "I broke her heart in the worst way possible. I got your mom pregnant."

"With me. Damn."

"Yeah, she left after that. But she came back when you were four. Your grams offered her a job she couldn't resist. It wasn't easy for any of us, though. I still loved her, and she loved me, but by then I was married, and she still hated me for the pain I caused her. We tried to pretend it didn't matter, but it was impossible. The resentment, the unspoken words between us, it was like a shadow we couldn't escape.

"It got to a point where she actually quit. She packed up and was ready to leave again, but you… you begged her to stay. You were so small, clinging to her like she was your whole world, and by then, she loved you so much she couldn't walk away. So she stayed, stayed for you.

"After that, she and I made a deal. We would only interact when it came to you and Paisley. She hated me, and honestly, I couldn't blame her. But no matter how much we resented each other, we both agreed that we didn't want you kids to be affected by it. So we put on a smile. We played nice, for your sake. It was the only way to make sure you never saw the cracks."

I shake my head. "She doesn't hate you, Dad. I don't believe for a second that a woman who raised and loved your kids as if they were her own, knowing we were a constant reminder of what she lost, could ever truly hate you."

He dismisses my words with a wave of his hand, but I can

see the weight of his feelings for Josephine pressing down on him. "Anyway, enough about that. What's done is done." He shifts the conversation, though the lingering pain is evident. "I'll see you in a month…" His words are cut off by my phone ringing.

Frowning, I answer it. "Kingsley Ashford."

"Good evening, Mr. Ashford." A calm, polite voice greets me from the other end of the line. "I'm calling from the Alzheimer's Research Foundation here in Minneapolis. We wanted to thank you for your incredibly generous pledge of two million dollars toward our fundraising campaign."

I freeze, caught off guard. Two million dollars? What the hell is she talking about?

"I'm sorry," I say slowly, my mind spinning. "Did you just say *two million dollars*?"

My dad, sitting across from me, shoots me a confused look, just as puzzled.

"Yes, sir," the voice replies. "The pledge was submitted earlier today by your fiancée, Miss Inès Dubois, on your behalf. We just wanted to confirm it before processing the donation."

My heart stops. No, it literally stops. Fiancée? Did she just say fiancée?

"Did you just say *fiancée*?" I ask, standing up, needing to move, to walk off the shock.

"Yes… Is that not, "

"Did she actually use that word? Verbatim?" I press, the word echoing in my head.

"Yes, sir," she confirms.

A grin spreads across my face, slow and unstoppable. Inès put me down for two million dollars. Of course she did. And she called me her fiancée.

"Yeah, that's correct. She's my fiancée," I say, my voice

steady now, more amused than anything. "Please go ahead with the donation."

"Thank you, Mr. Ashford. We'll send the paperwork to your team for confirmation. Have a great evening."

As soon as I hang up, I'm shaking my head, a quiet laugh slipping out as I sit back in my chair. Two million dollars for Alzheimer's research. It's a cause close to her heart, so I know she didn't make this decision lightly. But still, I wasn't expecting it at all.

I send a quick text to my assistant, instructing him to handle the donation, before turning to my dad. He's still staring at me, eyebrows raised in confusion.

"What was that?" he asks, still bewildered.

I can't help but laugh. "That was Inès punishing me for keeping the engagement from her. She just pledged two million dollars on my behalf for Alzheimer's research."

"And judging by the look on your face, I take it you don't mind?" A knowing smile tugs at his lips.

"Not at all." I shake my head, sitting back down. "Do you know what this means? There's hope. She just gave me hope, two million dollars' worth of hope."

God, I miss her.

I lean back in my chair, staring up at the ceiling, letting out a deep breath. Inès has always been one to surprise me, to keep me on my toes. Even now, with all this distance between us, she's got me wrapped around her finger.

But the best part? She knows it. She called me her fiancée, and whether she's ready to admit it yet or not, I know she's coming back to me.

It's only a matter of time.

INÈS

TWO MILLION REASONS TO FORGIVE

"Y ou *what*?" Camille screams through the phone so loudly that Beau stirs in his sleep, his little body shifting against me.

"Attagirl! I taught you well!" Meghan cheers, her excitement spilling through the screen.

I'm on FaceTime with both of them, nervously sharing how I pledged two million dollars for Alzheimer's research on behalf of Kingsley. I've been so worried about how he might react, he *had* to know by now. But all I got from him this morning was a text, and while it was sweet, it didn't provide the reassurance I craved.

> **KING**
>
> Hey, just wanted to check in. Today was brutal without you. Miss you, beautiful. Beau must be keeping you company, huh? Tell him I miss him too. I know I messed up. I hate that I hurt you, but I'm here whenever you're ready.

That was it. I didn't respond, but I felt giddy seeing his words. I miss him so much that I'm starting to dream about him, dreams in which longing and heartache blur together.

"Meg, don't encourage her! Do you guys know how much a million dollars is let alone *two million?*" Camille counters, her voice laced with disbelief.

"What's a million dollars to a billionaire? He's not hurting for money, trust me," Meghan replies with confidence.

"Yeah, but maybe I should have asked him first," I admit, running a hand through my hair. "And definitely not have done it in anger."

"Anger or not, it was a powerful move," Meghan chimes in. "It shows him you're serious about standing your ground. Girl, make his pocket hurt."

I bite my lip, uncertainty flooding me. "Have you seen him today?" I ask Meghan, trying to gauge where Kingsley might be. She's back in Boston, and I can't help but wonder if he's there too.

"I haven't seen him since the night of the gala. I think he's still in Quebec," she replies, and I feel a pang of disappointment. I wish he were here.

"Have you forgiven him?" Camille asks, and I fall silent. I'm still angry that he lied to me, but I miss him and want him back more than anything.

"It's okay to forgive him, you know. It's okay to miss him," she adds.

"I do miss him a lot, and I do forgive him," I admit, letting out a heavy sigh. "But I don't want to be lied to again in the future."

"Wait, didn't you lie to him, too about dating your professor?" Camille counters, raising an eyebrow.

"Yes, and I got spanked ten times with his belt for it," I say, crossing my arms in mock indignation. My tone is half-defensive, half-amused as both Meghan and Camille burst into laughter.

"I'm so glad my pain provides you two with such quality entertainment," I add, pretending to pout, though the corners of my mouth betray me with a grin.

"The things I would've given up just to be a fly on the wall," Camille manages between giggles, wiping tears of laughter from her eyes.

"Can we be serious for a minute?" I say, trying to sound stern but failing miserably as a laugh escapes me, making all three of us dissolve into another fit of chuckles.

"Okay, okay," Camille concedes, still chuckling. "But in all seriousness, from what I'm understanding, you lied, he punished you, and forgave you by moving on, is that right?"

"Yes," I say.

"Well, didn't you just punish him by spending *two* million of his dollars? I think you're even now," she quips.

"That's one way to look at it, I guess," I say, shaking my head, a small sigh escaping my lips. "But honestly, I didn't mean for it to come across that way. He knows how serious I am about Alzheimer's, it's something I'm genuinely passionate about. I just wanted…" I pause, the words catching in my throat as I debate whether to lie.

Finally, I shake my head and admit, "Okay, fine. I wanted to punish him. But at least I picked a good cause, right?" A faint, self-deprecating smile tugs at my lips. "I'm just worried he'll think I'm trying to manipulate him, and that's the last thing I want."

"Then you explain it," Meghan suggests. "You tell him the truth. You can't be responsible for how he interprets your actions."

I take a deep breath and nod, grateful for their support. "Thanks, guys. I really needed this."

"We'll always be here for you," Meghan says, her expression warm and sincere. "Now, go do something nice for yourself and Beau. You deserve it."

With a newfound sense of determination, I end the call and look down at Beau, who's now wide awake and wagging his tail, ready for some attention. "Alright, mon amour.[1] Let's go for a walk. We need some fresh air."

When I finally return to my room, I find my phone buzzing with a message. It's from Kingsley, and my heart races as I open it:

> KING
>
> I know things are complicated right now, but I want you to know I'm thinking of you. I miss you more than I can say. Let me know when you're ready to talk. Take all the time you need. I'll be here.

Reading those words makes my heart swell and ache all at once. I can feel the connection between us pulsing stronger, a reminder that we're still tethered, despite the distance and the misunderstandings.

The next morning, I drop Beau off at daycare, my stomach twisting with a mix of anxious anticipation and resolve. Once he's taken care of, I head back to the hotel and step into the shower, determined to shake off the lingering weight of yesterday. The warm water cascades over me as I take my time, methodically washing away the tension. I run a razor

---

1. My love.

over my skin, every stroke feeling like I'm reclaiming a little control, preparing myself for what's to come.

Afterward, wrapped in a towel, I glance at the bedside table where the small box of lube I bought yesterday sits. My cheeks flush as I pick it up. With a deep breath, I decide to give it a try. The butt plug he had bought feels unfamiliar but not unpleasant, and as I adjust to the sensation, a strange confidence blooms within me. The sensation is oddly empowering.

Once dressed, I pace the room for the better part of thirty minutes, rehearsing everything I need to say to Kingsley. I run through the conversation a dozen different ways, my heart hammering in my chest. Finally, I grab my phone, fingers trembling as I dial his number. No turning back now.

On the first ring, he picks up. "Butterfly?" He sounds breathless, and it feels like he's been waiting for this moment as much as I have.

"I reserved the most expensive room at the Blackwood Hotel on your card," I say, keeping my voice steady. "You have three hours to come find me if you want to be forgiven."

He chuckles, a sound that warms me from the inside out. "I'll do you one better. I'll be there in thirty."

Confusion flickers through me, and I frown. "What?"

"I've been in Minnesota since yesterday," he says softly, almost shyly. "Waiting for you to call."

My heart skips a beat, and I sit up in bed, my mind racing. "You… what?"

"I didn't want to be far from you," he admits, voice filled with sincerity. "I know you needed space, but I couldn't leave you. Not really."

Tears prick at the corners of my eyes, and I bite my lip, trying to hold them back. "You're an idiot," I whisper, though there's no venom in my words, only the ache of relief and affection.

"I know," he murmurs, a hint of a smile in his voice. "But I'm your idiot. And I'll see you soon."

As I hang up, a wave of lightness washes over me for the first time in days. The anxiety that had twisted in my stomach begins to unfurl, replaced by a sense of hope and excitement. I can hardly believe he's so close, ready to come to me.

In just half an hour, everything could change. I rush to get dressed, choosing something that makes me feel both confident and beautiful: a fitted dress that hugs my curves just right.

Less than thirty minutes later, there's a knock on the door. I school my features, taking a deep breath to steady my racing heart. I head to the door, and when I open it, I don't linger. I turn on my heel, walking away and letting my hips sway, reveling in the sound of Kingsley's low growl behind me.

I stride into the bedroom and stop, turning to face him with my arms crossed, trying to project confidence. "Are you still engaged?" I ask, needing to clear the air first.

"No, I'm not," he replies, taking a step closer, his gaze unwavering.

"What are you doing?" I ask, my voice wavering as I hold out a hand, as if the small gesture could somehow stop him. I'm supposed to be in control here, at least, that's what I keep telling myself. But every time he's near, he shatters that illusion effortlessly, stripping me of the defenses I cling to.

"I missed you," he says softly, his voice heavy with emotion. Before I can respond, he takes my hand, his touch tender yet deliberate, and presses it to his chest. My palm rests over his heart, where my name is etched into his skin, a permanent mark, as if claiming me was never a question but a certainty. The rhythmic thud of his heartbeat beneath my hand betrays his vulnerability, and for a moment, I forget why I wanted to act tough in the first place.

"You lied to me." My voice barely rises above a whisper, trembling with hurt.

His eyes soften as they search mine, as though trying to piece me back together. "I know," he whispers, his voice a confession etched in regret. "I know, Queen…"

I shake my head, the title ringing hollow now. "If I'm your queen." My breath hitches, fighting to hold steady. "Then why…"

He interrupts me, his voice filled with desperation, his words tumbling out like a prayer. "You're not just my queen," he breathes, squeezing the hand still on his chest. "You're my religion. The air I breathe. The light I can't live without. I failed you, I know, but losing you would end me."

The weight of his confession settles over me, warm and consuming. His words wrap around my heart like a balm, softening the ache I swore I'd hold on to. I should stay angry, I want to, but the way he looks at me, like I'm his whole world, makes it impossible.

A slow, sly smile curves my lips, though my heart beats erratically in my chest. I tilt my head, fixing him with a devilish gaze. "If I'm your religion," I say, my voice low and teasing, "then worship me properly."

He blinks, caught off guard.

"I want you to ask me for forgiveness," I demand. I see the tension ripple through him as he grits his teeth. I know how much he hates being told what to do. But I also know he'll give in; he'll let me feel like I'm in control, even if it's just for a moment.

"I'm…" he starts to say, but I cut him off.

"On your knees, King. I need to feel that you're actually

sorry." My demand hangs in the air, laced with a hint of cruel satisfaction. He raises an eyebrow, a smirk tugging at his lips.

"What my queen wants, my queen gets," he replies, a teasing light in his eyes. Slowly, he sinks to his knees in front of me, keeping his gaze locked on mine. I'm surprised he actually does it; I half expected him to resist.

"The last thing I ever want to do is hurt you," he begins, his voice sincere. "All I've ever wanted is to keep you happy and safe, but I've failed. For that, for ever causing you pain, I am deeply sorry. I vow to you that from now on, every decision I make will be guided by the hope of never causing you harm. Your happiness will be my guiding light."

Kingsley on his knees for me? This is straight out of a book.

"I'm sorry for making you cry, Queen," he adds, and I believe every word he says.

"Hm, I don't think you're truly sorry," I reply, pretending to maintain my anger, but the corners of my mouth twitch in amusement.

"Is that so?" he asks, his voice low and sultry. "Well then, I guess I should stay on my knees until I've proven just how sorry I am." He leans forward, grabbing my waist and pulling me to him with an urgency that takes my breath away. "So fucking sorry."

The sudden closeness sends a thrill through me, I can feel the heat radiating from his body as he holds me there, his eyes dark with desire and remorse.

"King," I warn, but my tone lacks the seriousness I intend. The sight of him kneeling before me, looking so vulnerable and determined, makes it hard to keep up the act.

"Please, Queen. Let me make it up to you. I'll do anything you want," he implores, his voice softening as if he's laying bare his soul.

"Anything, huh?" I raise an eyebrow, feigning skepticism, though my heart races at the thought of his willingness to submit to my desires.

"Yes, anything," he insists, his gaze unwavering, full of sincerity and longing. "I'll show you how deeply sorry I am. Just give me the chance."

With every word, my resolve weakens. The power dynamics shift, and I can feel the weight of my earlier anger dissolve completely, replaced by something softer, something I've missed far too much.

"Okay, but don't think this lets you off the hook just yet," I say, my voice low and teasing as he gently pushes my dress up until my underwear is exposed. I relish in the way he watches and touches me.

"I wouldn't dream of it," he replies, his smirk returning. His confidence is a reminder of the man I fell for.

For now, I'll let him say sorry. But deep down, I know it won't take long before I'm the one begging him.

KINGSLEY

SUPERHUMAN STRENGTH

"Magnifique,"[1] I whisper, my eyes devouring every inch of her almost naked form. Dress bunched around her waist, a barely-there thong, her high heels accentuating her long legs.

Her body is a masterpiece. A slim hourglass figure, with curves that drive me wild. And her ass, fuck me, what an ass, perfectly round and full, a stunning contrast to her petite frame. I'll never tire of looking at her, touching her, claiming her as mine.

"You're exquisite," I murmur, pressing gentle kisses on her stomach. "Every inch of you drives me wild, Inès." My voice drops as my hands slides up her thighs. I hook my fingers into her black lace thong and slowly peel it off. The intoxicating scent of coconut and her unique musk fills my senses, and I can't help myself, I lean in and take a deep breath, savoring the aroma of her arousal.

---

1. Stunning.

"King," she moans. My already hard dick gets impossibly harder at the sound of my name leaving her lips.

"Yes, Queen?"

She looks at me with so much lust and love that it almost knocks the breath out of me. "I need you," she murmurs, her voice thick with desire.

Without hesitation, I stick out my tongue and give her slit a tentative lick, sampling her taste. A groan escapes me as the flavor of her floods my mouth. She's better than anything I've ever tasted, a heady mix of sweetness and passion.

"Oh!" she moans, her hands tangling in my hair as she shudders under my touch.

"You taste like the rest of my life, butterfly," I murmur against her skin, my voice rough with need. "Hold on to me tightly."

With that, I dive in again, my tongue pressing more firmly against her clit, savoring every tremble of her legs as she reacts to my touch. The power I have over her, the way she responds so perfectly, is intoxicating. I grab a handful of her perfect ass, squeezing it possessively as I suck her clit into my mouth, my tongue teasing the sensitive nub with expert flicks.

As I spread her cheeks, my fingers trail to her ass, and I groan in raw satisfaction when I feel it, her butt plug. The realization sends a jolt of desire through me. She knew exactly what she wanted when she called me here today, and damn if I'm not ready to give her everything she needs.

I press lightly against the plug, testing her reaction, and her body clenches instinctively. Her sharp intake of breath is music to my ears, her moans unraveling every ounce of restraint I thought I had. I know her, every curve, every sound, every tell, and I use that knowledge to push her further, reveling in her surrender as she teeters on the brink of release.

Her moans grow louder, her fingers tightening in my hair as she rides the waves of pleasure I'm giving her. Every sound, every tremor, only fuels my desire to make her feel even more. I won't stop until she's completely undone, until she's crying out my name in ecstasy.

"Oh, King, I'm almost there," she cries out. I glance up at her, head tilted back in pleasure, fingers teasing her nipples. The sight of her lost in pleasure is something I want etched in my memory forever.

I release her ass and slide two fingers inside her, her wetness coating my hand and running down my arm. My dick aches, begging for attention, but I push my own need aside. My queen needs to come first. I curl my fingers, pumping in and out of her, hitting that perfect spot.

"Kinggg, please," she moans, her voice breathy and desperate as she starts to ride my fingers and face. "King... I... I'm coming!"

I don't stop, and I don't slow down. Instead, I double my efforts, licking and sucking with more intensity. Her body begins to tremble.

"God!" she cries out, her body convulsing as she rides out her orgasm. Her juices flood my mouth and fingers, and I savor every moment, every sound she makes.

I pull my fingers out and stand up, capturing her lips in a searing kiss, letting her taste herself on my tongue. "Such a fucking good girl for me, aren't you?" I praise her, my voice rough with satisfaction.

She starts to drop to her knees, but I stop her. "I'm not going to last, baby, and I need to fuck your ass," I tell her as I remove her dress completely. Her eyes lower to my dick, and she licks her lips. "I'm guessing you have some lube in here somewhere?" I ask her, and she nods.

"Yes, on the bathroom counter."

"Get on the bed, on your hands and knees, facing the headboard," I command.

She obeys immediately, her trust in me absolute. I rush to the bathroom in search of the lube and find it immediately.

I return to the bedroom, and the sight of her, waiting for me, her perfect ass in the air, sends a jolt of desire through me. "Fuck, butterfly, you are my favorite picture." She's on her hands and knees with her ass up, everything on display from the glinting jewel on the plug to her dripping cunt. It's a sight to behold. I undress as quickly as I possibly can. My hands are trembling with anticipation.

I waste no time and rush to her, getting behind her instantly. I can't resist and spank her hard. Have I mentioned I'm totally an ass man? And Inès's ass is to die for.

"King!" she cries out, and I spank her again and again until she's writhing and panting. I then spread her ass cheeks and grab the plug.

"Relax and breathe for me," I instruct, my voice low and commanding. She obeys, her breaths slowing as I begin to pull the plug out, inch by inch, savoring every moment until it's completely out. "Fuck me," I groan, unable to contain my reaction at the sight before me. This woman is going to be the death of me.

I place the plug beside me on the bed then bury my face in her ass, licking her hole with a primal hunger.

"Oh my God, King, no," she protests, trying to push me away. "That's dirty."

Without hesitation, I deliver a firm spank to her ass. "Hands above your head, and do not move them again," I command, my tone leaving no room for argument. Reluctantly, she obeys, her hands moving above her head. "Good girl. Now I'm going to eat this ass, because it's mine and I love it, got it?"

"Yes, King," she breathes, her resistance crumbling as she surrenders to me. I continue to worship her ass, licking and sucking until her protests are replaced by needy moans.

"You like that, baby girl?"

"Oh God, yes," she moans, her voice filled with pleasure.

I Unscrew the lube bottle and pour a generous amount onto her ass, the cool liquid trickling down her skin.

She tenses up when I press a finger to the rim of her hole.

"I need you to relax for me, okay? I need to make sure you are prep and ready to take me."

"Okay."

"Play with yourself for me." As she follows my instructions, I breach the first barrier. "Fuck, you're tight," I say, pumping in and out of her with one hand while my other hand holds my aching dick, trying not to bust a load. A few more strokes and I add more lube before inserting another finger.

"Oh, King, that feels so good. I want more," Inès cries out, so I give her a third finger.

"So full," she moans. I need to be inside her, right the fuck now.

She hisses when I remove my fingers. I add more lube, rubbing some on my cock, positioning myself behind her, I take a deep breath. "Ready, butterfly?" I ask, my voice thick with need.

She nods, her body quivering with anticipation. Slowly, I press into her, oh my fuck, I'm definitely not going to last with the way her ass is choking my cock, and I only have my tip in her.

"King!"

"Fuck! Breathe, baby. Holy fuck, you're tight and hot as

fuck," I grunt, adding a few more inches. It's hard to talk, to breathe. I feel like one wrong move and I'll come embarrassingly fast. "You're taking me so well, baby. I'm so fucking proud of you," I praise, stroking her back gently, lovingly. I keep it up until I bottom out, balls deep in her tight hole. "Jesus, fucking fuck!" I bellow. The tightness, the heat, is almost too much to bear.

"You're mine," I whisper in a low growl. "Every part of you belongs to me."

I can't move, I'm too close to the edge. Her moans and gasps are too much for me. This moment, this connection, is everything.

"I feel so full, King. God, you feel so good," she cries out as she begins to move, squeezing me even more than she already is. Holy fuck.

"Babe, hon, stop... arrête.[2] Don't move," I warn.

"Why? It feels good, s'il te plait,"[3] she whines and keeps moving as if I didn't just tell her not to.

"And you feel too good. If you keep moving, I'm going to come before I'm ready," I say, gripping her waist to stop her from moving. But I don't know if I've gotten weak the few days we've spent apart or she's gained some superhuman strength because, despite my grip on her, Inès moves hard and fast. So hard and fast, in fact, that our skin begins to slap together loudly. "Inès, putain.[4] Fucking hell, I'm..." I can't finish that sentence as I lose control, meeting her strokes with harder ones, and come in her so hard I start to see stars. I collapse next to her on the bed, breathing heavily. What just happened? That has never happened to me.

---

2. Stop.
3. Please.
4. Fuck.

Then Inès starts laughing, as in out loud, actually laughing, and I can't help but laugh, too. I roll on top of her and begin to tickle her relentlessly. "What's funny?" I ask, still tickling her.

"I just... I didn't think I could make you come in less than a minute. I love that for me," she says, smiling with so much love in her eyes.

"Yeah? Well, I'll make you pay for that."

"Promise?" she asks, and I kiss her.

"For the rest of my life, Queen," I murmur, brushing her lips in a tender kiss. The softness of her skin, the taste of her mouth, it's like coming home after being lost. I've missed her so much; I don't think I can ever be apart from her again. Not like this. It might actually kill me.

We lie there, our bodies still humming in the aftermath of our love, wrapped in each other's arms. She fits perfectly against me, her head resting on my chest, listening to my heartbeat.

"Two million dollars, huh?" I say, teasing, once the haze of our high starts to fade. She shifts in my arms, turning to look at me with a small, remorseful frown. "That's what pissing you off costs me?"

Her bottom lip pocks out, and I can't help but find it adorable. "I'm sorry... I wasn't thinking. I was upset, but I also really wanted to donate, "

"Hey, it's okay," I interrupt softly, stroking her back. "Honestly, I'm not mad. In fact, I'm happy you did it. It gave me hope... fiancée," I tease with a grin, making her groan and roll her eyes.

"They told you about that?" she mumbles into my chest.

"They sure did." I chuckle. "Maybe we should just make it official... you know, since you've already started calling yourself my fiancée," I half-joke, but there's a part of me that loves the idea.

"Don't even think about it," she warns, lightly swatting my chest. "I only said that so they wouldn't think I was suspicious."

We fall into a comfortable silence, her hand tracing lazy circles on my skin. But after a few moments, she looks up to me again, her eyes soft and thoughtful. "Ask me in five years," she whispers.

I raise an eyebrow, surprised. "Five years?"

"With my calculations, I should be done with my first year of residency by then," she explains, her voice full of dreams. "And though I'll still have more years to go, I think I'll be ready. To say yes."

"Five years," I echo, my heart swelling at the thought. "In five years, you'll wear my ring."

"And I'll wear it proudly," she replies. Her eyes shimmer with the promise.

I pull her closer, our bodies tangling together as we settle back into the pillows, feeling more connected than ever. The room feels warm, safe, like nothing could ever come between us again. Her breath is soft against my skin, and I can't resist pressing my lips to her forehead, savoring the sweetness of the moment.

"Five years," I whisper again, more to myself than to her, already imagining the day she becomes mine forever.

She lets out a content sigh, and I think she's about to drift off to sleep. But then, with a mischievous glint in her eyes, she leans up and kisses me again, slow and soft. My heart skips a beat, and before I know it, that simple kiss has me stirring back to life.

I groan as I feel the rush of desire all over again, my body

327

responding instinctively to her touch. She smirks against my lips, clearly noticing the effect she has on me.

"Really?" she teases, as she pulls back just enough to look at me.

"What can I say?" I grin, pulling her closer once more. "I'm always ready for you."

She laughs softly, the sound like music, and I realize in this moment how lucky I am, how I'll never stop wanting her, needing her.

INÈS

*TRUST YOUR GUT WHEN SOMETHING
FEELS OFF*

I hurry up the steps to my apartment, the familiar creak of the stairs echoing beneath my feet. It feels surreal to be back here after what's happened, like walking into a memory that doesn't quite fit anymore. Everything looks pristine, the way it always did before my life turned upside down. King had sent cleaners once the police gave us the all-clear, and for that I'm grateful. Without their help, I'm not sure I'd have had the courage to step through this door again.

It's been a couple of days since we returned from Minnesota, and I've come here to grab a few things before meeting King for a date. I didn't tell him because he'd insist on coming with me, but it felt unnecessary. I was already on campus tutoring, and I had my car. This quick detour made sense at the time. Now, standing here, I'm not so sure.

I take a moment to look around, soaking in the familiarity. It feels wrong, though. Too neat. Too untouched. My gaze falls on the living room rug, slightly crooked, and I wonder if it was always like that. Or maybe the cleaners shifted it? My mind drifts, restless with questions that have haunted me since this nightmare began. Why was I targeted? The police didn't find anything to connect anyone to the scene. Could it all have been a mistake, a terrible case of someone picking the wrong apartment?

I wander toward my room, thinking of how much things have changed since the last time I stood here. My fingers trail over the desk where I used to study, the lamp King bought me still perched on the corner. The air feels heavy now, thick with memories and unease. As I step inside, something catches my eye, the light in the bathroom. It's on.

A chill runs down my spine. Did the cleaners leave it on? Or…?

I take another step, but my gut is already whispering what I don't want to admit. I shouldn't have come here alone. My hand trembles as I run it over the edge of the bedpost. The arrangement of items on my nightstand feels subtly wrong, but I can't place how. My heart pounds as I tell myself I'm being ridiculous. Yet, every fiber of my being is telling me to leave.

I turn to go, pulling out my phone. King. I need to call King. The thought alone steadies my hands enough to dial.

"Hey, Queen?" His voice filters through, calm and warm, underscored by laughter and muffled voices, poker night with his friends.

"King…" My voice trembles as I whisper into the phone, the syllable barely audible. I make my way back toward the door, my fingers just inches from the handle when it happens.

A hand clamps over my mouth, the grip like iron. A chemical-soaked cloth presses against my face, the sickly sweet smell filling my nostrils. My phone drops to the floor with a heavy thud, King's voice calling faintly from the other side.

I twist and struggle, kicking out with all my strength, but the grip on me doesn't loosen. My head feels light, my vision narrowing as I try to scream against the cloth. Through the haze, I catch a fleeting glimpse of something, glasses reflecting the light from the bathroom. A pang of recognition shoots through me, but it's too late.

The world tilts, my legs giving out beneath me, and as darkness consumes me, my last thought is: I should have told King.

KINGSLEY

The room buzzes with laughter and the sound of shuffling cards. Poker night with Calvin, Desmond, and Justin is in full swing. We've been talking more than playing for the past hour and a half, teasing Calvin about his impromptu engagement that none of us except his brother knew about. It's been a while since we've all gathered together, and I miss my guys. But even in this moment of camaraderie, my thoughts keep drifting to Inès. My queen. She's supposed to be at school tutoring, but we have a date planned for tonight. The anticipation of seeing her is like a sweet ache in my chest.

My phone buzzes on the table, and Inès's name flashes on the screen. I smile as I pick it up, ignoring the teasing coming from my friends. "Hey, Queen," I greet, but instead of her usual cheerful voice, all I hear is a crackling silence. My heart instantly tightens with unease.

"King…" Her voice is barely a whisper, laced with terror. My heart stops. The world around me blurs.

"Inès? What's wrong?" I demand. The room falls silent, my friends' eyes fixed on me with growing concern.

The only response on the other end is the sound of the phone clattering to the floor, followed by muffled noises, and then… nothing.

"Fuck!" I bolt upright, my pulse racing the thought of her in danger twists my gut in knots. I frantically dial 911, my hands trembling. "This is Kingsley Ashford. My girlfriend, Inès Dubois, is in danger. I don't know where she is, the last time I spoke with her she was at school…"

"Meg says that Inès went to the apartment to grab something," Justin says, causing my head to snap in his direction, and I see he is on the phone with who I'm guessing is Meghan. I narrow my eyes and clench my teeth. I told her, I told her not to go back to that damned apartment. Fuck!

The 911 operator is talking and asking questions, but I interrupt. "She's… she's at her apartment." I give them the address. "There was a break-in a few months ago with no leads. Get someone there now!"

Desmond is already on his feet, grabbing his keys. "We'll drive. Cops will take too long."

I barely register his words; they're just noise in the background. My mind is solely focused on Inès. The fear gnaws at me, sharp and unrelenting, threatening to consume every rational thought I have left.

The car ride feels endless. Each second is a fresh surge of panic, each mile another reminder of how far I am from her, from protecting her. My grip on my phone tightens as I scroll through her unread messages.

Every worst-case scenario plays out in my head, each one worse than the last. The weight of not knowing is suffocating, but there's no room for breaking down. Not yet. I have to get to her.

I call the cops again, my voice sharp and unyielding, barking orders like my life depends on it, because it does. I remind them exactly who the fuck I am, pushing past their procedural nonsense.

For the twelfth time, I dial her number, gripping my phone so tightly my knuckles ache. The line goes straight to voicemail again, and the sound of her automated message guts me. My hands tremble as I open the app linked to her glucose monitor, praying for something that could give me a clue. But everything looks normal, steady levels, no spikes or crashes. A small relief, but it doesn't tell me where she is or if she's safe.

"Come on, Inès," I mutter under my breath, my voice cracking with desperation. "Give me a sign, baby. Just something."

When we screech to a halt outside the apartment, I don't wait for anyone before I dart out of the car. But Calvin, who drove with his brother, gets out of his car as well and gets to me before I can open the apartment building. He grabs my arm. "Kingsley, we need to be smart about this. Let's wait for the cops," he tells me.

I shake him off, my vision red with fury and fear. "She might be in there. I can't just stand here." Even as I say it, a part of me knows she's not in there. Still, I wait for no one as I sprint inside.

As we approach the apartment, the door is ajar. The sight sends a chill down my spine. Inside, everything looks clean, almost too clean, but my instincts scream that something is wrong.

"Inès!" I shout, desperation thick in my voice. As I walk inside looking for something, anything, but everything looks perfect. Nothing is out of place.

The police arrive, guns drawn, moving through the apartment with precision. But it isn't enough. I feel useless standing here, my fists clenched in frustration.

Desmond's hand on my shoulder brings me back. "We'll find her. I know a guy. He'll know what to do."

I nod, barely hearing him, my mind a whirlwind of fear and anger. The thought of Inès, my beautiful, strong Inès, in danger is unbearable.

The cops take our statements. I tell them about her diabetes, and they promise to do everything they can, but it isn't enough. It will never be enough until she is back in my arms, safe.

INÈS

DELUSION CAN BE DEADLY

I wake in a dimly lit room, my head throbbing with a dull, relentless ache. My mouth is dry and bitter, and the taste lingers like old metal. What happened? My thoughts swim through a murky haze, trying to grasp on to something solid, a memory, an explanation for the heaviness in my skull and the bitterness coating my mouth like ash. I try to move, to sit up, but something holds me down. Confusion flickers in my chest, quickly turning to dread as I look down and see why.

I'm seated on a metal chair, my wrists and ankles bound tightly. The rough bite of rope against my skin sends a surge of panic racing through me. My heart hammers against my ribcage, wild and erratic, and my breath comes in short, shallow bursts. I force myself to remember what happened last night, Was it last night?, I can't be sure how much time has passed. The memories begin to seep back in. My heart races even faster, oh my God, he took me, he drugged me, and… I'm going to be sick!

Get it together, Inès, now is the time to focus. You can panic later, but right now, you need to get the hell out of here. I take a deep breath to try and focus. My eyes finally adjust to the faint light, and I take in my surroundings. The room, if you can even call it that, is small and suffocating, the low ceiling making the air feel thick. It smells damp, like rotting wood and wet soil. I'm in a basement. I can feel the chill of the earth pressing in from all sides. The walls are made of rough stone, moss creeping between the cracks. The faint light flickers from a single bulb hanging from the ceiling, barely illuminating the room. In the dim glow, I can make out a set of wooden stairs leading up to what I assume is the main level of whatever this is.

I pull harder against the ropes, desperate to free myself, but the bindings keep digging deeper into my wrists. My hands ache, raw from struggling. The panic builds and builds, tightening in my chest like a vise. I try to steady my breath, but it's no use. There's no way out. Just cold stone, shadows, and silence.

"H... help," I rasp, but the word barely escapes my lips, more a wheeze than a scream. My throat burns with the effort, whatever he drugged me with is still in my system, slowing my movements, clouding my thoughts. My muscles feel like lead, every breath an exhausting effort. Tears blur my vision as a wave of helplessness crashes over me. My body trembles, shivering from the terror coursing through me.

I blink back the tears even as they continue to fall, my emotions as uncontrollable as fear suffocate me. "Hello? Pleas... please, somebody help!" My voice cracks, hoarse and barely audible, but I scream again, desperately, though I know it's futile. Exhaustion overtakes me. My energy is spent, every movement is a struggle, and my muscles ache with fatigue. I try one last time, mustering every ounce of strength to scream, hoping, *praying*, that someone, anyone, nearby will hear me. "Please!" I scream though it feels more like a desperate gasp. "Somebody…" But then a voice cuts through the darkness.

"Save your energy, amore mio.[1] No one can hear you."

I freeze, my blood turning to ice. That voice, it's smooth, calm, and far too familiar. Slowly, emerging from the shadows at the far end of the room, I see him. Dr. Salvatore. He steps forward with an unsettling ease, a small, leather bag dangling from one of his hands while he drags a chair across the stone floor with the other, the legs scraping in a long, shrill noise that sends a shiver down my spine.

"Dr. Salvatore," I manage to sneer, my voice filled with disgust. I figured he was the one who took me. The glasses and the embroidered psi handkerchief were a dead giveaway I should have noticed the signs! How could I have been so naive? So stupid?

He chuckles softly, the sound dripping with condescension. "Ah, Inès. There's no need to be so formal." His voice remains smooth, too smooth, like he's rehearsed this moment in his head countless times. He sits down in the chair, crossing his legs and regarding me with an unsettling calm. "Please, call me Nathan. 'Dr. Salvatore' feels so impersonal, don't you think?"

I glare at him, my heart racing as fear and rage churn together in my chest.

"That look on your face tells me you knew it was me before I came out, what gave me away?"

"Why?" I croak, ignoring his question. "Why are you doing this?"

---

1. Italian for: My love

337

He sighs, almost as if he's disappointed, and sets the bag on the floor beside him. "Don't insult either of our intelligence by acting as if you don't know why I did this. It's beneath you."

I glare at him again even as I shake. It's true I made an educated guess based on everything that has happened so far and came to the conclusion that he is somehow obsessed with me, though I still don't understand why, why me? What about me says *kidnap me and bring me to wherever this is and tie me up*? That's what I want to know, but it's not what I say next.

"Dr. Salvatore, you have to let me go, now. You need to release me." I tug against the ropes again, but they hold firm.

He starts looking through his bag as he speaks. "I can't do that, amore mio. We are going to stay put until I can take you home to Italy. You will love it there, it's truly beautiful. Our home is surrounded by beautiful flowers and water. You will feel at peace there, I promise."

My eyes widen. This is not happening! I am really trying not to panic right now, but I'm losing that battle. "What? What are you talking about? I'm not going anywhere with you. Please, let me go!"

He takes my right hand, ignoring me as he silently takes out an alcohol wipe and starts wiping my finger. Is he going to cut my finger off?

Of course, when I actually think about it, it doesn't make sense, but it's as if the logical part of my brain is shutting off. Panic takes over me again, and I start tugging my hand away and screaming, but his grip on my hand is far too strong.

"Stay still, baby."

Baby? Oh, God. He's even more deranged than I thought.

The probability of making it out of here alive is slim to nothing. Statistically, my odds of survival are shrinking by the second, and the numbers… they don't lie. I feel a sharp prick on my finger. I flinch and instinctively try to pull back, wincing, but he holds firm. Looking down, I see a blood glucose meter in his hands.

"I know you've got a Dexcom on, but I had to get rid of your phone. I'm sorry, amore," he says, his voice disturbingly gentle, almost affectionate. "I know how much you hate needles, but once we get home, I'll make sure you have a new Dexcom." That softness in his tone, it unnerves me more than anything else. It's the calmness of someone who thinks this is all perfectly normal. And it makes my skin crawl.

"H… how did you know I hate needles?" I ask unsteadily as he waits for the meter to finish reading my blood sugar.

"The same way I know you're diabetic," he says casually, not even looking at me.

"You've been watching me."

"That's something we need to discuss," he says firmly, but, laced with concern. "You made it far too easy. You need to be more aware of your surroundings. When you're studying, you shut everything out, completely oblivious to what's happening around you, and that's not safe."

My stomach turns violently, bile rising in my throat. I barely manage to turn my head in time before retching all over the cold floor. I heave and gag, my body trembling as dry, painful spasms wrack through me until my stomach clenches with nothing left to expel. I figured he has been watching me, which also means he was the one who broke into my apartment, but hearing him admit it out loud makes me want to vomit all over again. The reality is far worse than the paranoid thoughts I'd tried to dismiss.

"Looks like your levels are a bit high," he says, as though nothing is wrong, as though I didn't just puke my guts out inches away from us. He kneels beside me, stroking my arms with slow, deliberate motions. The sensation is revolting, like tiny insects crawling over my skin. "But that's normal, given the stress you're under. Still, you'll need to eat soon." I recoil at his touch, trying to pull away, but the ropes bind me in place. My body shakes uncontrollably, panic closing in from all sides.

"S... stop," I plead, my voice barely more than a whisper. "Please... you can't do this to me. I don't want to be with you. I have a boyf..."

The crack of his hand across my face silences me instantly. Pain explodes in my cheek as my head snaps violently to the side. For a moment, everything spins, the world turning into a blur of colors and sounds. My ears ring from the force of the blow, and I'm left gasping, struggling to regain my bearings. I taste blood. My cheek throbs, the sting of his slap still fresh on my skin. I blink, disoriented, tears welling up in my eyes. My heart races, but this time not just from fear, from shock, from the sickening realization that I am completely at his mercy. The silence that follows feels heavy like the air has been sucked out of the room.

"Fuck!" he says. Then that sweet, gentle facade slips right back into place, as though the violence was just a minor inconvenience. "Shh, amore," he whispers, brushing a strand of hair from my face with his hand as if he didn't just struck me. His touch, once again gentle and disturbingly affection- ate, sends chills through me. "See what you've made me do? It's okay. You don't need to be scared, but do not ever mention that illiterate in my presence ever again, okay?" he asks, and I nod my head before he gets up and leaves me all alone again.

Oh God... oh God... oh God!

What do I do? What do I do? My heart pounds like it's about to explode out of my chest, and I frantically look around the room, desperate for anything, anything at all, that could help me escape. But there's nothing. I squeeze my eyes shut, trying to stop the flood of tears threatening to spill. *Crying won't help. Think, Inès, think.*

King. Oh God, he must be losing his mind right now. My family, they must all be so worried, wondering where I am. I have to make it out of here. I have to. Of course, I had to catch the attention of a psychopath. But why me? I mean, it's not that I'm ugly, but there are hundreds of beautiful people on campus.

We were only on one date. So, why me… Did I say something? Did I do anything? My thoughts race as I recap the times we've talked, the classes, and that's when it hits me! *My brain.* He must think we belong together because of our IQs.

This is the first time in my life I hate that I'm smart, but maybe I can use it to my advantage. Now that I know what he wants, I can try to outsmart him. After all, my IQ is higher than his!

My thoughts race as I sit there in the suffocating silence, left alone in the dark with only my fear to keep me company. Time blurs, and I don't know how long I've been waiting, minutes, hours? My nerves are frayed when I finally hear the sound of footsteps approaching, heavy, deliberate steps that echo down the stairs. The door creaks open, and a shaft of light spills into the basement, blinding me momentarily.

"Come on." Dr. Salvatore's voice cuts through the stillness. "Let's get you upstairs." He steps toward me, pulling a pair of cuffs from his pocket. I swallow hard, my throat dry. I don't know what's upstairs, but whatever it is, I don't want to know. I need to buy time, get him talking. Anything to stall, to figure out my next move.

"Please," I say, my voice trembling but determined. "Help

me understand your mind. Why me? That's all I ask. Just tell me why."

For a moment, he pauses. The silence stretches between us, heavy and suffocating, and just as I'm about to speak again, desperate to keep him talking, I'm bathed in light as he switches on the overhead bulb. I wince, blinking as my eyes adjust, and when I finally open them, he's standing in front of me. My stomach twists painfully. He looks scarier now than ever before, his face half in shadow, half illuminated by the harsh, unforgiving light.

"You want to know why I chose you? What drew me to you?" He steps closer, his eyes locking onto mine, dark and intense. "It's your intelligence, amore mio. Your mind is beautiful. You were made for me. I've been waiting for you my whole life."

My breath catches in my throat as his words sink in, dread tightening its grip around my chest. He truly believes this. He thinks we belong together.

"We can be happy together, Inès," he continues, his voice low and disturbingly calm. "I can give you everything you need. I can protect you from the world. You'll see, in time, you'll come to love me."

I want to scream, to claw my way out of this nightmare, but my body feels frozen, paralyzed by fear. His words hang in the air, poisonous and suffocating. I try to steady my breathing, willing myself not to give in to the panic. I need to stay calm, need to keep thinking.

Dr. Salvatore leans in closer, his breath warm against my skin, his eyes flickering with a dangerous intensity that makes every hair on my body stand on end. "Don't do anything stupid," he whispers low and menacing, like a predator playing with its prey. Slowly, methodically, he begins to undo the ropes binding my arms and legs. My muscles scream in relief as blood begins to circulate freely again, but that brief sense of freedom is short-lived. Before I can even process it, the cold, unforgiving metal of handcuffs snaps around my wrists.

The audible click echoes through the room, sealing my fate. I bite down the rising panic, willing myself to stay still. He tightens the cuffs, and the cold metal digs into my skin, pressing against bone. I swallow a gasp of pain, determined not to show him how much it hurts. His hand reaches for my face. I flinch before I can stop myself, recoiling from his touch. My body betrays me, reacting on instinct. He ignores it, his fingers brushing over my cheek with a sickening gentleness, tracing the line of my jaw as if he's savoring every inch of my skin. His touch is repulsive, sending waves of nausea rolling through me. Before I can react, he leans in. His lips press against mine in a deep, lingering kiss. My stomach churns, and I fight the overwhelming urge to puke again, my entire body screaming to recoil, to pull away, but I don't. I can't. I force myself to stay still, biting down the revulsion, knowing that for now, my survival depends on keeping calm. It's a miracle I don't throw up again right then and there.

INÈS

THERE'S NO VICTORY IN DESTRUCTION

D r. Salvatore leads me upstairs, and as we emerge from the basement, I get my first real look at where I am. It's a cabin. I can tell by the wooden walls and the rustic, old-fashioned feel of the place. He walks me into a medium-sized bedroom, sparsely decorated with a bed, two vintage nightstands, and a dresser. Everything looks old, worn but preserved. The bedspread is a faded floral pattern, the kind you'd expect to find in an old country home.

Dr. Salvatore gently pushes me toward the bed, and I sit down stiffly, my heart thudding in my chest. He uncuffs one of my wrists, only to thread the cuff through the metal bed frame and secure me again. My stomach clenches with dread as I watch him, my mind racing for an escape plan. On one of the nightstands, I notice a tray of food, grilled cheese and tomato soup. The sight of it makes my stomach growl involuntarily, reminding me that I haven't eaten since before I left for school. *God knows how long ago that was*. But there's no way I'm eating anything he gives me. He could've drugged it, or worse.

Dr. Salvatore picks up the tray and sits beside me on the bed, holding the sandwich close to my lips like I'm a toddler. "Open up," he says, his voice deceptively soft.

I narrow my eyes, clamping my mouth shut. There's no way I'm playing into his sick game.

His lips press into a thin line, but he sighs, like he's trying to keep his calm. "Come on, Inès, you need to eat. The sooner you eat, the sooner we can head to bed." His words send a fresh wave of dread through me. *Bed*. I don't know what he plans to do to me, but I certainly don't want to find out. The thought alone makes me sick, and I instinctively pull back, determined to stall for as long as I can.

"Let me guess…" he chuckles lightly, "you think I would poison you?" He says it like it's some kind of joke, but I don't find any of this funny.

I don't respond, knowing that any word out of my mouth might give him an opening to force-feed me.

He sighs again, clearly frustrated, then dips the grilled cheese into the soup and takes a bite. "See? Now, open up," he demands, holding it out for me again.

When I still refuse, his eyes darken with annoyance. The sigh that escapes him this time is laced with irritation. Without warning, he reaches behind him. My eyes widen, and my blood runs cold as I see what he pulls out: a gun. I don't know why I'm surprised. Of course, the man who kidnapped me, who's been stalking me for months, would have a gun. But seeing it in his hand, pointed right at me, is a terror I wasn't prepared for.

Tears fill my eyes as my entire body begins to tremble. I've never seen a gun up close before, aside from on TV, and the sight of it aimed at me is worse than anything I've ever imagined.

"Now," he says calmly, his voice devoid of emotion, "you can open that pretty mouth of yours and eat, or I can force you. And I promise you, you won't like my methods." Fear tightens around my chest like a vise, squeezing the breath from my lungs. Every instinct screams at me to fight, to resist, but I know he's serious. I've seen the lengths he's willing to go to.

My voice trembles as I grit my teeth and hiss, "Fuck you," but even as I say it, I reluctantly open my mouth, knowing I have no choice. He smiles, smug and satisfied, as he gently places the food in my mouth.

"You're far too intelligent to use that kind of language, but I'll let it slide this time," he says, like a parent scolding a child. "I understand you've surrounded yourself with illiterate imbeciles, and they've been rubbing off on you. Don't worry, amore. All of that will change once we get home. You'll love it there. We'll be so happy." He keeps talking, rambling on about the future he's imagined for us as if any of this is normal. All I can do is glare at him, silent tears streaming down my cheeks as he feeds me. I feel the food slide down my throat like lead, each bite harder to swallow than the last. "You're so beautiful," he murmurs, almost to himself, his voice soft and filled with a twisted affection. He strokes my cheek again, and I try not to flinch, though my skin crawls with every touch. "I can't wait to make love to you. I hope you want a lot of kids, because I do. I want a house full of them. Our children will be so beautiful." His words hit me like a punch to the gut. My stomach churns violently, but I force myself to stay still, to keep my breathing steady, even though all I want to do is scream. I feel like I'm trapped in a nightmare, and I don't know how much longer I can hold on.

When he's done feeding me, he picks up the tray, glancing at me. "Stay right here. I'll be back soon, and then I'll take you to the bathroom. After that, we can head to bed."

"Where would I go?" I yell, anger and frustration bubbling up, but he only smirks, walking out and closing the door behind him. I wait until I hear his footsteps retreat before I start desperately tugging at the cuffs again. The metal digs into my wrists with every pull, but I suppress the urge to scream in frustration. I'm cuffed to the bed frame behind me, making it impossible to see what I'm doing. Still, I'm determined to get free before he comes back. Leaning my entire body forward, I try to yank the cuffs with as much force as I can. Maybe the old bed frame will give out, or maybe the cuffs will break, something has to give. But all I manage to do is tear the skin on my wrists.

"Putain!" [1] I curse, whimpering in pain. "One more time," I mutter, already sweating. This time, instead of pulling slowly, I lunge forward with all my strength. Snap. Pain shoots through my shoulder as I feel it dislocate, a white-hot flash of agony that makes me scream into the mattress spreads through my body. Tears stream down my face as I cry out in misery. The door slams open, but I can't lift my head; the pain is too intense. I can hear hurried footsteps before I feel the cuffs being unlocked.

There's relief in no longer being bound, but the searing pain in my shoulder swallows it. "Come here." He grabs me by my good arm, lifting me. I want to scream, plead, anything to make him stop, but when I lift my head, I freeze. He's holding the gun again, but this time, it's not the weapon that makes my blood run cold; it's the look in his eyes. Panic.

"Fuck, fuck, fuck!" he curses, looking around frantically,

---

1. Fuck!

his manic gaze darting across the room. Something's wrong. The pain in my shoulder momentarily forgotten, I realize why he's panicking. The cops. They're here. My heart skips a beat. They must be close, maybe even right outside.

King. Relief and terror collide inside me, but I know I need to be smart, this could turn deadly in an instant if I don't play my cards right. "Nathan?" I call out, my voice as calm as I can manage, even though every nerve in my body is screaming in fear. He's like a bomb about to go off, a nuclear bomb.

"I can't... I can't let you go," he mutters, his voice shaking as his grip on my wrist tightens painfully. "You're mine! Mine!" His eyes are wild, and I know one wrong move could send him over the edge. "They'll never understand people like us, Inès. We're a different breed. I wish we had more time, more time to show them how powerful we could be together. We would've taken over the world, you know that, right?" He's speaking in past tense. My stomach twists in dread. I need to stall, he's on the verge of something catastrophic. "I love you so much, amore,[2] maybe in the next life..." His voice wavers, his hold on me tightening. "Just... don't fight me too much when we're there."

I shake my head, my heart racing. "I understand now. Nathan, I understand now, you've always seen me, haven't you? You saw what no one else could: my mind, my potential. You're right, we're not like them. But think about it, if you do this, no one will ever understand why," I say calmly but with urgency. "They'll label you as just another criminal, another man who couldn't control himself. They'll never know the truth, the brilliance behind your actions. We're too smart for that." I pause, carefully watching his reaction as he

---

2. Love.

watches me. I can tell he doesn't fully trust me, but the parts of him that think I was made especially for him want to believe me, so I continue softly. "If you end it now, you'll be giving them the power to control the narrative. They'll erase who you are, who we could have been, reduce your genius to a moment of madness. But if you let me go, if we walk out of here together, I can help you tell the world what you've really been trying to do. They'll finally understand your brilliance, your vision. I can be the one to explain it. We could be partners in this."

"What are you trying to do? If you're trying to manipulate me, it isn't working," Dr. Salvatore growls, pressing the cold barrel of the gun against my forehead. My heart hammers in my chest, but I force myself not to flinch, knowing that showing any fear could be my undoing. He watches me, his finger twitching on the trigger. I meet his gaze, steady and calm despite the storm raging inside me.

My voice is soft but firm, laced with empathy I don't feel. "You know, true intellect isn't just in the brilliance of ideas, but in the mastery of timing and perception. Right now, Nathan, you're poised on the edge of something historic, but the narrative can still shift." I lift my free hand, trying desperately to hide its tremble, and gently cup his face, forcing myself to look into his eyes with the kind of tenderness he's been craving. "There's no victory in destruction. The real victory is in control. We can turn this into something extraordinary, an intellectual masterpiece, a triumph of manipulation, power, and brilliance. I can help you, but only if you trust me." His eyes narrow as he stares at me, searching for any sign of deceit. "You've already outsmarted everyone else," I continue, unwavering. "Don't let this be the moment where emotion defeats intellect. You're too brilliant for that. *We're* too brilliant for that." I can feel him falter, his grip on the gun loosening slightly.

For a moment, the room is silent, the tension thick enough to suffocate. His eyes bore into mine, still probing, still doubting. But I hold firm, standing by the lies I've spun, believing them with every ounce of my being. Finally, after what feels like an eternity, he lowers the gun. I resist the urge to collapse in relief, knowing it could shatter the fragile trust I've just built. But then, without warning, his lips crash into mine, a brutal, possessive kiss that leaves me frozen in place. My body stiffens instinctively, betraying me. I can lie to him all I want, say the things he needs to hear, but my body has never been good at lying. The moment his lips touch mine, I know he senses the truth. He knows everything I just said was a carefully crafted lie. I can feel the anger radiating off him like heat. His body tenses, and I know what's coming before it happens. Everything is a blur, the sharp, cold slam of reality as he pulls away from me, the sudden intensity in his eyes shifting from hurt to pure rage. There's a loud crash, and the door bursts open, shattering at the hinges.

"FBI! Drop the gun!" a voice booms through the room, authoritative and commanding. The air is thick with urgency, but Dr. Salvatore's eyes stay locked on mine, wild and wounded. For a split second, I see the look of betrayal in his eyes, as if I've just shattered his world. But then, the anger overtakes him completely. In one swift motion, he lifts the gun, pointing it directly at my head. Everything slows down. My heart seizes in my chest as I try to react, but it's too late.

Bang!

KINGSLEY

HER NAME, HIS ANCHOR

"Fuck!" The word erupts from my throat as the glass of whiskey shatters against the wall, the amber liquid dripping down like the blood in my veins, hot, furious, and ready to ignite. It's been fifteen hours, thirty-two minutes, and twenty seconds since someone snatched Inès from her apartment, and we're no closer to finding her. I've thrown money at every top investigator and used my resources, but it's like she vanished into thin air. The police have no leads; it's as if Inès simply ceased to exist, and it's driving me to the brink of madness.

Inès's parents and sister arrived this morning. They are currently staying with Meghan at the penthouse. I've had to send Beau to the dog hotel, so he is being well taken care of while we are going through this nightmare. I've been avoiding Inès's family, too ashamed to face the questions I don't have answers to. How can I explain that I failed? I was supposed to protect her, but instead, I let someone take her right under my fucking nose. The helplessness is suffocating, but all I know to do is throw more money at professionals, praying they'll succeed where I've failed.

"Kingsley, you need to calm down, man. My friend is doing all he can, but there's nothing to go on," Desmond tries to reason with me, referring to his friend, the so-called expert who's been working the case. But from where I stand, he's a useless son of a bitch. Don't get me wrong, I'd spend billions without a second thought to get Inès back, but I need her back safe and sound, now.

"Don't fucking tell me to calm down!" I roar, pacing the room like a caged animal. "What the hell is taking him so long if he's as good as you say?" I drag my hands through my hair, my nails digging into my scalp. I haven't slept, haven't eaten, haven't even showered. The only thing in my head is getting Inès back, holding her again, and knowing she's safe.

"He needs something to follow, but right now, there's nothing. No cameras in or outside the building, and no witnesses. Inès is well-liked, has no enemies, and no stalkers. There's just nothing to track. You've got to give him more time," Desmond explains, his voice calm, like I'm the one who's lost.

I slump into a chair, my chest heaving as the weight of reality crushes me. "I can't lose her, man. I just... I can't..."

"I get it, but you're no help right now. You need to go home, get your shit together, maybe take a nap. I'll call you with any updates. We're going to find her." Desmond's words barely register, but I know he's right. I'm no good like this, a shell of myself, consumed by fear and rage. I have to pull it together, if only for Inès.

Reluctantly, I take his advice and head home. As soon as the elevator doors open to my penthouse, I'm greeted by a room full of worried faces, Inès's family, Meghan, all of them looking to me for answers I don't have. Meghan is the first to see me, her eyes wide with hope as she rushes into my arms.

"Any news?" she asks, her voice trembling as she clings to me.

"Nothing yet, but everyone is working on it," I mumble, placing a kiss on the top of her head before releasing her. As I look up, Inès's mother, Hélène, approaches, and I brace myself for the slap, the accusations I know I deserve. But instead, she pulls me into her arms, holding me tight.

I can't hold back the tears that spill from my eyes, the weight of it all crashing down on me.

"Oh, baby," Hélène whispers, pulling away just enough to cup my cheeks and wipe my tears. Her eyes, red and swollen from crying, mirror my own pain. "It's going to be okay. Everything's going to be okay," she soothes, pulling me back into her embrace.

When she finally lets me go, Camille and Jonathan both hug me, too their silent support overwhelming. I'm drowning in guilt, but their kindness keeps me afloat.

"I hope you don't mind, but I couldn't just sit here doing nothing, so I made some food. Justin told me you haven't eaten since last night," Jonathan explains gently.

"I don't mind at all. Please, make yourselves at home. But I don't think I can stomach any food right now," I admit. The thought of eating turns my stomach.

"You need to eat something, fiston.[1] Come on, I made chicken gnocchi soup. Just try a little," he urges. Just as I open my mouth to politely decline again, my phone rings. I don't even bother checking the number, clinging to the hope that it's good news about Inès.

"Yes?" I answer hastily.

---

1. Son.

"Mr. Ashford, your parents are here. Is it okay to send them up?" comes the voice of the building attendant. Disappointment surges, it's not news about Inès. But then his words sink in. My parents?

"Uh, sure, that's fine," I reply, hanging up with a lingering frown. I hadn't expected them. I did call my father after Inès was kidnapped, he helped get the FBI involved, but I didn't think they'd come here.

"Is everything okay?" Jonathan asks, his voice laced with concern.

"Yeah. My parents are here, apparently," I say, making my way to the elevator. I feel everyone's eyes on me as I step away. When the doors slide open, the first face I see is my Daronne,[2] Josephine. Worry is etched across her otherwise elegant features. The moment she spots me, she gasps, rushing toward me with open arms, leaving my dad trailing behind.

"King, we came as fast as we could. I'm so sorry, baby," she says, pulling me into a hug only she can give, a hug that lifts some of the weight off my shoulders.

"What are you doing here, Mom?" I ask, and I can hear Camille behind me repeat the word *mom*, clearly confused. Josephine pulls back just enough to cup my face, her gaze steady and comforting.

"I will always be here, no matter what," she says firmly. And I know it's true; she has always been there.

I press a kiss to her cheek before turning to introduce them. "Everyone, this is my dad, Atticus, and my Daronne, Josephine."

"Please, call me Josie," she corrects, flashing a warm smile.

---

2. Mom.

Inès's family stares at me, bewildered, so I add, "Our house manager."

"Oh," Camille says.

My dad shakes hands with Jonathan while Josie gives Hélène a heartfelt hug.

"I'm so sorry your family is going through this. If there's anything you need, please don't hesitate to ask," Josie says sincerely.

"Thank you. That means a lot," Hélène replies softly.

"I was just telling Kingsley that I made soup. Please, join us, you must be hungry," Jonathan offers, gesturing toward the dining room.

As everyone moves to take their seats, my dad lingers, pulling me into a firm embrace. For a moment, it feels like old times, like I have my dad back, not just the business partner he's become.

"She'll come home, son. I promise," he murmurs.

We settle at the table in tense silence as Jonathan serves the soup. I lift the spoon to my lips, but the food tastes like ash in my mouth. My mind won't stop spinning, stuck in an endless loop of worry for Inès. Her diabetes... Has she eaten? Is she safe? The thought of her suffering is unbearable, a weight pressing heavier with every second.

I'm only able to take a few sips of the soup before putting my spoon down.

"What is it?" Meghan asks, concern etched across her face.

"Nothing," I lie, pushing away from the table. "Thank you for the soup. It was delicious. I need to take a shower. I've got a meeting I forgot about." I rise from the table before anyone can question me.

Feeling like I can't breathe, I take a deep breath as soon as I enter my office. My mind is racing, thoughts swirling in a chaotic storm. Inès has been missing for hours, and every second without her feels like an eternity.

"What do you need?" Justin's voice pulls me back to reality. He's followed me in, of course he did. My best friend knows me too well.

"I don't know yet." I exhale, sinking into my chair. My legs feel like they can't hold me up anymore. "Right now, I need someone with the family. Anything they need, make sure they get it.

"Of course... They'll find her, Kingsley. One way or another, they'll bring her home," he says before leaving me alone with my thoughts again.

My chest tightens with a bitter mix of hope and helplessness. I grab my phone, making call after call, pushing everyone to move faster, dig deeper. Anything, *anything* to bring my Queen back to me. But it's not enough. I slam the phone down, my fists clenched, shaking with frustration. I've never felt so useless, so damn incompetent.

Every second without Inès feels like a slow death. I clench my jaw, refusing to let despair take over. I won't stop. I'll keep pushing until she's back where she belongs, in my arms, safe. And whoever took her has already signed his death warrant. He'll wish he never laid eyes on her.

The hours crawl by as I pace my office, calling and calling, desperate for something, anything that might lead me to Inès. My office is dark, save for the cold glow of the computer screen casting long shadows across the walls. I barely notice the passage of time, the minutes blurring together in an endless cycle of fear and frustration.

I all but pounce when my phone buzzes on the desk. Desmond's name flashes on the screen. I snatch it up, hoping he has something to give me.

"Desmond, talk to me," I demand, my voice tight with anxiety.

"Do you know a Nathan Salvatore?"

"Nathan Salvatore? No, I…" Then my eyes go impossibly wide as it hits me: the psychology professor, the one who went on one date with Inès. "Yes, actually, I do. He is her professor, why?" I ask.

"We might have something," Desmond replies, his tone serious. "Maybe you should sit down for this…"

"Des, I'm in no mood, just tell me," I say, making him sigh.

"Well, my friend looked through hours and hours of security footage of Inès at school and around the city," he begins tensely. "He noticed someone always lurking in the shadows, watching her. After running some facial recognition, he was able to identify the person clearly, it was Nathan Salvatore. And from there, it all came together. He hacked into his home laptop, and, well… Nathan Salvatore has been stalking Inès for months. Watching her every move. Following her everywhere. He has a dossier on her, Kingsley… from what I'm seeing, he's obsessed with her."

His words hang in the air like a storm cloud, suffocating me. My grip tightens around my phone, and it takes every ounce of self-control not to hurl it across the room.

Stalking her? For months?

That son of a bitch.

The thought of Nathan watching Inès, lurking, studying her, invading her life without her knowing, makes my blood boil. My chest tightens with a rage I've never felt before.

"His bank statements show that he has been renting a cabin in Berkshires, completely off the grid."

A surge of adrenaline courses through me. "Where's the cabin?"

Desmond gives me the location, and I pull up a map on my phone, pinpointing the spot. It's remote, surrounded by miles of dense forest, perfect for hiding someone. "I'm going there now," I say, already heading for the door.

"Kingsley, wait, "

But I hang up before he can finish, my thoughts already on the next step. I rush to my safe and grab my gun. I've never killed anyone, but there's a first time for everything, and Nathan Salvatore needs to die.

"What's going on?" Justin asks, walking into my office.

"I know where she is," I tell him, my voice shaking with a mixture of fear and determination. "That son of a bitch got a cabin in the Berkshires. I'm going there right now to get Inès."

"Who has her?" he asks.

"Her professor, Nathan Salvatore."

Justin grabs my arm before I can storm out. "Hold on, you can't just rush in there without a plan. We don't know what we're walking into, and if Salvatore is dangerous, we need to be prepared."

"I'm not waiting," I snap, trying to pull away. "Inès's in there, and I'm getting her out."

"I know," Justin says, his voice firm but calm. "But we need to do this the right way. Call the police, give them the information. We can't just walk into that cabin alone. What if he's armed? What if there are traps? We can't risk her life, or yours."

His words cut through my haze of anger, and I realize he's right. If something goes wrong, I could lose Inès forever. The thought of her being hurt, or worse, because of my reckless-ness, makes my blood run cold.

"Alright," I finally concede, my voice barely holding steady. "I'll call Agent Callahan. But I'm going with them. I need to be the first one to hold her." In the first few hours after Inès was kidnapped, the local police were doing everything they could to find her. But it wasn't enough. I wanted the best, the FBI. Even though it's not technically their jurisdiction, my father has connections, and SSA Jack Callahan owes him a favor.

Justin nods, visibly relieved that I'm thinking clearly now, even if part of me is still on the edge. I take a deep breath and dial Callahan's number. My fingers are shaking as I explain the situation, how Inès has been taken, how we know it's Nathan Salvatore, the professor who's been stalking her for months. I try to keep my voice calm, but the urgency bleeds through. Callahan listens carefully, absorbing every detail. His tone is measured but intense when he finally speaks.

"Alright, Kingsley. We'll send a team out to the location. We'll handle this, but you need to let us take the lead."

"I'm coming with you," I say firmly, leaving no room for argument. "I won't get in the way, but I'm going. No one touches her but me." There's a pause on the other end of the line. I can tell he's weighing the risks, but he knows there's no point trying to stop me.

"Fine," Callahan says after a moment. "But you stay back until we secure the area. No exceptions. We'll handle the operation. You just stay focused on keeping it together for her."

"I will," I promise, though my mind is racing. I'll keep it together long enough to make sure Inès is safe.

The drive to the Berkshires is agonizing. The only sounds in the car are the low hum of the engine and the occasional murmur from Justin as he coordinates with the police. I grip the steering wheel so tightly my knuckles turn white, and my eyes are fixed on the road ahead.

As we near the cabin, the road narrows, the trees closing

in around us. The isolation of the place is unnerving. My heart pounds as we pull to a stop a few hundred yards from the cabin, hidden from view by the dense forest.

The FBI team is already there, their vehicles parked discreetly along the roadside. I step out of the car, my pulse thundering in my ears as I approach SSA Jack Callahan.

"You can stay right here. Agent Carmen will stay with you until we secure the area and get your girl back. Do not make me regret this, Ashford."

"Just get her out safe."

"Alright, let's move!" Callahan barks, and his team snaps into action, falling in line like clockwork.

Adrenaline surges through my veins. I can feel the intensity building around me. My heart pounds as the tension in the air thickens. Through Agent Carmen's radio, we hear the soft, urgent commands as the team fans out, each step calculated, each breath measured. They're positioning themselves around the perimeter, ready to strike. Every rustle of the leaves, every whisper of movement, sends a jolt of adrenaline through me. I can feel the weight of the moment pressing down on my chest, my pulse hammering in my ears as I wait for the signal that could change everything. My mind is overcome with fear and hope battling for dominance within me as I pray that Inès is inside, alive and safe.

Suddenly, the door bursts open, and the police flood inside, their shouts echoing through the trees. My heart pounds in my chest as I wait, every muscle in my body coiled like a spring, my focus solely on what's inside that cabin.

A deafening bang echoes through the air, and every cell in my body freezes. A guttural sound escapes from my throat, something raw and primal that I don't even recognize. Was that gunshot for her? My heart slams against my ribcage, my mind racing. Is she okay? I don't even realize I'm moving until a heavy hand grips my shoulder. Without thinking, my instincts kick in. I whirl around, grabbing the hand in a flash and twisting it at a vicious angle before slamming the person into the hood of a car. It's only then that I see who it is, Agent Carmen.

My chest heaves as I recognize him, but I don't care. "Never put your hands on me!" I growl, my voice dangerous.

"Kingsley, let him go!" Justin's voice snaps me out of it, but not before I get a good look at Carmen's face, embarrassed and angry. His pride took a hit, and he doesn't like it. As soon as I loosen my grip, Carmen twists out of my hold, pulling out his gun, the barrel trained right at me.

"Hands where I can see them!" he barks, his face tight with rage. The fact that I, a young guy barely out of college, had him pinned in seconds doesn't sit well with him. "I don't care who your daddy is, put your fucking hands up!" But I just stand there, staring at him. I don't have time for this pissing contest. My eyes are locked on the cabin, my fists clenched at my sides. If he thinks I'm backing down, he's dead wrong.

Justin steps between us. "I wouldn't do that if I were you, Agent Carmen. You like your job, right? Your life?" He gives Carmen, who's still shaking from the humiliation, gun trembling in his hand, a pointed look. Before he can respond, the words I've been dying to hear cut through the tension.

"We've got her. She's alive." Those words ring through my mind, obliterating everything else. My legs move before my brain catches up, my heart thundering in my chest. Inès is alive. I need to see her, to hold her. As I burst into the cabin, the scene before me is almost too much to bear. Officers walking around, a body on the floor, but I barely pay attention to it as I see Inès curled up in the corner, her clothes disheveled and her hair a tangled mess. The sight of her, my

Inès, looking so vulnerable yet alive, makes my breath catch in my throat. Her eyes meet mine, and in that moment, everything else fades away. I sprint toward her, my heart racing. I drop to my knees beside her, my arms instinctively reaching out.

When I pull her into my arms, the tightness of her embrace and her pained wince tell me something is wrong. I feel a pang of guilt and helplessness as I hold her. "Butterfly, what happened?" I ask, trying to keep my voice steady despite the fear rising in my chest.

She pulls back slightly, her face contorted in pain. "My shoulder," she gasps, her voice trembling. "It's... It's dislocated. It hurts so much." My heart drops at the sight of her suffering. I gently examine her shoulder, being as careful as possible not to make her pain worse. Her face is pale, her eyes glassy with pain.

"We need to get her to the hospital," a paramedic says urgently as she approaches. The seriousness in her tone makes me feel better. I know she'll take care of Inès. I nod, trying to stay composed despite the turmoil inside me.

The paramedics work quickly, moving with practiced efficiency. They stabilize her shoulder and prepare her for transport. I stay close to her, holding her hand and whispering reassurances. "I'm here, papillon," I murmur, my voice steady despite the tight knot of fear in my chest. "You're going to be okay." Her grip on my hand is weak but determined.

As they carefully load her onto the stretcher and into the ambulance, I follow closely, my mind racing with worry but focused on one thing: getting her the best care possible. Inès is safe now, that's the most important thing. And no matter what, I'll be by her side, every step of the way.

INÈS

SAFE HAVEN

FOUR MONTHS LATER

The early June sun streams through the windows of Dr. Hamilton's office, bathing the room in a soft, golden light. It's a peaceful setting, yet the tranquility outside feels worlds away from the turmoil that still occasionally grips me. As I sit in the familiar chair, I trace the stitching on the armrest with my fingers, grounding myself before I speak.

"Sometimes it's hard to believe that I was actually kidnapped," I begin quietly, almost as if saying it out loud might make it real again. "There are moments when it feels like a bad dream, like it couldn't have really happened to me."

Dr. Hamilton nods, her gaze steady and comforting. "It's normal to feel that way, Inès. Trauma can make reality seem distant, like it's happening to someone else."

I swallow, trying to find the words to describe the strange

duality of my experience. "During the day, I can almost convince myself that it wasn't real. I go through the motions, laugh with Kingsley, spend time with my family, and for a while, I can forget. But then... then I wake up screaming in the middle of the night, drenched in sweat, my heart racing, and I'm reminded that it *was* real."

My voice wavers, and I take a deep breath to steady myself. "Those nightmares... they pull me back, make me relive every terrifying second. I see his face, feel the fear, the helplessness. It's like I'm trapped there all over again." Although Dr. Salvatore is long gone, shot by one of the agents who rescued me that night, I still get anxious when I leave the house, thinking he is there, following me, stalking me, even though I haven't left the house alone in four months, until today.

Dr. Hamilton's expression softens, and she leans forward slightly, offering silent encouragement. "Nightmares are your mind's way of processing the trauma, even if it's painful. But it's important to remember that they're just that, nightmares. They can't hurt you."

I nod, understanding the logic but struggling with the emotional reality. "I know that. But it's hard to convince myself of it when I'm jolted awake, my pulse pounding in my ears, the fear still so real."

"What do you do when that happens?" she asks gently.

"Kingsley... he's always there," I say, a small smile on my lips despite the heavy topic. "He holds me until I calm down, whispering that I'm safe, that he's got me. He means well, and I'm so grateful for him, but..."

"But?" Dr. Hamilton prompts.

I bite my lip, trying to articulate the conflicting emotions I've been grappling with. "But sometimes it feels like too much. After it all happened, he became so protective, almost smothering. I know it's because he loves me and wants to keep me safe, but it felt like I couldn't breathe at times, like I was losing myself."

Dr. Hamilton nods thoughtfully. "That's understandable. It's common for loved ones to become overprotective after a traumatic event. But you've also been through something that changed you, and you've needed space to figure out who you are now."

"Yes," I agree, feeling a sense of relief at having voiced it. "That's exactly it. I love him so much, but I did not want to feel so smothered all the time."

"So how did you approach that with him?" she asks, her eyes kind but probing.

"It wasn't easy," I admit, leaning back in my chair, the memory of that conversation still vivid. "He's not used to being told what to do, especially not when it comes to protecting me. But I told him he had to loosen the reins a little and that I needed space to heal on my own terms. He didn't love it, but he understood. He backed off, just enough for me to breathe again."

"That must have taken a lot of courage," Dr. Hamilton says, her tone admiring. "And it sounds like he responded in a way that respected your needs."

I nod, feeling a warm sense of pride. "He did. It wasn't perfect, we've had our moments, but we found a balance. He's still there for me, still my rock, but he's given me room to heal. And in doing that, we've grown stronger together."

Dr. Hamilton smiles, and I can see the approval in her eyes. "That's a big step, Inès. Healing isn't linear, and finding that balance in your relationship is a testament to both your strength and Kingsley's love for you."

I smile back, the weight on my chest lifting just a little more. "It's been hard. I'm not the same person I was before all this, but I'm learning to accept that. I'm learning to love who I am now, scars and all." Before everything, my only issue was my diabetes, but now on top of that, I've been diagnosed with anxiety and PTSD, too. I'm also very paranoid.

As the session wraps up, I leave Dr. Hamilton's office with a lighter heart, feeling more at peace than I have in a long time. The road hasn't been easy, and there are still nights when the darkness closes in, but I'm moving forward. Today is a special day, my twentieth birthday. Despite everyone's best efforts, I know about the surprise party Kingsley, Meghan, and Justin planned. I also know that my family flew down to Boston for it, and I couldn't be happier. The thought of seeing everyone, of celebrating after everything that's happened, fills me with a warm, almost giddy excitement.

As I step into the penthouse, the comforting aroma of my favorite dish fills the air, instantly bringing a smile to my face. Papa knows me too well.

"Surprise!" Their voices are soft, almost whispering, and I can't help but smile at their effort not to startle me. They're trying so hard to be cautious, and it's endearing.

"Oh... wow, how... I... what?" I stammer, knowing full well that I'm the worst actress alive.

Meghan, her hand resting protectively on her growing belly, lets out a sigh. "You knew, didn't you?"

"The smell of gratin dauphinois was a big giveaway," I admit with a playful grin. "But that doesn't mean I'm not overwhelmed with gratitude."

I move around the room, giving each of them a hug. When I reach my mom, she holds me a little tighter and longer, and I cling to her, savoring the warmth and comfort of her embrace. Her hugs have always been my safe haven.

"I told you she'd know you were here if she smelled her favorite food," my mom teases my dad with a knowing smile.

Camille steps up next, her arms wrapping around me as she chuckles. "Please… you knew we'd try to surprise you long before today, didn't you?"

I laugh, leaning into her. "In my defense, Meghan doesn't know how to keep a secret."

"I do!" Meghan gasps, feigning indignation, though her playful tone gives her away. We all exchange glances and burst into laughter.

"No, you don't," we all chime in unison.

"But we love you regardless," my mom says, pulling Meghan into a warm, reassuring hug.

"Yeah, you just need to work on your poker face before you become an attorney," Avery teases, flashing a mischievous grin as Meghan playfully swats at him.

As they continue to banter, I feel a familiar warmth encircle my waist. Kingsley pulls me close, his presence grounding me in the best way.

"How was the session?" he asks softly, low enough for only me to hear, even though everyone here knows about my therapy.

"It was good," I say, smiling up at him. "I didn't cry once."

"And the drive there?" he asks, his voice gentle but curious. Leaving the house had become one of my biggest fears after the abduction, a paralyzing anxiety that gripped me for months. Thanks to King, I was able to do my classes and therapy sessions online until I was ready to face the world outside. Even then, King never let me go anywhere alone, he drove me everywhere, making sure I felt safe. But today was different. Today was the first time in four months that I left the house on my own.

Did I almost have a few panic attacks? Yes. Did I feel like I was being followed? Absolutely. But I did it. I made it through, and that's what matters.

"Scary, but fine," I reassure him, meeting his gaze. I know he's searching my face for any sign of unease.

"Are you sure?" he asks tenderly as if he's trying to protect me from the memories that still haunt me.

"Yes, I'm sure." I rest my chin against his chest and look up at him with a smile. "I'm fine, King. I promise."

He holds my gaze for a moment longer before he leans down and gives me a soft, lingering kiss. It's the kind of kiss that says more than words ever could, an unspoken promise that he'll always be there for me. When he pulls away, I'm left wanting more, my heart fluttering in that familiar way only he can cause.

"Happy birthday, Queen," he whispers, brushing a strand of hair behind my ear. "Tu es incroyable, mon amour."[1]

"Merci,"[2] I whisper back, feeling a surge of affection for the man who has been my constant through it all. "But you're pretty incredible, too."

"I love you," he tells me, making me smile again.

"I love you more."

Then I hear a familiar bark as Beau comes bounding out from wherever he was hiding, nudging my leg. I frown in surprise as I bend over to pick him up. "Beau? What are you doing here? I thought…" I look around, confused. I was sure King would send him to a doggy daycare, especially since my mom is allergic.

---

1. You are incredible, my love.
2. Thank you.

"I took a shot before I came over," my mom explains, smiling warmly at me. "I didn't want him to miss your birthday because of me."

Her words make my heart swell, and I mouth a grateful *merci* to her before pressing a kiss to Beau's soft head. "Hi, mon amour,"[3] I whisper to him, cradling him close. He licks my cheek in return, and for a moment, the warmth of family settles over me like a comforting blanket.

Just then, my dad's voice booms from the kitchen, cutting through the cozy moment. "Who's ready to eat?"

The room erupts in excited chatter as we all make our way to the dining table, the smell of the delicious food making my mouth water. Kingsley keeps his arm around me, and as we sit down with our family, I can't help but feel a deep, overwhelming sense of contentment.

Even though I already knew about the surprise, the moment still feels special. There's a deep, abiding happiness that bubbles up inside me as I look around at the people who've stood by me through the darkest of times.

As the evening unfolds, we laugh, talk, and celebrate, the room filled with warmth and joy. For the first time in a long while, everything feels right. I look around at the faces of those I love, my heart swelling with gratitude.

---

3. My love.

KINGSLEY

EPILOGUE

Five years. It feels like a lifetime and the blink of an eye all at once.

Inès is sprawled next to me, her head nestled on my chest as we lounge in a private bungalow on a hidden stretch of beach. I run my fingers through her dark curls, marveling at how much life we've built together. Five years, and yet every time I look at her, I still see that bright-eyed freshman girl who stumbled into my life and completely turned it upside down.

Except now, she's not that shy, tentative girl anymore. Inès is a force. Confident, brilliant, and a breathtaking woman. She just completed her first year of residency for neurology, and I couldn't be prouder of her.

She yawns softly, her fingers tracing slow circles on my chest. "This is perfect," she murmurs, her voice drowsy from the heat and relaxation.

I smile, pressing a kiss to the top of her head. "You deserve it, papillon. You've been working too hard." I glance out at the clear turquoise waters of the Maldives. Yes, I spared no expense for this trip. Nothing is too much for her. Nothing.

The sound of the gentle waves lapping at the shore, the faint scent of salt and coconut in the air, everything about this place is paradise. But it's nothing compared to her.

Inès tilts her head up to look at me, her brown eyes twinkling with mischief. "You're one to talk. When was the last time you took a break? I'm surprised the office hasn't fallen apart without you."

I chuckle. "It's still standing. I've got a good team." Since opening up the office in Boston, things have been busier than ever. But I've learned to delegate, sort of. I'm still a control freak, especially when it comes to her, always.

She stretches, her curves accentuated by the way she moves, and I can't help but drink her in. Inès has always been beautiful, but she's grown into herself in a way that takes my breath away. Stronger, more confident. And it's sexy as hell.

"Are you going to swim with me or are you going to keep staring at me like that?" she teases, her full lips curving into a playful smile.

I sit up, grinning as I take her hand. "I'll always stare at you like that. But yeah, let's swim."

We slip into the warm, clear water, the reflections of the sun on the surface looking like diamonds. Inès lets out a delighted laugh, splashing me as soon as we're deep enough. I chase her, dunking her under the water for a second before pulling her close, my arms wrapping around her waist. She squeals, but her laughter is infectious, making my heart swell.

She wraps her legs around me, her eyes locked on mine. "I love you," she whispers, her fingers brushing the back of my neck.

My throat tightens. Every time she says those words, it hits me in a way I can't explain. "I love you, too, papillon.[1] Always."

We float together in the water, the gentle ebb and flow of the waves making it feel like we're drifting in a world all our own. The sun dips lower on the horizon, casting a golden glow on the surface. It's just her and me, wrapped in the calm of the moment, the rest of the world fading away. It's been like this for years, just the two of us in our little bubble. No one else exists in these moments, and it feels like it always will be this way, like nothing could ever break the quiet connection between us.

When the sun is completely down, we make our way back to the bungalow, the evening air cooling against our skin. Inès towels herself off, her hair still damp from the ocean, when her phone buzzes on the nearby chair. I watch as her face lights up with a grin that makes her eyes crinkle at the edges. "It's Meghan," she says, her voice bright with excitement.

Meghan and J welcomed their son, our Godson Ethan, four years ago, and they got married a few months after his birth. Life hasn't been the same since, in a good way. Meghan, juggling law school, and J, running his sports agency out of Boston, somehow manage to give Ethan all the love and attention in the world. He's the kind of kid who lights up every room he enters, with a grin that can melt your heart. Every time we see him, it's like a ray of pure sunshine, and I know Inès feels it even more deeply than I do. She loves that little boy like he's her own.

"Hey, you!" Inès answers the FaceTime call, her voice warm and full of affection.

---

1. Butterfly.

"Hey! I hope I'm not interrupting," Meghan says in a teasing tone, which makes Inès playfully roll her eyes.

"Shut up, do you think I would have answered the phone?"

"Hey, I don't know what you guys are into, I'm not one to judge." Meghan laughs, which causes Inès to laugh with her.

"You are awful. Anyway, how's my little man doing?"

"He's been running around all day with Beau, talking about superheroes and supervillains; they wore out J by lunchtime, as you can imagine. He's been asking about you two, though. Wanted to call and say hi." Meghan's voice is light and a little tired, but happy.

"That sounds like our little guy. Let me talk to him." There's a brief shuffling on the other end of the line, and then Meghan speaks.

"Ethan, come here, love. It's Auntie Nés!" When Ethan started talking, he couldn't say Inès, so he just started to call her Auntie Nés. A moment later, Ethan's tiny voice bursts through the speaker, full of excitement.

"Hi, Auntie Nés!"

Inès's entire face softens as she listens. "Hi, sweetheart! What have you been up to today?"

"I played with Superman!" Ethan shouts into the phone. "And my Spider-Man! I was jumping really high like Spider-Man, and then I jumped and Dad caught me!"

"Wow, that sounds amazing!" Inès says, her voice full of admiration, feeding into his excitement. "You're getting so strong, Ethan! Maybe you'll be a superhero one day, huh?"

"Yeah! I'm gonna fly like Superman and jump like Spider-Man!" His little voice is so full of enthusiasm that it makes me smile from ear to ear. "Where's Uncle K?" he asks suddenly, his voice softer but still full of that eager energy.

I chuckle and step closer, leaning in so he can see me.

"I'm right here, buddy! How's my superhero doing?" I ask, my voice filled with excitement.

"Good! I saved Beau a lot today!" he exclaims proudly, his little chest puffing out.

I play along, my tone turning playfully serious. "Oh wow, that's a big job, buddy. I'm impressed!"

Ethan grins widely, and then he turns the camera, revealing Beau sprawled out on the sofa, looking utterly exhausted. Beau adores Ethan, but every time they spend the day together, he's completely wiped out by the end of it.

"Say hi, Beau," Ethan says, nudging the sleepy dog.

Inès and I share a look, grinning, and together we both say, "Hi, Beau!" in unison.

"We miss you so much," Inès adds, blowing a few kisses at the screen.

Ethan giggles at that before speaking again. "Okay, I have to go now. Mommy says it's bedtime," he says, bouncing with the excitement of the day.

"You're amazing, Ethan," I tell him, my heart swelling with affection. "Keep being good for Mommy, okay? We'll see you soon. We miss you, and we love you very much."

"Love you, too!" he shouts before the screen goes black.

Inès laughs, the glow of that call lingering in the air. Her expression remains soft, her heart so clearly full of love for that little boy. She looks over at me, and for a moment, I can see the future so clearly in her eyes, one where she's a mother, loving and patient, just like she's always been with Beau and Ethan.

For a moment, I just watch her, taking in every detail of her face, the way her lashes flutter, the gentle curve of her lips, the faint blush that still lingers on her skin from our time in the sun. She's so beautiful, so perfect, and I can't believe how lucky I am to have her. To call her mine.

I brush a strand of hair away from her face, and she looks up at me, her eyes soft and filled with the kind of love that always makes my chest tighten. "What are you thinking about?" she asks, her voice barely above a whisper.

I smile, my thumb brushing over her cheek. "Just how much I love you," I murmur.

She smiles gently and leans up to press a soft kiss to my lips. "I love you, too, King," she whispers against my mouth, her breath warm and sweet.

I deepen the kiss, slowly, tenderly, as I pull her closer to me, feeling her soft body against mine. "Show me how much you love me," I say, pulling her to the bed and laying her down, pressing my body against hers. She melts beneath me, her arms wrapping around my neck, pulling me closer. The connection between us is effortless, like two pieces of a puzzle fitting together perfectly.

My lips trail down her neck, planting soft kisses along her collarbone as I take my time, savoring every inch of her. This isn't about hunger or possession, it's about making her feel what she means to me. Her skin is soft beneath my lips, warm and familiar, and the way she sighs softly, her fingers threading through my hair, sends a rush of warmth through me.

I meet her gaze as I lean back slightly, and the look in her eyes, so full of trust, of love, nearly knocks the breath out of me. I take her hand, lacing my fingers through hers as I press a kiss to her palm.

Slowly, I take off her swimsuit. She shivers slightly as I bare her skin to the cool evening air. The way she looks at me, eyes half-lidded, lips slightly parted, her chest rising and falling in a slow, even rhythm, pulls at something deep inside me. Every inch of her body is familiar to me, yet every time I touch her feels like the first. I take my time, kissing a path down her body, worshiping her the way she deserves. She's everything to me, my heart, my soul, and I want her to feel that in every touch, every kiss.

She lets out a soft gasp as I press a kiss to her hip, her hands fisting the sheets. She's already so sensitive, so responsive, my slut.

Her scent fills the room, and it pulls me in like a magnet. I'm hovering above her, my fingers grazing her skin, and I can feel the heat radiating from her body. Inès's eyes are locked on mine, filled with both trust and desire.

I trail my lips across her stomach, taking my time, enjoying the way her body responds to me. Her muscles tense slightly under my touch, anticipation clear in the way she bites down on her bottom lip. I'm in no rush. I want to make her feel everything.

I kiss the sensitive skin of her inner thigh, her body shuddering at the sensation. My hands rest on her hips, my thumbs brushing just below her waistline. She lets out a soft moan, her legs parting just enough, an invitation I can't resist.

I move lower, pressing kisses along the inside of her thigh, drawing out her anticipation, feeling her body tremble beneath me. Her scent is intoxicating, and I let it consume me as I lower my mouth to her. I pause, just for a moment, hovering over her, feeling the heat of her, and then I lean in, pressing my tongue against her, slow and deliberate.

The sound she makes, half gasp, half moan, goes straight to my hard dick. I feel her hands reach down, her fingers threading through my hair, pulling me closer. I can't help but smirk against her, enjoying the way she reacts to me. I push deeper, my tongue exploring every inch of her, savoring her taste, her warmth.

Her hips lift slightly off the bed, trying to press closer to my mouth, but I hold her down with my hands, keeping her still, teasing her with slow, deliberate strokes. I want to drive her wild, make her beg for more. I want her to feel how much I need her, how much I want to see her come undone beneath me.

I move faster now, my tongue flicking against her with more purpose, and her moans grow louder, her breath coming in quick, ragged bursts. Her legs begin to tremble, and I can feel her getting closer, her body tensing, her grip tightening in my hair.

"King…" she breathes, her voice filled with need.

I glance up, watching the way her head tilts back, her lips parted in pleasure. I keep my eyes on her as I bring one hand down, slipping two fingers inside her, slowly at first, feeling the way her body clenches around me. Her moans become more urgent, her hips bucking against my hand, her body begging for more.

I curl my fingers inside her, finding that perfect spot, and she cries out, her whole body arching off the bed. I push harder with my tongue, my hand moving in sync with my mouth, driving her closer and closer to the edge.

"Let go, Queen," I murmur against her skin, my voice rough, the words vibrating against her. "I'll catch you."

Her response is immediate, her body tensing for just a moment before she unravels completely. She moans my name, shaky, breathless, as she comes undone beneath me. I can feel every tremor, every spasm, as her orgasm crashes over her, her legs trembling around me, her hips bucking wildly.

I don't stop. I keep going, drawing out her pleasure, making sure she feels every second of it. I want her to know that this is just the beginning, that I'm going to give her everything, over and over again.

When she finally collapses against the bed, her chest

heaving, her body spent, I press one last kiss to her, gentle and lingering, before pulling back. I crawl up her body, kissing her softly on the lips, tasting her, tasting us, before resting my forehead against hers.

"I love you," I whisper as I lie next to her and pull her to me.

She smiles at me, her eyes soft and full of love. "I love you, too, Kingsley," she murmurs, her voice filled with a warmth that wraps around my heart.

I pull her closer, holding her tightly against me as the sun finally dips below the horizon, casting the room in the soft glow of twilight. In this moment, everything feels perfect, like we're the only two people in the world, wrapped up in each other's love.

And tonight, when I propose, I know she'll say yes. Because what we have, this love, it's forever.

I've been planning this for months. Technically, Meghan, Camille, and I have been planning this for months, making sure everything is perfect. The timing, the setting, the moment when I'm going to ask her the most important question of my life. But I've been thinking about it for years, and if I'm honest, since we first kissed on our first date.

I lead Inès to a secluded spot on the beach, where a private dinner had been set up just for us. The table is adorned with candles, soft music playing in the background, and the scent of the ocean filling the air.

Inès's eyes widen as she takes it all in. "King, this is… this is incredible."

I shrug, trying to play it cool, but inside I'm a bundle of nerves. "Nothing but the best for you, Queen."

She laughs, shaking her head. "You're too much, you know that?"

We sit down, and as we eat, we talk about everything and nothing. She tells me more about her plans for her clinicals, her excitement and nerves, and I listen, hanging on every word. I love hearing her talk about her passions, seeing her light up as she describes the future she's building.

When dinner is over, I take her hand and pull her to her feet. The sky is dark now, the stars twinkling above us, and the sound of the waves is the only thing we can hear.

"Inès," I start, my voice steady, though my heart is racing. "There's something I've been meaning to ask you."

She looks up at me, her eyes wide. "What is it?"

I reach into my pocket and pull out the small velvet box I've been carrying with me. Her breath catches as I drop to one knee, the diamond catching the light from the candles around us.

"Inès Dubois," I begin, my voice trembling with the weight of what I'm about to say, every breath soaked in the love I have for her, "you've been my best friend, my confidante, my partner, my everything, for more than five unforgettable years. You are the center of my world, the person who makes everything feel possible. Without you... I can't even imagine it, because the thought of a life without you is no life at all. You've shown me what it means to love without limits, to give yourself completely, and I want nothing more than to spend every day proving that I can do the same. So here I am, all of me, asking you, Inès, will you marry me? Will you let me spend the rest of my life loving you the way you deserve?"

For a moment, there's nothing but silence. Her hands fly

to her mouth, her eyes welling with tears as she stares down at the ring. It's massive, sparkling in the soft light, but that's not what matters. What matters is her, and the way she's looking at me like I'm her whole world when in reality, she's *my* whole world. My lover, my other half. I can't tell where I end and she begins because we're so intertwined, so perfectly in sync. When she smiles, it's like the sun just decided to rise in her eyes, and when she's sad, it feels like my heart's bleeding out. I don't think you can even grasp it the depth of what we are. It's not just about love, it's more than that. She knows me in ways I don't even know myself. And when I hold her close, it's like everything in the universe makes sense, like I've finally found the place where I belong. There's no room for doubt, no space for fear. Because with her, it's always been more than just love. It's… destiny.

"Yes," she whispers, her voice trembling. "Yes, King. Of course, I'll marry you."

Relief floods through me as I slide the ring onto her finger, standing and pulling her into my arms. She's crying now, but she's smiling, and I can't stop kissing her, holding her as close as I can.

"I love you so much," she murmurs against my lips, her voice shaky with emotion.

"I love you, too, Queen," I whisper back. "Forever."

We stand there for a long time, wrapped up in each other, the world around us fading away. It's just us, like it's always been and like it always will be.

Forever.

THE END

WHAT'S NEXT

Thank you so much for reading *Loving Queen*, book one of *The Heart Lies* series! If you enjoyed the ride, please consider leaving a review, it means more than you know and helps other romance lovers find their next favorite read.

Want more of King and his Queen? Sign up for my newsletter and get a bonus epilogue of them.

Curious what's coming next in *The Heart Lies* universe? I've got more forbidden drama, bratty heroines, and dangerously charming men headed your way. Come hang out with me on

Instagram at @author_saffron. You can also pre-order book 2 of The Heart Lies Series now!

Until next time,
   Bisou,
   Saffron Brooks

ACKNOWLEDGMENTS

To my husband, my rock, my cheerleader, and the person who quietly (and not-so-quietly) made sure this book actually made it out into the world, I owe you more than words on a page. If it weren't for your relentless support and patience through all the late-night writing marathons and your gentle "Did you eat today?" reminders, this story would still be in my drafts, collecting dust. Thank you for believing in me when I didn't, for reminding me that I could do this even when I was absolutely sure I couldn't, and for loving me through every draft, plot hole, and dramatic character arc (mine included).

To my family: If you're reading this… well, that's brave. I hope you skipped the spicy scenes. If not, well, the next family gathering should be entertaining. But truly, thank you. Thank you for loving me and encouraging me. Your love and support mean the world to me.

To my sisters and Noumou, thank you for letting me talk endlessly about my characters as if they were real people we were all somehow raising together. Thank you for nodding along as I pitched ideas (good, bad, and chaotic), for letting me voice-note you long rambles about plot twists, and for never once making me feel like I was annoying or, dare I say, slightly unhinged. You made me feel seen, loved, and supported, and that means the world.

To Kai, thank you for being the ultimate Kingsley and Inès hype squad. I don't know how you do it, but your enthusiasm was like rocket fuel for me. Thank you for answering every single one of my *many* questions (bless you), and you did it with the kind of energy that never made me feel judged. You're the kind of friend every writer dreams of having.

And finally, to every single person who believed in this story before it had a cover, a title, or even a decent ending, thank you. Your belief made this dream feel real, long before it was.

ABOUT THE AUTHOR

Saffron Brooks writes contemporary romance full of heart, hope, and the kind of love stories that linger. A lifelong daydreamer who finally decided to put pen to paper, she's all about crafting swoony plots, heartfelt moments, and characters who feel real; flaws, feelings, and all.

In every story, you'll find a world that reflects the one we live in: beautifully diverse, rich with different cultures, and always brimming with love in all its forms. And if you notice a little French sprinkled in, consider it her signature.

When she's not writing, Saffron's probably spending time with her family, planning her next getaway, or getting lost in a book that makes her laugh, cry, and blush (preferably all at once). She believes the best stories are the ones that make you feel, and she's just getting started writing hers.

www.ingramcontent.com/pod-product-compliance
Lightning Source LLC
Chambersburg PA
CBHW020013120726
47903CB00004B/1259

* 9 7 9 8 9 9 8 6 5 5 7 0 8 *